THE LAST



Upamanyu Chatterjee is the
*of Indira Gandhi,* which was chosen for 'Best Short Stories of 1986', and *English, August: An Indian Story*. He lives in New Delhi, India.

*by the same author*

ENGLISH, AUGUST:
An Indian Story

UPAMANYU CHATTERJEE

# The Last Burden

faber and faber
LONDON · BOSTON

First published in 1993
by Faber and Faber Limited
3 Queen Square London WC1N 3AU
This paperback edition first published in 1994

Printed in England by Clays Ltd, St Ives plc



A CIP record for this book is
available from the British Library

ISBN 0–571–17155–9

2 4 6 8 10 9 7 5 3 1

for Anne – while the going is good

*Acknowledgments*

I thank the British Council (New Delhi), the Charles Wallace Trust (India) and Darwin College of the University of Kent at Canterbury for enabling me to spend the Michaelmas Term of 1991 at Darwin College as a writer-in-residence. A large part of this book was worked on there.

# 1

# AUGUST

For four slow and secret days, Jamun reads Robert Payne's life of Mahatma Gandhi, while outside August slips into a closed and equally febrile September. The on-off rains are warm, troubled, and touch off a dreary ache in the small of the back and a flame beneath the skin. When he gets the telegram calling him home because of his mother's heart attack, it has been raining immoderately and the electricity has gone off. 'The sky's an old old kidney,' Hegiste has said, leaning as far back from his ledger as equilibrium permits, arms snarled yogalike over his head, neck angled, eyes half-closed, dreamily sniffing his own armpit.

Jamun books a call, waits for two hours, hears Hegiste abuse the operator, and then walks to the Vayudoot office. In the rain he feels hot and somehow full of blood. From a crushed dog on the road, blood plays like an effluent. Its eyes are blue-white and pupilless, transcendent, frightening. He waits fifty minutes before the besieged bastard can place him on the flight four mornings away. '. . . Such a demand . . . Festival . . . Rush . . . '

In the four days Jamun emerges at twilight for cigarettes and potatoes, milk etcetera. Otherwise in the white rooms of his flat he reads the Gandhi life and hears the rain. In the afternoons the waters slip away under the cauterizing sun. Then the white rooms glut with the exhalations of mud – of fish and sea, the beach and the wet. In the early mornings, from his verandah he observes the cream crabs in the ooze on which the block of flats has been erected. Later in the month, the river will balloon and Hegiste on the ground floor will share his flat with it. At night he hears the polite tap-tap beyond the windows, in the swelter, in the rain. Not frogs; too well-mannered – perhaps the crabs clucking to one another before coition and proliferation, or perhaps a tiny dinosaur with a second-rate larynx wooing admittance through the window so that it might read a book. In the primal slobland and prodigious heat, all is potential.

Burfi's letter has preceded the telegram.

Ma might have rectal cancer. It sounds dreadful and is very likely much worse. Haldia said this evening that a lump in the rectum at her age is 75 per cent cancer. He wants to operate. His eyes shone at the money he'd pick up. Baba predictably has already suggested that we should divide the bill by five. He telephoned Chhana, who of course is rushing here with opinions.

When Jamun had last seen his valetudinarian mother, he had said, 'I returned because I was afraid that I would not see you again,' but his father had not been touched. Yet his father himself has often murmured, with a kind of distaste, while his mother naps on the sofa in front of the TV, 'She will not live long.' She herself has contended the same for the last twenty-two years. She has also said, fitfully, 'I want to go and stay with you, Jamun.' But he has circumvented. Rectal cancer. If she endures, she will trail around with a polythene bag affixed – something like that. Because Haldia will take away her sphincter and perhaps hawk it to a snooty restaurant, where it might well be used for an hors d'oeuvre, a phrase which its customers will not fathom unless pronounced as whores dee overs, like Punjabi streetwalkers at cricket. Plus, Jamun's mother also has had to combat her hypertension, her piles, corns, arthritis, heart, marriage, her mind.

Jamun hasn't written home for a while out of listlessness. They haven't written either. His father's last letter, now quite old, has run on an on about his *own* listlessness.

Here in this boomtown waste Jamun has bought the same brands of refrigerator and geyser as at home, and has also struggled to debar the blues from his white rooms. At home, depression wafts out from the whitewash downstairs, but Burfi's rooms on the first floor, in contrast, like Hegiste's flat, have always seemed to exhale light.

The third evening, on the roof of the building, draughty, forehead cooling. Pretty sick of Robert Payne, watching the river, orange and thick, recalling his mother in the kitchen, pottering. 'Jamun, the anger of parents is never anger.' All at once a white bird the colour of cold milk, gliding across the wet verdure of trees between river and gynae hospital. The wings wave in silent, tireless eurhythmy like ballerinas bidding farewell.

Just then, down the ramp of the hospital comes a young woman – hand gripping railing, pendulating clumsily on splayed legs, enfeebled, in pain, groping – perhaps walking was prescribed. She wears a pink salwaar kameez and a black chunni – an ineffable Muslim mien – and Hegiste has time and time again said that untaxed Gulf money has raised the hospital. Without warning, Jamun pines to procreate too, to feel an illimitable and unfading, secret agony, then nothing, then to crawl gracelessly out and see a new world. He sees the bird and the woman and knows that in biding his time for four days, he has sinned profoundly.

Dinner with Hegiste the first evening. 'Spoke to Burfi at last, it's only the heart attack, thank God – I mean, not rectal cancer. She's still in Intensive Care. My father said I need not come if I find it difficult to get away.'

Hegiste and Jamun step out for cigarettes at six. Hegiste's son, three and a half, endomorphic and captious, wants to go too. He puts Jamun in mind of one of his own nephews, Doom, aged four, though between the two there is no specific likeness. On his last visit, on the last day, on his way out, he had gaped at Doom kicking up a big big fuss. 'I want to go with Jamun, I want.' No Uncle, nothing, just Jamun. And with each 'want' Doom's head bobs. Everyone is amazed, for Jamun is not irresistible to children. Jamun is unduly touched and mantles with delight. This *hankering* for his company – who has evinced it? Kasturi? His mother?

Or even his father? Consummately smashed, head undulating, AWOL three nights running in one of those cold sweat years – late teenage, hadn't it been? When he came in, and his mother had shifted from anxiety to anger, and no one was listening to her, his father said, sombrely, 'In your whole life, no one will wait for you as we have waited, as tensely, with as much anguish. No one else will be as happy to see you. To no one else will you matter. Never again will anyone want you like we, or start at the sound of your voice, or your step, in all your years.'

Hegiste has moved up from Gold Flake Kingsize to Classic. 'If you'd made an effort at the booking, whipped up your anger, or wept and wailed a little, you could've caught this evening's flight.'

'Two women ahead of me in the queue conceived dead fathers. One was to zip straight to the ghat from the airport. In comparison, my mother was merely dying.'

A cola for the kid, who bubbles into the straw. 'But it's good that the whole family is together. Except you, of course. Like the joint family of an earlier generation. Especially in a crisis.' Hegiste is comradely and outgoing, and avid about others. 'And your parents are clocking their years out with *all* their immediate family, in a house that they themselves built. Not many can end as fortunately.' Decent of Hegiste to catalogue the pluses. 'For them these things cast a long shadow. Partition, refugees, trauma and all that, redeemed in time with a crumb of earth.'

'Slightly more than a crumb. The house is not large, but it's restful.' One's own fallout shelter, a funkhole from wayfaring. Jamun has wanted to have done with the journey even before setting out. At which his mother has times out of number expostulated, 'But after we go, your father and I, how will you exist alone! In some sort of love with a married woman. Who will shoulder you? Your brother? Will his wife allow it? He himself?'

Still, on these occasions, she has reprehended falsely, only because it is incumbent upon her, or so she surmises. To tell the truth, no one pays any heed to her mind. To her, Jamun is boring but he is secure. The others are ever so often boorish and uncaring – but he yet evinces concern, possibly because he hasn't married thus far. She is very afraid that he will slip away and leave her alone with her husband.

In the afternoons the sun's white flames at the frosted glass of the windows, and with the windows closed the white rooms have a genial, opalescent glow. Jamun, with beside him a cast-off Robert Payne, mulls over satyagraha in South Africa, and *the* Gandhi battling like mad, as though hooked on mutiny, for emigrant strangers, and all the while perhaps undutiful to his family, because later his eldest son turns Muslim to gnaw him. Evidently, he, Gandhi, has found the wider world more vital, more deserving of his care, than the vicinal.

The evening before, Hegiste of the Gioconda face, hairless and artful, has cooed to his child to put out of its head a second cola.

But the child is mulish, and most articulately, in Hindi, 'No I want another just just now no you said.' Arms bobbing about, body out of true, face constricted and the maroon of beetroot, stomping on the pavement. Jamun marvels at the bewitchment of articulation – precisely when did the child master the words 'another', 'just', 'now', and learn to thread them coherently? Thus Burfi's son Doom too is daily being moulded. With a child's rotten memory, he might now find me a perfect alien; but (Jamun reminds himself) a four-year-old nephew's forgetfulness ought not to upset an adult, and in any case, Time will cicatrize all the lesions that it has made.

He recalls the time when Doom first sprang underripe Hindi on his aya. The child has marked that her pitted and usually nonplussed face becomes even more befuddled whenever she hears English; he has therefore registered that the one language that simply will not do for his mother – Hindi – is the sole one for his aya, who is practically his fosterparent. When Burfi witnesses his son bossing his aya around in Hindi, and otherwise wobblingly utter sense (lallate, for instance, buddyfukka – no guesses – at his uncle), he tastes both a parent's loss and the consummation. The ripening child is both a mission accomplished and a dream dispossessed. An allegiance towards *all* flesh must always abide within one (so Jamun ponders), but in extremity one's duty must hurl one first towards one's blood. To hold true to one's blood is more noble than to combat General Smuts in a remote country. Hearken unto thy father that begat thee and despise not thy mother when she is old. So Kasturi had cited. That night she had also given a fleck of her self away. 'In my pregnancy I am safe, I feel defended, only here, at home with my mother.'

After dinner Mrs Hegiste sighs. She takes stock of the untidiness around her, the child under her nose with rice ringing his plate and curd in his left ear and her husband freeing his belt to grant his tummy parole. 'I so wish I could go home,' she tells Jamun in her bumbling Hindi, and grins – 'home means parents, of course. When your parents pass away, you have no home at all – only your children do.' She then struggles to hinder the child from careening his toy car through his rice. 'Home is the hanky-panky of memory – honeyed, quilted – a fabulous once-upon-a-time lull.'

In his excitation Jamun reckons that it is his mother's self-pity that cries out for him. Yet time and time again, he himself, with a child's raw sentience, has itched to be there. He can't situate her in hospital but when he at last contemplates her in Intensive Care – gunmetal skull on green pillow, stertorous, terrorized exhalations, brow rutted with veiled agony – he recognizes anew her method of living: a bullheaded and dreary conflict because she discerns no choice, in the main with head down and neck steeled, but botching and ebbing decade after decade, the point of the struggle progressively disputable, never taking stock because her mind could unplug, and after it does, what endures is this gentler submerged strife amongst the shards of her self. But you unhoused me, he tells the fluttering eyelids. Yet I shouldn't've slipped away. They say death crops up for all. They say all things must pass. Yet here you breathe, out in the cold, excluded as ever.

But life will always ambush with its burlesque, won't it. For

Hegiste's child indicates and fishes for immediate enlightenment on four donkeys (mules?) fucking in the dead centre of the road. Two overloaded sand trucks have stopped, perhaps to clock them. A liver-coloured Fiat honks petulantly. Jamun is positive that he has never spotted two pairs before, in parallel cadence, and particularly in the evening. 'This is known as an orgy,' expounds Hegiste to his son in Marathi. 'Orgy' is the one word for which he doesn't dig up any Marathi equivalent; the brat reruns the word once or twice but looks dissatisfied in between looking bewitched. The donkeys' wangs are enormous, and faintly incurvated and tapered, like a lance, or a preposterous nose. They take Jamun back to the cover of the Classics Illustrated Comic of *Cyrano de Bergerac*. The donkeys' cocks are contoured like Cyrano's nose, only farcically longer, all but a foot. Jamun's father'd times out of number bought the comics for his two sons, but they'd favoured *Batman* over *Taras Bulba* and *The Apprenticeship of Miles Standish*, and he'd been crestfallen. But the comics abided, because nothing was ever cast away in their house – rickety chairs, sweaters, decrepit spectacle cases, and stapled to each item an evocation – icons from another time, gaining smudges over the decades as they witnessed a family bicker and grow. At diverse flecks in time the sons happen on the comics in unlooked for pockets – Jamun aged nineteen raking everything over for his charmed dice, Burfi at seventeen quarrying in a cupboard for mislaid condoms – and for a point of time (grasping the tatters of *Robur the Conqueror* or *Kit Carson*), they are scratched by a wistfulness; and later still, Burfi seeks to introduce his own young to Hiawatha, but somehow the knaves plump for Spiderman.

The donkeys then frolic, hoist their hind legs at one another, whinny, shut their eyes, pirouette their heads up to the gathering sky, disclose their gums and overgrown yellow teeth, and look humanly hideous. The males angle for to swarm up again. 'Now baby donkey will pop out, but won't play with you because he doesn't like children who mewl for two colas in one evening,' plumes Hegiste.

Hegiste to Jamun, again in Marathi. Hindi and English are not for the exchange of weighty ideas. They are used in the unthinking life – for office, to snarl at queuebreakers at the movies, against a spouse when the argument is lost, that sort of thing. 'Okay, are you ready for Drama In Real Life? Good. A widow, two children, not angelic but mortal kids, with snot and conjunctivitis. She has just enough money for respectability, but the imps have to lick their plates clean even when it's spinach. The youngest needs surgery, say at Tata's, an extortionate operation, not a footling sprain or something. A hotshot doctor, maybe a tiny Parsee with degrees like the alphabet, a dynamo with no time to shit. He warrants to the widow that the operation will not under any circumstances more damage the son. Either her child will turn as right as rain, or status quo. Cost a lakh or two. Widow irresolute, her liquidity versus the child's *mañana*. Grave shilly-shallying. In the end she borrows promiscuously, right and left, derangedly. The operation concludes in good time, and the child snuffs it. The Parsee debouches from the OT – or the scene of the crime? – eyes his watch, says, "Oho, I am delayed for Strasbourg," and takes wing with Carl Sagan for a metagalactic symposium on Bioplast in the Afterlife. The widow beholds the meagre Parsee hindquarters twinkle into a Volvo. Well? What now for her?'

'She should strip. Peel herself of her clothing, blindfold herself in white, brace the remaining son on her shoulders – the last burden – I presume that she's strong and sexy – and stride out for an interminable walk. She's almost free.'

Then in the air the remote, namby-pamby siren of the Municipality, tipping off its taxpayers that the river is ascending. The embryonic moon, the springtide, the exuberant rain, and the town lying in a hollow – so the waters ascending. 'Crocodile time,' says Hegiste. A yarn of the town, that in another decade the spate had jettisoned a baby crocodile of the salt flats into the gynae hospital, and that its daddy had shadowed it, in quest. But the flood alert doesn't faze the traffic one bit. The auto-rickshaws continue to squirm through, like flitting lifers ducking flak. Their hooters are ear-detonating whistles, catscratches on the eardrum.

In the verge beside the liquor den, a girl and maybe her younger brother play frisbee. The girl is in salwaar kameez and runs about crabbedly but blithely. The boy likes missing the frisbee and darting after it with weak squawks.

The oldies, cordially tipsy, loll in the courtyard amidst the enormous moss-green leaves. Mrs Hegiste's grandfather – gums, baggy chest skin, yellow-and-white-striped drawers with a front pocket – says hello and checks out Jamun's mother.

'She's in Intensive Care with a heart attack. Numb.'

Jamun and Mrs Hegiste's grandfather are chums, although Jamun fathoms his speech but poorly. His nose is even, but the rest of his face has slumped. Desiccated skin and cannonball knees. He wiggles his finger at a neighbouring antique and warbles (so Jamun hears), 'Bong suitcase leapfrog in Africa.' Jamun beams at him. They now and then rust together in Hegiste's verandah and observe the crabs. The grandfather has onetime told him (or so Jamun got hold of). 'You are good. You must visit *me* and not always only Satyavan. If you don't come and visit me, then I'll visit you!'

'Your mother will not be taken.' Fossil eyes with capillaries like red-hot webbing. 'For where in the womb of time will she meet with another son like you?' The other wrinkled lushes amen.

Daybreak, the tint of ashes. The impatient honking of lorries at the liquor joint – truckdrivers topping up and laying in for their stretched day's journey into the shadows of the next dive – disturbs Jamun's frightful nightmare, the rubble of which nevertheless rattles him all day. Nothing in his perception connects with it, yet its matter seems intimate, and so more frightening.

He is in a kind of rowing boat, closing in on the waterline of a river, or a lake. Everything is in focus, the keen night, the deathliness, the swish and suck of the oars and the water, the hush. Then the clotted ooze of the bank, like phlegm and mud. The lights on the salt knolls loom ice-blue in the moonlight, the livid white of the tubelights hemming the road pale into the wetlands. Other contours in the boat, intimate yet shadowy. Jamun is wearing his customary clothes, jeans etcetera, and somehow knows that in everyday light the sand will be oyster-grey and not brown. (How was he privy to those settings, runs in his head hourly – why had he sensed that on those flats he was no stranger? Perhaps he tacks on some minutiae later, in the discursive light, but the gooseflesh defies the day – he had trodden those sands before; on that ashen alluvium he had not lurched.) Perhaps the hours just before dawning. The two boatmen (Jamun is an extra for that one particular crossing) are of a piece – diminutive, swarthy and rock-hard (like those labourers who transit past his kitchen window at daybreak tea on their route to some sweat-and-blood slog. Jamun observes them over his teacup. Tits of black plastic like large headphones, and eyes stale, absent, with a strain of amber). Jamun and the two boatmen beach, and with the oars start to bludgeon the heads of the others in the boat. The oars are ponderous, and as he pivots and lunges, Jamun slumps in the wallow. His crazed gasps clash harshly with the stodgy thud of wood on forehead bone. None demur, but all look thunderstruck. Jamun knows them all, but for the life of him cannot recapture a sole face in his waking hours. He jets sweat, but the oarsmen are passionless. Next, with the punts they are ramming heads into the ooze, like shepherds mustering a flock, and striving to extricate themselves from the talons of frenzied arms. The heads struggle up again and again; about six or seven of them, less than ten at any rate. Their features are veiled, but the victims are indeterminately rural, in dhotis and short saris. The boatmen have butchered before – their looks, as deadpan as their biceps, are witness – but whether Jamun too has been so hellish, and whether he has commissioned them, is not plain. Do the heads all scuttle? But he is swarming up a sandbank hand over fist, a precious few feet, white with panic, as though one of the heads has hinged itself to his leg like an auxiliary knee. Steps, inexpertly incised in the mud. He senses gore on his person, manifest to all but himself, on his shirt front and chin, like milk from an upended cup at the lip. On the knoll (is the sand hump by the river artificial, a boneyard?) is a cottage, and a splendent sulphur light from a box-like verandah, tiny and featureless, of perhaps a Lower-Income-Group flatlet. A door creaks into a newish and characterless bathroom – but Jamun is positive that underfoot and beneath the tiles and pipes slink the snake and the scorpion. He must scour himself, but which portion most feverishly his terror cramps him from tracking down. And then a female frame at another door, somewhere, in a transparent dress, with a rank and succulent thatch full up to the navel, and she grimaces, and he tries to hide. Then the truck horns hit upon him at the end of a warm, flesh-pink tunnel and yank him out to the slate and steel before sunrise.

He opens his eyes and tastes an illimitable and opulent easing which stills him for most of that third day. Yet quick as thought, he time after time experiences his hands weighted with oars whamming heads into pap, and is rattled by the sleep that can spawn such bogeys. Complicity and fright squawk in his brain – these ogres of randomness and he must connect somewhere, in some hoop, for otherwise how did they slink past his forehead?

But to Mrs Hegiste in the afternoon, when he goes down to phone, he merely chinwags. He dials a clear line quite soon. 'Burfi? Jamun. How's she?'

No tangible alteration. She has groaned once or twice, and threshed her head about in some iceberg world, but her pulse has not steadied. Burfi sounds distrait and ineffably rushed, as though the exchange with Jamun is stretching beyond forbearance a raving urge to piss. 'You should know – she in fact died. I mean her heart stopped beating and she was just dead. Then we thwacked her chest like in a roughhouse, and her heart kicked off again – like an Ambassador taxi. We'd determined to give you the details when you came, but you're so long coming. Baba boohooed like an infant when her heart started up again – his breakdown was a crumb of comfort.'

At the time the attack comes about, Urmila is alone upstairs, in that jittery slumber particular to mortals on the wane. An inflamed late-August afternoon. Burfi's elder son Pista returns from school, saunters about the house to circumvent his lunch and the aya, sheds his uniform in a hideyhole which he doesn't reveal to her until her fury seems authentic enough to menace him just a bit, and pushes on to rouse his grandmother to irk her into dabbling at chess with him. He calls, next hoots into her ear, jerks her. Shyamanand downstairs is hauled out of his fretted torpor by the shrill pinging of a bell. Pista stands hard by him with the bell that is customarily at Urmila's beside, staidly pronouncing, 'Thakuma has snuffed it.' Shyamanand takes unconscionably long to get there. He stares at her and with the first spasm feels as though, somehow, an ice-cream sky with tendrils of chilled cloud has ambled into the room. With his right fist he bludgeons and pounds her heart, the bile of panic vaulting with each thump. He then slumps on to the floor and breaks down. Pista could never have conceived his grandfather in that situation. He goggles at his grandmother inhale and wheeze like snorting wheelwork. He is instructed to telephone his parents' offices. Neither is in. Shyamanand's tears frighten the boy; he scampers to Aya. Both, after boundless rummaging, exhume Dr Haldia's telephone number, whose answering service enchants Pista. Shyamanand, run-down on the floor, waits for some being to relent and be benign. Aya brings water and wad for Urmila's brow. Pista wishes to listen to the answering service again. Aya tramps out for counsel from her neighbourhood comrades. A timorous Pista dogs her. Shyamanand watches the water drip from the wad into the ashen hair that camouflages the ear, the rictus mouth, the slate skin at the temples, the gashes on either side of the mouth scored by exhausted time, the crescents of ivory where the unseeing eyes lurk beneath the lids, the penduline skin at the throat, the disordered sari, the naked gasping, the wasted, scissioned hands, the pewter-and-burgundy bangles. He trembles with helplessness and almost craves to be in her position where doubtless this exhaustion would not harrow him. He has not the self-mastery to rise from the floor. Two sons and a bloody daughter-in-law – but where are they now?

'Burfi. Are you high? You sound strange.' Jamun is mindful that they have already expended ample long-distance time on Mrs Hegiste's telephone.

A tee-hee, discomposing. 'Baba and I have squabbled, so what's new. This afternoon Joyce had almost agreed to look in at the hospital, but he carped, it isn't proper to send her, I should go in her stead, Ma at this hour should not be girdled by outsiders, by Christians who do not care for her, even in these circumstances don't her sons rank her worth their time – his usual drivel, but so untimely in this wretchedness that I – well – let fly.'

Jamun is fearful. Burfi has always been hot-tempered, and in his tizzies has ever so often flattened out only other people's belongings. But his essence, his marrow, is buoyancy, and he ordinarily inclines to break with the past. He is in this manner distinct from his father.

At their last booze bout, on his birthday, Burfi, sozzled legless, has stretched out a hand towards a disinclined Joyce, and blazoned, 'I don't hanker after a single breath of my past, not a sole second.'

Nobody heeds his words, or so it seems, until some prattle later, Shyamanand without warning says, 'Why should you be hungry for your past, you who like a darling pet has been tutored to forget?'

Urmila, strained and miserable, has lain down betimes, to writhe and twitch on the bedlinen till morning, as is her custom. Shyamanand thinks ill of drinking, yet is intent on brightening a birthday with his sons. Tippling at least congregates them. Otherwise for days he doesn't come upon them at all, scarcely sights them as they bundle off to and fro office, or some errand, or scurry downstairs in the mornings for the newspaper.

The geniality dissolves at Shyamanand's remark. Joyce shifts to wooden and quits the room. Jamun bides equably for Burfi to cut up rough before following her. Burfi's face stales. He crinkles his lips and glowers, circumventing other eyes. 'You've again squashed our spirit, our good humour by your rottenness.'

'By saying what's correct? Why should you languish for your past – your puppyhood and your pubescence? Your wife was no chunk of that.' Shyamanand's head wobbles in extravagant disillusion. 'Underling, bodyservant. Chattel, instructed not to remember.' He flails out in this style, head to wind, whenever he is tight.

Burfi breathes a squirt of abuse, muted but unmistakable, then trudges upstairs. Jamun smirks to himself, with unwitting guile. The sons are regularly chuffed by the dispraise of their parents, and once in a while stoke it. Jamun says, 'Now you can let your bile boil over on me.'

So parent and sons chat, shabby to one another without motive or zest. When Jamun plods up to get his spectacles, he overhears Burfi summing up to Joyce, ' . . . is past bearing! Inly he's so misshapen and scrunched up that as a father . . . ' Burfi decrees thus about once every fortnight.

Joyce declares, 'Not mad, but mean.' She half-relishes and half-rouses her husband's choler against the family, in particular when their boys are listening in.

When Jamun goes down, Shyamanand is loudly reminiscing to the supine Urmila in the adjacent room. He is addicted to sporting with memory. '. . . put a sliced egg in each of their tiffins. I wrapped salt and pepper separately, in Britannia Bread paper – Jamun never tried the pepper; in the evenings in his tiffin the tiny wad was all along unopened, but when I discontinued the pepper he was bitterly resentful: Burfi's tiffin has pepper, why have you denied me mine? Occasionally I salted and peppered the bread-and-butter. I furnished Jamun his lunchbox for roughly a decade. Burfi scorned tiffin when he was about twelve – too old, he said, which actually meant that his contemporaries were ragging him for being so dull as to cart food from home. In place of tiffin, he claimed cash.'

To jolt the chatter on and so to gladden his father, Jamun

asks, 'It was you? But I somehow recall Ma handing over our tiffins – we bypassing baths and ever so often toothbrushing too, and squelching our hair down by dabbling water on our heads, and she in that first light half-gloomily bellyaching of scant time and little help while cramming eggs and the night before's dinner into our two Kookwel aluminium boxes. Yes, Burfi mutinied in good time against tiffin, and also stopped recognizing me in school; confessing to a tiffin-chomping, bespectacled sibling was even more embarrassing than being a boy without a father, like Kuki.' Jamun is on the divan, frolicking with a derangedly overjoyed Doom.

His hush (but Jamun doesn't mark it) is a statement of Shyamanand's befuddlement. 'Your mother?' he in the end falters. 'Very well. Excellent.' He gazes at the convulsed Doom. Jamun is chivvying the child's yielding, perfumed belly with his nose. 'Is your memory *that* supple? Your mother made over your tiffin! How can you expunge me in this way? She laid out your breakfasts and uniforms while *I* crammed your lunchboxes.' As usual, he is dreadfully stung.

'How does it matter?' Jamun chortles boozily. 'Practise to forget. In our prankish memories, you can't win over Ma, in spite of your extended ratfight to woo us away from her. You should've spawned daughters in our place.'

Yet on that late-August afternoon, forsaken on cement flooring, with his wife outmatched and insentient – the whispers from an ice-cream sky and outside, in a lucid light, the cawing of a million birds – he, Shyamanand, sweats to rescue her for the twinges of mortality. She cannot escape. He pulls away her pillow, aligns her head, strives to knead her feet, chill and lumpish, wets with the wad her desert face and tries the phones again. Dialling is all but hopeless. A clear fear has clenched him. The notion baits him that his sons and Joyce have juggled matchlessly to incarnate before him their mother's conviction that in extremity, when he craves them most, they will vanish; when thus forlorn, his vanity in his wealth of sons will atomize to stubble. He explains birdwittedly the emergency to a voice in Burfi's office. With his faculties pirouetting, he converses with an intelligent daughter in Haldia's house and receives phone numbers that he cannot retain. He hobbles and subsides leadenly beside his wife's head. Her exhalations are sweet, like purulent molasses. Next, Time mislays its meaning till Aya and Pista flood in with a knot of locals. Still, easing swells through him like maiden rain on desert sands. Now he cannot be upbraided for her dead heart.

Jamun's eyes ache. Very likely because of the rot on TV, he says to Mrs Hegiste's grandfather, and wanders out to the verandah. He slips off his spectacles and enjoys the matt-finish rain. His eyeballs itch to twist themselves free. He hopes that his vision isn't worsening. In twenty years, near enough as many opticians have pronounced that sight wilts leisurely, but that with him, the decline should've ended with adolescence.

How memory twines and enlaces value into the slivers of one's past. Whenever Jamun wonders about his eyes, he involuntarily rakes up a green blackboard and copperish pubescence on buttermilk skin.

He is eleven, and he has almost conceded to himself that his vision is falling apart. For several prefatory months, he hasn't been able to read the blackboard from the terminal rows in class. In these circumstances, he's censured the teacher's handwriting to his classmates. After the vacations of summer, the new blackboards are bottle-green in colour. On the first Monday, the sun singes but the skies rain too. Jamun is yet taking to the new board when the initial drops sprout on the windowpanes with a rat-tat that he takes a breath or two to match with them.

'Ohhh, rain!' whoops Kuki in the bench ahead of his and next the window. Very unforeseeably, Kuki bobs up and sets to shedding his uniform! The class gapes. Copper-brown shorts and cream shirt are abandoned on his Radiant Reader Part Two. Jamun notes that Kuki does not believe in undies. Then the play of light on a toasted fleeciness, on the flour skin at the crotch, as, naked, Kuki corkscrews to the window. He means to scurry off to cavort in the rain, but the thunderstruck teacher butts in at that instant. She is Mrs Jeremiah, meaty and baleful. Jamun abhors her with the ecstasy that one tastes with those whom one derides by day and is hot for in the camouflage of night. She is perhaps (alas, who can tell?) turned on by Kuki's nakedness, for she lumbers up to him, whinnying with arousal, and thwacks him a sledgehammer on his right ear. Kuki begins to pule some seconds before the clout; after it, he, yowling, lurches away from Arsehole (thus Mrs Jeremiah is felicitously named), across the room and out the door. Mrs Jeremiah brays that he be intercepted, and twenty-seven scholars leave their seats for the exit, of which twenty-four are dissuaded by her succeeding snarls.

It is in this atmosphere that Jamun is directed to rise and fill in the blanks on the board. He is unable to read a single letter. He stirs from his bench to make towards the board but his steps markedly exasperate Mrs Jeremiah. 'You'll stop right where you are! Read from your place!' she bawls, and struts up to him, udders and hams jouncing like ill-congealed pudding.

'We are now starting an eye test,' she proclaims to a breathless class, and positions an exercise book over Jamun's right eye. 'Read!' But his eyes are stitched to the spectacle of her hunk armpit, inches from his thorax, a meaty spread of talcum and sable stubble.

Mrs Jeremiah deduces that Jamun is being saucy, therefore she clobbers him till her meatloaf arms enervate and he mellows into a puling ruin, his lubricity having pelted Kuki's way with her very first whack. In his school diary, she carps, 'Has taken to impertinence lately. Also has some difficulty with his vision. Requires an eye check without delay.' To Jamun she suffixes, twitching a cautionary forefinger like a prick in rut, 'You'll get the bashing of your life if you don't show up with spectacles tomorrow.'

Neither parent endorses Mrs Jeremiah. In the evening, Urmila is sluicing the washbasin, office sari kilted at the waist. 'Ma, Jeremiah said today I must have glasses.' She stares at him, dismayed in an involuntary sort of manner. Shyamanand is gasping and glutting himself with the chill leavings of a watery lunch. 'Nonsense. But what roused her to say so?'

'No idea.' After a pause, without enthusiasm, condensedly, recapturing Jeremiah's uppercuts and maledictions, 'But I can't make out the board too clearly from where I sit.'

'Can the others?' Afterwards, Shyamanand bears up a newspaper a few feet from Jamun and invites him to read an ad. Jamun crooks his head left and right, elbows his chin out, then into his throat, withstands the itch to slither two paces forward, and is mute. Shyamanand is bitterly surprised, somewhat malcontented, and wavers awhile that Jamun is befooling him. Finally, 'We'll undergo an eye test at the KGH this week.'

Dinner is zestless and incidental, drudgery. Aya irks in the kitchen, half-fudges a tantrum, and flits. Urmila's face tousles. Burfi is enmeshed in Kuki's house, playing high. Shyamanand samples the dal. Its tastelessness goads him into murmuring, 'Everybody's eyesight in my family is first-rate. But Jamun at age eleven needs spectacles.'

Urmila checks her nibbling and stares at him. Her gullied brow is margined by oversize livid veins. Her mouth warps and she mewls, 'No one in my family puts on glasses either!' In reply, Shyamanand budges slightly to squint more finically at the afternoon newspapers. Urmila feeds herself through her tears. Jamun exits to frig on the roof underneath a hyaline night sky; Kuki has enlightened him, and he has accepted, that his onanism and his flaccid vision are twined together, but at that moment he doesn't upset himself with the notion. He routinely vanishes for his handpractice when he intuits a wrangle between his parents. Urmila evacuates the table. Her abandon has fattened and pulped the skin beneath her eyes.

The next Saturday, dawning. Shyamanand, Burfi and Jamun in their charpais on the roof, comatosely witnessing the sky slide through her tints. Jolted by the bellow of dogs from the Sikhs' house, whose border wall (snips of glass sitting on its ridge like a crew cut) has elbowed forward to gulp the road-shoulder into the house lawn. In the spectral light of every daybreak and dusk, the dogs yawp evenpacedly. Shyamanand has distended and jolted the imaginations of his sons with, 'It is possible, isn't it, that those Sikhs have no hounds at all? For the dogs that *can* hustle them up the ladder would be too costly. Far cheaper to arrange for tape recordings of the baying of mongrels, some hellish streetfighters. Our Surds play back the tapes to deflect the unwanted – neighbours poorer than they, schoolchildren hawking lottery tickets. Plus, for ultra effect, they rerun the cassette at those moments of the day when the world seems at anchor. Now, shut your eyes and focus on that barking. Well? And none of us has ever spotted one of those Surds with a dog, have we? Yes?'

Thereafter, at a thousand and one unannounced moments in his life, the neck-and-neck baying of dogs dredges up for Burfi the halcyon-day-image of roguish male Sikhs, with hair stumbling loose like an avalanche to the shoulders – perhaps a crystal holiday morning, and the males have earlier fumigated their scalps abreast of blue buckets in the garden – now crouching over an upmarket stereo system (whose speakers skulk in the prodigal moneyplant that fawns on the wise pipal by the gate), index fingers taut above the buttons Rewind and Play, about to unmuzzle the whelp snarls at Burfi vacillating at the gate, wiggling in his hand the raffle tickets pressganged on him by the Jeremiah who bullied him four years before she baited Jamun.

'Poor vision can be inherited, like diabetes and the assorted lunacies, from our parentage. The eyes of somebody or the other in your mother's family or mine might have been sickly. This is not good. In manhood, some spheres will not be for you – Air Force, certain engineering careers. Let's see how you handle today's eye test. Yet I can't think of a sole example of excessive myopia in either family.'

So the King George's Hospital at eleven. A Raj structure; with time, the verandahs have been blinkered with humpbacked plywood for more space. Public Works has slapped on the exterior a rust-red that scuffs off on the domes and shoulderblades of the drones against the walls. Like the average mortal, Jamun resents hospitals – the squeeze, the infestation, the torpor on hardwood benches, the trepidation at the malodour of purulence.

They have determined to reach by nine. For both Urmila and Jamun, the greatly loathesome excursion is a little uplifted by the fellowship of the other. They cadge with and scramble into an auto-rickshaw because both quail at buses. Urmila is also somewhat uncertain about her adroitness to prance on to a bus. 'The conductor waits till my one foot remains on the road, then the bus reels away. The steps are very skiddy and high. My legs are columns of mucus,' she inventories proudly as she gathers her sari about her and shortsightedly examines the floor of the rickshaw for crud. Jamun corkscrews and, through the oval hole in the rexine behind his head, waves to his father. Time after time, Shyamanand scans from the verandah when one of the family sets out of the house.

At the hospital, Urmila trudges crabbedly, drearily, clutching tongslike Jamun's wristbones for reinforcement. Underneath her sari, her legs will be wan and spongy, with veins varicose like a bluish subcutaneous skein. One foot forward; next, the rear foot inches abreast as though she is always fording chancy stepping-stones, and wishes not to wet her feet at all. When she walks, she scrutinizes the ground with the vigilance of a child sleuth with a magnifying glass dogging Professor Moriarty. 'Corns and arthritis, but when I was a schoolgirl, I was the wind!' After every few steps, she halts, reconnoitres her surroundings, wheezes and clacks, 'Your father was surveying us, wasn't he? To check that I don't mess things up? That we cross the road safely, that I pick an honest auto wala? How shabby he is. Why doesn't he escort you himself? When you grow up, you'll realize – he's unforgivably idle and self-absorbed. No, much cushier not to help in any way, instead to inconvenience and belittle till your wife wants to die, yet not permit her enough time to die.'

Urmila manifests not acrimony, but a kind of blithe untrammelling, a garrulous sunniness to an on-off listener. At the OPD, she unlatches her bag for her spectacles. Jamun gazes at small change, derelict one- and two-rupee notes, two or three rectangles of folded paper – recondite, with smudgy creases – the Lakme face powder compact with its fractured rose-plastic top on which Jamun has gummed a sticker of Batman, one flesh-pink, two-inch disc of the edible clay to which she is addicted (the sons have fitfully nibbled at some – paradisal!), two ponderous swarms of keys, the travel soap that couches in the lining solely to transude its balm, her scarlet Parker fountain pen with which Jamun secretly tests his calligraphies, a scalloped kerchief sulphur-yellow with desuetude, the carmine lipstick that like all other shades of red looms discrepantly against her etiolated skin (the same shade that Jamun, in his fantasies, tarts up on his bum-pulsing schoolmarms in their sunglasses and nylon stretchpants, sleeveless caftans, high-noon boobs, pruned armpits and hairdos the size of a bucket), (Urmila illumes with her lipstick only on signal events – when her kin overrides and tows her to the cinema for *The Sound of Music*, or on a Sunday afternoon with the grandsons on the beach – perhaps once every three years, maybe twice), a talisman of rudraksha beads, and *The Good Earth* by Pearl Buck – the job-lot of her portable world.

Eye tests at the KGH are scrupulous. They are also gratis if one vouches that one's family earnings are preposterously humble. Everyone fibs with felicity on the blanched old-ivory forms. Timeless laps in convoluted queues – Jamun quails whenever Urmila diffidently tries to pioneer new Ladies Only queues – toadying to unshaven bespectacled clerks, exploring the hospital for a loo that will not enrich Urmila with some ghoulish chancroid fester. The woman ophthalmologist is laidback, rotund, with a bobbed beehive hairdo, bull lips that will not bestride her teeth, and a tumid face that for the burgeoning Jamun resembles the nob of a sprouted phallus. He can't read the final three rows of the illuminated box chart. He sidles up to it while Urmila natters to the doctor and tries to mug up the lines. The penultimate line is peculiarly naughty –

C O Q C G O. To his vision, the letters look like a file of minute black quoits.

The doctor dashes off a prescription. Urmila condoles with Jamun, and airs a brief mortification. 'Spectacles don't count. Brainy persons put on spectacles. Perhaps you read again and again in minimal light, and earned your poor vision. Henceforth you'll always be propping up eyeglasses, deadweight on the bridge of your nose.'

The basement shop within the hospital compound offers spectacles at some concession, or so their billboard announces. Urmila and Jamun are jittery and morose, as seconds before one's set piece at an elocution contest. He ventures on a gold frame and inspects the bespectacled twin unknowns in the open-book looking-glass. The gold frames are overly costly. 'You look so elderly,' grimaces Urmila dispiritedly, and commends without fervour a biscuity Clark Kent pair. Neither bestirs him/herself immoderately over the choosing, and Jamun in addition feels both abasement and an undefined complicity. He returns for his spectacles six days hence. They aren't done. He, with deliverance vibrant on his skin, does not go back for the tryout until a fortnight after, when the assiduous Jeremiah hustles his recall with a rally of stunning haymakers.

Thus for Jamun, a miraculous virginal world careens into focus at three on one ordinary, false-monsoon afternoon. Each atom of the stuff of existence around him is transmuted, steeled and fissioned, is a deflector of a crystalline light. He feels wobbly. The ground appears to lunge towards him. Demeanours and vegetation, stray dogs and the waterfall-blotches of a million micturitions against compound walls, crows floating like black hang-gliders on a candyfloss sky – all contours have diamond lines, and the light is cusped like broken glass. Each leaf is an entity, and all creation looks scrubbed and lacquered with dew. Yet Jamun plucks off his glasses. For he feels etched upon, spotlit, as acutely edged as what he beholds; he is marred for life, he thinks, and for a flicker mulls over which parent is to be arraigned.

In a few days, he starts slipping his spectacles off whenever he is distressed, glum or enervated, is with persons whom he thinks are goodlooking, or aspires to dazzle, or whose traits he wishes to commandeer. In such contexts, his bedimmed sight rallies after a fashion his spirit; with the years his vision slumps in leaps and bounds.

'Going home?' The woman, sixty-five-ish, on Jamun's left in the plane, percolates through his pesky half-snooze. She has earlier softened him into ceding to her his window seat ('I've a soft spot for the sunrise') and has powdered her mug all through takeoff. 'So drearily lower-middle-class, Ma, to powder your face – oof, makes me unwell,' so Burfi has chorused for years on end, actuating his mother not a bit. For Jamun, powdering the face and neck is a deed not of womanhood, but of motherhood, executed (in the seconds pinched from the treadmill) to camouflage the chinks in a doleful housewife face. The ritzy perfumes from Dubai and Singapore that Joyce gifts Urmila in succeeding years are all pickled in her black trunk, and enjoyed on incomparably momentous jubilations – Burfi's civil marriage, for example, for which Urmila swaddles herself in Benares silk and where she grieves only because she feels that she has to provide her spouse companionship.

Yet Kasturi powders her face too. 'Much cheaper and much less hanguppy,' she retorts to a sardonically diverted, knottedly concupiscent Jamun contemplating her floundering with a sari in the darkish light, some seven months ago. In the looking-glass, she dabs and smothers with the puff. In that second, that she is older than him cannons into his skull anew.

'But I've all along bracketed it with mothers, Boss. When women who haven't hatched use face powder, can't one deduce that they tacitly *yearn* to bear kids?'

In response, Kasturi inexpertly lights a Wills and exhales a haze of smoke at him.

'Yes, I'm on my way home.' The window-seat-hijacker is grey and patrician. She is Mrs Shireen Raizada, she gabbles. She is petrified of aeroplanes, and to outpace her cold feet jabbers the hind leg off a donkey. 'My youngest has flunked three times in the Ninth Standard and once again in the Tenth now. How much more will his father have to satisfy the school with to hold him in there? Truly, living is null – like mud – when one's children are one's misfortune. Everything feels ill-spent – dust. But one twitches on. Good blood is the real fortune. I don't suppose he's dense, but what tension in the house whenever the exams are louring! How I quail at his Progress Reports. And then I'll cop it and some petticoat will roost on his head and milk out my sap. All he achieves day by day is exercise, three hours in the morning and two more hours by nightfall. He's soured on those days when he can't strain and gasp for that long. Nothing else upsets him.'

'I'm positive that all children dismay their parents now and then,' assuages Jamun vacantly, with a smart-ass smirk that connotes that he considers himself exempted. But for sure he isn't, and his words are more accurate than his smirk. Because memory is a crank, he does not remember the cold sweat that he and his brother have touched off, a million times, on those who cling to them. They've never threshed about for their parents with any remotely comparable strain. Burfi has scarcely troubled his head about them, or so Jamun reckons, with the entangled malevolence of the younger sibling. Yet parents can lacerate with equal virulence, so Burfi avers. 'You must recall – on the morning of my marriage, and Joyce within range, fixedly simpering and steaming in her Kanchipuram, weighted like bedding, Ma distrait and asking whether what I was about to sign held the provisos for divorce.'

Of course, Jamun too has triggered off enough disquietude in his parents. In his early pubescence, for instance, he has temporarily – but deeply – strained his mother with his clumsy itch for the grocer's boy (a man, really – old, malodorous, balding, buxom). Subsequently, as a hugger-mugger bisexual adult, he now and then remembers, with a feeling of lost blessedness, his unpolluted and stark, axial rut of those weeks. While the house had dozed, in the inflamed afternoons, he had waited, aguish with lust, for the buffeting on the back door.

Towards which he scampers, from whichever part of the flat he is in, to simper a welcome at Garam Gandu – Kuki's name for him (Hindi: meaning Hot Arselender, according to Jamun, and Hot-Arse Lender, according to Kuki). Jamun observes the plump frame of the shopkeeper's assistant, and randomly touches his bicep, and adventitiously rubs against his thigh, and bulges rasher and rasher every afternoon, and is tantalized on the days of the man's truancy; he is finally impeded, one day – 'Shall I tell your father that you don't know what to do with your hands?' – at which, in bafflement and funk, Jamun strafes him with a squirt of the newly learnt bawdry that is a feature of growing up. Bewildered, distressed, that evening, he is revealed to his mother. 'You'd better watch your second son.' Urmila is too shut in and fatigued for the stricture actually to register before Jamun is quaveringly confuting it. 'But, Ma, he broke two of our eggs, right before my eyes, and crammed them raw into his mouth – I only called him, bastard – his hands were all gooey with the yolk, and he wanted to fondle my face with that glueyness – so I called him sonofabitch. And he said, if you asked about the eggs, I should say *I* boiled and ate them.'

Urmila cautions neither; presumably, she just wishes the unpleasantness away. Jamun and Garam Gandu backslide into familiarity, into the itch, the irksome incontinence, the second-rate frottage, the limp menace of disclosure, till divergent yearnings tug the mellowing boy away.

Afterwards, Jamun, once in a way, broods on how much his mother had distressed herself over the affair of Garam Gandu, whether and how often she remembers the matter, and how marvellous she is to tend her son's secrets, for certainly she couldn't've divulged his proclivity to any soul. Or could she? At these moments, he vows to requite her caring, and for a time strives to be heedful of her numberless, paltry, annoying wants. Of course, he falters in honouring his vow; with him, as with many others, the allures and undertakings of the fleeting world bid fair to prevent duty (or contrition, if you prefer).

Mrs Raizada is still chinwagging when the plane begins its descent. Her eyes are glazed and infinite like the crushed dog's on the day of the telegram. Those eyes had ricocheted on to the rich, almost chewable, pages of the Bodley Head Robert Payne, and beyond the book on to the gossamer hexagons of the mosquito net, and the albumen-white of the ceiling, unmarked yet by spider and lizard. Mucus eyes; they had far transcended this life. For a moment or two, Jamun had watched the dog's head in the fading rain, slackly attached to some wads and dollops of flesh, and the blood slowly and without end poisoning the water.

Jamun considers (an idiosyncrasy of his, to sport with the features of his kin) whether he would've preferred his mother to look like Mrs Raizada. Like his mother, she also appears equably vain about the inwrought comeliness, underneath the powder and crannies, of her face. Urmila is placidly certain that no matter what she wears, no one can doubt her ingrained gentility. Yet one afternoon, decades in the past, Kuki's mother, out of the evanescent rancour that one neighbour feels for another, had flabbergasted her by mistaking her for their communal sweeperess.

The sweeperess has decamped the day before with one of Aya's male friends, a scraggy, peevish wolf called Kishori. The fuss over their moonlight flit impedes Aya from even thinking of the stodginess of housework. She, on the rooftop with her remaining chums, is in a huddle over the misadventure. Urmila screeches and yelps for her for some time. She will never be forceful enough to compel a toughie like Aya. Then Shyamanand begins to carp about the racket. Temples turgid at their insouciance, Urmila totes the garbage bin out.

'Oho, Laxmi,' miaows Kuki's mother to Urmila's back, 'the refuse of other houses is much more important than mine, is it – oh, it's you, Mrs – from the back I thought – with the rubbish pail – '

From the verandah, Jamun spots in the ice-blue of the road

tubelights his mother stumping arduously away. He glides out after her, past Burfi at this desk practically swooning over the newborn incubus of logarithms. Stalking Ma is initially more diverting than Hindi homework – easier too; only after a time does it drag. She wends at a foot's pace, does not look up or about and, Jamun recognizes at once, is not going to any specific place. Feebly trying to give her existence the slip, at least for a time. Dinner will wind her in, or the responsibilities of feeding a family, so she befools herself. For when she doubles back, her husband, ramping against his stomach ulcer, will have sated his jaws with whatever his fingers fumble on in the fridge before reverting to his divan. Burfi, study and dinner mopped up helter-skelter, will be in Kuki's house, clipped round-eyed to their TV. Jamun the gourmandizer will have guzzled once with his father and once alone, hating Burfi for having (while moseying past the table, aware that only Urmila and Jamun have yet to eat, and that his mother will never bleat over the dole of a leftover dinner) crammed down the best of the mutton. If there *is* mutton, when Urmila eats alone, wretchedly, she gets much gravy and many potatoes.

Her footfalls are uneven in the dispersed blue-ivory light that makes Jamun feel that he has slipped on sunglasses at nightfall – a tread more rickety than expected of her age, incarnating her infirmities and her cheerlessness. She does not trudge very far. She squats on the culvert by the lane, within earshot of the cigarette-wala from whom Burfi has lately, cloak-and-daggerly, started buying Gold Flake Filter Kings, parroting the adult world. She shows no wonder at seeing Jamun. Sluiced with sobbing, her face is voided and sacramental, as a landscape after a cloudburst.

'Come, sit.' Jamun sits, wondering whether any of the ambulant louts are going to be offensive about his mother perched alongside the lane.

'I rise at four-thirty every morning. Long before the sun. Every morning. Holidays, Sundays, nothing, no variation. Four-thirty, in the murk I ooze out of a bone-wearying sleep. Lurch in the kitchen, warm the milk, make tea for myself, skull pulsing. Scared of going to the toilet because of my piles. How to explain, and who shall listen? Every morning, how to express, that I blench at the thought of the lavatory, the abasing ignominy, the pain. In there, twenty minutes, now and then forty, face gnarled with exertion, once in a way tears, my calves and hams bubbling with fatigue. Five-thirty or so, back to the kitchen. Yell myself hoarse for Aya, who shall never descend before seven – from time to time she shrills at me not to disturb her. Tea again for your father – nowadays for Burfi too, he avows that he's come of age. Wake the two of you up, beseech and plead, please get up, you're going to be late for school, please wake up, your tea is becoming cold. Then wait, for you both to be indulgent with me and forsake the snugness of your cots. Possibly yet another intolerable visit to the lavatory. Pour out for your father his tea, detail the two of you for your baths etcetera. Bawl for Aya afresh. Screech at each of you through the doors to wash properly and not to fool yourselves. Whip up your breakfasts – eggs, porridge. Pack your tiffin boxes, lay out your school uniforms. Try to parry your vexing questions on your clothes – Ma, where's my left sock? Ma, why's Burfi not loaning me his other shirt? Park the bucket out for the sweeperess, make over clothes to the laundry boy, fish up the exact small change for the milk boy. Exhort you two to mop up your breakfasts in the moments remaining to you, sweet-talk you into not leaving your tiffin boxes behind. Lend Aya a hand in scrambling some breakfast for your father and me – and herself, and her several playmates – clout the beds into shape. Stow lunch for your father and me, hand on money to Aya for the cooking gas or the shopping, check with her what to buy – pointless, of course, for she buys only what her chum-of-the-week craves to eat – endure Aya's cactus patter on my stricken life while my temples flutter with the knowledge of the lifelong deficit of money, money, money.

'Then office. Meanwhile, your father, lolling in bed, has sipped several teas and inspected the newspaper with disrelish, grieving once in a way, perhaps, that the tea has cooled. I bathe and breakfast, virtually at the same time, scamper to the garage over the stabs of my corns. Forbear your father mouthing in assorted heinous ways that *I* delay him for office, the beast. Shut the doors of the garage after he sucks dry some *ten minutes* to back the car out – I stand and wait, my tummy tight with disquiet, wrath and worthlessness, why can't he ever precede me to the garage, even one single morning, why do only *I* have to shut the doors after the car? He could save me ten whole minutes.

'In office – borrow money and evade the loansharks. One or two peons will mince in, bank their hams against my desk, chomp paan and review my refunding power. In every chat, every exchange, I'm blemished – I've borrowed and have paid back or have to pay back, or I've wheedled to borrow, and he or she has begged off, perhaps with restraint, very likely without, but has noised abroad the titbit over the tiffin boxes: she's *still* cadging. Or I will borrow in good time to repay an earlier loan – or I will doubtless borrow in the long run. All day this tingling – this guilt and fretting – muddling with the leaden routine of office. I hate money because of the domination that it – it *squats* over me. Lunch with your father, at which, over Aya's vapid cooking, he recycles his strictures.

'Back home at six. I long to finish everything, scurry through everything, *conclude* it – feeding, trudging, clothes, being – so that at the end I can anchor; but where is the lull? In place of stillness, I reap only Kuki's mother designedly mistaking me for her sweeperess. Feed and distend once more your father – else the ulcer in his belly detonates through his jaws. Put up with Aya's gripes against her chums. Pass over the lurching in my skull, speculate about dinner. Food, all the time, food – consider all day what to feed others, yet perpetually bear their censure, stinking of an open-mouthed belly. Aya might not have gone to the market at all – some tip-top alibi – her menopause that's been obliging her now for some years, her kidneys, her breathing – meantime, she would've hobbled off for a matinée cinema show – nothing in the kitchen to cook. Tea yet again! And again the apprehensions of the lavatory. Your accusations against the day –

Kuki cheated at badminton, and jostled your elbow so that your orange bar fell. Burfi not at home for hours on end, another wellspring of misgivings – who are these friends that he doesn't bring home, are they lost souls or what? In particular that Assamese. But now the day is breaking up, and my corns are spiking me. What to ram into these greedy-guts? Who will help me to sate them? By and by, one of Aya's fan club will saunter to the market. From his bed your father will cavil – I never check the accounts, so how am I convinced that he's not swindling us? Of course I'm not convinced! But why doesn't your father oversee the house himself? Oh, he's shameless, hopeless. Make the beds, tidy the rooms. By the time dinner comes around, you'll've mewled fifty times to me that we should eat like Kuki. Very likely, you'll glide away to Kuki's and cringe before his mummy, bob around her, bear with and even thrill to her churlishness about me – can't I even sustain my own litter that it should cadge for grub in the houses of neighbours! By dinner time your father's belly will've thickened with snacks. So I eat by myself. Exhausted, skull on pillow, sleep evasive, waiting for Burfi, where is that son?'

Jamun glowers at his mother's profile. He has from time to time been informed that his features are hers, and Burfi's Shyamanand's. Jamun is guilty and jittery that his mother has intuited right about Kuki's mother. Urmila's sapience vexes him. Indeed, in the preceding one year Kuki's mother's meaty upper arms, inch-long rose-pink fingernails, lifebelts of lard underneath the restraining blouses, grandiose yet skittish buttocks of lime-green georgette, have unmuzzled a warm sap in Jamun's lower belly that eddies into his scrotum and about his coccyx.

He gazes at Mrs Raizada's face against the ellipse of the aeroplane window. Beyond her coiffure is the silver of the plane wing and the arid turf of the airfield. So. Back home after seven months, in which time his mother has suffered one piles operation and one heart attack, and he himself has picked up Kasibai and her lovechild Vaman, who is thick-ribbed and slow, and is charmed by mirrors.

# 2

# A MAROON CINEMA HALL, AND AYA'S PASSING

Kasturi beyond the thick glass of the airport, in a baggy coral-and-sulphur kameez that effectively keeps in purdah her pregnancy, plumpish but restive – no more mopish pallor. Jamun touches her elbow and sights Chhana ten feet away. He introduces them. 'Chhana, my cousin, my father's niece. Kasturi, my friend.' Chhana is still bespectacled and meagre. The sun is temperate and wholesome. The palms that fringe the airport road lurch in the gusts from the sea like spellbound women votaries with haunch-length hair, bedevilled by some shaman's philtre, corkscrewing their heads and arms about to a bacchic drum. Death simply could not be in this fair weather.

'Shall we drive straight to the nursing home? She's on the mend. She floated up out of coma last evening. She recognized me. She couldn't speak, though. Her eyelids shuddered. Your father's at the hospital too, though I urged him not to exhaust himself. She in fact croaked! Her heart knuckled under. Your father's catnap was disturbed by the tinkling of Pista entertaining himself with her bell. How long was she dead? A minute? Ten minutes? One hour? Maybe she'd been kaput an entire hour and nobody realized. Wonder how this'll affect her. I picked up somewhere that the brain can be choked for keeps if we don't provide it oxygen for a minute. She should never've undergone that piles surgery. That ghoul Haldia – doctors will *slay* for money – steadily tittering and fibbing, their forefingers and thumbs moist and expectant, itching for notes. The sight of her is grisly. All the time she has globules of some fluid on her temple. I imagined water from swabbing. But they were perspiration – swollen pellets of cold, cold sweat.'

'If you're driving straight to the nursing home, you could drop me off on the way,' proposes Kasturi. 'Only family should be with her. Outsiders would be cramping.'

The red lettering on the glass swing doors asks Jamun and Chhana to shed their shoes and slippers outside the cardiac wing. While Jamun, squatting on an invisible bench, back sheer against the wall, right ankle positioned on left knee, tugs at his shoelaces, a hospital attendant, hirsute and ruffianly, swishes past him and through the glass doors (the whine of which decelerates to a hushed groan, recalling for Jamun a gramophone ditched by electricity), bearing a covered rust-and-enamel bedpan that perhaps retains some festering offal, with his leather slippers squeaking like rats making whoopee.

A moderate cubicle, about twelve into ten. On the white iron cot, amidst chalky bedlinen and dun blankets, upended glucose bottles and tubing (like an aerial vista of a lattice of motorways and bypasses), in harrowed repose, a face the colour of mouldering teeth. Tall windows of tinted glass. Beyond, one more donkey-grey building with air conditioners embedded in it like cheese canapés poked into a cabbage at the centre of a feast. Wires from her brow shimmying to the corner, to an apparatus with a black screen that charts some electronic cardiograph. Beneath it, sunshine-yellow digitals whiffling helter-skelter .. thirty-seven ... twenty-nine ... fifteen ... one hundred and two ... The graph itself will, all at once, paroxysmically, yoyo up and down like the work of a toddler (wielding a pencil clutched like a dagger) being inspired to draw. On the dun blankets, derelict, an overblown and squelchy forearm, bluish. Through and above it, more rubber, steel and glass. The back of her hand is livid, but the fingers are chilled ivory. A frightful convulsive breathing, like being riveted within the breast of a beast by its amplified death throes. Her eyelids flicker unremittingly, unsettled moths. Her mouth gapes, as though composedly waiting to be fed. The ellipse from the edge of her nostrils to her chin protrudes simianly, shoved forward, as it were, from the root of the skull by the heel of a strong palm. To Jamun, his mother seems a vacant incarnation of a being till recently familiar. We are all like this, he mulls confusedly, sinking monkeys.

He lightly strokes a brow that is wheelmarked in gagged agony. Warm. Disorderly salt and pepper hair that she, in vexation once, had snicked off at the neck. In the air an inapposite redolence – oh, Chhana's scent. 'Burfi's just driven your father back. She's asleep. She's now conscious – has mumbled from time to time, but incoherent. Gibberish,' says Chhana, grimacing, gnawing her underlip.

A silver sheen on Urmila's cheeks. Hair, white down. Jamun is positive that it did not exist before. To him it augurs death.

'Your Baba's in wretched shape. Like being thwacked with a hockey stick. He senses it, if she breathes her last, no one else will suffer his antics, the house will just cave in.' Chhana trails about the bed, fretful, fearful, eyes so distended with contrition and irresolution that Jamun can't grapple with them. 'I'm going out for a cigarette.' Chhana withdraws swiftly.

'Ma.'

Ma, I, Jamun. I deferred for four days. I'm sorry. Befuddled, he smoothes down the grey strands over her ear. Like Chhana, he feels eerily vulnerable and does not know whether he should weep in atonement. Her turgescent, dogtired face is a mask. Her torso alone spasmodically leapfrogs for air, an old machine. He tips over and kisses her cheek, reflecting that it is due from him and perhaps he should have kissed her much earlier. He dazedly hankers after prodigious slabs of Time, weeks and years, in which he can indolently natter to her, lounge with her in pink-stone benches beneath the palmyras by the sea, evoke for her the trajectory of his day and, with the swish and rustle of the white horses of the sea, listen to the yarns of her yester-years.

'One day, when I am at ease and not tuckered out, I shall recount to you my life, what actually occurred.' Thus a good many times, across the years, Urmila has, singly and together, vowed to her incurious sons. 'Perhaps not to you, Jamun, you are too passionless, unforgiving. Maybe I shall tell Burfi. For all his unsteadiness, he will salute my survival, he's warm.'

'Burfi!' Jamun's pique spirals with the slump of his self-restraint. 'Burfi a responsive audience!' He struggles to explain. 'A listener should be painstakingly picked. The good listener invests esteem on both the fiction and the raconteur. But Burfi! He'll merely be prurient about the sex and the scraps, so that he can recount the ruttish details to Joyce, suffixing a "See! Even my parents are with it! The proof's these peccadilloes from the bloom of their lives – my mother was no gentle sufferer, and they married for – well, *not* for caste, and took to separate beds soon after – isn't that modern, Joyce, and aren't you dazzled?"'

A meaty nurse chugs in, stalked by Chhana, asking questions to her back. Meaty looks down her nose at her watch, twitches a tube out of that bulbous and torpid forearm, punctures in an injection, shoves a paper at Jamun, yawps, 'Medicines. Required at once. And Accounts Branch has conveyed that of the initial deposit of four thousand rupees for the patient, you've only paid two hundred. Treatment might end otherwise,' and chugs out, churlish and invincible.

At home, in the driveway, with a tennis ball and a child's cricket bat, Burfi (flared jolted eyes in a tight-knit, stable figure), Pista and Doom are playing cricket. Shyamanand sits, expressionless, in the verandah. Doom is bowling to Burfi. Pista, at ease under the umbrella of the neem tree that Shyamanand and Jamun had sown eleven years ago to shield the south-west wall from the malevolence of the afternoon sun, is cackling outrageously at Doom's manner of bowling. In his hilarity, Pista cants forward till his nut closes in one his knees, somewhat like a perpendicular foetus, or shudders back and forth, pitches his arms about, embraces himself, as though the jollity is an incubus that needs to be exorcized. His mirth further exhilarates Doom, who scuttles back to his bowling run on his dumpy, precarious legs, each unerring, twinkling step a marvel, twirls, draws up for an instant to paw the ground and glower at the batsman (as he has divined from TV, after the fashion of Pista's godlings, the doyen bowlers of Pakistan and the West Indies), then trundles forward like an irate crank to within ten feet of a theatrically intimidated Burfi, and, face wine-dark with excitation, intentness, and mirth, bungs the ball about ninety degrees wide of target. Impenitent, he and Pista then spurt after the ball, whinnying. After every such perpetration, Burfi, to encourage the ringing of the laughter of children, feigning an affronted prowl around an imaginary batting crease, hewing the pigmy bat about like a twig scooped up on an open-country, after-a-cloudburst tramp, bewails, 'I'm not playing with you jokers,' and, 'You ninnies are the worst players in India, the baddest cricketers in the Milky Way.'

Burfi and Jamun embrace cordially. The children wait, irresolute for an instant at the snap abolition of their sport. 'Hi,' smirks Pista bashfully, and, slewing round, 'Doom! Jamun's here!' Doom finds in the statement an additional stimulus to yelp and scurry back to the crest of his bowling run. Jamun touches his father's feet. 'We went directly to the hospital from the airport,' declares Chhana. 'No difference. But that safari-suited whale with the Americo-Chandigarhi accent – who flogs his own thigh with his stethoscope while discoursing – said, no deterioration either. We are on our guard, he announced, as though my aunt was the adversary.' Chhana, grinning demurely, then joins the cricketers.

The lawn, notes Jamun, their twenty-by-fifteen segment of desert scrub – what Burfi has named 'our bloody rock garden' – appears to have been poorly irrigated in his absence. The saplings that he had untidily planted during his previous stay – a tulsi, a white bougainvillaea, a eucalyptus, a shockheaded palm, and alongside it a hibiscus – are dead: bleached sticks and shrivelled tassels. Only the mammoth cactus in the further corner (two storeys tall, sentinel) and some undying, random scrub remain, an obdurate, arid green. In the years that he has lived in this house, with an ignorant and fitful zeal, Jamun has struggled to make fecund their patch, and time and time again failed. Shyamanand has tried too. So has Urmila, inundating the plot once in a way. The sight of the dead plants and the dusty soil dispirit Jamun, naturally. His parents and he, overly worried only about themselves, seem never to have succeeded in giving life to anything.

Except, Jamun half-smirks to himself, for the cactus. Which wasn't even truly theirs, since they hadn't planted it – not initiated it, at any rate – had simply dislocated and transported, and eventually transplanted, it when they had moved, roughly a decade ago, from a government flatlet to their own crumb of earth. The cactus had been part of the flatlet, a two-footer in a jumbo tub on the terrace, abandoned by the earlier occupant. Jamun's aya and her assorted chums, over the years, had desultorily nurtured the plant to more than mansize; it had been disregarded by the family till the week before departure, when the sentimental ache that is roused when one quits a nook that has fostered one for years made them view rosily whatever did not, or could not, accompany them – the leaky, blackened kerosene stove, the cracked pail beneath the dripping cistern in the toilet, the Public Works Department armchair in the verandah, the enormous cactus on the terrace.

For the first time in a decade, Jamun, fagged out by the tangle of packing, mooching about among the transporter's coolies, notices the symmetry of the many arms of the cactus. 'Baba, can't we take this with us? It'd be a continuity. These guys could easily yank and haul it on to the truck.' Shyamanand, forever loath to forsake even a shard of his past, assents.

Shifting the tub, however, proves to be a killer. The coolies, for starters, decline to touch it, contending that it is not furniture. Then everyone starts to dispute with everyone else, glad to escape the decisions of cramming in and putting away. 'These slobs need to be informed,' squawks Jamun's aya at Urmila, 'that they are here to fetch and carry, and not to argue. And that *of course* the cactus *is* furniture, since it has as much sparrow shit on it as our dinner table and the chest of drawers.'

Two removal men finally begin to shove and tug at the iron tub. A third is hindered from a handhold by the thorns of the plant. He disappears to smoke and cough. Progress is fraught. With every gasp and snort, the cactus teeters like a child learning to rollerskate. At the doorway, they discover that its arms and some two feet from the head will have to be sliced off. One coolie saunters away to forage for a weapon. The second tries to light his bidi, but is instantly prohibited by Shyamanand's baying that he can't puff under the noses of his superiors.

'Look, Baba, can we call this off? I didn't realize that this damned thing was so bloody heavy, unwieldy . . . However will these buggers cart it down the stairs? Especially those bends? . . . And now he's going to hack away at it, and lop off large chunks – what's the point? And after these guys've chopped it up, whatever remains will be further thwacked about while they're staggering down the stairs with it . . .'

Shyamanand's face pronounces that he takes a dim view indeed of Jamun's backing down after suggesting what might very likely turn out to be an A1 domestic adventure, and particularly one which is beginning to give him a chance to bully some lumpen. The first coolie returns with a rusty toy saw and, while Shyamanand yawps his astonished delight ('But that saw! My god, it's from the carpentry set that I presented Burfi on his tenth birthday! Amazing how one unearths the oddest things while moving house. Oye you! Wherever did you get hold of that saw?'), starts on an arm of the cactus. Jamun gazes at the milk, dribbling like blood from the wound of the plant, and plods on, 'We *could* live without this giant in our new house, you know, and could plant something else instead, a palm or bougainvillaea or . . .' His knowledge of flora is at this point exhausted.

He recalls that he had, well, sort of chickened out just then, and had shambled off to pester his mother to make some tea. He had felt that standing about to witness the amputation of the cactus would be intolerable; so would the passage of the tub down the stairs. When it jammed at one of those bends, and when one of the plant's vestigial arms grazed its spikes against someone's skin, Shyamanand's bile would spurt forth, and Jamun wished to be absent when the coolies reciprocated his father's churlishness. Perhaps, most oppressive of all, their resolution and endurance would crock up midway, and his whimsical, sentimental suggestion would be abandoned.

Cup in hand, but unmindful of the tea, he has ears only for the hoarseness, the turmoil, on the stairs. Shyamanand squawks at his wife, 'But where *is* Jamun? Ask him to show himself at once! *He* should be wrangling with and overseeing these numbskulls, not me. After all, this demented proposal is his, isn't it, to ferry a plant the size of a bloody tree . . .' Then an abrupt screech of panic: ' – Mind that corner – on your left, you donkey, your *left* . . .' From the stairwell, a deep, heavy thump, and some noteworthy Bihari vituperation. '. . . God, can't you tell your left from your right?'

When he is certain that he won't be spotted, not even, somehow, by the mutilated cactus, Jamun sidles over to the head of the stairs to register better the sounds of the descent; he is nervy and half-believes that the enterprise can still stall. From the balcony, he observes them sweat blood to heave up the cactus into the truck. The plant looks woebegone. Shyamanand takes time off from his disparaging superintendence of the coolies to squint up at his son and scoff, 'So we've won, but no thanks to you. Try and not cavort through life with the fickleness that you've shown today, Jamun. You wanted an outcome, but you couldn't even witness the donkeywork for it, like craving victory without wishing to watch the savagery of battle.'

They had not expected that the cactus would thrive in the new house. 'It's too old to be transplanted,' Shyamanand pronounces, 'and the hole that Jamun's dug just isn't deep enough. Homo sapiens is much more resilient than plants, you know, and can outlive all sorts of changes.'

But the robust cactus belies his conclusion and, over the years, grows, thrusting out new arms to compensate, and scabbing over the scars of the old with a marred, charcoal-grey skin.

'For how many days will you be with us? Chhana could only collect ten days. But a week should serve, to settle your mother's case.'

Doom is rebuffing Chhana's jabs to seize the ball from him.

'No no you came just now! You can't bowl just when you come! You have to field! It's the rule!' With both hands he rams the ball tight into his pot belly, and jams against the wall his forehead, nose, chubby beetroot lips, tummy and smutty knees.

'But I know one way, Auntie, to prod him to let go the ball,' snickers Pista affably. 'You should bully with, if you don't drop the ball, then you'll be turned into what Thakuma became the day we shoved her into hospital.'

A routine lunch, gelid, all anyhow, eaten in slovenly ones and twos, off a marigold decolam surface, on which the X-ray of the two o'clock light from the windows betrays, like the splotches of a lively contagion, the crud of numberless comparable meals. 'At the nursing home,' launches Jamun, 'we've to pay some four thousand rupees more.'

'Oh, much more. When the bills show up,' jeers Burfi – but his derision is beamed not so much at Jamun as at a dispensation; he is fuzzily discerning that the money that plunges pell-mell into the pockets of doctors' safari suits, plausibly to cure one's kin and certainly to heal one's *own* contingent distress, complicity and fatigue, is so thoroughly ineffectual; that the affliction of a relative, its spinoff on one, and the damned costs of alleviation – all mingle into some Deceiver's extravagant, contumelious performance – and that money yet allures and abides, useless but magnetic – 'for the cabin, the Intensive Care, quacks' fees, medicines, the solicitude of those pig nurses, the foolery of betterment, then you'll understand. Thousands and thousands more.'

'Yes, of course,' reacts Jamun, restrainedly, shrouding his choler. Like others, he dislikes being addressed as though he is slow-witted. 'Meantime, this four thousand should be settled. In one letter you let out that we were bickering over who ought to share how much, should we split the costs by five, why should Joyce contribute. One of us can clear accounts now, afterwards we can square up.'

'How could you write that?' demands Shyamanand of Burfi,

glancing up from the stupendous mass of rice on his plate, brow incised in ire. 'Yet only you could have.'

Burfi's face dulls with umbrage. 'Don't talk shit. I wrote no such thing.' He whams a tablespoon down on the table, at which Chhana hollers, 'What happened!' from a peripheral room.

'My mistake,' owns Jamun, detesting himself for relishing their friction. 'I confused matters. You'd written that Baba'd proposed that we should divide the piles surgery costs, not this stroke.'

'And that we haven't!' snaps Shyamanand spleenfully. 'I forked out the full amount, only to watch her cave in three days after to this frozenness.'

'But who bears the expenses of Ma's medical care is definitely not the issue,' remonstrates Jamun, peeved, endeavouring to sound measured.

'Well – did I trigger it off?' Shyamanand surveys his plate and again ponders why he has lumped food on it so edaciously.

'It shouldn't be an issue at all! She's *your* wife. You hatched her maladies. You should pay for them.' Burfi nettles and bridles like clockwork. He almost roots about for pretexts to explode, for he half-divines that in his other tempers he commands no attention.

'But you're her sons! Are you not her sons?'

'That's not the point, either! Thirty years hence, if Joyce is dying, will I angle for money from Pista or Doom for her pulling through? You're gibbering.'

'And you? Thirty years after, Pista should *jump* to contribute for his mother's healing. Otherwise, you'll provide further proof for what is already conspicuous – that your and your wife's style of moulding children is disgraceful.'

'Meanwhile,' Chhana speaks in a designedly audible aside to Jamun, '*I'm* buying all the medicines. Somehow medicines are never urgent when anyone else is visiting.' She snickers brashly at Burfi. She is forty-fiveish and speaks pantingly, as though she has never mastered the coordination of utterance and respiration.

Four o'clock tea before the next circuit of the nursing home. Joyce returns early from office, for the reason that her mother-in-law could be dying, and debouches from a bathroom after epochs, etiolated, blinking as though her eyelashes are immutably weighted with waterdrops; she is older than Burfi by three years, so Burfi time after time, but cunningly, underlines.

Boisterous family prattle over the marigold decolam after months, blithe emissions of homecoming, reunion and amity, while Shyamanand sips his tea, alone, in the soft-focus light of the drawing room. When Jamun steps in to check whether he needs a second cup, he is sitting in Urmila's chair, gazing at the TV's cataract face, twiddling Urmila's bell, bemusedly raking his fingers through his beard. In that indistinct light, in his presence, the jollity from the proximal room is the peal of vileness. Jamun twitches with guilt. 'We're leaving now. Would you like some more tea?'

'Your gaiety will fade when your mother and I are dead. This roof itself will moulder. Strangers to one another, with nothing in common, congregating once a decade, then how will you giggle?'

Jamun is hotly stung. He strives to clarify. 'We were chuckling about other matters to divert our minds from Ma – ' He stalls at the falsehood. For those trivial minutes, they had all outright blotted out Urmila. 'We were joyful – we were just glad to be together.'

'Doubtless, the company of your dazzling sister-in-law is altogether preferable to that of your half-dead mother.' At that, their eyes sheer off each other and their faces mantle with a shared remembrance.

Of the foregoing year, early autumn. Burfi has just returned from his maiden tour of New York, bewitched, and with baubles for all. A Friday. An after-dinner champagne bout to jubilate his homecoming. 'Ma? Champagne! Baba?' proffers Jamun. 'Won't you? Champagne?'

No, too late. Their disinclination dispirits the junket a bit. Possibly, all would've been pleased to rejoice together, without abrasion and discord. But a swarm of explanations behind their abstention, about which the sons introspect a while, waveringly, with abating impetus, investing the reluctance of their parents with less and less priority. Perhaps the parents intuit that the daughter-in-law will not welcome them and therefore neither will the two sons. Or maybe they, with the grumpiness that is the sensitivity that age doesn't smother, wish to be the hub of the joviality and are huffed at being solicited as an afterthought. Perhaps they wish to be wooed, for which the sons have no time. Possibly, they might've been pleased had Burfi rather than Jamun coaxed them to sip and are miffed that he has not budged. Maybe they imagine that he considers that champagne bought in New York will be squandered on them, who've never been overseas. Perhaps they truly are convinced that the time is too late and they too wrinkled to revel into the dead of night. Too late. Jamun attempts once more, flaccidly, from the dining room doorway to his father's sluggishly receding back, 'Positive? Not even one?'

'They won't, Jamun, all right,' trills Burfi from behind, half-waspishly; to Jamun, his inflexion seems to utter, why're you wasting time, rush and join us, and listen to my yarns of 52nd Street and Park Avenue. Jamun intuits that his father hears the same meaning in Burfi's voice.

Through the exhilaration, the dry wine, the vignettes and the Marlboro smoke, Jamun fancies that he hears his mother call, a removed but indomitable bawling. He shuffles to her room, traversing his father's. From his bed, Shyamanand pronounces, 'She's been bellowing for you for the last ten minutes. We could turn to dust here and you in the same house'd never be aware till disturbed from your carousal by the stink.'

'I've been hollering and hollering for you for the past twenty minutes, and from his bed your father's been hooting at me not to bawl and swamp his reading. Will you please lessen the speed of the fan? I guess the night'll get chilly afterwards. I've just been floundering here like a fish, waiting for some soul to scale down the fan for me. You know that if I reduce it, the fan's so prankish that it'll promptly stop dead. I only need it a bit less.'

Jamun twiddles the speed regulator of the fan a few times. He is feeling a little sinful at not responding sooner to his mother and a little piqued with himself for feeling sinful. 'If you twirl the knob only clockwise, the speeds usually don't go haywire.' They both contemplate the ceiling for a time, like believers waiting for some portent from a doom merchant.

'Isn't that now too slow? If the room gets too stuffy, then I'll perspire, won't sleep, I'll catch a chill from the cold sweat. Of course, I can't open even one window because of that maddening black cat – it'll saunter in, fishing about for a nook to doze in – you all are greatly entertained – but you should instead find beastly – the thought that more than once I've been hauled out of a rare sleep by a stinking, footloose cat trying to wrap itself around my face. Yes, my face! At least the cat finds my face appealing, unlike your father.'

Jamun spins the knob once more. They both wait again, Urmila recumbent, Jamun upright, wishing to teeter with the champagne, ogling upwards. 'It was at 3, I moved it to 1, this is now 2.'

Urmila murmurs, with ample misgiving, 'This can't be 2. See – isn't it stopping altogether?'

The fan groans more torpidly and sonorously. Its axial disc, like a giant, waxen carrom striker with three fine, concentric, silvery hoops, and its circumambient chalky blur, which is like a whitish gramophone record when at superspeed, decelerates to a three-limbed figure cartwheeling at the same spot. The brims of the arms of the fan are maculated with measureless fly droppings. At the close of several winter afternoons, Jamun has observed scores of flies rendezvous on the verges of fans, commingle and parley, as in a congress of houseflies.

He clicks the switch to 3. The groans of the fan spurt into full-throated whines. 'The knob's now veered round to where it was. 1 is too slow and 2 doesn't work.'

Urmila vents the tuts and clicks of discontent. 'I've reminded you all time and time again that this fan regulator needs repairs, but if others ever listened to me, this'd be a different world.' In dereliction, she swivels her neck and slumps her face against her four pillows. Jamun manipulates the knob once more and hopes that he isn't going to get cross over a matter so footling. Yet what chafes him ever so often is the defencelessness in his mother's utterance, the leverage over him that she and his father command through goading his pity. For more than sixty years, he muses untidily – gazing at the meagre, rickety neck, the askew sari, the calves the tint of old newspaper, the frowzy, turgescent feet, the soles scissioned like famined earth – you have lingered, laboured, ripened, mated, tussled, hated, and nurtured two children, and yet the selfsame you has to clamour for me to adjust the speed of the fan above your bed.

'I'll leave it at 1.'

He's at the door when Urmila implores, 'Can't you open the window just a little? So that the cat can't breeze in? You could twine the window handle to the grille.' She adds when she glimpses his face, 'I'm sorry for vexing you.'

'Where'll I find some string?'

'All right, forget it.'

'No, just point out to me some string.' Blood swirls into his temples, and all at once he is set upon honourably concluding the matter witout articulating even one syllable of acrimony. He battens down his teeth till he feels a sort of hardness against his eardrums and half-believes that one jaw will dislodge the other.

'On the second shelf in the J. B. Mangharam box. If the twine isn't there, then forget it.'

The whole task is executed in roughly two minutes; the two inches of open window hint at a night breeze, Urmila purrs in expectation of ease, and Jamun is happy that he has won against himself. Release and triumph make him motherly. 'Anything else? Are you positive?' He kisses her forehead.

From his bed, Shyamanand, not removing his eyes from the

science quarterly to which he has subscribed ever since his adolescence, probes, 'What was the problem?'

In his ascendancy, his tenderness, Jamun is luxuriantly insouciant, light-minded. He simpers and drawls, 'Oh, Ma was being her usual, exquisitely infuriating self. She was squealing for the fan to chug around at a speed that doesn't exist. Yet marvels do happen and she's at ease now, content.'

Shyamanand rejoins, sedately by design, 'How brazen of her, to let her distress yank her son away from his merrymaking, and from his sister-in-law.'

Jamun is stunned. His ears flame with blood and a pinhead of ache bulges deep underneath his left nipple. His wellbeing fissions; choler inundates him. 'That's gibberish – ' and then, for he hasn't voided himself enough, 'Only you, lout that you are, could've mouthed that – ' and again, because Shyamanand doesn't rebut and his own bile doesn't abate, 'I'm – we all are – so disgraced by you. When will you understand that?'

Shyamanand lays his magazine and his reading glasses aside, and hauls himself upright in bed, as groundwork for interminable hostilities. 'What I utter, certainly, is a disgrace, and what you do, of course, is praiseworthy. You should, for sure, feel ashamed for me while I should, doubtless, swoon with rapture for you, thus is your generational canon. Your own mother merely appealed to you to flip a switch to help her to pass a comfortable night, but that makes her "exquisitely infuriating" because it muddles for a minute your tippling some champagne, and impedes you – for a moment! – from those fulsome anecdotes of your paradises and the society of your Christian sister-in-law, whom you nibble on the cheek when you greet and nibble when you part – that should not be you! She already reigns over your brother's face underneath her – but you!' Shyamanand's face glows with blood. The veins in his temple now sprawl like maggots of sputum. Evocation has hacked away all mockery from his features and his voice. He quavers, in a tongue tinny with fury and indelible abasement, scrabbling for articulation, 'They've nonstop been so horrid to us, your mother and me – they bake and sauté a good many savouries upstairs – all those smells drift down to us, but they've never offered us any, never! They've coached their boys to keep away from us. Whenever Pista or Doom is with us, he's becked upstairs by the screeches of the aya or the mother – you know that, you've witnessed that yourself countless times –'

'But you're insane! Joyce does detest you and Ma, but only in jerks and snatches, and not without basis, and she's congenial with me. And her churlishness with you has no link with Ma's fan!' Even in his resentment, Jamun perceives that they both are bearing themselves idiotically. One element in him hopes that the other inhabitants won't overhear their deranged tussle; yet another that they will, will flurry in from diverse parts of the house, wary at the voices spiralling to hysteria, will stand about superfluously, and unwillingly salute his chill articulation under stress. Urmila has resumed her sapless and fidgety mewling, 'Jamun! What's wrong! Jamun!'

The stub of his reason importunes him to quit the room, but the blood in his skull, the breathlessness, quickens him to be glacial and barbed, to waste his opposer with the balefulness of cogent argument, to reinforce his self-discipline with the debris of the restraint of others. Urmila's disquiet goads him the more. 'She was cheerful a minute ago, and now you've launched her off afresh.' He stretches his voice for the further room. 'No, Ma, nothing, merely Baba's routine depraved thinking.'

Pista's Corporation Bank footrule – cast off every day in the least foreseeable crannies of the house as slag from his homework, a withering token of his pick of place of work for that afternoon, the selection itself intimating his derision at the very idea of homework, the dereliction in addition offering him a stratagem to defer his homework on the succeeding afternoon, when he will bum around the house ruffling everyone by dolefully enquiring whether they have sighted his footrule anywhere – is now in Shyamanand's fist, bobbing like a chastiser's irate forefinger. 'Depraved, oh yes, I am so and you're not. You warm to those who spurn your parents, your fount. When they kindle our death, over our pyres you can clink glasses of the champagne that you couldn't share with us tonight. Depraved – you pig, I ask you – who is depraved! You procure your love-boys from the wastepipes of slums, survivors with scabby skins and ancient eyes, who squirm their waists in front of your face for your money – you sleep in their diseases, you cheep and baa over them and feed them like a woman – and I'm depraved?' The sallow, agape befuddlement on Jamun's face infuriates Shyamanand the more. 'You itch for that artful Joyce – I know it! You hurtle home every three months for her. Your goofy mother presumes that you scuttle home for us, for her, but the quarry is Joyce – hapless Burfi, noosed between unrivalled wife and brother. You'll die fumblingly, of some contagion that your traits'll sow in you –' The penduline flesh beneath Shyamanand's beard starts to shudder unrestrainedly.

Noisy oversize inhalations, tears jolted out of him, sweat irking his armpits and collar, and a lumpish fury within Jamun that now intends to hack apart his sinful flaccid body, and spirt out. He is queasy, as though a vigorous talon has gashed through his muzzle down to his belly and is foraging in his guts. His calves bubble but the warm tears feel easeful, like cleansing. His father looks shrivelled and appalling, but something baneful and primal in him craves to flail back, monster versus monster. He snarls snatchily, spite stifling rage, 'You bastard – we should thank God that we are sons. If you'd hatched a daughter, you'd've bedded her – you fucking ingrate – this as recompense for what I've done for you –'

'Jamun! Have you no shame!' Urmila, buoying herself against the wall – appalled eyes, but her voice conveys more dread than indignation; she censures somewhat dedicatedly, as though she will be chided for not excoriating with sufficient zest, panicky in the meanwhile that without warning, without motive as usual, both husband and son will enervate each other and instead beleaguer her.

'Oh, hold your tongue – ' for through his sniffles and gulps, Jamun tastes solace when he carps at his mother; because in his animus, carping is easier than winnowing those words for his father that are sure to stab; yet he detests himself when he recognizes on her face the blind slackness of deep hurt, and he knows that he will loathe himself even more when Shyamanand at last is also gutted by the prongs of his son's words.

'Savour your handiwork, our sons. Fostered for decades to hate me. Like a perfect mother, you've kneaded them against me. You're the saint and I the demon, but notice, they damn you too.'

Burfi hears some of the particulars of the squabble and snickers, 'My bout next, I imagine, with Baba.' The next morning, Jamun, in the verandah beside the kitchen, liking the sea gusts on his inflamed forehead but not conceding so even to himself. A leaden, toss-and-turn night for Shyamanand and Urmila, in their shunned rooms, but Jamun has enjoyed the numbness of the sozzled and overtired. Urmila in the kitchen, pottering, warming milk for her husband and herself: 'Jamun, he's a worthless husband, but a good father. Jamun, the anger of parents is never anger.'

'You suppose she'll die? Or return?' To use the word 'die' for his mother is hard, but for Jamun the euphemisms – 'pass away', 'breathe one's last' – are impossible. From the gate Shyamanand and he gaze at the car that carries off the others – Chhana, Burfi, Pista's aya – and Pista and Doom too, who beseech, are rebuffed, wail, are screeched at, blubber, pule and are finally permitted – to the nursing home. Shyamanand doesn't respond. 'She looked so . . . meaningless this morning, like . . . Burfi said you'd told him that you were convinced she'd mend. I hope you're correct. She looked so ill.'

Shyamanand hobbles away from the gate. Jamun stalks him. Shyamanand was too exhausted to go to the hospital. As is his nature, Jamun felt uneasy at forsaking him, and remained behind too, deeming that his father would be covertly glad for his fellowship. In like conditions, Urmila would have been patently so. Plus, Jamun wished to converse and himself be allayed.

They subside in the uncomfortable garden chairs. Shyamanand has no idioms of solace for anyone. Too old. Jadedness has coated his soul. 'Just five days. Getting through to you was hopeless. So we despatched the telegram. Chhana was much easier to contact. Within a minute. On the first night, Burfi stayed till sunrise in the car in the hospital parking lot because she was on the edge.' Shyamanand slackens off. Enunciation is bone-wearying. He craves to be in a warm snugness, in darkening and silence. 'I should die before she does, that is my leading, hoggish thought.' Jamun wonders how he had looked for alleviation from his father who so bitterly needed alleviation himself. He feels silly. The deathliness that soaks down into them is chafing, a sandpaper presence. He intuits that he should sneak off from Shyamanand before their dispiritedness pricks them into words that they'll afterwards unwish. 'I'm going to doze,' he mutters. 'I'll be up before dinner.' On his pillow, he feels sinful that he is trying to snooze when he should be heeding his sinking mother.

Twilight. Beyond the window grille six feet away, the heavens like the sea, leaden and minacious, like the back of a torpid beast. A figure against the sky, sloping against the railing of the verandah, gazing seaward. Without his spectacles Jamun can't discern who it is. He can fuzzily distinguish a sari the shade of dusk. He is positive, without reason, that the form is smiling. For the one unearthly instant upon waking at an unfamiliar hour, before the understanding clicks into position, he imagines that the shape is his mother, in good heart and euphoric, grown larger because of ruddiness. A section of the form stirs up and down unhurriedly, in intervals. In another second he spots the tip of the cigarette, in his bedimmed vision like a fulgent tangerine snowflake under a microscope. He puts on his spectacles for an instant and verifies that the contour is Chhana, puffing bemusedly against a cavernous, half-dead heaven. Tousled thoughts hustle one another when he is once more in the twilight blur of his vision. Is this a harbinger of some ghoulish eventuality, his imagining a shape in the half-light to be a restored, healthy version of his dying mother? From whom none could be more different than Chhana, surely. His sickly sight, his snap awakening, the receding span of day, the sky like a gunmetal sea – all these have hampered him from recognizing her. Chhana. Who has mothered Urmila's firstborn. Who is arid, unwed because she was born without a womb, a freak of sorts.

'So you are up,' gleams Chhana. 'Your mother's now conscious. Was asking after you.'

On the wall beside the elevator that always appears to run only for the liftman's guffawing cronies, sags aslant an oversize photograph of a ponytailed girl. Her eyes gape like ink spots on white saucers, or black poached eggs, her dextral forefinger presses against her roseate, schnozzle lips, tip of finger upending nose, her fist like a bubo on her chin – fervidly shushing the world. The legend beneath the photo enjoins: 'Learn to exist with silence.'

'How mournful!' warbles Chhana, warping her features to nudge her spectacles up for a better squint. 'But doesn't that snap recall Belu – the same lips and expression?'

Shyamanand doesn't react, concentrates instead on negotiating the hospital corridor. Jamun scrutinizes the picture anew. Belu as a duteous pigtailed girl? Belu is just one of the numberless relatives whom Jamun (and Burfi) have never met, whose photographs they have never viewed, who have never visited and have rarely corresponded, yet whose nicknames have bobbed up from time to time in the retrospections of their parents, and who have been mentally modelled by the listeners after those particulars of the recollections that have hoodooed their imaginations. Over the years, Jamun has hatched Belu to be fleshless, sombre, introspective, with mines for eyes, a creature in a grievous romance.

Urmila's tale, unfolded now and then, whenever she is at ease in her immediate woe, to whomever chances to be within hearing.

'In the age when I was idiotic – the feverish mugginess of a midsummer in Calcutta, sweat spiking yesterday's sweat – your father and I were rendezvousing thick and fast, he befuddled, occasionally disinclined – before office, during and after too, ambling on Chowringhee, scrabbling for an unoccupied bench in some park, just tramping because there was no spot where we could be alone. Nearly everyone at my house disliked your father. But my sisters detested me too. Moni spited me further that April to August because your father was good looking. But Belu was almost afraid of him. Belu was the sole person in my family who cherished me, and not the salary I carted home – all, all family narratives are despicable, hideous – if they're faithful to the essential life – aimless rancour for one another, the most guileless event milks from us our watchful malice – living together merely to thrill in unkindness, marrying, mounting and spawning because we're all afraid of being corporeally alone. My sisters derided Belu, were ashamed of a brother, supposed him crazed, because he hadn't voiced a word for some twenty years, vowed to silence after that rat-poison episode – you recall that? – he burned for some beastly slut, lowly caste, pined to marry her – "Baba, I can't live without her!" – huh! – my father lashed him with a fine bamboo switch, for hours, I was seven then. We all watched. Belu's twiggy forearms twitched – like exhausted butterflies – to shield his face and skull. His saffron kurta ripped inch by inch. Flitting about in thirty square feet of space, bawling, sobbing, pulling, "Ma! Ma! Release me! Ma!"

'"Yes – I shall pound you enough for your shrieks to retrieve the dead!" So my father snarled with each whack, but he also was weeping, and, "I'll purge the harlot out of you. She's in your blood, you swear, but your blood's mine, isn't it –" And the scourge whistled down, over and over, like stealthy, camouflaged queries from beyond your window from a chum whom you're prohibited to meet. My father tired, pulled up to wheeze. His heaving mingled with Belu's blubbering, the gasps and snivels whamming against my eardrums, no other vibrations in the universe. Moni time after time was needling my father, murmuring, atremble, "The sides. Lam the ribs. From the top you're just smacking his forearms."

'Hours, perhaps one. Belu slumped into a clod on the floor, a knot of bloodied shreds, hair. My sisters cuffed me about lightly, forbade me to help Belu. I didn't. I was utterly terrorized by the trouncing, the screams, the disarrayed pile on the floor, like clothes for washing, its stillness. I gaped. I was summoned away.

'At some juncture Belu hobbled and tottered away to drink poison, to requite himself. After these years I don't accurately remember how he got the poison, or what it was. Luckily, he panicked almost instantly after. He lurched towards the courtyard, spluttering my name. Amidst the weals and drying gore on his face trailed pellets of cold sweat. We couldn't puzzle out his slur. His lips spumed, and his exhalations ferried a dreadful stench. He had to be hospitalized. My father laid out sizeable amounts of cash to bribe our neighbourhood police, the Station House Officer especially, not to register a case of attempted suicide.

'Belu was half-paralysed. Nonstop aching since then, and creeping involuntary movement, for more than fifty years now. He settled in his bed, his room, hushed. Would infrequently come out at dusk, or after, like a wraith, perhaps to stare at the rain. He conveys the essentials through practically unreadable notes. His survival intensely discomposed us all. When we weren't writhing with guilt, we were half-yearning for his death. He's the Chhana of our family, the grand embarrassment. I scarcely ever ventured into his room. Throughout my girlhood, behind the grass-green doors of his room sneaked the ghouls of my twilight, the bogeys that bullied me in sleep. When I suffered my first period, the maiden blood, even in my bewilderment, my terror, I was convinced that the gore had dribbled out from behind Belu's doors and into my guts.

'On the single occasion that your father visited my family, Belu was in the courtyard. Owl-light, late evening. I couldn't introduce *him*! He lingered in the gloom, like an incubus biding its time. That night he sent me through the cook a note: *Do not marry that evening-man*, and at the foot of the fragment, as a tailpiece: *Remember the picture* – is it picture, or portrait? – *of Dorian Gray*. The words "Dorian Gray" were in English, I think. I wasn't even sure if those were exactly his messages – Belu's script had become so unreadable. In his normalcy he'd once in a while echoed from that book – *How horribly real ugliness made things* – something like that. He'd all along recoiled from and discredited goodlooking persons. After two or three months of my marriage, I wrote to him sketching it – a ululation from a dungeon to the one least likely to snigger on hearing it. He didn't reply for months. Then suddenly another note: *You used to bleat, to flit from my family, I'd even wed a demon. In your husband you have a better dispensation*.'

Jamun has time out of number been the audience for the parable of Belu. To him Urmila has sometimes appended, in a coda, 'But you oughtn't to judge all marriages by the corrosion of ours. I *know* – that you don't wish to marry because you dread that you'll tail off like us.'

'And if I don't marry,' banters Jamun, 'I'll end like your Belu? Really, Ma – you flatter yourself. You and Baba haven't contaminated me that much! And you reap what you merit – why did you marry in the first place?'

'Don't counsel like a grandmother. Now and then I imagine that you're faintly scornful of us because we married even when we were so inconsonant. But not to have married would've been unthinkable – we were everywhere together – I would've gained disrepute, a thirty-plus woman, perhaps thumbed and dumped – you remember the buzz about Kuki's mother, and she was only a divorcee. I too was incubated in that middle-classness – no oddball outsider, me!

'Jamun, inly you're so puffed-up! Being unmarried, you suppose, makes you objective, the deadpan eyewitness, but bachelordom'll bleach you.'

With his mother Jamun is softened, but does not expose his

chastening. To Burfi, however, on a different occasion, he comments, 'Ma is no rebel. She herself sweats the same prejudices that she grieves squelched her in her youth. No one learns. You'll never forget her outcry at your marriage, as though you were hitching up with Whitney Houston or something.'

'And she wasn't,' rejoins Burfi, 'turning any younger. She was thirtyish then, which for her generation connoted forty. She must've funked. But her perspective's so queer – I pattered to her once that remaining single was simpler nowadays, and she replied, of course, but that's also because we now stay in houses that are set apart, and not snarled into one another.'

At the glass doors of the Intensive Care Unit, Chhana sternly impedes Shyamanand from shedding his sandals. 'You look old and adequately eminent, so the underlings won't block you. If they do, try to look even more eminent.' Within, behind inky glass and nondescript tapestry, in a creaky, seared voice, subterraneanly familiar, like an intimate ditty on the brink of one's hearing, Urmila is catechizing the meaty nurse with certain exacting questions. 'Why haven't I seen you before? Who's changed these curtains? When did this hurt in my left arm start? Why don't you respond instead of just skimming about like a mosquito? What's the date today?' Blessedness and grief eddy through Jamun at the slurred, unnatural tones of her remembered voice.

Urmila's eyes are now leaden, with unfocussed dots of amber. The striated desert face, toasted gashed lips that won't cap her teeth, and the extremity of a whitish tongue that whisks over the ruts of her lips like a gecko's. Shyamanand evens the silvered hair away from her forehead. 'How long you all took to come and see me,' she mumbles. Jamun nears the top of her bed. She pirouettes her head at the movement. 'Jamun?' Her eyes centre above his left shoulder, but for an instant her features splinter into a childlike smile. 'Jamun.' An ashen hand on the coverlet throbs heavenward. Jamun touches it. Her fingers hug his like chilled talons. Chhana detonates into sobs. A sliver of Jamun's mind ruminates whether it's right that a husband's niece rather than a son should, at such a moment, bawl so.

'You're going to bounce back. You're going to snap out of this.' Shyamanand is gabbling, clenching Urmila's shoulder like a predator. He raises up her frozen hand and inspects her decoloured fingers. 'Then when we reach home, we'll blink at the TV, and if Jamun can spare us so many hours, we'll play Cutthroat Bridge before dinner. You'll sham an unwillingness to join, and all through'll never concede that you enjoy it. You'll bellyache for the thousandth time that you vehemently resent chess and bridge because Belu and your father both were such zealots about them that they skimped the remainder of living. And if a tipsy Jamun entreats us to swill a peg or two of Burfi's fancy New York stuff, we won't decline, even though you'll continue to tch-tch in reproof. When I gain a rubber, you'll grouse of giddiness and twinges in your chest, and I'll gibe, "Oho, the green-eyed monster, so this is your gimmick to jam the game!" You'll be miffed, and we'll bicker. But hereafter, when you grumble about your ill health, we shall all consider you soberly, and Burfi won't twit, "Oh, leave off hamming like a hypochondriac," or, "like an untended grandmother in some factious joint family!" And we'll all bear ourselves so caringly that you won't need to slide back into hospital merely to point out to your family that it's neglected your danger signals.'

Endearing prattle, and exceedingly rare, as Shyamanand scuffs around the bed, impeding the nurse, badgering her about the readings on the electronic cardiograph, scrutinizing his wife's limbs, spiking diverse localities of flesh with his index finger to verify for hollows, carping about the airconditioning, the water carafe, the pillows. Urmila's smile is a snarl wedging apart her jaws; at the same time, the halves of her face appear to be skewed, as though it had cracked down the middle. She doesn't register three-quarters of what Shyamanand babbles. She surrenders Jamun's hand. Her tongue darts over her lips without stopping. Jamun introspects, as he has done before, gazing at his parents, one with her bubble life, the other mentally worn, futile, too late her protector, which of them will be the first to slip away, and which of them he will ache less to see off first.

Across the years, he has time after time imagined himself alone in a modest, maroon cinema hall. Time has made the sequence more distinct by accretion. He is seated in the geometric centre of the auditorium, clearly visible in the reflected, ice-blue lambency of the screen. Usher-like shadows seem to huddle at the doors. The screen displays a gargantuan close-up of a man's face – small, mellow eyes, a ten-foot-high nose, lips like violet pythons. Jamun recognizes him to be a celebrated cinema villain of a previous age. He speaks to Jamun in donnish Hindi, in the gentle, prudish tones of a specious believer in persuasion through methods other than thuggery. 'Jamun, sweetie, you understand that your dear mother and father are being indecently tortured even now in this chamber. In a moment the camera will rove to bare to you what is being done to them. Such feral acts sicken me. We have slashed off the sound so that their shrieking and puling do not divert you from me. That would vex me with them. We could halt if you divulge to me which of your parents you hate more. We would then fix just that one. All mortals hate one parent less than the other. Raise your right hand for your mother, left for your father. If you cannot decide because you are squeamish, then we shall have to kill both. If you crave more time, I could grant you some, though you should be able to resolve this promptly.' The fiend's mien modulates from august malignancy to finger-wagging, chiding naughtiness. 'I realize what you are imagining, you darling corrupt boy, that what if you put up *any* one hand only to settle your macabre bewilderment, and we fathom your gesture, and realize that you have despatched a parent to his – or her – or is it his? – death without even fretting yourself with brainwork, and, to chastise you, choke the remaining parent too? Would that be better? Or shall we leave the survivor be? How will you confront her – or him – and yourself? Quick, which hand now?' The face falls back gradually. Jamun spots a whitish jacket lapel and cravat, and about the ears an indeterminate sky-blue backdrop. 'To help you to select, we will now show you your parents.' The face swerves to off-screen. The voice edges to command. 'On sound.'

The hallucination routinely peters out at this point, presumably because Jamun wishes to know no further. He can never recapture precisely when he visualized it in its bud, and how. Very likely in pubescence, that dishevelled season of awakening, perhaps in one of those numberless, exquisitely perturbing dreams. He is not unduly discomposed by this one, for he has visioned a good many hideous things. He isn't even certain whether the minutiae that he has afterwards crammed in are the upshot of cognitive and slothful musing, or are the disclosures of assorted nightmares. In his earliest recollections, for example, the seats in the cinema hall were toneless and sombre; some time later, he notices that they have shifted into maroon. However, what the hallucinations, or the nightmares, do tousledly urge on his soul is that the duty of waiting for the extinction of one's source is unconditional, and that such passing sires a desolation that would never fade, were it not overlaid, mercifully soon enough, by Time's desert sands and the accretive lumber of living.

The fat nurse is cranking up to shoo them out. 'Enough now. Patient must rest.' But Dr Haldia twiddles in then, in an opulent-yellow safari suit, suave, lubricious, like a freshly opened can of cheese. 'Hello, hello, and how're we this morning?' The fat nurse tries to look demure and dextrous at the same time and nearly drops a bedpan. 'We're chatting unsparingly today, aren't we?' Dr Haldia tilts against the head of the bed, crosses his legs and simpers dotingly at Urmila, like the besotted and knavish lord of a fortress and Urmila his tearful hostage, recaptured after a shot at deliverance. Dr Haldia has been to Europe and the United States umpteen times. After virtually each visit he has had to reprint his visiting card, and jack up his consultation fees. He returns radiant from his jaunts, clutching four or five letters of the alphabet, seemingly selected out of a hat, and the abridged name, in brackets, of (presumably) a European or American centre of learning. The letters and the abbreviations are tacked on to the others on his card, like extra bogeys for a slow train. Thus FIVN (Zur.), DBTP (Lond.), MAKG (Berne), OCSE (Bos.), etcetera. His six telephone numbers have had to be hustled to the reverse of the card. 'We're fairly set upon recovering and buzzing off from Dr Haldia's today itself, aren't we?' (His idiom, expectedly, exasperates Burfi. 'Where the fuck did that shaved arsehole pick up his English? Unless one of those degrees is for a course in Bedside Manners – Take Their Money, Not Their Shit. Isn't he an FRCTTMNTS (Edin.)?')

'An admirable recovery, Mr –' to Shyamanand. 'She' avuncular chucking under Urmila's chin – 'grappled with her disorder like a redblooded boy.' They meander out like a politician and his groupies. Outside Intensive Care, Dr Haldia discourses to a dozen strangers – relatives and sympathizers of those held in his half-nelson, their faces naïve with anxiety – while Shyamanand, Chhana and Jamun wait. At last Chhana asks when they can shift Urmila home. The good doctor chortles, pronounces nothing, motions to them with his stethoscope to go and sit in his office, and joins them there, refulgent, after thirty-eight minutes.

Dr Haldia has no time to be genial with those who have waited long for him. 'Hahn, your Mrs's case . . . infarction . . . angina . . . coronary thrombosis . . . intense hypertension . . . clot . . . embolism . . . dyspnoea . . . cardiovascular murmur . . . phlebitic arteriosclerosis . . . arteritis . . . high blood pressure, dogtired heart, pacemaker . . . surrogate, standby, booster . . .'

'Is my mother strong enough for the operation? You remember, you cleared her for the piles operation, and she caved in because of the strain. How much'll this one cost?'

'I see no alternative,' declares Dr Haldia glacially. The glabrous cheese surface gullies. 'There was no choice to the piles operation either.'

Shyamanand is somewhat twitchy on the way home. 'Twenty-five thousand for the pacemaker. Does she need it? Can she bear it? We should consult a second specialist.' Through the car dawdle the drugged, moist breezes of September. 'I don't have twenty-five thousand in ready money. I'll be forced to break a bank deposit, borrow – and pay interest to the bank for using – my *own* savings.' He shrugs dispiritedly.

'Before we do that, let's just check – with Burfi – how much we can pool. Doubtless we can –'

'Burfi! Huh! My child, isn't he.' After a while Shyamanand adds, 'You ask him. I won't. Also confirm with someone else this pacemaker business.'

'I'll sound him this evening. If you recall, you wanted to amble in the Municipal Park today. We could drop you there, and on the hospital circuit I'll discuss the contributions with Burfi.'

Dusk by the time they leave Shyamanand, Chhana, Pista's aya, Pista and Doom at the gates of the Municipal Park. Shyamanand is downhearted. 'Too late to enjoy a stroll here. Please return in good time. Too often've you discarded me in different gardens for what has seemed aeons.' The women and the children pad into the park. Shyamanand plods towards a towering pipal beyond the gates.

'Ironic,' decrees Burfi, as he forages in a picnic basket at his feet. 'Baba's first love, his money, will now be gobbled up by this hocus-pocus to extricate his first hate, his wife.' With a 'tch' of incontinence he evicts from the basket and dumps on the car seat a coppery flask of mutton broth, a turquoise flask of milk, and a canteen of a milk-and-banana mash. With an 'ah' of accomplishment he educes whisky, water, glasses. He pours himself a peg. Jamun waits until he's certain, then asks, 'Won't you pour for me? Or put back Ma's dinner in the basket?' and yanks the basket over to himself.

'Cheers. Here's to things mending,' proffers Burfi. After a while he runs on, 'Baba's already paid out a good many thousands in the piles fuckup. He'll disgorge more yet – his is an old chastisement. You and I remember Ma boiling over time and time again, gnashing her teeth – Pista does it too, identically – she'd then curse, "His money'll damn him," and, "As though he's going to carry his money over with him when he croaks." None of us has any accurate idea of how much cash Baba's squirrelled away in his bank deposits. The sum'll be lightweight, nothing to holler about – one lakh or so – the lifetime hoard of a commonplace creature, who never had the daring or the adroitness to speculate. Oof, such a dismal lower-middle-class exercise, a babyish sport – to mothball the interest on a Fixed Deposit – never to wade into it – with that interest after months to archly open a Recurring Deposit, and with the interest of the Recurring Deposit to start some Term Deposit, or National Savings – like playing Trader or Monopoly.'

'Rubbish. Let Baba and his money be,' retorts Jamun, shifting his eyes off the road for a swig from his glass. 'Even if we were on the breadline, Burfi, you'd never lay out a pie to pluck any one of us back from death, except possibly Joyce, and that only after she overrides and shushes your protests.' Burfi grins like a bashful cherub and bawdily ups his thumb at Jamun. Jamun continues, 'Phew, you and money are like a junkie and his fix. Do you remember, on my last visit, one usual evening, you and I imbibing upstairs – as Chhana would say – steaming bloated weather, skin like a fine cactus, but you were beaming – what's a sandboy? – in the Bermudas that you'd bought in Kuala Lumpur. You'd proposed that the three of us – minus the brats – should dine out, and then your mug showed that you'd begun to worry that if we did eat out, who'd foot the bill? From another room we could overhear Joyce fulminating against Pista.'

Well, Burfi half-remembers, but is certain that, since the recollection is Jamun's, it won't be to his credit.

Pista's aya has complained to Joyce that in the afternoons Pista never alights at the apposite stop from his school bus, but gets down instead with friends at *their* stops. Pista's aya then wastes a wearying half-hour on the telephone trying to ferret him out. Pista has already had his dome chewed off for this failing, but since it's chiselled out of adamant, this time Joyce is underlining the terrors of being kidnapped. 'Hellish men will twinkle at you, offer you lollipops and toffee, and carry you off from your bus. Nobody'll protest because you're *always* getting off the bus at the wrong stops.'

'The lunch that those men'll give me will any day be better than what Aya gives.'

'Ha! For lunch they'll fatten you with beatings, for tea and dinner also.'

Pista is silenced, then, more considered, balancing the unknown horrors of days of thrashing against the ascertained horrors of his aya's lunches, 'What kind of beatings?'

'First one villain – looking much like your Hindi teacher, what's his name? – will hack apart your mouth and bully you into draining a hundred large glasses of milk. Next, twenty-five injections, one upon another, half of them in your gums –' From the squeaks and squawks that succeed, Burfi and Jamun gather that Pista has leapfrogged on to his mother and is pummelling her. Then Joyce runs on, primly, like a godfearing Catholic schoolmarm – she uses the identical tone with Burfi too, frequently – 'Pista, you must promise me that you'll never ever straggle anywhere else from school without having earlier informed one of us in the morning.'

At that moment, suddenly, Burfi bobs up and tramps in from the verandah to instruct his wife and child on the cardinal point that she has omitted. 'But consider the money, Joyce! Listen, Pista, you piglet, if you're abducted, do you know how much *cash* we'd have to fork out to retrieve a bugger like you? You're not to greet any stranger or bum around anywhere with anyone, ever! My God – they could exact lakhs! In a burst all, all our savings gone – plus, we'll be driven to borrow! We'll be paupers, rag-pickers – and we'll have *you* back – some solace! – gadding about with new strangers, who'll be coolly hatching a second abduction just so that we can be flattened out for ever and ever.'

At which Pista, 'Will Mama also be flattened out, or only you?'

Jamun sniggers callously at the memory. 'Neither Baba nor Ma, fortunately, believes in primogeniture; otherwise, if they will the house to you, the instant you possess it, you'll bundle me out and sell it, eh, Burfi?'

'My attitude to money isn't the issue, you bugger – the question is, what's Baba doing with his cash? Both of us, at different times, have hissed at him, with varying intensities of rage, that we won't miss his money. Maybe we won't, really – even though a windfall of money is one of this world's appealing things – because somehow we've made it, even you, you fuckpot – even though you angled for a really weird deal with Baba, ha-ha. You remember? You can't forget! He was so nonplussed when you proposed. "You make over your money to me, and I'll remain with and foster you and Ma for the remainder of your lives, but I'll need to be financially independent" – some compact for a joker in his twenties! Of course he refused – "Don't be so slothful!" – and you gravely pronounced, while everyone else was holding his sides, "Even when I urgently need money, I shall not thumb yours. When you feverishly need me, I won't be within reach," a forecast that didn't awe Baba much!

'Look – we've felt the pinch – Ma and Baba have, and because of them, I as a college yob – but the terrible years are done, and the future now is no more the withered winter for which Baba had to salt away – just pull up somewhere for cigarettes, Jamun . . . thanks . . . Gold Flake, twenties, are now so bloody expensive . . .'

Jamun remains quiet as his brother rambles on. Like his mother, he is wary of money, for he too has witnessed its bestial clutch on others.

Nearly two decades before, Urmila had stayed alone in Bhubaneshwar for about a year. She was transferred there. Missing her children, she remitted them the fare for the train tickets so that they could spend part of their school and college vacations with her. Jamun recalls that in her absence their government flat became drearier, more dishevelled and soulless, like a slummy hostel. They must have pined for her too.

But Burfi didn't go because he snapped up his ticket money in staying alive with his prodigal chums. Shyamanand wheedled a few days' leave to convey Jamun to his mother.

From that holiday, the scene that abides with Jamun for years is Shyamanand's leave-taking of Bhubaneshwar.

A Saturday forenoon. The adolescent and his parents stand in the sliver of lawn outside the tidy, diminutive house that Urmila has had to rent for a considerable sum. Shyamanand and Jamun are about to start out to scout for a rickshaw when the unshaven, cross-eyed postman flings in a letter at the gate. It is to Urmila from Burfi.

The familiar, ingenuous long hand on the envelope greatly disquiets Jamun. That his brother communicates with his mother independently of their ritual, joint, monthly letter ('Dearest Ma, How are you? I am fine. Yesterday, at badminton, I thrashed Kuki 15–10, 15–7, even though he cheated . . .') in itself is astounding; it seems inconceivable that between two habitants of his intimate world might exist a link of which he is unaware. The concomitants of Burfi's handwriting – his sallow, breadstick fingers, Urmila's scarlet Parker pen that he's snaffled, his desk that he won't humour his brother to touch – are lacking; instead, there is the wispy grass and the gulmohar tree.

But that is not all. Jamun intuits that Urmila is loath to let Shyamanand read Burfi's letter. She doesn't open it there and then; indeed, she doesn't even appear especially pleased to have received it. Shyamanand has unthinkingly stretched his hand out for the letter, but Urmila affects not to notice. It is at this point that his parents, the most familiar shapes of Jamun's world, begin to look unaccountably unfamiliar to the boy.

He isn't accustomed to seeing his parents in any surroundings other than those of their shabby flat. Unmindful of the sun, he watches them in the shade of the gulmohar tree, down which pelt two squirrels, and behind which is visible their neighbour's kitchen window, from which eructs the trendiest Oriya film pop. All at once, everything seems unprecedented – the lawn, the house, the mould around the tap in the boundary wall, the faces of the neighbours, the lingo on the roads – everything. They even cause the heavens and the sparrows to appear newfangled. The diverse, extraordinary components of the entire setting are telescoped in his parents looking like strangers. He senses, fuzzily but forcefully, that he doesn't know them *at all* – not their essentials – their past, whom they yearned for at fourteen, and what they dreamed of at thirty-one – the kernel of their humanness; creation itself then seems without context. Jamun feels as though he has been cosily swimming underwater, and on gushing up for air has faced an altogether new world, and an outlandish light.

'So,' says Shyamanand pawkily, returning the letter, 'after dissipating the ticket money that you posted, Burfi now implores you to "be a sweetie, a sugar" and send him "at least two hundred", since the issue is of "life and death, and bloody Baba'd never understand". Certainly, Baba doesn't understand, not when life is jiving till dawn in some discotheque, and death is deviant sex with godforsaken hippies. As the world's champion mother, you're bullied by your conscience, no doubt, to exhort Burfi to carry on; especially when, as an upshot, he detests his father even more for not being like his poppet mother. Do despatch him the cash. What's two hundred rupees in these days of inflation? Borrow from peons and typists, thresh about under their oblique derision, but feel saintly, bolster yourself with: I distress myself so that my deserving son can hold his head high in a discotheque. Five years later, will Jamun be as profligate as your elder son?'

Urmila is weeping by then. Her children have seen her sob night and day; to them, her lamentation has become piffling – now and then bothersome, vexatious.

Since that forenoon in Bhubaneshwar, Jamun has time and time again speculated on Burfi's improvidence and Urmila's outlook on money, for the attitudes of both have irked him. When he wasn't yet ten, he would listen with rapt horror to Burfi, then thirteen, composedly cobble together – to bare acquaintances, to anyone who couldn't verify – the most preposterous yarns about their wealth at home, or homes, for he endowed them with several: a kind of ranch outside New Delhi, with its separate swimming pool for the servants; a sort of chalet in Ooty, to which they retreated in the summer; a six-bedroom penthouse suite in Cuffe Parade; etcetera. His father, who smoked a pipe, planned to buy a building or two in Manhattan, but his mother wouldn't allow him, because, she asserted, how would the nation press on if we showered our money upon foreigners? Of course, Burfi next had to compose sinuous excuses to stymie his disbelieving auditors from visiting him at home, or homes. Jamun would hear his brother fabricate with the misgivings that one senses when a loved one, unready, performs on stage.

When he was nineteen, Burfi's buddies were the anglicised, modish children of rich men. The affluence of his friends made him sneakingly ashamed of his own family. On weekday afternoons, since his parents would be at office, he and his girlfriend, or a hippie-adventurer, would frequently fetch up at the flat for an hour or so of coupling. They would habitually encounter Jamun, aged fifteen, dawdling in the house in shredded vest and discoloured undies. The sight of him always discomposed, dampened and peeved Burfi. He would bellyache in the evenings, ''Why can't he dress less like a servant? He's embarrassing.'

'Why should I stew all afternoon in pants and shirt just to appease Burfi and his soulmates for the one second that they glimpse me?' Jamun, disputatious, would demur. 'They can shut their eyes and sniff their way to his room.'

At fifteen, and at twenty-eight, Jamun recognized the disparity in what money denotes to him, and to Burfi – rather, at fifteen, he was witheringly certain; at twenty-eight, he fancied that a difference in their attitudes might exist, but also that it might not matter. He himself gauges money to be wily. If he has the money, he'll buy chewing gum, or condoms, or a refrigerator. If he doesn't, he will muzzle himself to do without; the self-discipline becomes in itself quite piquant. But for Burfi, deprivation is failure, a cudgel to his self-esteem.

'Why don't we suggest to Baba that if he truly can't manage the pacemaker business by himself, we'll both pitch in?'

'Obviously,' snorts Burfi, as they drive into the hospital, 'but you pitch in first.' When they park, he reminds Jamun, 'Check with Kuki about the pacemaker.'

That night Jamun reports to Shyamanand that his sons will share the costs of Urmila's healing. Jamun himself can immediately part with twelve thousand rupees. 'Yes,' falters Shyamanand, 'that'll greatly help.'

After dinner Jamun trudges down the back lanes to the beach. Past the fisherwomen and the offal, through the fetor of the sea, of fresh and putrid fish. The heavens black and lumpish, the waters thin and scummy, like black kerosene in a wobbling, transparent can. Through the night rovers, the queens, flashers, gynanders, old-world floosies, the lonely hearts, Jamun casts about vainly for a sequestered, unsoiled nook, from where sky and ocean will appear to be one, like a boundless cinema screen seconds before the show. Maybe he will be treated to spangles of lightning, beguiling advertisements from some other life.

He is very happy that he has given Shyamanand twelve thousand rupees. He feels unburdened, blessed. He believes that in the nursing home his mother somehow knows what he has done, and is smiling in her numbness. He plods on, wallowing to his ankles in the sand.

Whenever Urmila has lacked cash, Jamun has reminded her of the crisp, virgin banknotes entombed in her trunk. 'Every time, over the years, that you've received a brand-new note, of whatever value, you've interred it in your trunk, never to use it. You must have more than a thousand in there, among the folds of saris and the leaves of unread, sacred tomes.'

'No, Jamun, I can't spend money that looks so clean. These notes are like starched, lily-white saris after a cosy bath on a warm winter morning.'

Urmila's views on opulence and solvency have been moulded by the innumerable beastly humiliations that she has twitched under for need of money. In her later years, when money is no longer anguish, she feels towards it contempt, and sometimes repugnance. She begins to live freely; money is vital no more. 'You'll notice, Jamun, money's never within your reach when you need it the most. I've witnessed how the itch to hoard dominated both my father and yours. I merely hoodwinked myself – that if I spent bountifully on the deserving things, then somehow my kitty would be replenished. That happened just once – remember? – when I parted with three thousand to your aya for that Kishori rape incident? I was left with about five hundred in the bank, and the whole month to see out. I borrowed, of course – and, ludicrously, from Aya! – but soon after, a cheque for more than eight thousand – from Moni! that viperous crosspatch – my share for some lands of ours in Balasore that I didn't even know of, that were bought by I don't know whom – most sisterly of Moni to spare me my portion, but God knows what I was entitled to. I gawped at the cheque, I wanted to whoop and coo – and instead, burst into tears. It appeared such a victory for me, though the event was no victory, of course, merely a miracle, never repeated, though it should've been. For I don't spend on myself – you can't deny that, Jamun – but to reap some stillness, respite, caring – these *can* be paid for.'

'This morning's horoscope in the *Express*,' responds Jamun, 'states that Sagittarians are total lemons with money. That fits you – zip through the cash in your hand, and *mañana* to the leftovers.'

'Because of previous debts, I'd no money in that racking year in Bhubaneshwar. I was alone, utterly friendless, away from my children, in a defunct, unfamiliar town, regularly pondering why I was living, and every time prompting myself – oh, who'll then see to your children, and, more to the purpose, who'll then pay back your borrowings? Next, when your father was transferred to Jamshedpur, he famished himself to stow away some money towards building this house. He too was alone, friendless – but he adores squirrelling, and salting away.'

On the beach, Jamun recalls that both Urmila and Burfi are

positive that, for Shyamanand, conserving money is exhilaration – 'his bank deposits are his uppers' is Burfi's vitriolic remark. In his retirement, forenoon upon forenoon, unbathed, with his vitals paddling in litres of tea, Shyamanand has calculated and notched up figures in a large black diary, and has striven to sway his sons into sharing his enchantment with those numbers. The diary contains the particulars of his bank accounts, tidily jotted down in distinctive inks – green for name and location of bank, blue for rate of interest and duration of deposit, red for amount deposited and date of maturity, black for the run-of-the-mill reckoning, the withdrawals and accretions. Shyamanand jabs away for hours at the pocket calculator that Joyce has half-sardonically gifted him; now and then, never failing to jolt, like thunderclaps of delight, he will plangently whack his thigh or the table if his summations are roseate – if in May, they indicate that by July he'll've scooped together a few more thousands in interest to open yet another account. If his computations augur against him, Shyamanand will remain glum till his further study of them touches off a new brainwave to swell his revenue by a thimbleful.

The costs of Urmila's rehabilitation have already blighted Shyamanand's savings plans. Yet no one condoles with him in the least. He bickers, noon and night. 'Don't you follow? If I discontinue a deposit today, *I* pay the bank to allow me to touch my own money, whereas as soon as the deposits mature, I'll repay you bloody all.' And, 'Isn't my money yours? After I die, won't my money be yours?'

'We don't want your money. Not that compellingly anyway. Wade into it now, when it's needed the most.'

Kasturi's telephone at eight-thirty the next morning. 'Hello, Jamun here . . . Thanks for waking me up . . . Sorry, I couldn't contact you earlier . . . Oh, she was yakking chirpily last evening. They mean to hustle a pacemaker into her . . . I'm meeting Kuki about that this evening . . . will you come too? I could pick you up.'

He isn't certain that he's glad at Kasturi having called. When he's away from her, he believes that their friendship should moulder to nullity. They've been intimate for over a decade. After her marriage to someone that her grandfather found for her, Jamun's slept with her twice, frenziedly, without fondness, trying to bludgeon with his phallus his own tension and rage. Neither much relishes alluding to those two misadventures, though silence will never whittle down their import. Yet every time that either's taken a break at home – he, in particular, when repelled by his Kasibai life – one has dropped a line to the other, not to hint at a rendezvous but just to inform of one's whereabouts, as a compliant child will to a domineering mother. But when they meet, their talk is just flotsam.

Urmila despises Kasturi, without intelligible cause. Kasturi's maiden visit to Jamun's house, years ago, was a catastrophe.

A holiday, about four in the afternoon, tea. Jamun's parents are at the dining table. He introduces Kasturi.

Shyamanand behaves with his wonted civility towards guests. 'Do please sit down, Kasturi . . . Are you two in the same college? . . . Ah – Political Science, certainly a formidable subject . . .' Urmila doesn't acknowledge Kasturi in any way, and, after the preliminary chit-chat tapers off, woodenly observes, 'I've no more tea.' She then rises to her feet and starts to clear the table.

Kasturi, wholly taken aback, begins to disclaim that she needs any tea. Jamun, to cover up, patters, 'Oh, I'll make some more. Baba, woud you like another cup? Ma?' and steers Kasturi to the drawing room. 'Perhaps I should leave,' offers a still startled Kasturi.

'Rubbish. If you slink off, imagine how tickled pink my mother'll be.'

Jamun's sangfroid seems further to madden Urmila. When he crosses her with the tea, she remonstrates, in a stridor squawky enough to carry to Kasturi in the other room, 'Those biscuits are not for that woman. Put them back!'

Jamun can devise one explanation for Urmila's conduct, but is sure neither of its accuracy nor its need. Why should he at all interpret his mother to Kasturi? To himself, he therefore defends himself by arguing that locution and inflexion are slippery matters, and that he might misrepresent one woman and rile the other. Kasturi remains composed through her tea, and does not touch a single biscuit. Jamun doesn't insist.

He doesn't badger Urmila either, later that evening. He prefers, like his father, that his silence should voice his contempt. After dinner, Urmila, penitent and prurient, murmurs, 'Your Kasturi looks much older than you. In a few years, the flesh on her jowl'll slump, like toffee in the sun.'

To disconcert and distress her, Jamun declares, as though inadvertently, 'True. But Kasturi's terrific in bed.' He then discerns the wound of affront on Urmila's features and knows that he has deeply wronged both his mother and his friend. (At the same time, the imp in his head reminds him – with a snicker – that Kasturi is *not* terrific in bed; she's bloody passive and shy – and unwilling to learn; the only things going for her are her coffee-with-milk skin, and its tremulousness.) Infuriated with himself, he detonates at her, 'I know you too well. You observed Kasturi for an instant, and, from the way I spoke to her, baselessly deduced that she's dazzled me, that I burn to marry her. That dismayed you. Not only because every parent recoils from the marriage of his son, loathes the pliancy with which he yields to his interloper-wife. But because *Baba*'d sneer, how shoddily our sons've married! Their wives're older than they – and one's even a Christian! Our grandsons're being reared as Catholics, have been baptized, and their measly father has not demurred! Now Jamun's scented out for himself another nymph. First-rate. *Then* Baba'll arraign you, his whipping boy. *You*'ve goofed everything. You've not fostered your children rightly. They've discounted their traditions, culture, parents – because of you. As a mother, as a mortal, you're a disaster. Task consumated, Baba'll then roll over in bed, fart, and return to his journal. Instead of hissing his twaddle back at him, you'll start sobbing – because you'd snivel even if a toddler accused you of bumping off both the Kennedys.

'Therefore, to stall – or just to defer – the next squirt of Baba's toxin, you were so uncivil to a stranger, a guest, this afternoon. Under Baba's nose, at the start, you wanted to manifest that you disliked Kasturi, so that – you reasoned – even if Jamun marries her, you could never be reproached with having encouraged us. "I? But I behaved so wretchedly with her the first day! However could I've put heart into them!" But creation is much larger than Baba's sentiments. I know you to the core, Ma.'

'Set against you, even your father'd pass for a cherub.' Urmila's face, like putrid fruit, has pulped with gall and misery. 'You are the cruellest person I know. As though in my womb you'd laved in venom.'

In the car, Kasturi maunders about her husband and herself but, weltering in his inexorable retrospections, Jamun hears not a phrase. '. . . will turn up for the last weeks of my confinement. But you won't remain here till then. And you haven't met him since the wedding. When d'you return? Of course you can't foretell, how silly of me.'

Kuki has ballooned in the months that Jamun hasn't met him. His blowzy, stretched skin looks about to slit, like a mouth for a yawn. Over whisky (and a nimboo pani for Kasturi), Kuki exhibits to them a thin, dove-grey, two-inch metal case, like a ritzy cigarette lighter. 'This is the pacemaker. The cobbler that Haldia gets for the job'll position this just beneath the collarbone.'

To discover how it feels, Kasturi props the dummy pacemaker underneath her collarbone. 'As a wily trafficker in medical gear, Kuki, you might even know when a pacemaker's truly necessary. Or are we just easy money for Haldia? And for you!'

'No one jokes with stuff like pacemakers, oaf. Your mother must need it if her heart's kaput. Haldia's reputation is top-notch. Mind you, a pacemaker can never harm. Of course, the combination of Haldia and pacemaker'll be extortionate. Are the costs stinging you?'

'No, certainly not,' demurs Jamun, and focuses on his fourth peg. He and the others of his family would have been harrowed if, by and by, they themselves began to assume that they were bedevilled more by the expenses of Urmila's healing than by the uncertainty of her restoration. To enquire about the pacemaker is just to flabbily betoken to themselves that, even in an extremity, they stay composed enough to probe the fitness of each counsel. The truth is that the rut of the preceding one week – the two trips every day to the hospital, the arranging for Urmila's particular diet, the superintendence of the house in the desolation of her absence, the comfortless palavers with Haldia and his lieutenants, the sons' imperceptible shunning of Shyamanand's despairing mien, and the evocations of the hospital itself – the pale corridors dully dispersing the ice-blue of the tubelights, the pong of carbolic, the careworn faces of those who wait in the bucket seats outside Intensive Care, the sly orderlies Argus-eyed for a fast buck, the grudging, strutting nurses, the unpunctual specialists, Urmila's ashen wrinkled face, her gripes about agony and neglect, her accusations of their tardiness which irk them because true – have enervated and bludgeoned them to automatons. They persevere in their new routine, outwardly, in Chhana's phrase, 'hoping for the best and ready for the worst', but inly, too inert to speculate. At home, the void of Urmila's absence is abominably dislocating. Each thing – tea in the early morning, the sere flowers in the vases, the dust on the face of the TV, the reckoning of the dhobi's monthly dues – reminds her husband and her sons of her. But the remembrance of her is now unbiddenly embroiled with the impressions of the nursing home. Hence their entire existence seems to recall only their visits to the hospital; to summon up with solace the trip just completed, and with gloominess the trip to come.

'Haldia and his kennel,' states Kuki, dallying over his second peg, 'will flip in the pacemaker in a day or two, as soon as they fancy that your mother's fit enough – or when they urgently want some money.' He smirks. 'I'll telephone you when. Will you pay cash for the pacemaker? Then I'll charge you about two thousand less.'

'No . . . Kuki' – Jamun struggles to crystallize his foreboding – 'how can we be certain that this damn snuff box is not a wholly *unnecessary* precaution? After all, it involves yet one more operation. Is she fit enough? If I sound Haldia out, he'll just fondle his own balls and split. Can we call in some other quack? That'll look bloody weird, won't it – Haldia's hospital, but not his advice.'

'Yes – and there's a limit to the weirdness that he can take.' Kuki simpers in remembrance. 'I was craving to film one of his pacemarker insertions – Oh, but you haven't' – He bounces out of the sofa – 'even seen my latest thing.' From his cupboard, from behind the hundred hanging shirts, he heaves out a greyish duffle bag with several scarlet zips. It discloses a compact video camera, a bit larger than his hand, and its accessories. 'It's far out, this Sony Handycam. I picked it up in Singapore – and I can't look at my Nikon again.' He begins to click into place the several attachments. 'If you can spare twenty minutes, I could put on what I trapped two weeks ago – after midnight, the male sluts in Dost Garden, leching away.' He starts to scrutinize, through the Handycam, the room, the contours and expressions of Kasturi and Jamun, murmuring all the while, 'Like a high . . . you yearn to capsulize your . . . unkempt, soulless universe . . . for your home video . . . in these . . . tidy frames . . .'

Back in the car, euphoric with whisky, Jamun stretches out and tucks behind Kasturi's ear a wisp of hair that has straggled across her cheek. His fingers tingle the downiness of her neck. She stares at him with pawky amusement, and asks, 'In that dump where you work, what's your recreation? Your company?'

'Ah – a purposeful shift of subject. The cook. A meaty, middle-aged Kolhapuri jade and her lovechild. They aren't there now. They've scooted to their backwoods village for some crisis.' At the adduction of Kasibai and Vaman, Jamun's wits – for one week convulsed by his mother's affliction, and at that moment pulsing with sottishness – welcome, like an enslaved satyr his fornicatress, the evocations of their bodies – Kasibai's titanic soufflé thighs, Vaman's blubber-lipped smile, bashful. Inflamed, he clutches Kasturi's warm forearm. 'Will you drive with only one hand?' she murmurs drily.

'If you indulgently raise your right leg, then your toes can replace my hand on the wheel. If a cop objects, I'll point out that the left hands of bachelors whose mothers are bedridden appear, on steering wheels, like womanly right feet. And doesn't he know how addictive desire is, and how fulfilling caving in to it is, like the silence after a fever? Oh, but you snicker at mine, and piety mauls it.'

'Tch-tch, poor Jamun.' Kasturi giggles. 'Did you scurry home for your mother, or for me?'

'Scurry?' He drives off slowly. 'I took four days.' A minute later, he chortles tipsily, 'My father would've asserted I stampeded home for Joyce. As though in my case there must needs be a reason.' Yet without a summons you wouldn't've returned, he catechizes himself voicelessly. I shan't come back until you clamour for me, he had willed to himself at his last homecoming. I need to break free. I must relish another life, other bonds.

At two one afternoon, in office, on a faultlessly languorous day six weeks ago, with all the king-sized windows yawning, and a warm, moist breeze on their skins, with a post-lunch paan from Hegiste glutting his mouth, a notion, like a windborne seed, had floated to Jamun that in the few months in his new post he had educed a tenuous – and ethically suspect – delight from electing to be away from where everyone fancied he pined to be – from thus, in likelihood, effecting heartache and concern in parents, sibling, lover and himself. He had found the notion nicely perturbing.

Yet on the third evening after the telegram informing him of his mother's heart attack, on the roof of his block of flats, he had recognized that in biding his time for four days, he had sinned profoundly. He'd then determined, in penitence, that he'd stay with and foster his begetters till they died.

'A friend of mine, Satyavan Hegiste, always uses the phrase "native place" for "home". A matchless phrase, isn't it – the only place where one is truly a native, and can mooch about in a lungi. Everywhere else, one is a migrant, marking time. And Mrs Hegiste equates one's parents with one's home, the base to which one regresses by reflex when blitzed, where your arrival is jubilantly welcomed for its own sake. That nonplussed me, and I joshed her, So you have no home, despite husband and son? And what of the lonely hearts like me, spouseless and bratless? She rebutted: man, woman and litter in themselves are just nomads, in caravans across the desert . . . Kasturi, am I gibbering?'

'Yes indeed, but delightfully. I'd relish your babble even more if your hand didn't, under its cloak, amble over me proprietorially. Mrs Hegiste must've married precociously – is she very young? – and like a patriarchal Jew out of Genesis or Jeremiah must hanker for her native place. Weep ye not for the dead, neither bemoan him: but weep sore for him that goeth away: for he shall return no more, nor see his native country. Isn't that an entirely Indian sentiment?'

'Your Bible quotations are generously multipurpose. No doubt your fondness for them harks back to your green years, when the nuns of your school so inspired you that you actually wanted to convert – to float about like them – lay sister, lay! – in white, colourless, serene, with Jesus's candle in their crotch. But I adore the Bible too, and exploit Corinthians against my mother whenever she perorates about my unmarried state, and my father wields the *same* lines against my brother whenever he mopes about *his* married state. But I would have you without carefulness. He that is unmarried careth for the things that belong to the Lord, how he may please the Lord: But he that is married careth for the things that are of the world, how he may please his wife.'

In the previous year, when the entire family had lived together, before Jamun had chosen to be transferred, Shyamanand had been distinctively vocal on the subject.

On the sporadic Saturday, the two brothers, the one wife and the two children ebb away the whole day loitering, window-shopping in the ostentation of any one of the city's voguish bazaars. Shyamanand grouses to Urmila, 'Your daughter-in-law adores this loafing about in glitter and gloss, trailing two goodlooking men, wearing clothes too youthful for her, slopping money on frippery, glutting her brats with candy and other junk, triumphantly islanding her husband – and even brother-in-law! – from us even on a holiday.'

Jamun presumes that Shyamanand's gripe is only huffiness at being neglected for these Saturday jaunts. So he invites his parents time and time again to join them (while simultaneously reminding them how boring and fatiguing these outings in fact are – 'we return every evening with foul tempers and aching calves'), but Shyamanand consistently rebuffs with, 'Your sister-in-law'll demur against my presence,' and Urmila declines with, 'No, please, I'm too fagged, but please, please lug your father with you, so that I may unwind at home by myself.'

But by that juncture of his life, Burfi has become inured to Shyamanand's opinions on his wife, and on all other issues – or almost inured. Husbandhood and Joyce's unremitting, subdued disdain have secretly seared him; now he usually feigns to disregard all the opprobrium against her that doesn't pointedly discredit his own sagacity in picking such a spouse; and yet, at the same time, the most elementary parley, with parent or with wife, appears to have become a potential spark for factiousness.

In the lambency of marriage's initial years, the discord would have germinated differently. Burfi had all but shouldered his father out of his house once. 'He's nuts. He wanted to bed down in my room and wished Joyce to sleep alone in the spare bedroom.'

Burfi's account. Joyce's too. Shyamanand presents no version because he is never so importuned. His account will doubtless be more vapid, and which audience relishes the etiolation of an unwholesome yarn? Burfi's auditor is his brother, who threads his recital to the corpus of unfilial anecdotes that kith cannot forbear from recounting about kin.

'You must remember,' advises Burfi, 'that those days, Joyce and I rendezvoused only on intermittent weekends, in Udaipur, because she was stationed elsewhere. Baba arrived for his holiday, alone, his maiden visit after our marriage; I was glad for his society. I even made believe that during his sojourn his relations with Joyce would mend. He'd partner me on my tours, etcetera. But patently, I existed just for the Friday to Monday, youthful lust and all that. I'd allotted Baba the second bedroom, and he appeared to've liked it. At least, he didn't bleat for three days, not until the Friday when Joyce arrived.

'I'd brimmed myself with rum. Baba didn't swill at all. At dinner he and Joyce were starchy, but okay. Then we said goodnight to Baba, I puffed a joint, we tee'd up for bed – shadowy light, Joyce's notion of soulful music from the stereo, Perry Como crap – and a demanding thumping on the bedroom door. What the fuck, I spluttered. Who's it, I hollered. Joyce's face was a cartoon of frigid rage. "Your father," she spat, "can't stomach our being together."

'"Sorry to disturb," spouted Baba, but for sure he didn't mean it. He muttered that he'd panicked because of the scorpion in his bedroom. He looked genuinely scared, in a cold sweat. What the fuck, I groused to myself again, knowing that bloody Joyce'd censure only me for this dishevelment. Oof, I felt so pestered. "Won't you at least come out and help me?" asked Baba.

'The scorpion was monstrous and beautiful, a sable six-incher, between chair leg and chest of drawers, tail nutating like an acrobat on a tightrope, flawlessly poised. Killing a fucker like that isn't the smoothest stunt when you're stoned and've just been plucked out of humping. Baba carried on spluttering. "Don't approach it! Keep clear of it!" Apparently he's been stung once by a scorpion, as a cub, in his village, by the well or something. The terror and pain'd blacked him out. I bellowed for the menials. One of them, a tribal from a dot in Gujarat, simpered unabashedly when he sighted the scorpion. With a knife he snicked off the final quarter-inch of tail, and, smirking like a primate, he – phew! – hoisted the scorpion by the tail and, waggling it about, carted it to the wilderness of the compound. We overheard the other flunkeys chortling outside. Tizzy over, I was slipping back to Joyce, when Baba demanded, ruffled, "Where should I turn in? I can't sleep here."

'But where could I park him? That house was a tumbledown chateau of horrors, erected circa 1875. In the downstairs halls some snakes and their chums had taken up residence. As a choice for Baba, there remained only the upstairs verandah. He tacked on, "And your own bedroom."

'I sweated to cajole him to hang on in that same room. Scorpions don't intrigue and harry the same patsy in droves. We both began to bridle. Then Baba proposed, "Why don't you and your wife doss down here? And I in your room?" Boy!! Next – you won't believe this – in a modulated tone, the pharisaic inflexions of stratagem, he suggested, "If your wife" – never Joyce, always "your wife" – "can't sleep in the same room with me, then perhaps she can bed here alone." He scanned my face, and demanded spleenfully, "Can't you rein in from your wife even for one night?"

'I returned to my room, fuming, and latched the door. I could've whammed him. The idea of Joyce and me together was deranging him. For hours, until we crashed, we heard him clumping about in the verandah – the plod and shuffle by and by pacing my guiltiness.'

'D'you want to come in?' asks Kasturi at her gate, not looking at Jamun, abruptly, curiously formal. Jamun doubts whether, with Urmila not there, anyone at home'll remember to put by some dinner for him. He drily senses that their house no longer has a whipping boy whom they can all berate for such inattention. Kasturi then glances fugitively at him, gauges the yes on his face, grins and asserts, 'You won't accept when you realize that my younger sister's sharing my room.'

'Will you feed me something?' coaxes Jamun, laughing, as they go in.

Nearly midnight when he reaches home, fuddled and relaxed. In that mood, Urmila's affliction is not dismal, but inexorable. A soused Burfi has described the state, with which he himself is most intimate, as the Omar Khayyám blues.

The lights in Burfi's room and the upstairs rear verandah are on. That isn't extraordinary, since Joyce is a wholly nocturnal creature. Burfi, Joyce and Chhana are in the verandah, on the floor of which, in the slack gusts, dart – like wee, black-cowled, terror-crazed Inquisitors – shreds of charred paper. From the mien and attitudes of the three, Jamun senses that some unusual event has occurred. For one unhinged second he believes that they've murdered Shyamanand and triumphantly incinerated him in the verandah. 'Anything wrong?'

For a moment, none responds. Joyce cautiously steps past Jamun and goes in. Chhana glances at Burfi out of the corner of her eye, histrionically. Jamun knows that she has secretly enjoyed whatever has happened. Her wry mouth and her parabolic eyebrows, thrusting concentric ellipses of forehead flesh into her hairline, tacitly connote both scorn and amusement, and concurrently gainsay any possible complicity in the affair. Burfi intends to answer casually, but falters. 'Uh . . . Joyce suddenly started burning my things – my management textbooks, my new Jordache jeans, the Frank Zappa CD, two hundred-dollar bills.' He looks at Jamun shamefacedly and grimaces a smile. 'The kids were present. Even Doom pegged away at her – "Mama, why you burning Baba's things?" When I dashed to check her, she chucked at my face the burning jeans.'

'Shall we chat about this over a gin?' moots Jamun.

'A first-rate idea,' purrs Burfi, alacritous, even under stress, to quaff someone else's booze.

The brothers and Chhana deposit themselves in the verandah under a louring, starless sky. 'I half-felt like calling in the police. Doubtless the cops would've only tried to quarry some money out of us, but we should've summoned whoever deals with screwballs, and made her over – so what if she's a wife?' Opinion conveyed, Burfi declines into his basket chair, muses whether he's gaffed, and downs half his gin. Mindful of the silence of his companions, he then lights a cigarette. 'Nineish. Chhana and I'd just returned from the hospital. Joyce was fulminating because we were overdue for dinner at Rani's house. She ranted for fifteen minutes, clumping about the room like a foiled strangler, eyes debouching out like a nervous disease – I'm perpetually unpunctual, I forever delay her in every matter. Doom witnessed us from the bed, agape. I protested, I've barely got back from the hospital, they're sliding in the pacemaker day after tomorrow, we had to chat with Haldia's troupe. That was more important than dinner and prattle with her Rani. Then I reminded Joyce that she hadn't even once visited Ma in the nursing home, which is a revolting omission. At that, she boiled over again. Afterwards, Pista confided that he'd thought that the room'd burst, like a pressure cooker – his simile. Your mother hates me, Joyce screeched, why should I yawn about in a hospital watching a shrivelled cow die? If her two darling sons treasure her at all, they should be waiting their nights outside Intensive Care; instead, they look in now and then, as though she was a dragging Wimbledon quarter-final on TV. At which, I retorted that I would *not* chaperone her for dinner to her bloated, lesbian ex-beau, except that Rani's not ex. We bickered at that incendiary level for a while. Joyce then set fire to some of my stuff, and is now swanning off for Rani's house, never to return, which should mean Sunday.'

'Well, just this pyre of your belongings is new – she hasn't tried this one before. Ordinarily, your chats with Joyce on any subject conclude with her scudding off to her parents, Doom pursed into her armpit, being tossed out of there within three days, zipping next to her soulmate Rani. To all her cronies, she must be portraying her husband's family as these ogres who make life intolerable for such a young, photogenic mother – and one with earnings of her own, so it's clearly her niceness that enables her to endure her inlaws.' Jamun's temple pulses like a heart. He has had enough of calamitous marriages. 'Burfi, whether it be you or Ma, in a marriage, one crops exactly what one merits. A pity about your dollars, though. Didn't Baba double the hubbub by bawling from downstairs, "Who's fighting whom up there!" and, "How can Pista finish his homework in this din!"'

On the way downstairs to his bed, Jamun is checked by the vigorous reek of newly ground coffee. He subsides against the stair rail. Pista's aya is steaming herself a late-late-night cup. He craves for a large mug too, potent, sugarless, black, blistering, that'll detonate the crapulous ache in his skull, cauterize on his brain the truths that he ought never to forget: that his mother is eroding away in hospital and surely merits all his surplus time, that Kasturi is quite contentedly wedded to someone else, that Shyamanand is loveless and solitary, and needs solicitude, that, but naturally, marriage – which is as prodigal a corrupter as time – has altered both Burfi and Kasturi. Jamun ponders whether he can cadge some coffee off Pista's aya. She is generally damnably insolent, he is virtually a stranger to her, and he doesn't pay her salary. To brew himself a cup seems wearisome; to surprise her by asking for half of hers quite reasonable.

But marvellous, he ruminates sottishly, how each generation has its aya, how sequent ayas have always been a unit of the family, as household as the walls, the watcher of all, the curator of secrets. Burfi and he were fostered by one; she was also Urmila's confidante. Pista was reared by a second, who, of course, also helped with Doom. Doom finds it insupportable that Shyamanand, Urmila and Jamun call her Pista's aya (to distinguish her from the first aya, who was called simply 'Aya'), and not Doom's aya.

The nurture of his nephews has hoodooed Jamun, unveiled to him how alike generations can be. As a kid, he too was more intimate with his aya than with his mother. He had continually striven to wield Aya's fondness for him to prick Urmila's jealousy. Then, by degrees, with age, with the dilation of his frontiers, with school, playtime, companionship, with awakening self-reliance, he was participating in activities – school elocution, French cricket – in which his aya couldn't share. Next, without warning, she was no longer an aya and the surrogate mother of his nonage, but just a cook, who could be screeched at for slackness when a tardy lunch was delaying one from table tennis or rudimentary porn at Kuki's.

Now and then, bewitched, Jamun witnesses Pista and Doom enact random scenes from his own infancy, reincarnating the same themes, as though they are players in an extravaganza about Jamun's life. Doom, resentful of the quantity of chocolate fudge that Pista can shovel in, is a parody of Jamun's envy, of two decades ago, of Burfi glutting himself with halwa that would otherwise have swelled Jamun's portion. Pista, flaunting to an unlettered aya his freshly-won attainments in classroom English, appears to parrot Jamun trying to edify his own aya.

Who used, from time to time, out of monotony and mischievousness, to fib preposterously to the child Jamun. While he is tackling his homework beside her, in the sudorific kitchen of the government flat, Aya divulges – in her dialect that till school Jamun'd fancied was the 'correct' way of speaking Hindi – 'You know, Jamunya, you're *my* son, but your parents snaffled you because they yearned for another child. But I insisted that they employ me here as an aya, so that I could remain with my pet.'

Jamun, flurried, scoots to Urmila for illumination; she muddles rather than assures: 'Aya pretends to forget that we're *all* her children. Isn't she Sakti, the Celestial Mother of the cosmos?'

Aya died of diabetes, tuberculosis and neglect in a rundown charitable hospital. Jamun was eighteen then, and she ageless. She had never known the date of her birth, and had computed her years by the earthquakes and famines that she'd witnessed. For some months she disregarded the symptoms of her afflictions; when finally she couldn't ignore them, she hyped up her ailments. 'I'm dying, don't you know that!' she would scream at Urmila. 'Yet you bulldoze me to slog, slog, slog! Insufferable!' And she would hobble up to the roof, to puff a bidi and plan with her male freeloader cronies an outing to the cinema.

Shyamanand objects to Aya's continuance in the house and her unconcern for the doctor's injunctions. 'She could transmit her tuberculosis to us, to Jamun. She cooks our food. She coughs incessantly, a parched, corrosive hawking, as though sand and bonedust gnawed at her windpipe. She's losing flesh. Her skull's peeping out from beneath the pleats of skin. She hasn't dropped any of the taboos – bidis, rice, potatoes, sugar – doesn't take her medicines systematically. Yet pules nonstop that we don't look after her properly, that *we* are killing her. Can she or can't she conduct herself like an adult, a sixty-five-year-old? She is disintegrating. She must be admitted to a hospital, where she can't be fussy.'

Instead, Shyamanand, Urmila, Jamun and Aya move that monsoon from the government flat that they've nested in for a decade to their own house. They are among the pioneering householders in that mushroom housing colony, set up by the sea on gaunt, hardbitten soil, girdled by tipsy fishermen, harried by fetid sea breezes. Shyamanand and Urmila have scrimped and drudged to watch their house rear up, on their own clod of earth. They had wished that the whole family would stay there together, but their longing is not to be slaked for another decade; by the monsoon of their transfer, Burfi is in a job that has plucked him out of his hometown; he has also married. The nearest bus stop is a kilometre away; the closest paan wala doesn't stow Jamun's brand of cigarette. For the initial months, they live like refugees in a depot.

Shyamanand, Urmila and Jamun ferry a most averse Aya to the nearest government clinic, ten kilometres away. Shyamanand and Urmila have to skip office for the day; they are vinegary at the waste of a day's leave. Grimy benches of wood, an aeon of enervating waiting, Jamun flinching in the huddle of the infected, Aya's eyes tinted with emptiness, without expectation, her talon hand trammelling his wrist.

He dislikes sitting alongside her. She looks so servantlike; he is disquieted that he might be mistaken for her relative.

Recapturing the scene more than a decade after, maudlin, deflated against the stairs, without the energy to entreat a second aya for coffee, Jamun snickers woozily – and what of his Kasibai? A veteran scrubber from the intestines of some slum, whose most bountiful regulars were crimson-eyed truckdrivers – he now beseeches her for her bloated body; she constitutes one of his quadruple lives. To any fair-minded appraiser, surely Aya would've been signally less loathsome a human being than Kasibai? Yet he cringed away from Aya when she was dying; in her terminal months at home, a derelict in her charpai beneath the stairs, once virtually his foster-mother, he was revolted by her; a decade after, he is cringing anew, but this time sottishly, lasciviously, in a ruttish charade, in front of Kasibai's randy, bestial face. Perhaps the abettor of this degeneracy is that corrupter, the decade itself, and its expression that jocose snicker that once in a while nuzzles his ears. Oh, he should die, rackingly, with a dagger slash on his loins, devises Jamun out of contrition, and titters once more.

Aya is deserted at the government clinic. The doctor, a young dunce, is initially most unwilling. In the end, after Shyamanand effectively shams acquaintance with the entire Ministry of Health, the birdbrain concedes Aya a bed in the single befouled ward for the days that Shyamanand requires to admit her to a TB hospital. She is caddied through the ward in a tumbledown wheelchair. Her new neighbours gaze listlessly from their beds. 'You'll improve here, in no time. Then you'll return home . . .' They patter the last-minute pledges, the half-lies of a cursory grief prodded by alleviation. Aya remains quiet and does not glance at them.

She comes home the next afternoon, her triumph camouflaging her apprehension. She has dawdled out of the ward and hared into an auto-rickshaw. 'I'm not going back to that compost pit. This is my home. If you toss me out of here, I'll die at your gate.' She starts to bawl. Urmila, feeling blameful and now eased – indeed, delighted – begins too.

Shyamanand's features buckle in distaste. He stresses that

Urmila, Jamun and he should get themselves examined for tuberculosis. Urmila cavils vehemently. She is scared. They go, by and by, and are exculpated. To felicitate, they buy a kilo of sweets – sandesh and gulabjamuns.

In the anxiety before the results of their examination were disclosed to them, Jamun was fearful for his parents, particularly Urmila, who is infirm, brimful of symptoms, and Aya's soulmate. He is annoyed to learn that his parents were uptight for *him*. 'You *look* tuberculous, so skinny, and you smoke so much.'

Shyamanand and Jamun select the sweets, after ardent, loving debate. Jamun realizes then that this is probably the one occasion in the lives of his parents that they are rejoicing together. They never commemorate their birthdays or wedding anniversary. How peculiar a pretext for jubilation, smirks Urmila, that Aya has been unequal to transmitting to them her tuberculosis.

In the following weeks, Aya stays beneath the stairs and disintegrates evenly. From their offices, Shyamanand and Urmila haphazardly try to unearth a hospital, administered by government or some philanthropes, that'll remove Aya from them without levering out any of their money. They don't have thousands of rupees to spill for her nursing. The costs of her therapy oblige them to recognize that she is not a limb of the family. Her precise status has hardly ever preoccupied them before, although she has lasted with them for more than twenty years. Her husband had ditched her long before she had been recruited by Urmila. Her two sons – jewels both, she's sustainedly asserted – were mashed, aged thirteen and eight, in the landslide of an earthquake. In those decades with them, she never once holidayed by herself in some other town, or visited people out of her past whom Shyamanand or Urmila did not recognize, or – even at her most malcontent – repiningly conjured up a halcyon past that antedated her fosterage. Perhaps the past before her existent employment had just not been – or had been too hellish, or too nondescript. Nevertheless, she was not family.

From the beginning Aya is resolved not to leave her cot. She swears that she can't, but the family is cynical. Jamun buys a bedpan for her. Urmila wheedles with their sweeper to scour it periodically. He refuses, pithily briefing her that he considers the handling of the faeces of women degrading. So Urmila cleans the bedpan twice a day, before and after office. Aya continues to shun her medication. She also suborns the sweeper and the peevish maid to get for her paan, bidis and her pet jalebis.

Aya viperously berates Urmila whenever she sights her with the bedpan. 'Tch-tch, the madam of the house carting my dung! Because she's loyal to the faithful, isn't she! Then why did you slough me, my sweetie, at that cold government clinic? And on that single night that I spent there, you were easeful at home, weren't you, while I slipped on someone else's droppings on the tiles of that repelling lavatory, and lay in the feculence, voiceless, till the next piddler pulled in. You hanker after my death, no? But you wait, I'll endure on this cot for decades, and promptly after *you* cop it, I'll revive.'

Urmila will weep and call Aya an ingrate. Urmila's conduct peeves Jamun acutely. 'D'you know how ridiculous you look, snivelling, with a bedpan in your hand? You're bitter with her, so you blubber, but you're cleaning her shit at the same time.'

Jamun more or less ceases to acknowledge Aya. When he bounds upstairs, or slopes off through the side door, or ushers an electrician to the fusebox, he dissembles to himself that she's only an inanimate accumulation beneath the stairs, a truss of cast-off clothing, a few blackened sticks. Only her eyes, misted by infirmity and bitterness, jar him. In time, overlooking her existence becomes almost effortless.

Jamun has hazily (and fatuously, inspired by junk entertainment) fancied tuberculosis to be the ailment of the soulful, a contagion that yanks towards itself harrowed, beauteous nurses who weakly weep while the consumptive wheezes and hawks over his violin or his typewriter, his generative will befooled by his frayed lungs. Aya deftly blitzes this silly idea. Her coughs and groans, squeals and sputters, infiltrate the entire house. She – out of torment or boredom – rasps, chokes, screeches, for minutes on end, like a monstrous, lacerated bird. Covertly, Jamun gawps at her, spellbound by the stridors of agony. Certain spasms pluck her torso a foot off the bed, like a fakir's, bedevilled. Beside her charpai lie, side by side, her bedpan and her forgotten plate of food.

Aya's stridency brings Urmila scuttling to her. 'Aya, what's wrong? . . . Aya, sip some water? . . . Aya, shall I call a doctor?' Her questions are always answered by further, almost theatrical, racking coughs and howls. Urmila waits by the cot till her futility worsens to humiliation; then, snivelling, she veers round. Occasionally, before she's beyond earshot, Aya reviles her. 'Pig. Trollop.'

A formidable night, monsoon, abating to a sort of autumn. Urmila has that afternoon, at last, ferreted out a charitable tuberculosis hospital whose superintending doctor has assented to enrol Aya at seven hundred rupees per month. Rather, through a labyrinthine circuit, she has managed to entreat Someone in the Ministry of Health to bid an intermediary propose to a connection to nudge the doctor not to be irksome. Shyamanand and Urmila forthwith visit the hospital, thirty kilometres away. Clean enough, Urmila declares. Cleaner than our house, contends Shyamanand. They engineer with the doctor, a ceaselessly smirking Punjabi, a ruse to transport Aya there the next morning. Fortuitously, the following day, Burfi is arriving after months, on work. The first family reunion in their own, new house. Shyamanand, Urmila and Jamun would've honestly liked the real Aya to have participated in that reunion, but she appears to have been supplanted by an eerie, lookalike wraith, by her own skeleton shrouded in her own – but darkened – skin, commanding all her bane and none of her winsomeness. Unspokenly, they want this false Aya exorcised from the house before Burfi shows up. For at the news of Aya's hospitalization, or of her leaving, he'd be aghast – but only in passing, because he'd be more eager to natter of his new world. But to actually exhibit her to him – almost transfigured, a set of bones beneath the stairs – would be, somehow, grim on him too. He'd –

naturally – overlook Aya's kinks, her pigheadedness, 'd never spot the grit in Urmila's drudgery, and would almost certainly insinuate remissness. However could they celebrate Burfi's homecoming against the noises off of her groans and her corrosive cough?

'She's lived with us for over twenty year. She's part of the family. She doesn't wish to leave the house now. She wants to die at home, she proclaims, literally! She throws away or hides her medicines. Doctor, we can't suffer this to continue!'

The custodian chortles. 'In the Registration Card, in the column, Whom To Notify In the Event Of Death, shall we, Mr' – to Shyamanand's nostrils, from the doctor's mouth, flutters the sweetness of paan masala – 'write, Not Applicable? That'll officially docket the patient as Waif, and'll acquit you of all obligation. Then we'd just have to dream up how we stumbled on her. But if your names are entered as Family, then we'll have to, for starters, explain to Welfare how a patient with family's been registered in a hospital meant basically for the shelterless. Every four months, till my transfer, suspension, retirement, or death, whichever's the last, they'll despatch letters troubling me to explain.' The doctor's lips flag from a boundless grin to a fatuous simper.

'Can't we be written down as Ex-Employer, and Well-Wisher?'

Aya scents, the same night, the ruse for her removal the next morning. No one alludes to it, but she's always kept an ear to the ground. She slap-bang snatches her plate of food from Urmila and chucks it back at her chest. She'd aimed for her brow. Urmila snorts in shock and pain and totters against the wall.

Aya in her hysteria is a deal noisier, but less frightful, than Urmila in hers. As soon as Aya begins to ululate, Jamun frisks about the house shutting all the doors and windows. She yowls, whines, grunts, groans, brutally writhes in her cot for an hour or so, till exhaustion hushes her. Amidst the high, bestial squeals and base rumbles, she intermittently murmurs half-penetrable phrases about landslide and her pulped sons, herself as Urmila's companion, Jamun as a child, one of her chums Kishori. Spume at the mouth, pupilless ivory lunettes for eyes, above the snarl of a skull. 'Have sinned . . . sinned . . . seized my sons . . .'; such expressions are abruptly punctuated by weak squawks of fright as she delves her head away from some bodiless ghoul that pitches into her.

Watching her, Jamun battens down his jaws to repress his tears. To divert himself from his impulse to cry, he thinks that he should mouth something, anything; maybe he can ask, conversationally, d'you fancy she's shamming? No sooner has he opened his mouth and inhaled than the tears begin to dribble out, gropingly, like a reptile oozing out if its lair.

'Thank God the houses here aren't ravelled into one another,' mutters Urmila bemusedly, through her abated tears.

The ambulance pulls in two hours late the next morning. 'New colony, yours. I lost my way,' fibs the ruffianly driver. He's been instructed to sedate the patient, so that she doesn't kick up a shindy, and, when she surfaces out of insentience, initially doesn't realize where she is. 'But is that wise?' demurs Jamun, again only to squash an urge to cry. No one troubles to answer.

The subterfuge is needless. The driver, quite solicitously, lifts Aya and easefully lays her down in the ambulance. 'Don't fret, Mother, you'll be okay.' She, like a snapped doll, reacts to nothing.

Jamun is averse to accompanying his parents. He isn't doughty enough, he senses. Now that their distress is clocking out, his desire for its cessation has swelled insupportably. At the same time, he feels cold inside, as though each artery, each vein, in his torso has been sliced, and the gore has dribbled out and, torpidly, curdled about his entrails, smothering them in glacial jelly. Through the window of the ambulance, he struggles to smile at Aya, but she is looking away. 'Aya,' he whispers in someone else's voice. Her desert eyes swivel. She smiles gnarledly at him. When the ambulance chugs away, he's happy to be sobbing. He opens wide the side door, but the sun won't lick her cot.

Cutty Sark at sundown, for Shyamanand, Burfi and Jamun, while Urmila tries to suppress that she likes the shandy that Burfi's blended for her. 'This is what you've mastered at work, is it, to make your mother tipsy?' Expectedly, she's both extremely gloomy at Aya's removal and joyful at the homecoming of her elder son.

Burfi *doesn't* manifest much curiosity about Aya, and he *is* eager to gabble about his new existence with Joyce; for him, marriage'll gulp down a decade before it irks. He's also agog with the particulars of Joyce's recent sojourns in Vancouver and Dubai, and of Vancouver a sight more than Dubai. For him, Aya is the jetsam of an anterior passage. 'When she improves, she'll return, I imagine,' he voices in passing.

On her third shandy, Urmila, almost theatrically ruminative, scanning the condensation on her tumbler, murmurs, 'When I'm dying and you tackle me as we behaved with Aya, as though she were a mess on the floor, I must remember not to lament. I must wham into my head that we all, generation upon generation, peter out in that manner, with those we've reared absent, or impatient, or looking away.'

Shyamanand demurs. 'Why're you so upset? If we'd found a hospital earlier, we'd've removed Aya there before. We'll visit her from time to time, and every month we can send her a little spending money with an office peon – some trustworthy type who can't pocket the cash. Isn't Aya behind us now? Her recovery rests with God. Don't be morose. Consider the congenial things – your new house, the rare concurrent presence of your sons – and that'll become more uncommon as the years glide – their splendent futures, which'll crown our fosterage. Your mind has never stretched out for the agreeable things.' But, perhaps because he's beginning to be tiddly, Shyamanand's tone is singularly benign, and Urmila doesn't appear to resent. She doesn't seem to be listening either. 'Now's the moment to quiz Burfi when they intend their first child, and whether they dream of a boy. And when will Jamun marry? Has he met any appealing woman yet, anywhere? Will we have to scout for him, or will he too, headstrongly, ditto his elder brother, and blunder into a marriage of passion? Who knows – in the hours that he wastes away from the house and supposedly at college, he might already be leching around; in my time he'd've been "encountering life". Which is vital.' Shyamanand chortles like a man of the world and asks Jamun for a refill.

Any prattle about sex – *any* prattle – has always interested Burfi. He lauds, 'Excellent, Baba, that you commend sex before marriage. That's essential.' Then, with a smirk and a twitch of his eyes at Urmila, 'And Baba, you? You've never disclosed whether you were a virgin when you married.' A custom common to the brothers, to while away their time by discomfiting their parents with probing their sexual lives and tittering at their equivocal replies.

Shyamanand quaffs down half his glass before he responds, sententiously, 'No one, no male, is a virgin by the time he marries.' Though Shyamanand tipples like a novice, in huge inexpert draughts, he conducts himself well.

The sons glance at one another urbanely, simper, but voice nothing of their spice at their father's gaffe. For that he means exactly what he's uttered is inconceivable; to the sons it is incredible that their sedate, respectable father is in fact betraying that before his marriage he'd actually tumbled a woman; much more likely, silently smirk the boys, that Shyamanand, craving to be candid, barefaced, to be accordant with his sons by adopting what he fancies is their idiom, has assumed that a male virgin denotes, not one who has never copulated, but one who's never ejaculated, that is, simply a prepubescent stripling. Thus Shyamanand is only indicating, surmise his sons smugly, that before he married he'd known what his spunk looked like.

# 3

# CLOSENESS DIES

Burfi and Jamun go to bring Urmila home. Muggy late-September; should've been morning, for Dr Haldia was prepared to bundle her out then, but they can set off for the hospital only at noon because Burfi slopes off at ten to the dry-cleaner's for his Armani ensemble, which ruffles Shyamanand frightfully. He therefore wishes to accompany them, 'to remind you on the way of your mother and the object of your drive, and to restrain you from halting midway to windowshop for T-shirts and cassettes'. The remark and his tone, of course, peeve Burfi considerably, whose huffiness quite entertains Jamun; his jocundity in turn riles Shyamanand and Burfi. So Burfi informs Shyamanand that he shouldn't go with them, 'because Ma'll presumably have to lie in the rear and three of us'd be corseted in front. Then if that cadaver of a car of yours flops on the road, we'll have to fret about you as well as Ma.' Shyamanand's face exposes his wound at that comment; Burfi is vexed with himself, but can't display his contrition – in brief, their routine emotional vacillations.

The pacemaker's been slid in and Dr Haldia is still simpering, so everything was super. The matter of a second medical opinion has been pigeonholed; no one resurrects it, partly because no one's sure of precisely what to resurrect. ('Dr Haldia, we aren't certain that you don't mean to slice open my wife/our mother *only* for the forty thousand that you're picking up on the deal – but it's ludicrous, isn't it, to discharge her from here and admit her into the clinic of a second shark, just for his counsel, which could very well ditto yours, for who'd wish to forgo a tidy sum? . . . Would you mind if we invited another specialist to look in on my wife/our mother here? – Could you, by the way, recommend somebody else? – Someone trusted, of course, whose views you'd value? . . . ') They don't speak of the subject, half-believing that its urgency will dwindle if they don't refer to it. To be fair, the unusual and tiring rhythm of their lives in these weeks has hampered levelheaded thinking; machinelike, they can plod on till something happens to Urmila, but they can't will themselves to any resolve. The interviews with Haldia – some five minutes every three days – have afforded no guidance. 'Hallo, hallo, how are we? . . . No, not stable yet, poor thing, a restless night, fidgety . . . We'll wait, before we make that teeny-weeny nick at the collar – so, now that I've confined your mummy here, who's simmering the dal-rice at home, ha-ha! You look run down, pining for Mummy's curry, are you, ha-ha! Don't worry, be happy! And thank you for dropping in, my dear.'

Urmila is not overly keen to return home – an excellent augury, that her cognitive befuddlement and bodily distress have adequately decreased for her to discern the comforts of twenty-four-hour airconditioning, nursing, repose, silence, greyness. She's warmed to one nurse in particular – demure, efficient, flatchested – and has jocosely proposed her to Jamun as a potential wife. 'She's pretty and kind. While you introspect about the meaning of existence and eternity, she can look after your father and me.' 'We should pick for her a less boring husband,' suggests Burfi.

Philip Jonas sends luxuriant bouquets thrice. Urmila recalls him effortlessly and is charmed even in her debility because she loves gifts. Jonas also presents her, incongruously in Intensive Care, with a tin of Earl Grey tea, which delights Urmila even more.

Three days after the operation, she's been shunted to a peripheral, presumably less intensive, cubicle. Dr Haldia visits her much less frequently there. The flatchested heroine is recruited as a night nurse at a hundred and fifty rupees per ten hours, and twenty rupees for every extra hour; 'Like a bloody taxi kept waiting,' bellyaches Burfi.

Urmila remembers practically nothing of her immediate past.

She can't recall when she was carted to Dr Haldia's, and only fuzzily grasps why. Time has misted for her, and space too. 'Isn't my piles operation done? . . . If you help me to sit up, then perhaps I can stump upstairs and loll in the sun for a time, away from your father.' Her mouth stays open after she's tailed off, and her eyes constrict, her forehead corrugates, in puzzlement, in her tussle against opacity, to educe her past. But the dauntless Haldia bleeps that her memory, presumably a wine, will enrich with time.

No one knows how much to disclose to Urmila about herself. 'I really was senseless for days with the heart attack?'

'Uh . . . This curiosity of yours is a bracing sign,' sidesteps Burfi, who is for postponing all enlightenment until Urmila surfaces to normalcy.

'Why don't I remember? I recall returning home from the piles surgery and lying in bed, terribly weak – and next, nothing. How many days between the piles and this heart failure?'

'Three. You arrived home on the twenty-seventh, and were carted here on the thirtieth of August.' Chhana can never dissemble adroitly.

'August,' dittoes Urmila, unfamiliarly, trying to assign it, puckering her eyes at the Air-India calendar on the wall. 'And today is . . . My God, I've lasted with Haldia around a month!'

'She can calculate!' squeaks Burfi ebulliently.

'Certainly I can, goose . . . August.'

Pista is markedly crestfallen. 'Can't we at least tell Thakuma that for ten minutes she'd copped it, that Thakuda thwacked her chest and dragged her back to life? Please. She could even be interviewed on TV.'

In the further room Urmila has become a wizened, slack bag, professionally declared out of danger, because of which the visits of the final five days are noticeably more genial. For Pista and Doom, their grandmother all at once grows measurelessly more interesting; formerly the unassertive, unwilling fulcrum of the household, of whom none is seriously heedful, she is now the tousled drift of bedclothes in a chilled, sombre room, near whom they are shushed nonstop, and hindered from pawing unfamiliar objects, but who is still as delighted to see them, even though she appears ashen and unfocused. The incongruity between the two generations is hideous. Pista'll be maroon and sweaty from the football game from which he's been plucked *en route* to the hospital; Doom will be like a meaty peach, in the way of everyone's knees, trailing strangers into other rooms.

Doom, nose caulked with muck, breathing restfully and audibly through his mouth, the bridge of his interdigitated hands shouldering his chins, resting plump and caked elbows on the stool beside the bed, sallow rotund calves – with the scarlet streaks and stipples of nicks, stings, spills, scuffles – intersected at the ankles, drivellingly, to Urmila: 'Thakuma, Pista says you died, Thakuda whammed your chest and you came back to life. Now like other aunties you're going to TV.'

'Yes, Baby, I snuffed it, and while Thakuda was boxing me, I zipped off and met Heman and Skeletor. Skeletor sends you many smooches.'

Doom sighs and starts to dispute the story. His birth, four years ago, was fortuitous. Joyce wished to abort. 'We didn't intend this. Joyce doesn't want the load of a nursling right now.' Burfi defensively advanced to the rest of the family. He routinely has to vindicate his parents and his wife, one to the other, his parents and his wife seldom communicate straightforwardly. This aids the son, when vital, while bickering with wife or parent, to fudge his own disagreeable views as those of the absent individual.

'Abort? Why? You're married, aren't you,' carps Shyamanand, and to Urmila, apart, hyperbolically, 'We've hatched a killer.' She compliantly remonstrates with Burfi, 'You'll regret this abortion.' Next, both parents, mordantly, 'Can't you dictate your own hankering even once to your wife? Isn't the foetus yours too?'

Jamun probes Burfi. 'What d'you really feel? D'you itch for a second child?' He's truly interested.

'If I want my way, I should suggest to Joyce the precise

opposite of what I actually wish her to do,' jokes Burfi. 'I'm ambivalent about babies, Jamun. They're wholly unknown, almost extraterrestrial! Pista helter-skeltered our existence, rampaged through the ruts of our lives to the heart. He cradled the marriage – snared us *both*! Which is Joyce's signature tune – that she's been enmeshed, first by marriage, then by a kid. Modernity dribbling out of her boobs. But ever so often, I'd imagine – would be thrilling to sense a scrap of your flesh outside yourself, to nurture it, see it pule, laugh, argue, prosper, into a separate creature that was yet yourself. We all, from time to time, endure life's blues – it's null, etcetera – a brat provides not a reason, but a pretext – and for a time distracts you from those silly questions, and bluffs you that procreation in itself is an end.'

'"The wise men of old,"' cites Jamun joshingly, '"did not want children". 'What should we do with children,' they said, 'when we have Brahman and the world besides?'" Just the sentiment to echo to Baba when next he bleats that you're being deviant in not hankering for a second kid, in bereaving *him* of another grandchild. But I like him because he fattens on choler. He's corrosively dubbed you and Joyce "Grammy Sugars" – a delicious expression, isn't it? – for those who habitually gape at the Grammy Awards on TV, and who, Baba assumes, submergedly crave to resemble those freakish beings we glimpse at those awards – hair like aquamarine ropes, and windowpane skirts, no matter what gender! For Baba, both his sons are Grammy Sugars – they dote on the screech and squawk of bebop and covertly yearn to be – the horror, the horror! – Christians! Doubtless, Pista'll be even more of a Grammy Sugar. Would be ironic, then, to zap Baba by confessing that Joyce and you don't want to spawn, on the counsel of a bloody Upanishad.'

Now and then, in those terminal days in that further room, the family muses whether they are carting a stranger home. All, save Chhana, struggle to smother such introspection; the sons yield their mother altogether to time. For minutes she stares vacantly at the wall, or the lavatory door, the blue night lamp, or the aggregation of bottles and injections on the metal table beside her pillow, the desiccated skin of her forearms, or her drained hands and her temple ruts, her eyes dim with the remembrance of an anterior ache, but she won't, or cannot, share the evocation.

'Enormously expensive, wasn't it, my heart attack?' Urmila asks Shyamanand, her face buckled into a grin. 'Jamun tells me that you and he've divided the costs.' Shyamanand whooshes into his beard and says nothing. 'I'll repay you, whatever I own.' Shyamanand doesn't demur.

Burfi wheels her out. In the corridors and across the lawns, she gapes at the faces, the whirl and the sky, like a toddler confronting a new world, wondrous-eyed, mouth feebly slack. She's dreadfully frail. Her collarbones show like an ivory coat-hanger. Her features illume when she sights the car. Burfi cradles her in his arms and lays her down in the rear. She's weeping unashamedly.

Jamun drives. Urmila begins to waffle, fitfully, in a jerky, peaked, almost-cataleptic – but not distressed – manner. 'How much inconvenience I must've caused you . . . no matter how hotly we grouse, your father and I're fortunate in our sons . . . Next time this heart nonsense occurs, lodge me in a home for the aged, or whatever they're called . . . some must exist somewhere . . . a few might even be congenial . . . Your father's anxiety – and mine too for a season – was that we'd be discarded in a large house in the city of our lives, desolate, with an Alsatian for crony, like that stodgy Mr Naidu, whose children stay in Australia and Germany, and who takes six unending walks a day to flaunt that he isn't piqued . . . In our time, in how many homes do three generations stay together without baring towards one another a beastly malignity, like the mother-in-law histrionics of Lalita Pawar . . . For sure, Burfi and Joyce dream of their own establishment, and are rueful about living collectively . . . but instead, you should be proud and happy, because it's markedly rare . . . Why are the old abandoned? . . . In the paper last Sunday . . . no, not last Sunday, silly . . . I read that derelict parents nowadays are prosecuting their issue for maintenance . . . You must foster me, for I fostered you . . . For hundreds of years, generation upon generation, why've the old been abandoned . . . Pista and Doom'll shed you in a big house that you'll shout you erected for them . . . and next their young will . . .'

'Her wits are tip-top. Shush, Ma, enough, you'll flake out. Too torrid to chat.'

After they pull in at home, Urmila offers additional evidence that her thrombosis hasn't harshly altered her. The family seethes around her like water vanishing down the drain of a sink, while she: 'But the drawing room's noticeably untidy . . . the dust on the TV . . . Hasn't that woman been swabbing and whisking? . . . Nobody to thwart her from shirking, I suppose . . . ghastly, these servants . . . What d'you mean, I can't go upstairs, what doctor's advice . . . ' She is markedly jolted to learn that Dr Haldia has prohibited her from climbing stairs. She subsides in a mass on the divan. Pista and Doom subside alongside her, and instantly begin to bob up and down on the springs of the mattress. 'I'll lie down for a time. I feel dreadful.' She stares dismayedly at the faces cordoning her. 'If I can't mount the stairs, how'll I dodge your father when he resumes his sarcasm and rancour?'

That annoys all her listeners. 'Phew. Don't you have anything else to brood about right now?'

But Urmila has lain down on the divan, crabbedly, her neck askew as though it'd been snipped. Her eyelids shudder, and she is murmuring, 'God, I must die before he does . . . I must . . . Then he'll learn . . . '

Flatchested quotes two hundred rupees per ten hours for nursing at home. 'We ordinarily don't nurse our patients at their houses,' she simpers to Urmila, 'but with you . . . ' To tend an invalid away from the hospital is, ostensibly, obscurely degrading; at the patient's house, the nurse is presumably less a professional than a domestic. For Urmila, however, Flatchested consents. 'Nonsense,' dissents Shyamanand. 'Coax her to procure us someone much cheaper.' Flatchested complies glacially.

She presents Revati, an aya of a kind, elderly, civil, proficient, also flatchested.

Revati remains with Urmila for a month. She feeds, bathes, clothes, natters with and humours her. In the nights she naps – as snatchily as Urmila – in the same room. By degrees Urmila becomes totally dependent on her and, between eleven and eight in the day, feels tetchy and vulnerable in Revati's absence. Urmila's demeanour sneakingly vexes Jamun, even though he is plainly reluctant to, say, supplant Revati with himself.

Urmila cleaves to her bed all day. She snoozes wobblingly, like the damned, in the subtler hours, chats patchily with Revati (herself noticeably garrulous), gazes emptily beyond the window at the tints of green in their unweeded garden, hears the sea and, in the night, the lewd squabbles of the fisherfolk. As the days trickle by, the family appears to accustom itself to her seeming fairly content with the society of Revati; they, excepting Shyamanand and Jamun, begin to look in only now and then: they have their separate existences, they assure themselves that they are not essential, and convalescence, that lull after an extremity, is covertly dreary, a subtle comedown. Shyamanand, however, remains beside her for all the time that they do not wrangle. And to Jamun, Urmila shrivels to a supine, querulous contour in a crepuscular room.

Dr Haldia has prescribed a daily walk in the verandah and subsequently, sanguinely, in the neighbourhood park. Urmila dignifiedly sidesteps the advice. Shyamanand calls her lazy. Urmila's blood pressure zooms to the moon. She bawls. He remarks that she implicitly pines to regress into the morbid repose of Intensive Care. She screeches that he's expended his money to pin down her life because he needs a target for his barbs.

Chhana returns to Calcutta four days after Urmila's homecoming. 'I'll be here if anything happens. Don't fret,' she enjoins Shyamanand. 'You remember, I reached home before Jamun could.' No one save Shyamanand misses her, and he not for long.

Chhana is some sort of assistant in the Raja Rammohun Roy Library. She's also been studying Rabindrasangeet for decades. She's the only one of their relatives whom Burfi and Jamun meet – once in a way, about once every three years – and whom they can easily recognize. Because of the circumstances of their lives and their dispositions, Shyamanand and Urmila have swerved from their kin; hence, Burfi and Jamun are barely acquainted with their cousins. Among the kith that they've infrequently come upon over the years, they can't tally more than three names and faces, or deduce who has spawned whom. The next generation of Pista and Doom are not even aware of the existence of their father's kin, though they're notably chummy with their maternal cousins. This skewness pesters Shyamanand alone; to him it incarnates his most sombre forebodings – the total suzerainty over his grandsons of their execrable mother, the vassalage of Hindu husband to Christian wife, the dishonourable anglicization of his own sons, the erasure of the patrilineal family organization that he recognizes, the complete apathy of the others to these concerns.

Chhana and her manservant – fiftyish, bald, obese, Bihari, badtempered, flatulent – inhabit the first floor of a drab house in Baliganj. She manages quite nicely with the rent from UCO Bank for the ground floor. She began to smoke after her mother died. When the flunkey fetches the milk in the morning, he also picks up for her a packet of Four Square Twenties. Because she smoked Burfi concluded, when he was sixteen, that Chhana was panting for it. 'Bets that she'd dote on SM, a pounding with a leather belt,' he offers Jamun, who's startled and titillated by the idea. 'But she nursed you, Burfi!' he demurs involuntarily.

Burfi pauses, as though granting this image of the other Chhana enough time to flick open – in Jamun's brain – a shutter, to unveil to him the tortuous wine dark tunnels of adulthood. 'She brushes against me all the damn time. And why's she always hanging around while I'm exercising?' He shrugs his shoulders, a Not-even-God-can-help-my-sexiness shrug, and simpers. 'Someone must be regularly mounting her – maybe that fuckface slave of hers – these Bong spinsters can be desperately horny, and entwining with her menial'll spice it with extra kink – you know, caste 'n all. And she's wombless, remember, totally hasslefree.'

At Urmila's heart attack, Shyamanand entreats Chhana to come because he funks; all at once, he's not certain of his sons. They seem brand-new and alien, in jeans and T-shirts of dubious shades, and articulate a puzzling species of English; whereas Urmila and he had ripened in an earlier, illusorily genial world (in which Shyamanand and his siblings had nested together in parsimony, balefulness and rancour), wherein, mawkish that he is, he reckons that the bonds of family had been sturdier, and parents more revered. To him in his vulnerability, Chhana has at first seemed an unflinching figure from that world, but she disillusions her uncle.

Chhana'll handle everything, Shyamanand asserts – our meals, the kitchen, the household. Burfi, Joyce and Jamun await the marvel of her proficiency, but it stays undercover for the days of her sojourn. She appears to relish only ambling about the house in a crimson housecoat and her hawaii slippers – smacking them on the floor like wet kisses on a toddler's jowls – unconcernedly observing others at their chores, puffing away at her Four Squares (though not under Shyamanand's nose), gawkishly aping Joyce's manner of speech, imperceptibly annoying everybody. Daily, she bathes for an aeon, and for another brews and soaks up tea. Whenever Shyamanand troubles her for trifles, or what he rates trifles, to make him black coffee, or assist him with his walking shoes, Chhana starts amenably enough, but progresses so torpidly, botchedly – 'I can't find anywhere the tea cozy that we use every day, the one with lemon-and-pink spots, but I rummaged about and hit upon another one, green and shabby, so I thought I'd begin the coffee only after verifying with you whether I could use this green . . .' 'The laces of your left shoe are kind of queer, aren't they? I don't quite understand how they can squeeze through these eyelets and also skirt the back . . .' – that Shyamanand, exasperated, halts her midway and grouses at her to call Jamun instead. A few days of Chhana saps him; he'd never have accepted that the years would remould her into a vapid, bumbling stranger. While he observes her push her spectacles above the bridge of her nose to peer better at the muck on TV, the idea twitches within him that the being who riles him the least is Urmila, and she'd all but died. He feels scared.

Three hours after Chhana entrains, Joyce, clenching Doom's gummy forearm, simpering vacuously as she transits the supine Urmila in the drawing room, departs for Rani's nest for the weekend.

'And Jamun? When d'you go back?'

'Whenever you and Ma wish me to. I've already written for an extra month's leave.'

Neighbours, curious, civil, look in on Urmila. Among them, Mr Naidu the tramper. While his cur sniffs the petrified Revati's thighs, he gabbles. 'Pyne's litter hawked his house last week. The eighth house in my block to be sold this year. Twenty-five lakhs, is the whisper. A profit therefore of nine hundred per cent in one decade. What else could we do – doubtless they must've exclaimed. They last showed up in India for Pyne's final rites – you remember? the newspaper-wala located him outside the WC after ringing and ringing for the clearance of his bill.'

'Pyne's eldest daughter met Burfi or Jamun somewhere, and declared that they needed the money much more than their father's house.'

'So Pyne's clod of earth has now been ceded to the developers. They plan to raze the entire house and erect on that plot a four-storey block of eight dolly apartments, each of which will cost ten lakhs. However does the Corporation tick such plans? Pyne was a refugee too, one of us. He could stay just four months in the house that he built. Eighth house in my block this year – like the crust beneath you'd loosened itself, become an island, and the tides were gliding you and your home out to the sea lanes – that's how I feel. When we raised our houses here, we'd only the sea, the fishermen and these sapless sands. The house itself became a chunk of the family, the newest child.'

Mr Naidu interrupts himself to perfunctorily dissuade his hound from thrusting his muzzle up Revati's sari. Revati continues to appear to be transfixed. Mr Naidu runs on, 'When I stayed with my daughter in Munich, I'd once in a while telephone my deserted house here, just to listen to the distant burr of the instrument – next to the stairs on our scrapped dining table – and I'd hear the burr-burr with the receiver crushing my ear, with the enraptured, encouraging intentness of a parent listening to his infant turn articulate. Sometimes I'd even croon into the phone – how screwballish of me! – "I'm returning to you soon, kiddo!" Those days we had two phones at home – one was from my son's office, and those slothful buggers'd forgotten to retrieve it. I never rang my son's office phone, though, because the sound of our own, older phone was wondrously sweeter – hushed, well-bred.' Mr Naidu has thoroughly eructed himself for the time being, and so sighs with toilworn contentment. He then remembers the rest of the cosmos, squints at an abstracted, procumbent Urmila and brays, 'So? How's our Pacemaker Madam?'

She responds bemusedly, palpating her collarbone, staring at the ceiling. 'My pacemaker's detached itself.' She pauses to assiduously probe the tract around her collarbone. 'I can feel it, like a toad underneath the skin, eluding my fingers.'

From which Mr Naidu deduces that he should withdraw *forthwith*, and bounces up from his armchair, alarming his mongrel most of all. 'Up-shup – c'mon, kiddo! – time to halt your drooling all over this house! Bye then – I'm positive this pacemaker headache's no great shakes – just a little delicate adjustment required – like catching a radio station.' He waves to Urmila from the door like a prime minister bidding adieu to his fawners before ducking into an aircraft. At the gate he fashions for Jamun four or five facial expressions of neighbourly solicitude and distaste, perhaps wishing him to choose one; in the final contortion, Mr Naidu rams his sausage-lips against his livid nose and lavatory-brush-moustache, and faintly resembles the vitals of a lavish humburger. 'Tell me if you need any help for this pacemaker pickle. A sticky wicket, but you've the ' – Jamun twitches at his startling guffaw – 'balls to bat! So cheerio, kiddo, grand to see you floating about here and absconding from your post.'

'Ma, whatever did you spout to Chachacha about your pacemaker? A pickle and a sticky wicket?' But Urmila doesn't answer.

She's dead, intuits Jamun for a millisecond, at which a kind of balm sprinkles his entrails before contrition routs him. But Urmila is breathing, fitfully. Jamun watches her drowse, benumbed by the notion that at her death he'd probably, for starters, taste deliverance. Nothing is godly. They'd continue to shove damaging – at best ineffectual – chemicals into this capacious pouch of senescent skin, only so that it can flounder in this fashion, like an enormous heart. Under their eyes, in their fosterage, she'd crumble into a thing querulous and unrecognizable. What was uncertain was just the tempo of her deterioration. Their love, or tender scorn, would struggle against the fatigued distaste that the alien that she'd slump to would beget. She'd wail for succour, and her heirs would 'tch' with exasperation and pretend they hadn't heard. Their hellishness was even now demonstrated, when the youngest of them fancied his mother dead and, for an instant, felt eased.

'What's the matter, Jamun?'

'Oh, you're awake. Your pacemaker seems to be distressing Chachacha as much as you. What's this new nightmare?'

Urmila asks Jamun to palm her upper chest. 'See, it's loose, floating about.' He is extremely unwilling to touch her. Something'll snap, he is certain, and life will rush out of her as out of a balloon, she'll shrivel to a scrap of puckered rubber in his hands, because of him. 'No, Ma, my thumbing it won't help. I should inform Haldia at once.' At the evocation of Haldia and his hospital, and that entire exacting routine, dispiritedness shades their features.

Urmila continues ruthlessly to knead her collarbone flesh,

pulling up dollops of it like plasticine, eyes remote in concentration. 'Stop that, Ma, please!'

'I'm not returning to Haldia. Revati, water.'

'What of this pacemaker detaching itself?'

'Forget it.'

'Are you sure?' knowing that her answer will be yes. Of course, he's unable to forget; at unanticipated moments in that week, remembrance bobs up jubilant, a jack-in-the-box of an adversary, and pesters him with the conviction that he's ignoring her warning for his own comfort.

She can't reply with the glass at her lip. At their following consultation with Haldia, she doesn't initiate the subject. Her cagey responses to the doctor's perfunctory questions suggest the interrogation of an inept spy in a comedy, but Jamun discerns that she's truly petrified of being prescribed a reversion to Intensive Care. He suffers with her for a while and then, eluding her eyes, declares, 'Doctor, my mother's been murmuring that the pacemaker's somehow been dislocated. She's continually massaging and pawing that area – won't she disarrange . . . ?' He unfolds her and his anxieties, muddledly. Dr Haldia pooh-poohs and chortles, a crescent of a cackle being doodled on the face of cheese. Urmila is snubbed into an irate quietness. She begins to consult him less often. 'What's the point? He isn't interested in my case any longer. How are we, dear? Aren't we hunky-dory, dear? Just two hundred rupees, dear.'

'D'you want to consult some other vet?'

But Urmila seems will-less, not unconcerned, but both afraid and unequipped to decide. So appears the rest of the family. They're all wary of her affliction, and deport themselves as though they hope that if they ignore her infirmity it won't harass them anew. Stroking, pawing, massaging the flesh on her pacemaker becomes a solace for Urmila, even a fixation, like the thumbsucking of a nursling. Her left arm is forever up, communing with her collarbone, save when Jamun's in the room. His presence deters her. Undetected, he once in a way observes her – recumbent, unseeingly eyeing the fan, her left forefinger gently, ramblingly pirouetting about her collarbone, like a lone figure idling on a skating rink. An eerie peepshow – the waning room, and in it a blurry Revati gliding from cupboard to desk, stashing away clothes, tidying the drawers, pilfering cash. Jamun struggles to conceive how he himself would feel with a cigarette lighter embedded in his vitals, but can't. He imagines it as a clod in his windpipe that can't be prodded down. Whatever scampers through his mother's mind as she reclines and scans the ceiling, hour upon muggy hour? Then Revati notices the voyeur, and reveals him to Urmila by clearing her throat or asking him the time. Urmila's left hand whips back to her side, like some bloodsucking reptile rattled at its feeding. Jamun waits, irresolute, and at last slouches into the room, embarrassed, smirking vacantly, befuddled time after time that his mother has to be cautioned of his approach, and by a downright stranger, as though he were the menace. Yet who could one upbraid, since time helter-skeltered everything?

In her last days with them, Revati's attitude to her chores, of course, alters, and Urmila becomes more distraught at her approaching departure. Dr Haldia had proposed that if she mended evenpacedly, Urmila should tend to herself after about four weeks, but Revati asserts that *she* is quitting because she can't endure any longer Shyamanand's nitpicking and faddishness. She has in fact procured a more paying job, but must've decided to bleat about Shyamanand in transit, out of devilishness. Urmila certainly is for Revati and against Shyamanand, and wails day and night to Jamun, 'See *again* – your father can't stomach my being comfortable! He may seem solicitous, but inly he festers whenever he spots me at rest. The instant I pick up an efficient servant to somewhat ease my donkeywork at home, he begins to niggle and crab – only because I may catnap one afternoon or in front of the TV one evening. He's been like this for forty years – a purulence in my skull. You must remember that chain of servants – Kishori, Bhido, Ramteke, Chandan – that we had to help Aya. They all scrammed because they couldn't endure your father's prickliness – "Chandan! Five past one already! Lunch is five minutes overdue, you'll have to be more punctual, duffer!" "Bhido, you oaf, you should've tallied the entries in the passbook before you left the bank." Your father plainly doesn't know how to behave with domestics – it's his deep-seated boorishness. He bullies those whom he fancies are beneath him, and discovers in good time that they are not. And he, in this way, upholds caste, and rues that we don't come by a Brahmin cook. He's naturally a skinflint, and wishes to pay a servant by the rates of 1917, and then expects him to be grateful to us. And –' To Jamun, Urmila's ceaseless carping against Shyamanand has always irked; she observes the tedium on his features and starts to patter faster and more tinnily, straining to conclude before he quits the room. '. . . With Revati he's even more infuriated because her attendance benefits *me* specifically, and not the household in general. "You aren't punctual, Revati. We aren't paying you to uneasily wait for you every morning." "How dare you enter by the drawing-room door! A guest, are you, you bloody sow? The side entrance is beneath you, is it?" Your father should decide for good whether he wants me alive!' Urmila slithers to the edge of the bed to aim her last remark at Jamun's exiting left heel and calf.

So Revati departs, and Urmila reverts to fending for herself. Jamun helps, in the initial week or two, to escort his mother to the lavatory, to carry her lunch and dinner to her bed, to be with, and listen to her; but he's gradually enervated by the tasks of passive attendance, and begins slinking off from the room – to any nook beyond earshot of her – moments before he senses that he'll be needed. By the time he returns, Urmila has managed somehow, or has done without. Her vexation has surged. He counterfeits reasons and afterwards attempts to persuade himself, listlessly, that by wriggling out of his responsibilities time after time, he's helping his mother to be self-reliant.

November. A whisper of wintriness in the air. A long letter from Satyavan Hegiste. Jamun browses through it and recognizes that he has now to slide back to the antipodal life one thousand kilometres away, of Kasibai and the apartments on the wetlands.

He has to budge from home for a further reason too, he discerns sardonically. If he doesn't decamp fast, Burfi and Joyce'll very likely exploit his presence to once more try and shove off themselves. 'You seem to've anchored yourself here for keeps. So now at least we can scram from this cowshed, pick up some space for ourselves. If and when you decide to revert to your other responsibilities, and Ma and Baba remain alone in this house, don't harrow yourself, *we'll* care for them – telephone them every evening or something. Or we could entice that damn Chhana to wangle a transfer here – she and her fuckface could roost in the entire first floor – she'd freak out, luxuriating in these rooms, wholly unattached to the crises downstairs.'

Jamun and the others in the family have endured these opinions from Burfi numberless times in the foregoing eighteen months, ever since he, Joyce, the kids and their aya arrived on their transfer. They initially occupy two of the three bedrooms on the first floor; after Jamun leaves, Burfi reshapes the third into a den for deafening heavy metal.

After a crushing eleven hours in office – chitchatting, swilling barrels of tea, sauntering from one colleague's chambers to another's – Burfi comes home and glumly switches substandard gin for tea. He can't spatter his middle-thirties, sundown blues on Joyce, Pista or Doom, because the one overrides him and the other two are at their homework in front of the TV. Hence he sulks at his surroundings, buffets a few downstairs doors, hollers for his mother to help him unearth the pyjamas that he has (for dread that Shyamanand'll usurp them) interred somewhere, reclaims just *his* laundered clothes from the pile underneath the stairs, manages to dishevel the remainder, forages through the fridge for a snack to attend the gin, fulminates at the refrigerator for not stocking more alluring delights, totes upstairs the mutton (thereby effecting four fewer helpings at dinner), and with his second gin starts to whine to an audience of lamp, stereo system and one unmindful relative.

'What a septic tank. I've picked the shit end of the stick, hooked by parents into staying with them. They grouse day in and day out about Joyce and me. "You don't spend any time with us . . . Your wife" – never Joyce, fuck them! – "takes no notice of us. You whiz to work at eight every morning, and when you hobble back it's unduly late in the evening, your temper's beastly, and in any case, you plod straight upstairs, without a second for us. If we snuff it downstairs, you all, upstairs in that dinning rock music, wouldn't even know." I've suffered that one about a thousand times. Fuck, does anyone wish to hear such shit at thirty-four? So I've retorted once or twice, "Unlikely that both of you'll croak together. When one cops it, the other can ring us on the second phone upstairs, and then leave the corpse be, join us and let his – or her – hair down to some vintage acid rock." This sort of exchange can fuck you up for a week.

'By staying here, Joyce and I lose three thousand rupees every month as Residence Allowance! Baba should repay me that. Staying with them is screwing my marriage up.'

Whenever Shyamanand overhears Burfi in this tone, he soon after grumbles to Urmila or Jamun, 'What's preventing them from clearing out? Please beg them to leave. Why does Burfi pretend that we've manacled him to us? They could leave the brats behind. I'll nurture them.'

The listener placates Shyamanand. 'Never mind. Burfi's just a child.'

And now and then Jamun striates his brow and submits undecidedly, 'Burfi doesn't really intend to budge. Three large rooms for nothing – he won't have it so good anywhere else. When I arrive on holiday, it's a squash only for me. I survive out of a suitcase in the drawing room, and feel like I've registered in a camp for evacuees or something.' The bitter deadness on Shyamanand's face dries Jamun up. Shyamanand prizes the house that he's raised and any remark on its insufficiency stings him.

Indeed, for Burfi, staying with his parents is fairly gainful. For one, it is substantially cheaper. Until cornered, he never contributes any money towards staying alive; when he senses that he's going to be accosted (by Urmila, or by Shyamanand through Pista – 'Baba, this afternoon Thakuda handed me this water bill to give to you. Could you send someone from the office with your cheque?') he slopes off even earlier to work, remains upstairs, jerking his dome to the earphones of his Walkman, or, whenever he can't dodge his parents or his sons, gabbles, with a heavy, forbidding countenance, of the dreadful lumber of office affairs that's hampering him from looking to domestic matters. Burfi's chief bestowal on the superintendence of the household is his desultory censure; this taxes neither his mind nor his purse. Thus he never actually, determinedly, prospects for another house, though on weekends, now and then, eluding Joyce's eyes, he proclaims that he's off to househunt, and melts away for the day.

Other blessings too. He can evade the exhaustion and the costs of entertaining; when chaffed on the issue by his pals, he can, and does, reprehend his circumstances. 'No space, man, like living in those colossal PWD sewer pipes underneath some flyover. We live with my parents. They need me.' His grimace, his shrug, the lugubrious delivery, could've depicted the slaughter of an intimate.

And certain benefits of staying where they are Burfi and Joyce do not concede even to themselves. When they return from office, they are usually dejected with fatigue, and the twingeing in the skull that now a different life will have to be administered – Aya's crabbing against Doom or Shyamanand, and Pista himself – having outgrown his Aya, and being six whole years older than his brother – was the boy lonesome, and did he pine for his parents in the day? What did he actually do, and mull over, and makebelieve; was he burgeoning well, would he consummate creditably? Why didn't they command more time for him, and yet what span of time would be ample?

On some evenings, at their return, Pista is enjoying himself at chess with his grandmother. She sits shapelessly on the couch, while he bobs about the room, trotting up to hurl invisible, wicked balls at timorous champions among batsmen imagined against the walls, contorting his spine and skying his arms in yawps of ecstasy as their wickets explode – from all of which Urmila drearily lugs him back, again and again, for his next coup on the board. At the entry of his parents, Pista looks joyful enough, and skips up to greet them and be cuddled, but returns in a wink to the game.

'Chess is more lovable than your mama, is it?' grins Joyce, but Pista is more agog to exhibit to her how utterly he's drubbing Urmila in that tussle. Of course, neither player is at all certain of the elementary operations in chess, and Pista dabbles only with his grandmother, because she's the one adversary whom he's fairly convinced of trouncing – or badgering into yielding. Urmila detests the game because it summons up her brother Belu, but she never declines Pista, for only chess seems to bring the boy to her. Further, with the brat capering about, there is another being in the room to tug away Shyamanand's regard, which, when trained at her, customarily expresses scorn.

On other days, if they are early, their parents spot Pista and Doom in the straggling garden, planting saplings for their grandfather. Aya will be in the first-floor verandah, much like a muezzin on a minaret, yowling to the heavens for the children to be benign and come upstairs for the dual horror of warm milk and homework. Not to be winched up by her stridulation, to exile it from his universe, Pista clenches his jaws and savages the earth with his trowel as though she, Aya were spread in front of him. Shyamanand, guiding his grandsons, smirking, winking, proposes, 'If you disobey Aya, I'll reward you with chocolate or bubble gum, whichever you wish. If you remain downstairs till dinner, I'll gift each of you both.'

And Doom, Pista feels, though ridiculously young, does have his pluses. He potters about the house after Pista, hauled by the overriding enchantment of the four-year-old for the activities of the greenest of his elders, bawling when Pista apprises him that his tommy gun is immeasurably superior to Doom's idiotic Smith and Wesson, and that Doom won't be permitted to so much as touch it, squealing when Pista asserts that he's decided to be both Thor and Hiawatha, but Doom can't be anything because he's too young, short, fat and too dense, so there. On many a sultry afternoon, from divers corners of the house, this shrill wrangling of Pista and Doom, and Aya's screechy, disregarded shushing, filter through Shyamanand's half-snooze, and make him fuzzily marvel at the vitality in the young.

Urmila, Shyamanand and Doom: for a year and a half, Pista buds in warm company. His parents, however, never concede this notion, do not acknowledge it even to themselves as a ground for not shifting, that Burfi's parents are beneficial to their boys and so to them. For both, living with one's parents is a sort of embarrassment, a dreadfully lower-middle-class practice, like conspicuously relishing epic television soaps.

'Ma and Baba can't be discarded, Burfi, like rundown chappals. We could slice them, and one could be despatched to Chhana's. Baba, I suppose, since everyone else aches for a respite from him, Ma most of all. I mean, in a race for The Nation's Most Disagreeable Bong, he'd be streets ahead of the rest of us. You'd be second, though.'

'What about giving *us* a break, fucker, and packing both of them off for a time? In that peace, we could even overhaul the house, painting, with-it fittings, throw a party, let our hair down. But they'll never leave this house, even for a holiday.'

'Astute of them, if a vacation involves yielding the whole house to a sharper like you. When they return, you won't allow them in, or you'll exact rent or something. But jokes aside – a firstrate idea, to sunder them for a few days – they can rediscover how much they detest each other. I'll probe them.'

'A priceless suggestion, worthy even of Burfi at his most witless. You imagine that I'll abandon to him and his wife your mother in this state? You're very stupid, Jamun. When we hankered for you to bear us away with you, you seesawed, submitted rubbishy pretexts – that the climate there's noxious, malarial, the cook's boneheaded, there's nowhere to visit, we'd bore ourselves forthwith, we'd yearn for the snugness of this house, etcetera. Your lukewarmness crumpled up your mother – doesn't Jamun want us with him? He too? She was wholly correct. And now you propose that I should unwind for a bit at Chhana's. Whatever for? We don't need any breathers, thank you.'

The answer lies in part in Satyavan Hegiste's letter. Hegiste writes a cultivated Marathi, as one who aspires to polish his reader's knowledge of the language.

My dear Jamun,

More than two months've slipped by since you left. I received your letter, and by the time you get mine, I'm confident your mother will've recuperated greatly. My grandfather-in-law too is assured of this. In the evenings, lolling in his pet venue – the courtyard of the liquor den – he continues to proclaim to his comrades, 'Jamun's mother will definitely revive. For where in the maw of time will she happen on another son like him?' Awed by this proclamation, the chums then – as always – drain an extra peg to you.

Office has ticked your leave, most regretfully. Chhupa Rustam sanctioned it only when your beloved colleagues dared him to differentiate between your presence and your absence.

Your Kasibai and that teenage street arab Vaman returned one afternoon last week. They apparently possess a key to your flat. I was about to slip back to work after lunch when Kasibai fetched up at our door, mammoth and snuffling, perturbed. 'Where's Saab?' Presumably, the cobwebs and dust had told her that you weren't in office, or out buying cigarettes. Anyway, I left her to my wife. In the evening, a foxed Mrs disclosed that Kasibai had wanted to telephone you and actually chase you a thousand kilometres away to your parents' house! Well, well, well, well, well, well, well, well, well, well! – is what I observed to myself. However, my Mrs suggested, stalely, that you, muddled that you are, have probably not paid her for some months. She's informed Kasibai that pursuing you across the country wouldn't be necessary since you were returning within a fortnight. Aren't you?

In your flat they play the transistor day and night. Bhojpuri skits, or the weather in Kannada, or something, interrupts, once in a way, Bombay film pop. From the roundabout, through the yawning doorway, the sluggards (i.e. seventy per cent of our citizenry) observe Vaman the yahoo playact, to that howling from the radio, in front of your cracked mirror, the Hindi blockbuster hero. He jives and shimmies, shadow-bludgeons a hundred rogues, scrutinizes his braced muscles for that pit-a-pat effect, tries outlandish coiffures, declaims filmdom's ageless, purple passages, for hours without pause, in tight T-shirts and your – presumably junked – sea-green goggles. That bum's sole worth is as farce.

Whom do I play Drama In Real Life with, now that you're away? I've stacked some for your return. Take one.

A havenot – subsisting two kilometres beneath the latest Poverty Line – in a trashy town – like ours, for instance – soaks up buckets of venomous hooch on payday, and cops it. Two hundred dead in the country's worst liquor tragedy, squawks the press – the worst liquor tragedy since last Tuesday, that is. A pillar of the community ordains an enquiry, and an ex-gratia settlement of three hundred rupees on the kinsmen of each cadaver.

'Ex-gratia?' hoots the local Member of the Legislative Assembly, who is from the Opposition. 'Its idiom itself exposes this witless gerontocratic government to be still mentally besmeared by colonialism!'

That was local colour. Now, on with the tragedy. Our cadaver's son, aged thirty, befuddled and happy, capers off to collect the money, which he means to drain on vats of a rice beer the virility of which his defunct father had been scornful of. Ah well, will there never be any unanimity between generations? The local Revenue office implores him for a bribe. The goofy son starts to explain that he has no money to bribe with. 'What, not even a naya paisa?' demands the clerk, incredulous, his eyebrows like horseshoes. For them, quite often, it's not the cash that counts, but the principle. So, shaking his nut, and emitting clucking, 'poor you' noises, the clerk discloses to Goof that to process his case, he is required to submit, for starters, seven certificates, three affidavits and one testimonial, all in triplicate.

Next. An erring sister – HIV bubbling out of her pussy – affecting to be the liquor tragedian's loved one, turns up as a rival claimant for the compensation. She proffers herself most prodigally to the entire Revenue office. Afterwards, she peacocks past Goof, tucking the notes into her tits.

Now what should our protagonist the scion do? Should he dart after her, bleating that he too works in the Revenue office, but that he'd missed out because he'd zipped off for a shit while she'd been spreading herself out on the Head Clerk's table, and that it wasn't fair? Or is he tragic, and hence will he bend over in the courtyard of the office, tug down his striped drawers, and screech, 'Behold! Can you see the real me?' Your answer, as always, to be propped by forceful argument, please.

I hope to see you soon. Even my son appears to be missing your evening saunters with him. My best wishes again for your mother.

Satyavan

Now that Kasibai's returned, Jamun itches to go back. But forsaking his parents to Burfi he likens to gifting an heirloom – a grandfather's fountain pen, or the family gramophone – for a plaything to a three-year-old.

'Ma, I was considering returning to work. You've rallied now, and in any extremity Burfi's always here. I was wondering whether, for a change of scene, you or Baba'd spend a week in Calcutta. I sounded Baba, but he declined. Sarcastically.'

'Have you squabbled with him? Perhaps Burfi has. Because he edged in about half an hour ago, faltered about, and without warning urged that I revise my will, and not bequeath the house exclusively to you two – add me also as a beneficiary, he suggested, otherwise, if you predecease me, what's to curb my sons from turfing me out from what will lawfully have become theirs? Then where will I stray? he demanded histrionically. On the sands? "Whom have you bickered with now?" I badgered him. Incidentally, Jamun, where *is* the will?'

'Oof, Ma, I've no idea, and that's not what I want to chat about. Are you longing to laze about at Chhana's? *Without* Baba?'

'You do recall the will? Mr Naidu and your Kasturi attested it, around six years ago, and we continually wondered whether, since neither witness was a psychiatrist, the will would be illegal. Nobody seemed to know what to do with it, and now it's lost. But before anything else, will you find out whom your father's wrangled with? Never any peace in this house.'

Shyamanand has quarrelled after all, and with *two* people, and both on the telephone; long-distance with Chhana, and with Burfi in his office. Jamun is moderately riled. 'Scrap on the phone? Isn't it easier to disconnect?'

Dredging details out of a reluctant Shyamanand is particularly onerous. Nevertheless, Jamun fathoms that Burfi'd wished to inform them that his mother-in-law wanted to visit Urmila, now that Urmila had mended.

'So?' Shyamanand had asked, quite justifiably.

'Joyce spoke to me from Rani's a short while ago, to check whether her mother's dropping in on you all would be okay. Of course, I retorted, why shouldn't it be, but she sort of assumes that you detest her so much that you'll be stand-offish and inhospitable with her mother. This visit appears so totally dispensable – of course, that peeved Joyce considerably, because for her, Joyce Senior is a kind of matronly Jesus . . .'

An assessment of his mother-in-law that Burfi himself lukewarmly accepts. Jamun has for long been covertly appalled at the psychological governance of his brother by his wife. Burfi, in Jamun's expression, is a 'gone case'. His opinion on virtually everything – on every topic save money and sex – on education, religion, therapeutics, vocations, his upbringing, the family – has been recast by his marriage.

At a routine rum session, Burfi will proclaim, after the Old Monk has laved his tongue, 'Hard for us to size up our parents undistortedly. Ma and Baba, you realize, are really quite unexceptional – self-centred and unwelcoming. You notice how they've no friends? They haven't learnt to *give*.'

'Who has?' retorts Jamun vexedly, despite conceding the unsociableness of his parents. His booze carousals with his brother have steathily slackened after Burfi's marriage; by the time Jamun grows unconcerned at this falling off, he's started to brood, now and then, over how little he now shares with Burfi – only a handful of years of a past the import of which is ebbing apace, the seconds of which are cascading like sand through the sieve of memory. Doubtless that both have always lived their distinct quadruple lives, but once upon a time they'd also shared, or had appeared to share – or perhaps it now seems, and only to Jamun, that they'd once shared – a fateful chunk of living that had fostered their existent form, and that hence their present being was embedded in an affinity that it was wrongful of them to slight.

Jamun has noted that whenever Burfi bleeps the sentiments of his wife, he frequently glances out of the corner of his eye at her – as though for benediction. Perhaps, had he wheedled and supplicated Kasturi, and yanked her away for the nullity that she had wed, he too would've begun to view Urmila and Shyamanand in an unforgiving light, with Kasturi's eyes, be lorded over by her loins and her mind. Or he could peter out like his parents, friendless, inexpectant of the future, intuitive that the other's passing would wither the survivor, yet pottering about in a house all day to shun each other.

Closeness dies, between parent and seed, always. In his case, Shyamanand imputes this attrition in part to the uxoriousness of his elder son, and so abhors his daughter-in-law. Yet the unmarried Jamun also admits, but secretly, to the slump of his own fondness for his begetters. This acceptance melts and yet assuages, seems to release him. His brother has already whittled himself down to an acquaintance, his nephews command memories of no consequence, his mother is dying, his aya is dead; what remains for Jamun seems to be to front his father with his overblown trollop and her ragamuffin son. Grotesque.

'Next on the phone, Burfi proposes to me, his father, that I should *promise* to be cordial with his mother-in-law! Then he, like a trustworthy deputy, can report so to Joyce. Wouldn't you've bridled if your son'd called you boorish, particularly when he and his wife have a thousand times been unmannerly, even brutal, with you? I've been so disgraced by my children. When my daughter-in-law shames me, my son doesn't demur at all, yet he dreads that for some reason I shan't conduct myself with his mother-in-law. Why? Joyce baked a cake for Burfi's birthday and offered it to all save your mother and me. You sated yourself on it too, didn't you? I heard you, baying, "Fabulous cake, Joyce, way-out!" I questioned Burfi, why haven't you given your mother some of your birthday cake? He tched and oofed in annoyance, conveying, how can you beset somebody of my weightiness with such piffling matters? Your vexation means, I paraphrased for him, that you're too faint-hearted to ask your wife. Burfi next tried, "The cake's extremely rich – butter, sugar, cream, chocolate and all that. Disastrous for your and Ma's cholesterol." Two hours later, the leavings, the remnants of the cake – crumbs and butter paper – were on the dining table downstairs. I couldn't endure it. I ordered Aya to cart it upstairs again. I later probed Pista, my mole, on what happened afterwards. He recounted to me, relishing every detail, that Aya brandished in Joyce's face the litter of the cake that I'd returned. She whined to Joyce that I'd snarled at her and, typically, warped what I'd really mouthed. "I can't endure this obnoxious house, I simply can't," apparently snorted Joyce, over and over, padding about the room, Doom padding behind her. And now I'm to be the saboteur once more, for the visit of her mother.

'What *does* Burfi dread? His mother-in-law'll blow in and gush

– and I'll hold my tongue, kennel our chat to bare pleasantries, but that too'll rile Burfi, for he'll interpret my reticence to be churlishness. But why *should* I chinwag with Joyce's mother, when I don't wish to, when we've nothing at all to spout to each other, when both my taciturnity and my tattle will be misread as incivility, when my son itches to niggle at me because his wife's brainwashed him?'

And in the maiden flush of Burfi's marriage, to the startled Jamun, this effacement of his brother's mind appears total, like a spick and span blackboard for a fresh school term. Or how else to construe an enthusiastic Burfi exhibiting to Jamun, then in his teens, a flattering snapshot of a usually unphotogenic Joyce, and clacking, 'See, isn't she a wow? She's much more beautiful than I'm goodlooking,' and he half-glowers at Jamun, all but challenging him to dissent.

However have they arrived at such a situation, Jamun reflects then, wherein a human being, otherwise clear-headed, can conceive *and* voice such a fatuity: from certain photographs, one can infer that my wife is (basically) sexier as a woman than I am as a man.

Shyamanand is partly at fault. He has opposed the marriage of his son on all the grounds that he can dream up in the months between the declaration of the intention and its consummation. Joyce is so plain, he has cavilled, and she's a Christian! She'll appear terribly frumpish beside Burfi; does he wish his issue to be like their mother, dark and mousy? He and Joyce are virtually strangers to each other; how can one wish to wed a person one has known for only one messy fortnight? Especially a woman who lives apart from her parents for no discernible deficiency in them? And Joyce is older than the booby she's netted. And thus Shyamanand runs on, for years, hatching fresh protests against his daughter-in-law even *after* the marriage, enraged and befuddled at the rage and befuddlement of his son. Why wasn't Burfi, for instance, he demands, demurring against the fosterage of his children as Christians?; he is gnawed by his son's unconcern for the subject, and slips back to it again and again as a reassuring finger to the fringes of an abrasion.

Certainly all are to be reproached for the subsiding – or the suppressing – of closeness, of love, in the family. Burfi is to blame for disclosing, once in away, to his wife, Shyamanand's impressions of her. Perhaps Joyce has dunned to know; or maybe in the initial glow of his marriage of infatuation, the husband has – ingenuously, and for starters – determined to be on the square. 'Joyce, perhaps you could call Baba "Uncle" or something, and not "Mr—", which sounds sort of queer . . . Yes, "Uncle" is odd enough, but if you just can't call him Baba, then Uncle's better than Mr—, or maybe you shouldn't address him at all . . .' Such disclosures of Shyamanand's views help Burfi to shunt to him, whenever required, those of his own unpleasing opinions that need to be transmitted to his wife. 'Joyce, Baba was mulling over why, even after marriage, you whisk off time after time to Rani's and other friends' houses, trailing Doom with you. The kid's too young for late nights and offbeat living . . .' A share of this dishonourable transfer of opinion is unpremediated; most of it is utterly foolproof because Shyamanand's own views in general are discordant, untenable, displeasing.

Of course, the deleterious effects of his fault-finding are long-lived. Burfi, for one, for years remains flummoxed and stung that his father exhibits so straightforwardly his dislike of Joyce. Patently, Shyamanand's censures of his wife's attributes reflect unfavourably on Burfi's own appraisement of feminine attractiveness: what pathetic taste you must have if you were actually spellbound by a female as commonplace as Joyce. Only extraordinary maturity or indifference, or a singularly crass skin, can effectively breast this blitzkrieg against one's sensibility. Burfi, being a vain child, commands none of these qualities; instead, he ripostes as best he can: displaying to all, for example, like an elated kid, any snap that presents Joyce photogenically, and parroting her convictions at all times on all subjects – on the upbringing of Pista, the selection of a counterpane as a gift for Urmila, the care of the teeth, the knots in his parents' marriage, the primacy of Christian instruction as a guide for the stainless life. 'Church on Sunday,' Burfi'll observe, brow corrugated, lips skewed downward, expression stately because he supposes that they're discussing God, 'has been terrific for Pista. Has drilled him in the virtues – truth, kindness, charity, and all that crap. When we were young we missed that grounding, but Pista's well up on Ruth, Job and Solomon, and how Absalom vibed with Herod, or whatever. On Sunday afternoons, when he babbles to me, I recall that Baba never towed us to any temple, ever, or distinguished for us Shiva from Krishna, and Sita from bloody Savitri.

'Now and then I'd overhear, chancily, Jamun's aya evoking for him the yarns of myth – Sravan trudging to Benares, bearing his decrepit parents, and Trishanku excluded, out in the cold between heaven and mother earth. But by then I was old enough to be irked by the romances and parables of grannies and fostermothers. Pity.

'Doesn't Baba recollect that *he* enrolled us in a Jesuit school, where Catechism classes were obligatory, that he exhorted us to speak English even at home, with Ma too? When I'd come by a couple of friends who braided their manes, cosseted lice in their beards and sniffed snow, Baba never protested against them for the crazy pretexts that slapbang! became momentous only when he first saw Joyce, when, without warning, I was informed that I had to acknowledge my responsibilities as a practising Hindu.

'"A what?" I recall hooting. "Who the fuck cares? I just want to *marry* her!"

'More than a decade now, but Baba's still miffed that I married a Christian. What if Joyce'd been Muslim? Phew. Jahanara, or Jaaneman, or something. He's gnawed even more by the "waning Hinduness" of the family. Continually tries that hocus-pocus on us, that one doesn't have to perform any act to be a Hindu, one simply *is* one, Hinduness being intrinsic, inwrought, etcetera. Oof. Now he, off and on, exhorts me to revert our kids to our roots and all that jazz – so proposes that Pista should pick Sanskrit rather than French for his third language at school. Nuts. Who has the time, I pleaded, for bloody roots! To which Baba rebutted, But Joyce has the time for church! Precisely, I bawled, because with her it's the drill, like changing undies. She's been accustomed to church by her parents; why didn't you and Ma habituate us to whatever you wished? We were putty in your hands, as Pista and Doom are in Joyce's.

'*Before* she agreed to marry me, she'd asserted that our children should grow up as Christians. For sure I assented. Whatever had Baba and Ma enriched me with that I could demur?

'Then, whenever Baba's cheery and disposed to banter about his relations with us, he cites Genesis: Therefore shall a man leave his father and his mother, and shall cleave unto his wife: and they shall be one flesh. Which is damn annoying as well. I mean, if he's so bloody Hindu Mahasabha, then why does he know the Bible.

'The first time I heard that, I zipped to Joyce, braying, See, see, Baba's quoting the Bible! I was a little loony those days, foolhardily rooting about for something, anything, to reconcile wife and father, even the Bible would serve. But Joyce retorted, with smug triumph, "The Bible is an eternal work, consummate, for all seasons." Fuck, what an existence.'

Shyamanand is saddened, naturally, that his rapport with his eldest son crumbles with his marriage. Equally naturally, the birth of his grandsons – of Pista ten, of Doom four, years before – deflects his cognate concerns. Jamun secretly grieves whenever he notices his father trying to woo his grandchildren. Shyamanand's efforts are distressing because so abortive. All his conversation with Pista and Doom, sooner or later, directly or askance, ventilates his acrimony against the interceding generation. Parents during the fosterage of their issue fecundate their minds, naturally, and overpoweringly, compulsively. Children willy-nilly soak up from them their opinions, attitudes, biases, idioms, quirks. Shyamanand is galled by the certainty that his grandsons have begun to disregard – occasionally snub – him and Urmila because they've noted their parents behave so. Time after time he probes Pista, his nark, on what is being discussed upstairs. Perhaps the imp recounts without embroidery or guile. But Joyce especially seems to relish brutally debunking her parents-in-law in the presence of the children.

'She stayed glacial and closed, Pista described to me,' narrates Shyamanand, chafed afresh at his own evocation, 'till Burfi was obliged to ask what'd occurred. Your father is so beastly, ill-bred – Joyce seemingly jeered to him, then all at once started to sob – he spurned the cake that I'd baked for your birthday. Burfi, with a few pegs hyping him up, boiled over and foamed in his routine manner – to placate his terrific wife, reviling me with obscenities, audible enough to your mother and me downstairs. I'll slice the fucker's balls off, he screeched. You all heard him, no one chided him. And Pista and Doom listen to that about their grandfather from their father: What impressions'll they conceive of me? They learn that Burfi telephones me from work only to entreat me to be affable to an individual whom I've run into barely thrice in my life, with whom we've invariably been cordial, and whom the children idolize. What kind of ogre will they assume me to be that I've to be implored not to be loutish with such a darling, and implored even on the phone from office! They notice that their parents are perpetually churlish with us, that nobody admonishes them; hence they roll up their sleeves and begin too.'

'Never mind' – from her easychair, Urmila strives to assuage him – 'we'll both die in good time.'

'These matters are more important than death.' Shyamanand disagrees with Urmila whenever he can; where discord is unfeasible, he usually, derisively, marvels at her acuity. 'Since you've brought up the subject – you should alter your will, dispossess both our angels, bequeath the house outright to me. Yes, both, for Jamun is ours only until he marries. Perhaps we should've spawned daughters instead – I understand that they're more faithful to their source. Once you assign the house to me, I'll square these two fiends, who presume concurrently to live off *and* denigrate us. Just why're you smirking? This is comic, is it?'

'Even if Ma wills the house to you,' smartly intrudes Jamun to divert Shyamanand from Urmila's discomposing simper, 'you'll still be miserable and insecure, staying here with Chhana in vapid anxiety.'

Urmila attempts to shush Jamun. She then swivels her neck to Shyamanand and submits, 'Had Jamun been more alive to Hindu epic, maybe the dictates of fealty to his parents would've forced him to make war against his brother.'

A playful, even joshing, comment, but it disquiets Jamun somewhat; in thirty years Urmila has never manifested any instinct for wit or drollery. Whenever her sons have charged her with being too stodgily dour, she's parried that wifehood has pumped all the *esprit* out of her. 'Before I met your father, I was a charmer – sparkling, piquant sallies, always the core of a get-together. He's shrivelled me.' Her heart failure seems to Jamun to've unmuzzled her wits – but thank God for that, he points out to himself, smiling.

Burfi and Joyce come round the corner of the house. To fraternize minimally with her parents-in-law, Joyce often uses the side door, like a lodger who's behind with the rent. After a while Burfi, as is his habit, has followed suit. His parents at first are unduly pained by Joyce's shunning of them, and perforce have to persuade themselves that they abhor her very face anyway. In good time, Joyce and Burfi have convinced themselves of the same idea.

They are going to Pista's school, to attend some Parent Teacher Association meeting. Burfi is obliged to pout and carp because he's had to skip office for the day only to be updated on something as piffling as Pista's progress. His dress, however, contrasts rather fetchingly with his mien.

A cream and pearl-grey half-sleeves shirt, flawlessly casual Jordache jeans. Burfi doesn't look like the father of a ten-year-old; he seems instead practically a decade younger than he is. To Jamun, Joyce too appears captivating, in a lilac and honey salwaar kameez. Time has nurtured her comeliness, tutored her to accentuate her eyes and hair, to smile more often and without pretext, to remain hardy and robust, only by the might of will if necessary, to ensure that her sons cherish her more than their father, unremittingly to remind her husband, in a thousand ways, that she's in every manner more versatile and masterly than he.

Burfi glances doubtfully, once or twice, at his parents and brother in the verandah. 'Will you return for lunch?' asks Jamun, just to say something. In the preceding two months, he's settled into inhabiting the same house with his brother and sister-in-law and not swapping even one nod or a grin with them for days. They've nothing at all to intimate to each other. He's begun to feel as separated from his brother as his parents, and repines that neither Burfi, Joyce nor he have striven in the slightest to stall this waning of their amity. Psychologically, even physically, he seems to have hinged himself to his parents in a gang against the occupants of the first storey. Now and then – when, for example, Burfi is rabid and spitting abuse at those who don't answer back – he even feels that he has to shepherd his parents from the others in the house. Then, penitent about such thoughts, in expiation, when next he comes upon Burfi or Joyce, or even Pista or Doom, he sprouts fraternal prattle on any subject that flits into his head.

'Nothing definite yet. Put by some food for us anyway.' By which Burfi connotes: our lunching out is not linked at all to our lunching in. We – uh, Joyce, at any rate – contribute to the household, so we must have our due of food for breakfast, lunch, tea and dinner, no matter if we waste it. Which they regularly do. Platesful of untouched food lie in the fridge for a day or two before Shyamanand, Jamun or Aya – all three of whom abhor wastefulness – nibble, grimace and grouchingly toss the food away.

Burfi flails dust off their beaming Maruti and puts on his sunglasses. He abruptly smirks at his parents and Jamun. 'How at ease, domesticated, and cosily seedy you three look, like rheumy-eyed villagers around a hookah in the winter sun.'

'But when *we* presented ourselves at the Parent Teacher

get-togethers of our sons,' retorts Urmila jocosely, 'we looked less crotchety than you now.'

'What crap,' chortles Burfi through the window of the Maruti. 'For starters, in my eleven years, you didn't show up more than twice for my Parent Teacher do's, and that only because as a student I was a catastrophe, and the Principal sent you many notes of foreboding on the topic. But Jamun was virtually a whizkid in school – how many of his Parent Teacher functions did you grace?'

Astonishing that Burfi can recollect the minutiae of school life, but, Jamun reasons, everyone remembers if he wants to; even so, Burfi – childlike, forward-looking, well-favoured, once-uxorious Burfi – can never have been presumed to wish to recall the leavings of his uninspiring past. Yet Jamun is wrong.

And Burfi right. Jamun himself can remember his parents meeting his teachers just once. They had appeared grey, wrinkled before their time, overtired, careworn with themselves, and prodigiously, unutterably proud of Jamun. Their rapture in him distracts them, for the time being, from the dispiritedness of their selves, gleams on their features like polish on creased buff shoes. He is doubtless chuffed at their delight, exhilarated by its openness – and, in passing, assured of their solicitude for him. For he too has been bedevilled, at that point of his life, by the commonplace pubescent anxieties of filial neglect, and has been certain that his parents, at the least, cherish his brother considerably more than him; his aya has time after time affirmed such sentiments to him.

But remembrance is so capricious. He can't recollect with conviction whether at that Parent Teacher function itself, he was lurkingly rueful of the inconspicuousness of his parents, or whether that indistinct intuition of shame sprouted at a later date, with the fascination of Burfi's glittering friends, to keep pace with whom, for years, Burfi donned a disingenuous face, idiom and manner.

Yet, among the other parents, Urmila and Shyamanand *do* look out of place. Urmila doesn't elbow forward for Jeremiah's notice. She's not wearing lavender georgette, stupefying perfume, or chokers. Instead, she has smarmed down her face with Lakme powder and carmine lipstick. And Shyamanand, with his ivory-white thatch above a youngish, chubby countenance, his shabby clothes and scruffy shoulder bag, does not mingle either.

Jamun stands with them, futilely, vision cleaving to Jeremiah's waxen hardboiled thighs, mind turgid with concupiscence. That day in school has been seismic. Jeremiah proclaims in front of the entire class that in his new spectacles Jamun looks downright idiotic. She next is unforgivably endearing with Kuki, and thanks him for the chocolates that he's gifted her at Sunday church.

Church? 'You mean you waste your Sunday morning mooching about in church just waiting to suck up to Jeremiah?' Jamun is sneeringly enthused. 'It's easier, Kuki, to instead mug up to shimmy through your exams.'

No, discloses Kuki with a hint of a shamefaced grin, his mother and he attend church now and then because they are Roman Catholics.

Jamun is astounded. 'Beefeater?' And then, for that doesn't appear to sandbag Kuki enough, 'You're a fucking beefeater!'

In reply, Kuki, quite rightfully, whams him on his nose. Two hours before his parents turn up to chat with Jeremiah and co., he spends fifteen minutes in the washroom trying to plug the play of blood from his nostrils. From the smoky mirror goggles at him his wet, flummoxed face, with its handlebar moustache of watercolour vermilion. He'd expected Kuki to chortle instead of slugging him. Shock at Kuki's reaction greatly abates his hurt. In a blurred way he's also humbled. He can't even begin to conceive responding similarly if another were to decry the tenets of his own religion.

An education in a Jesuit school and college, the fellowship of friends who conversed on and thought about consequential matters principally in English, and in general the snarled ins and outs of their fosterage, have piloted Burfi and Jamun to discounting, even pooh-poohing, the worlds of their own languages. When Jamun's ranking in class slumps a rung or two because of a suicidal performance in Hindi, Shyamanand expresses no disappointment and does not exhort his son to concentrate more on Premchand and Kabir. When the Jesuits, without warning, aiming perhaps to cart Mother Mary to the lumpen, seek to alter the medium of tutoring to Hindi, and to set aside a quarter of the seats of the school for the children of the badly-off, they acutely discompose Shyamanand and the fathers of some two thousand other pupils. 'I do not pay your steep fees,' he impetuously writes to the Principal, 'just so that tomorrow my sons for a living have to teach Hindi in a tinpot primary school.'

His sons – Burfi in particular – have hobnobbed with, aped and envied cronies who usually were wealthier and more westernized than they; who, over the years, introduce them to hamburgers and porterhouse steaks, soufflés and blancmange, Levis, blues and heavy metal, hash and coke, and phrases like 'laid back', 'shit creek', 'a piece of ass'; these friends also make the brothers, with diverse intensities, at different ticks of time, veiledly ashamed of their parents and their home.

Because their house, wherever they roost, Jamun knows, is gloomy, joyless. The features of his parents have desiccated with the meagreness of delight; they used to glisten with a precarious rapture, once upon a time, whenever the children scampered home, from school or playground, with prime tidings and the avidity to share the news with their parents – 'Baba, I've been chosen Class Monitor again!' 'Baba, I thwacked sixty-seven not out, two sixes off Kuki in one over!' – but time winds up all that; the children, now adolescents, now adults, straggle up their dissimilar trails, scraping together on the way their differing powers of cognition and insight. Thus Jamun at eighteen can expostulate to Urmila, 'Don't wait, wait, wait for me all the fucking time. To return from college, to finish a chat on the phone, to double back from Kasturi's house, to tail off an evening amble with her, to dart back from a movie – for what?

To hear you bleat and whine against Baba, and him against you. Is that why you nurtured us, for our bloody ears? You just have to absolve and inure each other – this is priceless, a full twenty-five years after your marriage, to reap such counsel from your children.'

Urmila will definitely be sobbing by then. For some moments, while his gall surges, Jamun half-relishes her lined, forsaken face. 'I'm sorry – ' but he isn't, not truly. 'Our house isn't worth returning to. It's unhappy, dead. Kuki's, or Kasturi's, house is such a contrast. Banter, warmth, a sunniness. Her parents' friends'll be in the living room. Yours don't even exist. Kasturi's mother's face lights up whenever she sights me, a guest. I'm always urged to stay longer, have tea, participate in whatever the family's doing. The father's just bought tickets for a play for the whole family, her mother chaffs Kasturi's grandfather, everyone cackles – they could be on another planet. You and Baba don't even sleep or stay in the same room, unless the TV's on. God.' He switches off after he's heaved his pique out, but the sentiment – that its very inmates have ousted from their house the warmth and light of consanguinity – abides with him, like a lump, for all the cold sweat years that he and his parents live by themselves.

They occupy three different corners of the house, like three isolated angles of an uneven polygon. Once Burfi shoves off for the wider world, he doubles back only for fair-weather holidays, which, after his marriage, he has to further halve between his parents and his wife's. When he and Joyce finally pull in on their transfer, a decade, more or less, has glided by; in recompense for the years, they own a car, a good many thousands of rupees, and two sons. They breeze into the first floor, and without delay begin to grouse about being crammed.

Yet for Jamun and his parents, they are dearly welcome. They from the first appear to detonate the muteness of the cold sweat years. What the house seemed to hanker after most was the babble of a frolicsome child. And Joyce brought three, her spouse and her sons. Doom squeals at Aya not to distract him with spoonsful of tonic and other such piffle from the iron-willed tracking down of evil to a contour underneath his grandmother's bed. Burfi yowls out his version of the lyrics in exultant singalong with some rock'n'roll original on his stereo. Pista yawps and crows with rapture as he totters, trying to master the steps, as expounded by Burfi, of a shuffle called the Hustle. From the upstairs verandah Burfi, to Jamun in the downstairs dining room, brays his end of a conversation on the affinities, in general, between his stool and his brother. To Jamun, the rooms that Joyce and co. tenant seem to exhale light; the remainder of the house appears dank, leaden, without hope, like Urmila's features when he used to return eight hours later than expected from college, and that because the house and its residents were too cheerless to lug him back early.

'Who are these friends with whom you exhaust day after day?' Urmila will demand, tears tipping her eyes. Are they like Burfi's corrupters of six years ago, moneyed, unshaven, unrestrained? Are they worse? Why do you desert me for sixteen hours of the day? I can't tend to your father by myself. I shall snap.

Burfi's cronies were from the same Jesuit school, which was a first-rate institution, meaning that it was costly and that many of its alumni, under their own steam, performed superlatively in exams. They usually had mothers – some years younger than Urmila – who puffed long foreign cigarettes and tinted their tresses; or stepmothers whose blouses flourished their breasts, and fathers who tippled and chortled at the Club, wherever that might be. Their world, which Burfi was always hungry to sidle into, and in which, Jamun surmised, Kuki wasn't out of place, was expectedly removed from any spiritual impulse. One could contend that only Christianity decorated this world from time to time, and that only in the idiom of wonderment – Holy Moses and Jesus H. Christ!

'Fucking cow-sucker,' Jamun breathes to his befuddled reflection, testingly. It doesn't grate at all, and instead sounds quite comic. He snickers and, half-startled at himself, returns to cupping water against his nose.

Eight years after, in the ado of Burfi's civil wedding, amidst the exuberant bouquets, the perturbation, the household faces above the punctilious clothes, the fatigue unavowed beneath the steadfast smirks, Kuki dawdles up to Jamun and sniggers. 'Your turn now, you booby, to mate a second fucking beefeater. Wouldn't your parents simply freak out! You positive that your pigmy, Kasturi, didn't knuckle under her nuns and turn into a Presbyterian, or a Seventh Day Adventist, or something? She could then yak with Joyce about who fucks around the most in the Bible, though your new sister-in-law looks too erotic to be any good at chitchat.'

'God. Do you still remember that fucking beefeater affair? You bled my nose for it ages ago.'

'I could repeat that for you, if you wish.' They both titter embarrassedly. Beneath the varnish of his undemonstrativeness, Jamun is actually inconsistent, highly strung, inflammable. He leapfrogs over all ratiocination to the most freakish deductions. That Kuki can rake up a lightweight episode, eight years old, of Jamun jeering at his faith, that Jamun himself, now and then, can hiss at his own religion without being in the least disquieted, steers him to deduce, not that Kuki and he differ in their notches of forbearance, but that Christianity itself is better synthesized, more mettlesome; that its sway over its believers is a bit motherlike, kindling, at any gibe, even the dubious ones to its safeguard, leaving him to ruminate across the years whether, in the absence of a similar, external, cogent discipline, he in his fosterage has lost irredeemably.

'Will you be back by six?' Jamun sounds Burfi. 'Ma's to meet Haldia either this evening or tomorrow, and the Ambassador's misbehaving, so if you could loan us your car . . .' More than the Maruti, Jamun wants to delay Burfi's departure for Pista's school, to spin out these rare breaths of intimacy between parents and son, so that their sequent conversation, because so uncommon, itself will give Urmila and Shyamanand a subject for discussion (and eventual discord) in Burfi's absence: 'How time darts by. Burfi going to Pista's school looks so young and fetching. Altogether childlike, and characteristic, of him to bell-yache that he can fritter a day away in a thousand more pleasing ways than tuning in to the natter of Pista's schoolmarms. Ah well. I was nearly fifty when I used to meet Burfi's teachers –'

'But you grumbled just as much then as Burfi now. I had to lug you with me by bus, and you preferred the get-togethers with Jamun's class because then we could snatch a lift with Kuki's mother. But she'd always keep us waiting in her car while she drew up all over the city for God knows what work of hers – in Caulay Town and at the YMCA. Exasperated, you'd hiss, "This waiting for her is that sow's shoddy game. You're in my car, so you budge only when I wish to."'

To detain Burfi awhile, however, by asking for his Maruti is a cheap trick indeed. Burfi'd much rather hand over Shyamanand's blazer or Joyce's ballpoint. 'Six? I can't say. Why don't you instead drive the Ambassador down to the garage?' Out of habit, he glances for an instant at Joyce. Time and time again, when Burfi can't sidestep a request for the use of his car, he drives off, on what he asserts is a crucial task, an hour or two before the Maruti is actually required, fibbing and vowing to return in time. About a year ago, Burfi, twice in one week, manoeuvred in this manner with his father. By that Saturday Shyamanand, immeasurably wounded, bought a ludicrous Ambassador off Mr Naidu, which Jamun drove whenever he was around. For ten months of the year, the Ambassador moulders in the driveway, ahead of the Maruti. From time to time, Joyce's office chauffeur whisks its dust off, steals its petrol for his motorbike and takes Shyamanand and Urmila out for a spin.

'Both of you look super, like winter-ensemble-models on a honeymoon. However will you mingle with the frumpish parents of Pista's classmates?'

Burfi and Joyce simper. Burfi's face shifts from sulkiness to rapture like a before-and-after film ad for the alleviator of a stuffed nose, or for A1 undies. 'Yes, that's true,' he smirks, eyeing himself in the rear-view mirror, purring at what he sees.

They wave and drive off. Jamun glances at his parents. Both are watching the road, as though the Maruti is still visible. Urmila's armchair is between Shyamanand's and Jamun's. Her profile is incised on a background of ashen wall, the etiolated leafage of a money plant (that Joyce positioned there, beside the living-room door, when she came to stay and supposed that she'd belong. Objects in that house are scarcely ever dislodged from the nooks that they originally, haphazardly, occupy. Dressers, tubs for plants, settees, desks, root themselves wherever they are planted and, with the years, gather, like trees, reverence and dust), a once-white door, the pepper-and-salt tendrils of Shyamanand's beard. The skin of Urmila's face is fragile, slack, rutted, softened by brooding, the fatigue of age, and the recent, rare badinage with Burfi. Jamun remembers that Kasturi'd observed once, in the snug afterglow of coition, her fingernail sauntering down his nose, his abused contented lips, the ridge of his collarbones, his nipples, that he looked like his mother, while his brother took after his father. He hadn't been pleased with the remark and hadn't known how to react.

'Whatever are you mulling over, Jamun?'

'Oh, nothing, Ma, just hollow thoughts.' Nothing, at any rate, that he can share. It seems impossible that the old – the shrivelled, the senescent, the toothless – had once been nurslings and toddlers, that decades ago Shyamanand had been Doom's age, had played marbles, worn shorts, dodged baths. Time is the boss. Sometimes, when Urmila's expression is unmindful and still, Jamun notes, underneath the desolation of the years on the film of her skin, another face – of the same mould, but paler, tighter, more expectant – of someone she'd once been, now bedimmed by her puckered, translucent skin, the cerement of time.

Burfi and Joyce return at five, and Burfi seems to have no crucial tasks that evening.

Seven-fifteen. Urmila, Jamun, Pista, Doom and Aya in the

Maruti on the way to Haldia's house. Of late Urmila's met her doctor most erratically. She enjoys the car drives but shrinks from their objective. Her reluctance is in part her anxiety that Haldia'll insouciantly confirm her covert impression that she isn't mending. She in fact meets him only when she's even more unmanned by an abrupt frisson in the chest, or a leadenness at the root of her skull, or when she runs out of capsules, and Jamun proposes that the quack be consulted before his prescription's renewed, and she initially bridles, arraigning him with a minginess befitting his father's son ('I'm not spilling *your* money on my pills!'), and then, lukewarmly, acquiesces.

A snow-white, capacious waiting room, trendy murals on each wall, three ghastly electroliers, a handful of other invalids stoically waiting to be skinned, behind a white table an imperturbable woman with spectacles like the eyes of a mammoth dragonfly. 'Yes? Are you with an appointment?'

'Ohhhh – all white! So white!' trills Doom, chugging about the room. He pulls up beside the receptionist and explains, 'Thakuma's come.'

Forty minutes later. 'So hallo, how are we – my, we're looking tip-top, aren't we, my dear . . .' The pockets of Dr Haldia's ivory safari suit are patterned like fish scales.

He checks Urmila's pulse and blood pressure, and drivels away. 'My, our heart is like a GDR gymnast's, solid enough to bounce over the Berlin Wall . . . Appetite, digestion no bother? . . . Your piles shouldn't . . . sleeping well? . . . Can you please hold back that cub from raking through my medicines? . . . Thank you . . .'

Jamun answers several of the doctor's questions, because Urmila often prevaricates to evade admonition. 'No, Doctor, she hasn't dropped table salt yet. She only declares that she has. The phial of special potassium salt that we bought over a month ago hasn't been opened yet. I try now and then; she reasons, why should I deprive my taste buds in my last days . . . No, she isn't sleeping on any hard bed, her mattress instead is like a roly-poly woman, brimful of some sap . . . What, without pillows? She uses three . . . Exercise? Ma? Exercise! She hasn't shuffled out of the house since she returned from Intensive Care, six weeks now . . .'

Urmila remonstrates, but perfunctorily, because inwardly she gladdens at Jamun's motherly, finical grousing. To her it connotes that he cherishes her. 'What bunk. I lie in bed because I need to rest. And my eldest son calls me Kumbhakarna.'

Dr Haldia giggles obligingly and slides his stethoscope about her back like a vacillating reptile. Jamun wishes to underline the point. 'Ma's shown no zeal, Doctor, to recover. You can't contradict that, Ma. Your entire day's laid out in this creepy drowsiness in your twilight room. Whenever anyone unbolts a door, or tugs the flush in the loo, or dials a telephone number, you in your cot shudder and twitch, as though suffering a vision, and murmur, or sigh, "Who? Who's that?" without straining for a reply.'

At such moments, he feels that his mother has floated up from the dead, only to mutter gibberingly. Yet this impression, like several others of his, is more whimsical than accurate. For Urmila, time and time again, also discloses a mindfulness that jolts him. From her bed she'll, for instance, ask, 'Jamun, please check the kitchen chart and tell me when our gas cylinder arrived. Because in the last week I haven't, even once, heard on the road the plunk and clang of the gas delivery cart. I'm certain their supply's packed up for the millionth time. That cook'll sulk and grumble when we wheedle her to use the kerosene stove instead. We'd better book our cylinder in good time.'

Jamun is startled by these minor, yet revealing, instances that establish that Urmila's senses are finely attuned to the world beyond her mind, her person, her room; in those balmy, early-November afternoons, she's the only one who misses the everyday sounds that don't reach her, and correctly reads its import. But Jamun is also certain that in the weeks of rest after her heart failure, she's been bewitched by inactivity. Her relish for the agreeable activities of her past shrivels, then vanishes. She does potter about in the kitchen to make tea, slowly forage through her trunk for the bric-à-brac that yanks up some slivers of her past, compose incomprehensible letters of grievance to the Municipal Corporation against the scavengers of the locality – but not with her previous, or any, vim. Ludicrous, but true, for instance, that her tea, once an occult, heady blend, brewed with almost Japanese attentiveness, now has lost its savour. Her inertia is eerie, and darkishly suggests to Jamun that stir, the flurry of the lives of Burfi and Joyce, is vital only to bury the vanity of the hours, that existence can be rated a gift only when the impotence lurking beneath all action is accepted.

'We must begin a short stroll every morning, starting tomorrow. That's crucial. We must also meet more frequently. We are not cronies who gather once a month for bridge.' When they're at the door, Dr Haldia suffixes, not looking up from his desk, in a pitch outrageously casual, 'Ah . . . Mr . . . Will you wait a second, please? . . . No, only you . . .'

Haldia's consulting room has no cobwebs or smudges on its citrine walls. No matter where, Jamun always, unpremeditatedly, matches the room he chances to be in with those of their own house – for cleanness, for taste, warmth. Haldia presumably paid hundreds to some cocksure lackeys to empty the wastebaskets in good time, to clear teacups with treacly dregs off his table, to spot that the curtains ought to've been laundered weeks ago, to swab the flyshit off the fans. Would he've preferred such a room to be his own? With its burr of airconditioning and room-freshener-air? Jamun's questioned himself thus in a thousand rooms, and has always responded with a no; he's richly maudlin about the house that his parents've raised. He's lived with them in it for long, and their pride in their possession – for whatever it is – in their affixture on their mote of earth – has sidled into him as irresistibly as his past has soaked into the cupboards and the blotches in the whitewash, like winter benumbing one's bones; the house has not affected his brother so. Whenever he quizzes himself whether he covertly prefers other houses and rooms to his own, he feels sweetly sinful, as though in a fuzzy way, he's being false-hearted, unfilial; each such occasion overhauls his affection for all that's his own.

In fact, he can't even *see* himself tenanting a room as aseptic as Dr Haldia's. He's been fostered in, and so has become habituated to, has even, in a way, grown to cherish, this household world of bedraggled counterpanes, speaker tops so dusty that his finger doodles on them the serpentine courses of caravans across a desert, askew picture frames, lamps with fused bulbs, switch-boards with missing screws, clocks with dissynchronous faces, all out of time, walls that are canvases for the exploratory pastelry of burgeoning nephews, last year's newspapers yellowing in knolls underneath the stairs. Unlike Burfi, he's never hankered to inhabit the gloss of the rooms in an ad for distemper.

'Your mother's pacemaker batteries are leaking. I thought you should know. Of course, the patient mustn't be told.'

After a pause, Jamun, 'What does that mean? Isn't the pacemaker working?' His very first reaction is that Kuki, by dumping on them for twenty thousand rupees a dud pacemaker, has avenged himself too prodigally for Jamun's having once dubbed him a fucking beefeater.

'Now, we mustn't harass ourselves. When next you come, we'll examine her again, meticulously. Shall we put off our assessment till then?'

'Why did the fucker blab to me, Kasturi, if he isn't certain? What am I to *do* with the news? Tell Baba and observe his befuddlement? If I check with Kuki, he's sure to fib to shield himself. He'll assert that Haldia's mistaken; he'll then coax that testicle to concede that he is. After all, they've been accomplices in business for ages. Hence next week Haldia'll profess that the pacemaker's running tip-top, that this evening's diagnosis was half-ripe.'

'If the pacemaker's packed up, your mother's too feeble now, I guess, for a second operation – for a replacement.'

'A third. Before this pacemaker shambles, Haldia'd slashed her piles off. Perhaps we should call in another quack. But even for that, I'll have to confide in Baba.'

'You look as though you're going to eat here. Tell me, because then I'll scramble together an extra something. There's practically nothing in the fridge.'

'And all but no one in the house. If we can stash away your grandfather in the fridge, I could show you what I really want to eat. Isn't that a response worthy of the smuttiest adolescent?'

'And since when haven't you been that, sweetie? "Sweetie" is what my sister's new boyfriend calls her. He's bloodcurdling. D'you remember BF and GF? In our nonage? I was ardent about widening your mind, whammed down on you all kinds of books – potboilers, antinovels, opuses – but you doted only on Ring Lardner. Remember?'

'But your husband was for starters to've hitched up with your younger sister, no? At least, so your grandfather'd worked out. Queer how things ripen. He couldn't endure your sister's jabber, leered at you instead, and you peeled off your panties – you'd mooched about long enough with Heidegger and Max Weber.'

Kasturi's lips curl with minimal mirth. 'What stakes, please, that you'll start your pawing in ten minutes?'

Jamun stares at her from the verandah door, but she shuns his eyes. 'Why didn't you hold on, last year, when I proposed that we marry just after my parents die?'

For minutes the lull of recollected discomposure. He dawdles about the room, recapturing a white-hot afternoon, eleven summers ago, in this same room, when he'd gawkishly, naked, lain down in Kasturi's warm arms and had shammed that he'd tumbled and entwined with other women before. With his face weltering in the fleeciness beneath her ear, in the balm of the expectant, susceptible skin of her throat, the heat from her riven lips, ravished by the ecstasy with which her thighs'd scissored his hips in an intuitive, immemorial rhythm, bewildered by the notion that the miracle was actually, truly befalling him – him with his spectacles and womanish haunches – he'd, all at once, been stupefied by a thankfulness to her that'd felt like a double dose of molten blood in his forehead, and all over him, just underneath his skin. In his gratitude, the delirium of which'd waned with the shrivelling of his rut, he could've attempted anything, flagrant, infernal, to laud the bewitchment of the coffee-with-milk dunes of her body; could've bedecked her pudenda, tongued her leavings.

Later, languorous, he'd taken in the new world. The same four-poster had then faced the windows; the curtains'd been prettier, bleached-blue with flecks of white. The fan had gone off. Emboldened, he'd rolled over and tasted the sweat on her throat.

'I remember how you ducked my questioning. By citing Isaac and Rebecca. Slickly flipped the subject into the absurd. Is she gaga? Why the fuck does she connect with the Bible all the time?' At the remembrance he snickers like a ham, blood-and-thunder blackguard. 'And Isaac brought her into his mother Sarah's tent, and took Rebecca, and she became his wife: and he loved her: and Isaac was comforted after his mother's death. When you quoted that through your fake sniggers, you actually jolted me. Maybe she does believe that only after my mother snuffs it will I itch for another woman. Perhaps that's how I register with other people – as though always groping about for an udder to nurture me.' He halts in front of her, seated, with ramrod spine, on the bed, abdomen overblown, hard, like a mammoth globe. 'Why don't you lie down, Kasturi? Please?' He's taut with misgivings and hunger.

She simpers uneasily, rises from the bed like a beast of burden, murmurs, 'Don't be foolish,' and, with her heaviness, shambles towards the verandah. 'And the Lord God said, Jamun, it is not good that the man should be alone: I will make him an help meet for him. I'll have to station verses from Genesis between us to head you off from knowing me. Tch, you don't look a bit tickled. Why don't you marry, Jamun? Since you've been so solicitous for your parents and their sentiments, beseech *them* to pick a Mrs for you, so that you don't have to wait for them to croak before you can, as my husband says, get your sex on tap.'

They shuffle out to the verandah. The night gusts from the sea trace them among the highrisers.

'Shall we run up to the roof? Ogle at the stars and listen to your unseemliness?'

Among the forgotten junk and TV aerials of a hundred apartments, they share the stump of a lychee pudding. He watches her spoon pudding into her yawning mouth. 'Since when've you begun using your right hand for anything?' She's the most lefthanded creature he's ever met. He's never been able adequately to reason to himself why he's so extraordinarily charmed by her sinistrality. A warmth ruptures in his belly when he watches her do the most commonplace things – scrawl a telephone number down, brush her teeth, draw the curtains – only because she uses her left hand.

In an irregular line, in the bottom inches of a curtain of patchy blue-black, nod the motes of light from the tankers and liners too mammoth for anchorage in the harbour. A mettlesome breeze, and haphazard halfhearted stars. Traffic easing along hundreds of feet below like ants with torches, other overnight highrisers prodding the sky like the monumental, upraised arms of the contentious and dispossessed bawling for a chunk of the sun. Jamun banks himself against the parapet and inspects the vertiginous drop. 'Say something viperous, Kasturi, now that my mood's mending.'

She giggles and, from the back, enfolds him, lolling her head against his shoulderblade. 'Can't we be friends and enjoy a radiant relationship?' She sniggers again. 'Jamun.'

'Does Genesis have any of those? Male and female soulmates who don't hump? Unlikely.' He revolves to confront her. His rut has whimsically attenuated to a dryness against himself. Inwardly snickering, in a manner abashed, he deduces that he isn't going to mount anyone other than his matronly Kasibai, that he should hence return to her swiftly, that he should bear himself more charitably with her, in particular because he possesses no one else. 'Your Genesis is pretty ravening and queer, isn't it? You thwacked it on my head, hissing, read, pore over, evolve your psyche, its passions are most Asian. So I waded through it, and was overpowered, out and out, by the hard porn and the way-out dollops of fornication, harlotry, defloration, gang bang, buggery, pederasty, incest and bestiality. Wow, who doesn't, in the Bible?

'But its soul is not a bit Asian, I remember cavilling to myself; we – the humans I know – aren't like that in the least. Malevolent familial discord, the totally capricious, arbitrary conduct of kinsmen towards one another, one parent whimsically favouring one child, brother versus brother without any cause other than a communal blood – Esau and Jacob, Abel and Cain, Lot and his daughters – quite flummoxing. If we'd inhabited that world, Kasturi, and I'd there mooted to you that we marry just after my parents die, you, in the span of two verses, would've diced them up and whirled me off to bed, where you'd've commenced knowing me. Or if you'd married another, the dreadfully knotted life of this marvel in your tummy' – he palms her – 'of course hatched in possessed heat while your husband was away, would be vaticinated by the direst omens – black falcons tittering and crunching off the heads of infants, that sort of stuff. Aren't we much gentler than those patriarchs of the Pentateuch, more tolerant, and less sexy?'

'You've been with me, and absent from your home, for some three hours now. Unbelievable. Oughtn't you to scamper back to the arms of your drooping parents? Or have you miraculously reversed your trait of a decade – of fucking off instantly after either shooting off all over me, or as soon as you realize that that day'll be armistice? Or perhaps you're still waiting for me to knuckle under, to shimmy on the floor with desire? Since when has your other life – as you style it – stopped becking you back?'

'Fuck you, Kasturi, in as many ways as feasible.' He slants forward and kisses her warm cheek. He can still divulge those emotions to her that he can't to his parents or Burfi. 'In one of your sermons, you discoursed to me that when I feel love or its synonyms for someone, I'm disposed to secrete away or overlook the instinct, because at bottom I'm afraid. Don't you recall that afternoon?'

She squints at him for an instant, smirks.

'For sure you do. An infernal summer – when isn't it summer, Kasturi, in our city? I'd ferreted out a *tour de force* titled *Love without Fear*. Burfi's consistently and incisively disclaimed its ownership. One of the more delectable memories of those lurid undergrad years. Chapter Eleven was succeeded by realistic line drawings of some of the *Kama Sutra* catalogue. I was ghoulish about one position which required four roly-poly bolsters beneath the male. Nice bolsters.

'But you were considerably jittery about being the Upstairs Floosie. Doesn't your mother *ever* come upstairs? Only in the afternoons, to dodge my father, to grab some sun. But they must be curious about what the two of us've been up to in your room for hours. Kasturi's going to wrap up Hegel for me, so please don't disturb. I'm not your mother's soulmate, as it is. So you whined, bleated, croaked and wailed, and I struggled to divert you with proposals of the bolster callisthenic. You sweated to dodge me and zoom back home to – I imagine – Deuteronomy. I was breaking through, though, when you sprouted your homily. If I truly cherished you, I'd – instead of exhorting you to mount me – usher you home. I was propelled only by love for my own self. For my id or my ego? – but you couldn't illuminate. I must treasure the world outside me, the creepy-crawlies of creation. Masterly, because my hard-on puckered into my scrotum.

'You weren't, of course, mouthing anything revolutionary, but whether I'm here, or at my job, with Satyavan Hegiste, I find it a tenet too exacting.

'These last few months I didn't write very often to my parents or to you. Barely twice or thrice. There seemed nothing to convey save my trite ennui and my visor of unconcern. Then in snap spurts I'd dash off to them that I missed them. Now and then I even felt that I was declaring my yearning for them just to string out the letter, so as not to waste the rich, milk-white paper. I wasn't actually shamming, but I was professing that I needed them because there was nothing else to voice, no other sentiment or notion – the choice was silence. Now that I'm here, I'm not certain that I pine for them in the least – because here at home I don't spend much time in their company. I do mooch about a lot in the house, but am not with *them* for more than half-an-hour, totally, in the entire day. So, I muse, what then do I actually hanker after when I'm not here, am mopish elsewhere? Kasturi, you bitch, you're bored.'

'Only to a sort of death, sweetie. Which shouldn't distress you, since you all but chopped my skull in two last year when I disclosed to you my marriage plans.'

'What lies. You're a bloody fib factory.' He grins at her, but when he continues, his inflexions whisper at disingenuousness, as though he articulates on one subject only to forestall all allusions to another. 'And when I do sit with my parents, I feel as though I'm foundering into becoming like them. In the evenings they're positioned in front of the TV, and answer me in monosyllables, but if I shift channels they don't notice. They grouse gracelessly against whichever of their sons is absent – and chiefly because they in fact yearn for his companionship. And thank God our small talk is minimal, for any phrase, even the most aboveboard, can trigger off a blustery quarrel between any two of us; each of those slanging matches tails off with my mother sobbing, and her whimpers and snivels rile one of the other two to spatter any residual bile on her. So what's new.' Their ashen faces touch off in me many ugly ideas, so that I feel both rancour and remorse at them. If I marry, will I also clock out like them, sightless in front of a TV? Why won't I? The same blood, isn't it. Even Burfi's marriage is annihilating; he's glided out from beneath his wife's thumb for some systematic two-timing. So why won't I? Won't my life ripen after my begetters die? Be released? Will I be able to break down over their bones, when they are burning? 'I mean, love must be all, but it's awkward to profess – and easier from a great way off, than face to face. I've a hunch I must mend, Kasturi.'

'All in a good time, dearie. Do your parents still bully you emotionally with that tripe that used to screw you up those days – that no one else will be as happy as they to see you? What? Never'll anyone want your society like they? You replayed the phrases to me night and day, so they incised themselves in my skull.'

'We all seem to command the memories of either wise elephants or ninnies, depending on how much we wish to bugger the character we're chatting with.'

'I've harangued you a thousand times before, that if you'd kept away from home for a few of your seminal years, you wouldn't have this braindamaged idea of your familial responsibilities. Truly, in a sense, Jamun, your formative years haven't petered out yet. At seventeen Philip Jonas fluttered into Vietnam on hash and Haight-Ashbury, he said. Contrast yourself. At seventeen, had you weaned yourself off your mama's lap? That's why, after school, I scrammed from Calcutta and my parents, and fetched up here for college. We all just have to break away.' Next, in an everyday voice, 'Shall we go down now? We still have to figure out our dinner – and I've to bustle around my grandfather as well, while he stuffs himself with the food he criticizes.'

On the following morning, Jamun hauls Urmila out for the initial paces of a stroll. Commandeering her to consent is Hercules' thirteenth. Before he begins the gruelling process of prevailing against her, he divulges to Burfi Dr Haldia's disclosure of the evening before about the pacemaker.

'What the fuck does that excreta mean? Does he want more cash or what?' Burfi's just completed his forty-minute work-out and – as is his practice – is now scanning his torso, appraising whether its muscles can spellbind the world. Every morning, for five minutes or so, he poses for himself in the mirror. This is the single time of day when he can be reckoned to be in a good mood. 'Look, just look at that bicep. Wow.'

'Are you chatting with me or with your tit? Burfi, please be attentive. I'm confiding in you because I felt that someone else in the family must also know – I can't be on my own with this info. Sure, Haldia'll finally decide only next week, but don't we act until then? Consult some other charlatan, or cram Kuki's mouth with his balls, or something?'

'If Ma's feeling okay, then let's hold on for the second bout of Haldia's bullshit. Fuck, I must zip now. Shall we discuss this again this evening over a rum? Why don't you also sound Joyce out? That reminds me – since you loll about all day itching for that pigmy bomb and frigging, why don't you instead be helpful, amble out in the afternoon and buy a rum?' and Burfi glides into the bathroom behind Joyce. They frequently bathe together. 'Saves time, hot water and electricity,' is his reasoning. 'To save even more time, like a PERT CPM for our reaching our offices punctually, I even shit while Joyce showers.' He now and then divulges such snippets to disgust his brother. He usually succeeds.

'Help me' – on his way downstairs, Jamun invites his nephews – 'to persuade Thakuma to stroll down with me to the beach.' But the brats don't even hear him. They scoot to the closed bathroom door and huddle against it. Pista, in a raucous whisper, exhorts Doom to demand to be let in. Doom, globose and gullible, obliges. 'Mama! Mama, I want to see!' . . . 'Mama, please come out in your nightie! I want to see you please in your nightie!'

'The bloody horny bugger,' Burfi purrs half-appreciatively, 'panting for it at four.'

'Oof, kink and smut, does your skull store nothing else! To Doom, my nightie denotes that I'm not stirring out anywhere, and deserting Pista and him, that in my nightie I can curl up in bed with the kids, natter with them, answer who's mightier, Hanuman or Superman. Doom's a lonesome child.'

'Balls balls. You're just being churchy, too goody-goody to concede that the imp's plainly, naturally randy.'

The ground floor contrasts hellishly. Indistinctness, silence, dust. Urmila a death's-head on a weathered counterpane. 'Please get up. You and I'll step out for a very short stroll.'

'Not today, Jamun. I don't feel at all fit. Butteflies in my heart all morning. Simply because I never bellyache, you assume that I'm as hale and hearty as an American black at some Olympics.'

'Once, only once in your entire life, please listen to another human being. This seems the single aftercare with which Haldia isn't milking us. Unless he sneakingly plans to dump on you some gym shoes for five thousand rupees.'

'Let me see. Perhaps next month.'

'That soon? What about next decade? Or in the year 2525? Ma, just a hundred paces. Fifty. We'll use one of Baba's walking sticks. If you funk and pussyfoot, I'll board the earliest train to work.'

'Doubtless, merely to bounce off at the next station.'

'At this tempo, Ma, you'll in no time yearn for TV's nine o'clock slot for a sidesplitting turn. I'll inform Haldia next week that your bad heart's metamorphosed you into a desi Lucille Ball.'

'Huh. What do my sons know of what I might've been? Had it not – '

'Aha, that cataclysmic marriage, that impeded both your and Baba's blossoming into geniuses! Ma, if you yes a stroll, you'll at least dodge Baba for its span. You can also bitch about him till your heart's eased. I swear to snitch to him only the spiciest bits.'

By and by, Urmila submits. What finally prevails with her, perhaps, is Jamun's singular solicitude for her wellbeing. The news lugs her grandchildren down from Burfi's room, where, spellbound, they'd been staring at their parents dressing for office. 'Are you really?' demands Pista, smirking witlessly. Urmila's bashful nod pricks both the imps to dinning, deranged laughter, enchanting to hear. 'Stop that squealing,' grins Jamun. 'Instead, escort us on our walk.' 'Even if it's just to the gate,' snorts Shyamanand, coltishly jolly that his wife has assented to the inconceivable – a saunter towards her recuperation – but striving, out of habit, to muffle his delight.

# 4

# A WALK TO THE BEACH

But Aya stumps into Urmila's bedroom then, grinning ebulliently, two prodigal bouquets of wine-dark and white roses, like twin sucklings, in her arms. 'Happy Birthday of your marriage, from Joyce-ma,' she beams at Urmila and Shyamanand. On cue, Joyce sidles in after her, *en route* to her office car, breakfast sandwich in hand.

Urmila's jaws slacken in astonishment and pleasure. 'For me? Joyce, what exquisite flowers! Ohhh! Glorious, gorgeous . . .' Cradling the bouquet, she titters like a child at her daughter-in-law.

'For me? But I've never,' demurs Shyamanand, with a confused half-simper, 'received any flowers in my life. Why me? You needn't have, Joyce.'

'But isn't today your wedding anniversary? The thirty-seventh? Or have I goofed on the date? The eleventh of November, I'd thought.' She lists against the door and, to veil her sheepishness, tousles Doom's hair, and pushes a third of her sandwich into his unwilling mouth.

Shyamanand detonates into whooping, rumbustious laughter. With each guffaw, he seesaws like a puppet bowing to the hurrahs of encore. His face maroons, his spectacles perch awry, he all but overbalances. Yet his thunderclap hooting – which shudders his paunch like the touch of the electrodes of shock treatment, which nonplusses and even disquiets the children so that their half-smiles do not spread beyond uncertainty, and which Jamun sizes up as histrionic, overdone and selfish to the full – expires only when he begins to heave and wheeze.

Jamun explodes too, despite himself. 'For God's sake, Ma, don't blubber, he's *not* cackling at you!' Incensed with himself for boiling over, he then corrals her with his arm and tries to steer her to her bed. She is weeping mutely and unrestrainedly. She shuffles compliantly enough with him, the roses in her arms like a lifeless child. When he glances up, Joyce has glided away, the kids, pop-eyed, have edged closer, and Shyamanand's face is crimson and still.

'Why the hell does Joyce, without warning, give you flowers? She knows, no, that you've never celebrated even one of your wedding anniversaries or birthdays, even one, in all your lives, unless it be to bicker with more than everyday malevolence.' Jamun pauses to bridle his voice. 'Which other duo would acquit itself like this on receiving flowers on an anniversary – with faces like the tragic and comic masks of Greek theatre? What remains for you both now is to flail each other, maybe with these flowers for starters. We've never spotted you touch each other from fondness, you could instead begin with hate.'

He keeps his arm around Urmila, corseting her, silently willing her to stop sobbing, willing Shyamanand to quit the room. In the disagreeable silence beneath her snivels and the ephemeral sounds of the world, Shyamanand does hobble towards the door, but before he leaves the room, he haltingly swivels to assert, 'Your dishonest memories've always pampered your mother. She did lunge at me once – with a ladle – under *your* nose, just because I asked her why she was feeding me dead cockroaches – jumbo-sized, too. You ought to recall the incident, since you were ripe enough then to prance to her defence with the signal thesis that cockroaches are a significant source of protein. If your mother asserts that I've clouted her too, ever, then she, as usual, is fibbing. Everything about me gnaws her – my mind, my clothes, my condition – quite naturally, my laughter – the idea that I'm enjoying myself, am joyful – propels her round the bend.'

At his receding back Urmila snarls, 'I remember, even if Jamun doesn't! I remember each of your million feats of churlishness.' Fury dumbfounds her, like a child. Beneath his arm, Jamun senses her whole body tauten in the struggle for articulation. Her face buckles, her teeth chomp down again and again on her striving tongue. She starts to mewl the short, stealthy ululations of impeded rage. Though cramped by Jamun's arm, she also begins measuredly to reel back and forth. The domes of the brats wouldn't've twirled from her even if Joyce had minced past them naked, her boobs dunked in chocolate.

Jamun, miserable and unsympathetic, waits for his mother to recover. She, once in a way, is racked by assorted tantrums and fits, the existence of which has always been overlooked by all, probably because Urmila the human presence is so unaweinspiring, longsuffering, so lulling, that no oddity linked to her can ever kindle any disquiet in her family. In the core of a rare might, Jamun the featherweight sleeper might be winched out of slumber by the hushed yowls and yaps that she splutters in her nightmare. But no one's ever been unnerved by her; tch, it's only Ma, he'll dozingly enlighten his pillow. She herself, on the morning after, or at any other hour, never acknowledges her volatile paroxysms, her ravings. 'Don't discuss the matter with her,' Shyamanand has counselled his sons. 'Don't disturb her during a spasm, you might convulse her. In any case, she suffers these fits once in a blue moon.

'I did try to jostle her awake once or twice, in the first months of our marriage, when we still bedded in the same room. My God, I muttered to myself in a cold sweat, when I heard her pule, gaped at her shudder in her apprehensive sleep – my God, what've I married? I jogged her, and the throes stopped; she seemed to tumble from an immense elevation into an abysmal sleep. A sort of transition of colour – or light – or expression – percolated across her features, like a blackboard being swabbed, or a film of skin being peeled. I jerked and prodded her until her eyes opened. Her pupils were atoms of light in blobs the shade of evening, like the pinpoints from a liner on the skyline, winking at dusk. She appeared to be gazing at me from some other time. I probed her the next morning, but she couldn't remember. More wouldn't than couldn't, because she did stiffen at my questioning. I suspended it then, and supposed her seizures to be a sibling characteristic, a freakishness in their blood, for which there was her brother Belu to vindicate me.'

Urmila slackens against Jamun's shoulder as though punctured. He lays her down and hauls his unwilling nephews out of the room, wondering what stock they've taken of the bizarre.

'When Mama presented the roses, why did Thakuda laugh like that, Jamun, like a screwball?' Pista.

'Because Joyce – like some kneehigh buggers of this house whom we all know – forgot to scrub her feet before hopping into bed last night. As you know full well, toejam overnight comes by a life of its own, and by daybreak shapes itself into numberless, microscopic, woolly spiders which, snickering with delight at the windfall of life, scuttle away from the toes to new sanctuaries. This morning, they happened on – and lost their hearts to – Joyce's roses. You must remember that even after they become spiders, they preserve the pong of toejam; so they'd – naturally – idolize the balm of roses. From the bouquet they romped into Thakuda's beard, lips, nostrils – they adore the adventure of untried habitats. They also tickle and itch like crazy; so Thakuda wasn't really guffawing – he was yelping because the spiders'd begun to prickle him.'

Jamun watches his nephews dismiss his reportage of the world's workings; had Burfi sketched the yarn, they'd've bought it outright, for Burfi has a way of distending the imaginations of children, a wizardry that Jamun too has inherited, in some measure, from Shyamanand, who, in the nonage of his sons, scarcely ever enlightened them with the prosaic when the fantastical was accessible. Hence, for some of his unfledged years, for instance, Burfi accepted that only when, during a thunderstorm, a male and a female, standing naked – for whatever reason – in the open, cheek by jowl with each other, were whammed on their bums by lightning – only then were eunuchs born, or, more accurately, forged.

'But Thakuda and Thakuma don't celebrate their birthdays?

They do have birthdays?' Pista's inflection transmits a tinge of alarm at the inconceivable .

Yet at Pista's age, Jamun'd never reflected on why his parents didn't commemorate their own birthdays and anniversaries. He'd accepted that they simply didn't, just as he'd acknowledged that God was exactly what his Moral Science textbook imaged Him to be – chubby, in a white kimomo and a silver-wool beard that dribbled down to a sort of rope about His waist, sixtyish; with twinkling eyes and outstretched, welcoming arms, with woolpack clouds tingling His ankles, He perennially stood, simpering. Indeed, Jamun'd surmised that no parent, no adult, actually, ever observed such special days, that with Time the zeal to honour its passage ebbed. Thus he was baffled to learn that the world viewed the subject rather differently from his parents, that Kuki, for example, loped off on a unique day every year to buy for his divorced father a card and perhaps an aftershave.

'Don't you even *know* your parents' birthdays?' Kuki in turn is startled too.

'Of course I do,' fakes Jamun. 'Ma's is seventh February, and Baba's twenty-eighth October,' and he eyes with curiosity the downmarket aftershave in Kuki's hand; it betokens another universe. At home he badgers, 'Why don't we ever remember your and Ma's birthdays, and give presents?'

'Who's stopping you?'

Yet son is nearer the mark than father. Jamun's question is really one of a suit that recurs to him in a thousand contrary ways over the decade. Why don't you and Ma display at least some signs of intimacy, of charity, towards each other, acquit yourselves a little like some other married couples. Why don't you stop scuffling with each other for the affection of your children, and instead ferret contentment out of yourselves. Your brood is not yours just because you've fostered it. After all, since no wily go-between hitched you up, once upon a time, between the two of you must've lurked some kind of concupiscence; well, whatever happened to that heat, that lukewarmness. If it stubbed itself out, why didn't you cut adrift, instead of averring that parting is impossible once the litter is spawned. Or is your disaffection itself that cohesive a yoke. Is amen your retort to the other's silence, and do you both invoke Time's desert sands to be your buddy and your spouse's foe.

Unhurriedly, as though the years needlingly tug at a veil, Jamun fathoms that his parents share several ugly attributes of their marriage with millions of others. Some of this perception is disclosed to him as late as when he enlists in college. 'Certainly, my parents wrangle, day in 'n day out, you ninny,' snickers Kasturi at his ingenuousness, over their sixth cup in the coffee-house, 'because all couples abrade each other.'

'Yours too? But they certainly don't bear themselves like cat and dog.' Yet he grins involuntarily at Kasturi, because she's giggled, and he's been startled by a kind of easing that the shame of a joyless household doesn't sully him alone, that a matter as stealthy as parental incompatibility *can* be debated, and even partnered with smiles. He can't, however, gauge how much to disclose. 'Kasturi, my parents don't exactly bicker and wrangle – they don't chat to each other at all, not like other people, like you and I natter – of the day, of how horrid the bus conductor was, and how you had to flit from your tutorial because the rain was pummelling the windows and the tutor was so unsexy – my parents in contrast are sort of webbed in a glacial, spleenful hush. They swap just a handful of phrases per day. "Dinner is ready . . . Have you signed the cheque for the electricity? . . . This tea is cold." Beyond these expressions squats the silence. And the most inoffensive statement can sizzle in seconds into a brutal tiff, which routinely closes with my mother snivelling, and my father's brow crimsoning like a dam against the blood; then we assume that these rows wound her more than him.'

Too early in their companionship for him to divulge to Kasturi his parents' sexual relations, though he's all at once prurient about the intimacy between her mother and father. In his seventeen years, Urmila and Shyamanand have never gone to bed in the same room; in the tiny government flat in which the family whiled away more than a decade, Shyamanand customarily bedded down with Jamun; Burfi commandeered one entire room for himself, the ingress into which of his parents and brother exasperated him fiercely; Urmila turned in on the divan between the dining table and the Philips radiogram; thus, that innumerable wedded adults all over the world actually doss down together, in beds that are joined, night upon night, never dawned upon the subteenage Jamun.

He is spellbound when, with pubescence, he learns of sex, of copulation, how babies are spawned, when he twigs, open-mouthed, that Shyamanand must've mounted Urmila at least twice to hatch Burfi and him. The notion seems inconceivable, seismic, like the seas spiralling, out of hand, to peck at a skyline of skyscrapers. At first, Jamun balks at visualizing Urmila and Shyamanand together in one bed, mother naked, heaving, jammed; but he can't corral his fancy for long, and it prances back, time after time, to try and piece together, from the slivers of his apprehension, an abiding, tenable image of their coition; yet his imagination always sideslips to other countenances, other bodies, integrating the two to beget, not his parents, but the unbridled satyrs of burgeoning desire.

Shyamanand has enlightened his younger son on how babies are hatched. On the nights when the moon is full and simpering, Jamun, thousands of dwarfish, swarthy oarsmen forage through the damp shingle of scores of riverbanks for a curious species of minute, vermilion crab. Before the moon pales away, the boatmen scuttle about and flick the crabs down the nostrils and into the tummies of snoring, married women. The crabs that sneak in through the left nostril ripen into daughters; through the right nostril trickle in future sons. 'What about twins?' Obviously two crabs edge in simultaneously. 'Then why do we call *you* Baba?' Because before they withdraw, the sweating oarsmen purr into the ears of the napping fathers guidance for the morrow – on pocket money, homework, ablutions, fealty, football. 'Why boatmen? Why not batsmen?'

Because decades later, when you're taken, you'll need someone, and it'll be they who'll pilot you down the river.

Certainly, in the imaginations of his sons, Shyamanand's mythopoeism is to grapple with the waxing insights of boyhood, and erode in the tussle. 'You're a bloody motherfucker,' Jamun, aged nine, informs a scornful Kuki.

'Huh. You're a grandmotherfucker, greatgrandmotherfucker and a dogsucker.' Kuki leers at him with inexhaustible disdain. 'I bet you don't know what fucker means. I bet! You do? Yeah? What does it mean, fucker?'

'I won't tell you, why should I?' squawks Jamun in indignant panic. 'You can ask your fucking mother!' He's rather chuffed with the timeliness of his retort.

But not for long, because Kuki flashes back, 'You *don't* know, you don't know what fucker means! And until you tell me, you can't come to my house.'

Which is truly dire. Jamun will be bereaved of airconditioned afternoons, Monopoly, Yahtzee, outlandish foreign confectionery, the allure of lolling in other interiors, and the likely proximity of Kuki's mother, with her redolent odours and her upper arms that seem to thrust out their meat, like cheeks, into Jamun's face, no matter where he gapes.

Kuki and he have arrived at that age and mood when bawdry entrances, even when it is incompletely understood. For them, communication appears to slump to a pretext for the swapping of smut, the syllables of which titillate them into tee-hees. In time, ribaldry and the hams of Kuki's mother are augmented by Jeremiah's blubbery thighs, the inciting fetor and impudent simper of a grocer's handyman, the two issues of *Playboy* that the intrepid Kuki taps from his father's mine (along with a shrieking-coloured German glossy with foldout pages, each pleat of which discloses one smirking participant of a prodigal orgy, the whole of which splays into a chart of eight stripped, living souls twined to one another by vagina, mouth, penis, anus – the sight of which seems to crunch open Jamun's skull and stuff it with a kind of obscene turgescence) – and persistent, breathless parleys, speculation, joshing exegeses. In time, percolate into Jamun the notions that between a woman's thighs lurk neither a sort of ineffable maroon wodge, much like some primate's arse, nor a second bellybutton; that coition isn't quite Kuki's seismic theory of an ebullient penis gnawing apart a female navel furiously enough to hustle some shit through her anus; that everyone – his mother, his father, Jeremiah, Kuki, his aya, the ophthalmologist who examined him, the bilious driver of the school bus, their fish-wala, he himself – *everyone* had copulated, or would copulate, and that some of these numberless couplings would beget.

'I don't know, Kasturi, how you learnt about the carnal life – in the usual lurching way, I suppose – but isn't that really, truly the hatchet job on innocence? Just the knowing that these layers of clothing only veil a prick and a pussy made to lunge at each other – that that's the crux, the heart of the matter, the rest is sludge?'

'Phew. My parents do lunge at each other a lot, but not out of libido. Haven't your parents ever slugged each other? Mine swat 'n clout roughly once a week, as clockwork as shampooing your hair. They wouldn't brawl in front of *you*, but then who lathers his nut in the living room?'

'Well, in my presence, my parents – my mother in fact – let fly at my father just once. Some seven years ago,' in the summer when, having freshly stumbled on to the phenomenon of coitus, Jamun assiduously watches his parents for weeks for the most gossamer tokens – the graze of a touch perhaps, or a shared chuckle, an instinctive glance of communion, or an inadvertent hundred-pace stroll – the most shadowy clues to an extant comradeship, no matter how inert, that can be construed to be the precipitate of an expired infatuation. Of course Jamun senses no such sign. Urmila and Shyamanand comport themselves like two uncongenial hostelers constrained to room together for fifteen years. Certainly Jamun's never *really* expected – has instead only, fancifully, fitfully hoped that his parents, like some other parents, would be *observably* fond of each other –

that on an anniversary Shyamanand perhaps would take Urmila out to dinner and their third viewing of *The Sound of Music*. He's wished for a glimmer, a whiff, of an indication that between his parents had once lived a sensation more human than the periodic rut of primates, that Burfi and he were engendered by an emotion less evanescent than carnality. Yet he can't even envisage them prodded by lust to pat and cuddle each other, to cavort like donkeys on heat in the thick of a thoroughfare.

Midweek. A cauldron of an evening, when everything chafes like nylon on skin. Urmila and Shyamanand return from office, tuckered out, droopy. Shyamanand slips into pyjamas and subsides at the dining table to wait to glut himself to lull his peptic ulcer, rapping out on the decolam with fingers, spoon, ladle and tea-strainer a signature tune of impatience. Urmila sheds her handbag on the divan and sets to in the kitchen to worm some food out to cram her husband's maw with. Aya is AWOL, so Jamun informs her, has lumbered off to the movies directly after lunch to dodge the heat and her chores. The kitchen – minute, sleazy, fusty, vermin-plagued – at first glance seems to contain nothing edible. Like a harpy limbering up in his belly, Shyamanand's ulcer gnaws him increasingly every minute. He rises turbulently. 'There must be something, some leftovers from the afternoon – scraps. What did you lunch on, Jamun?' But Jamun can't recollect.

Her skull, it appears to Urmila, will, in a wink, gash open in a discharge of curdled blood. Her eyelids seem congealed, her head appears to wobble like a sentry dozing on his feet. The enervation of a long day, its sapping mugginess, the ineffable dispiritedness of a routine midweek evening, her piles, the abrasiveness of her husband's presence, the tension of waiting for the next squirt of his derision – all intertwine to make her sluggishly rummage through the kitchen without quite remembering what she's seeking. After some minutes she unearths, with a kind of unmindful relief, underneath a sloppily flung tea cozy, a plate of wizened chapatis atop a bowl of sour curd. The two've been abandoned there by a miffed Aya after they were spurned as inedible by her chum Kishori; to woo him anew, she's hauled him off to a blockbuster weepie.

Shyamanand dunks a good many spoons of sugar into the curd and, before plunging into glutting himself with it, debunks it as outright rancid. Near the bottom of the bowl, half-alive and certainly kicking despite a marathon smothering in a universe of curd, lie, on their backs, two enormous, mocha-brown cockroaches, their legs and antennae orbiting as though they're pedalling, upside down, two invisible bicycles. They look altogether content, all but about to coo to each other.

Urmila, in her blouse and petticoat, is at the door of the lavatory, clenching herself for the ordeal to come. Yet (like Jamun at that point of his maturation!) she, in a manner, *likes* to visit the loo more than once because, as she's times out of number apprised her tittering children, without any glint of waggishness, it's the one pocket of the house where she can be free of them and their father.

She pauses when she hears Jamun ask, 'But are they bad for the health? What if you fry them crisp, maybe they'll taste yummy, like fingers of chilli-chicken.' Chin on fists, elbows on table, tubby face scanning the cockroaches like Jehovah spying on Adam and Eve.

'Inform your mother, Jamun, that my food habits differ from hers. When I begin to relish cockroaches, I shall intimate her. Until then, however, she must not presume that we all will stomach whatever she smacks her lips over.'

Jamun snickers at Shyamanand's timbre – frosty, disciplined, like a champion skater on thin ice – and at his precision of idiom. With his wife Shyamanand is never inarticulate. He's most at ease with her, and hence most himself too, just as one doesn't square one's shoulders when one slips on an outworn, favourite dressing gown. Jamun glances at Urmila for her reaction and, foreseeably, watches her features buckle into tears. Even a mother's woe ceases to rend a heart when it becomes as commonplace a sight as the gashed graffiti on one's school desk. Her brood has viewed on Urmila's face a handful of the well worn countenances of grief; her wretchedness is not manifold enough to be perpetually appealing.

'I nibble at cockroaches, is it! After drudging in the office, I scoot home to chomp cockroaches. Yes! For sure! I manage to endure your loathesomeness only by spooning in cockroaches – live, baked, griddled, poached, minced, curried, stewed – an entire menu, along with spiders, toads . . .' Urmila ebbs away into hushed, unintelligible moans, like the soughing of the sea on distal sands. Measuredly, like a dulled, ironwilled drum, she begins to pound her forehead against the doorpost of the lavatory. The clockwork thud of bone on wood, the gentle mewling and spastic snorts for breath, the tears on her scorched-earth face – these vents of her inarticulation run on for some seconds, yet without sorely incommoding either husband or son.

Shyamanand then rises, murmuring, 'This is a real hoot. I'm a villain because I declare that I don't need cockroaches in my food. I'm still hungry, though. Is there anything in the fridge, Jamun, that I can chew these chapatis with? Cheese? Honey?'

Urmila shambles forward, atremble. 'But how can you be so beastly? To presume that I was trying to shovel cockroaches into you –'

Shyamanand screeches at her. Some particular about her, or her entire being – the thin, penduline meat of her upper arms and thorax, her unfailing expression of harassed grief, the ageing shapelessness beneath petticoat and blouse, the belly distended, thickened by parturition, the brow ploughed by the aeons of discord, the mulish, strangled psyche – galls Shyamanand to lose his habitual soberness. 'SHUT UP! I don't want to talk to you at all, on this or any other subject! Please get back to the lavatory, for that's where you belong!'

So Urmila sloshes his chest with the ladle of the curd bowl, unpremeditatedly. She could never've designedly clouted any creature; she's too chastened. The unexpectedness of Shyamanand's snarling nearly concusses her; in reflex, to stave off further horrors, she bats him with the first object at hand.

The cockroaches hotfoot down Shyamanand's vest (trailed

sedately by crawling driblets of curd), bound on to the table, and scurry away like two triumphant spearheads fleeing their demented fans at the cliffhanging close of a football tie.

Stillness, for a minute. Urmila totters back a pace or two, exhausted, appalled at herself. Shyamanand, almost as disturbed, stares unmindfully at the dabs of curd on his chest, resembling stranded alpinists on a precipice. The solitary thought in Jamun's skull at that instant is (in the manner that we have, when thunderstruck, of conjuring up only the ridiculous, the fantastic) that if Shyamanand thwacks Urmila in requital, she, infirm that she is, will never be able to retain her clenched sphincter.

'Oh, but that's no tiff, that's bloody foreplay,' pooh-poohs Kasturi, 'compared to how my parents maul each other. Though they still do have it off – maybe twice a month. I know, because I've spotted condoms in my father's wallet, in slithery pink plastic packaging. You positive that your parents don't sleep with each other, say, twice a year? At Diwali and Holi or something? So what if they're fifty plus? Because they all itch to mount and tup, even when they loathe each other.'

Jamun spends twenty minutes rooting about the house for a vase that won't leak and finally returns to Urmila's room with Doom's porridge mug. His nephews dog him like the bogies a train engine, and huddle around him, ghoulishly curious, to gape at him compose Joyce's anniversary roses. He notices that Urmila's eyes are open, that she appears to be observing him, but he says nothing. 'Aya'll be livid,' pronounces Pista joyously – 'livid' is one of Joyce's pet words – 'when she finds out that you've used Doom's porridge mug for these flowers.'

'What time is it?' asks Urmila.

The brats instantly forsake the roses to crowd her bed. 'Ten-fifteen,' replies Jamun. 'You must be feeling too flaked out to even contemplate that stroll.' Urmila pulps the meat about her right collarbone and looks befuddled, inert, far away, adrift; so he plods on, 'We could step just fifty paces – even twenty . . . We'll pull up the *instant* you feel wobbly . . . The kids'll accompany us, Doom could even ride his tricycle . . . The weather's terrific . . . The sea air'll fumigate your head, it's more wholesome than the jadedness of your room . . . Today'd be a super day to launch Haldia's cheapest advice on – your anniversary . . . Joyce's roses are even lovelier than the gladioli – weren't those lanky ones gladioli? – that Philip Jonas colour-washed your hospital cubicle with . . .' Thus he natters on, because Urmila voices not a word but, compliant like a sleep-walker, acquiesces in whatever he pilots her to. So she slips on Pista's gym shoes (which nip her toes ludicrously, but the novelty, the sentimentality, the bounty of the offer she'd never've been able to withstand), tidies up her sari, unsnarls her hair, practises her weight on one of Shyamanand's walking sticks. She vivifies and speaks only when Jamun hands her her spectacles. 'No, I don't need them.'

'Of course you do. You won't make out where you're trudging to, or on what you're treading. Spectacleless, you'll return with even your ankles daubed with the droppings of various organisms. To sidestep the turds of pissed fishermen is more important, wouldn't you agree, than to appear in front of them as evergreen, lustrous-eyed and sexy?'

'I am *not* exerting myself and stamping out somewhere only to goggle, in razor-edge focus, at the pus, sputum and nightsoil on these pavements. Spectacles aren't, at my age, meant to help me to peep at yuk, to wince, shudder and swerve!'

'But this is India! Heh-heh. Wisecracks aside, let's march. Your first constitutional shouldn't be stalled by either my measly wit or your worthless vision.'

He doesn't exhort his mother any further to put on her spectacles; he knows that she abhors her pair as much as he his, that she's, time and time again, sought to mislay them, shatter them, or forsake them in thronged places. In this matter, neither mother nor son are swayed wholly by vanity; they, ever so often, actually like the snugness of blurred surroundings, the fuzzy sensation of existing in a mammoth, tepid, soft-focus womb, wherein skulks no peril, for in that indistinctness – in which a fulgent sword and a silver hawk are one, and a human skull can well resemble a white clown in dark glasses – all contours of menace can soften to appear cosy, like those of a timeworn, favourite pillow with its individual smell.

'Besides, you'll be there, Jamun, alongside me when I totter and plod. Can't I trust you to keep me apart from the shit? After all, what are sons for?'

'Well, Baba isn't tagging along with us, if that's what you mean. Though he should – it'd profit him too.'

Urmila, Shyamanand's walking stick, Jamun, two gambolling, factious nephews and one cherry-red tricycle. Shyamanand shambles out to the ground-floor, and Aya to the upstairs, verandahs to spectate, root for, and chuckle. Urmila – shrivelled, roundshouldered, befuddled – falters twenty steps to the gate, halts and begins to plead exhaustion, giddiness, twinges in her joints, murmurs in her heart, proximal death. She and Jamun bicker till she starts to snivel; then, peeved with each other, yet muffledly pleased with their wrangling, continue their amble, down the lane, through the wicket in the boundary wall of the housing estate – and thence into the hurly-burly, the snarl, of the hutches of the fishermen.

Scattily mumbling and squeaking her strictures, Urmila, spectacleless yet Argus-eyed, inches past the hovels (of brick, mud, asbestos, pilfered boards, cardboard, canvas, jute sacking, motley flapping polythene, yesteryear's newspapers) crested by TV antennae, the yawning sewers of rank, pestilential ooze the tint of pus, the scrum of round-eyed urchins, with turgescent tummies and moustaches of snot, frolicking, playing hopscotch, marbles, a sort of cricket, the standby and laidup dinghies, scummy, mouldering, at close quarters disagreeably large and seemingly unwieldy; the fishing nets, their measureless rhomboids of cord somehow resembling a sea of sloughed off snakeskins desiccating in the sun; the paan stalls, all mirror and white tile, like a loo for the villain of a Bombay movie (but with a paan wala in it! – perhaps crosslegged on the commode, with his paan leaves in the sink), whinnying out the trendiest Hindi boogie-woogie; about the stalls, dawdling, the lotuseater generation, in Ulhasnager Calvin Kleins, painstakingly scruffy, mincing and posturing as though modelling for cigarettes, aftershaves, condoms, shunning till lunch their warrens, their mothers and the chores that've been deferred for weeks, clutching, cuddling, squeezing one another's hands, waists, thighs, arses, genitals, in that lubricity wherein anything will momentarily sate, even a straggling pig, as long as it tussles; the sickly, knackered palms; the yards of washing on the shingle behind the shanties; the squash of housewives in the quagmire around the handpump, scouring puling toddlers who forget to blubber when they spot Doom's tricycle; the fearsome pong of a billion fish parching on perplexing cement slabs the size of double beds; the stridor of shrewish bickering, of matrons snarling at plastered husbands, of a hundred bicycle bells, the unthinking yawping of dulled hawkers, cubs squealing bawdry and arraigning one another with cheating, the undying Hindi film muzak, which, by the time Urmila fetches up at the hem of the row, has melted into a syrupy ghazal with a timbre whose opulence seems to ooze from the wrinkles between the crooner's anus and scrotum; then, sensing before feeling on their skins the muggy breeze, they tack with the compound wall to squint at the calloused sands and a steelish sliver of sea.

'Oof. Some stroll,' bleats Urmila. 'I'll sink into this for just three minutes, try and revive before returning. Oof. Never again.' She and Jamun subside on to a pink-stone bench on which, over the donor's mawkish proclamation, has been etched by a zealot: 'JESUS IS COMING SOON', beneath which has been postscripted by a wag: 'TO HELP US CUNTS WHAM PAKISTAN IN CRICKET, AND HOCKEY, AND WAR'. Pista and Doom, tricycle forsaken, scamper away to gawp at the monkeys jig and whirl; rather, Pista lopes off and Doom wobbles after him, mighty dome and jumbo rump touch and go on his isthmian shanks.

Jamun watches him totter away. Doom's podgy gawkishness

irrepressibly reminds him of the distresses of his own puppyhood, when he too was derided for ungainliness, for nosediving without reason every five paces, for losing every single scrap that he was baited into, for bawling at all nicks to his body and his heart, for being hopeless at marbles, kiteflying, treeclambering, for being selected for a game always at the butt end, just to eke out a side. Jamun had assumed that Doom would intuitively cling to him, simply because Doom raked up Jamun's own puppyhood, and therefore in disposition they must be one. He's rancorously tickled to elicit from the years that tenderness between kin is never instinctive, never just a spinoff of cognation, that Pista and Doom do not adore him out of some fathomless consanguineous sympathy, that fondness – among uncle and nephew, and parent and issue – has to be assiduously fostered, like a dimpled babe on its back, on a fresh sky-blue sheet, ogling its mum and gurgling.

While Urmila natters on, unheeding whether Jamun listens, gratified (though she'll never concede it) to lounge in the sun and breeze of a tepid November, he, with a smirk of empathy, observes a maddened Doom frisk about the hem of the knot of slackers around the monkey-man, doing his damnedest to ferret a route through adult hams and adolescent haunches to the epicentre for an eyeful of the cavorters.

Filial love. To bewail its attrition is the singularity in Shyamanand that his sons, times out of number, have smirked at, cocksure that they themselves will never ache likewise, that cognate fondness is passé, outworn, hardly the burden of those who dab their armpits with Halston and encourage an illjudged Americanness to bespatter their enunciation when they converse with all foreigners: '. . . Jeez . . . shucks . . . bucks . . . geewhiz . . .'

Show over. The scroungers diffuse across the beach before the monkeys can paw them for a tip. From the dumbshow in the near distance, and from a commonality of experience (by which what befalls Pista and Doom at any sole instant only seems to rerun, in essence, what issued with Burfi and him some twenty-five years ago), Jamun recognizes that the monkey-man is trying to sweet-talk the brats to scamper across to the bench for a baksheesh for him. Doom, at ease, eyes Pista for guidance in the matter; Pista, recalling his father's derision of those who kowtow to pestering entreaties for tips, and yet joyously bewitched by the monkey-man's personality – the witchery of which is his livelihood – simpers witlessly at the universe. Tenderness goosefleshes Jamun as he watches his nephews scoot, and flounder, back to Urmila and him. Will his memory – as wilful as a circumspect cat – salt away this instant of his fondness, this frame of two laughing children haring across nondescript sands, against a shoddy sea, to meet him? Won't he rather smack his lips over the thousand inevitable instances of their heedlessness, when they've been too up-and-doing with living to remember to give tongue to love, have deemed that a grandmother or an uncle will eternally be there to ease the flapping of the heart, have assumed the philanthrope's bench across a few feet of sand?

Pista of course fetches up first, cherry-red, huffing, touches the victory post of Jamun's knee, and twirls to boo Doom's tottering progress – 'Roly-poly-snaily! Roly-poly-snaily!' Jamun is quckened to countermine, 'No, no, don't listen to him Doomo! C'mon Doomo, you're really zipping Doomo! Abibe Bekila, Doomo!' Chortling irrepressibly, breathless, with ecstatic eyes in a carmine face, Doom scuds up to tumble into his uncle's lap. Jamun cuddles him hard, and nuzzles the warm, plump, talcumed neck. Pista, needled perhaps by this show of love to a kind of neck-and-neck jealousy, disregarding Urmila's bogus protests against his weight, plonks down and starts to rock on his grandmother's knee. How piteous Shyamanand and his sons are, reflects Jamun turbidly – with his chin roosting on Doom's head, palm spreadeagled on the soft child-chest, feeling through the cotton the heart thudding like the diesel engine of a rice mill across miles of field – for nurturing their remembrances of one another on instances not of unprompted affection, but of putative affront – doubtless not wholly putative, which was even more piteous, that in one's fosterage, with one's blood, with whom one is entirely naked, one shows more balefulness than charity, just because with them one is snug, and can be oneself.

The notion didn't dishearten Burfi in the least. 'You take any fucker. Any fucker anywhere in the world, he's secretly vindictive, viperous with his what are called near and dear ones. It's natural – like shitting once a day if your tummy's okay. With those we're completely restful with, in front of whom we can loll and fondle our balls through our lungis – with them we're time and time again feral, churlish, baleful, till our vitriol pricks us to contrition and pity – which is what tenderness is when untouched by carnality. Libido brews well with loathing, don't you think, a sort of malevolent rage at the golden body that one hungers for. That's what I believe, at any rate – we find malignity comfy, we're rancorous just so we can goad ourselves into love. Thank God for the family. Without it, how could we grapple with the world?'

Flattered that Pista is comfortable on her knee, Urmila, with her shrivelled hands on his back, sighs and continues her natter. 'Have you read Chhana's last letter? No? You brothers've done with communicating with her or what? It arrived some four days ago. I know that Burfi hasn't riffled through it, your father refused last night to hand over the letter. "It's not meant for you, Burfi," he sneered, "it's only from a lower-middle-class niece to her lower-middle-class uncle." Of course Burfi mooched upstairs, quite riled. All this while we were wasting our time and money at Haldia's. Really, who's more infantile, your brother or your father? You do remember that rumpus between Burfi and your Baba?'

'Which of them, Ma? In the past twenty-five years, the rest of us together've achieved, on an average, one earthshaking and three frivolous wrangles with Baba per week. You and Burfi head the charts, neck and neck. The one about our letter-writing manners was ages ago, wasn't it, just after Burfi married, when the savour of Joyce's world seemed to grate him with what he concluded was the coarseness of his own past.' Yes, Ma, I remember. We *are* our parents' sons. If the recollection is ugly, we never forget: we tack it on to the anthills in our minds.

The family's always written common letters to one another. If from Amsterdam, for instance, Joyce addresses a picture postcard to Jamun, the other inhabitants of the house can rightly suppose that her 'Wish You Were Here' is equally meant for them. Burfi writes to Urmila, and Shyamanand replies: 'Received your letter of 16.4; your longhand's even more illegible than before . . .' They unthinkingly slit open one another's letters when they recognize the handwriting to be parent's, brother's, son's'. Envelopes from acquaintances who are aware of and beguiled by this communion in correspondence are sometimes marked: 'For Your Eyes Only'. Nobody in the family thinks the quirk queer, leave alone shameful, till Burfi marries, and Joyce, stupefied, gawps at Jamun rip open Chhana's letter to her husband.

Afterwards, Burfi, plainly goaded by his wife's derision, strives to expound to his brother how wedlock has refined him. 'You see, Jamun, people of class simply don't tear open others' letters, just as they don't burp and gurk in public like fetid volcanoes. I'm certain – '

'People of class? Phew. I'm appalled' – Jamun is now eighteen, when 'appalled' sounds really good – 'that I'm actually related to someone who can, without flagellating himself like a Muharram freakout, actually use the phrase, "people of class". Whom do you – '

'– that none of your soulmates apologizes after belching into your mug, and up your nostrils, perhaps because your face deserves it. But do they even *know* that to burp in front of others is as vulgar as to fart? Bet they don't. Not even that new bomb of yours, Kasturi, that squat one who wants bad. Her eyes become like damp pussies whenever she peeps at me. Have you fucked her yet? Bet she and you suspect that fuck means to burp into each other's noses without warning. Joyce was zapped – and how fucking embarrassing, that she had to hiss at me, "in the presence of my friends at least, please don't belch like a Guinness Book hopeful. Jesus, I feel so goofy proposing to a husband that he burp less, that he finish each eructation with an Excuse me, or Sorry, or something." Would you enjoy hearing that from a wife?

'Then Joyce has spotted Baba writing postcards to Chhana. Baba's not exactly her honeybaby, you know. Why doesn't your father, she asked, use envelopes and inlands? They aren't – she couldn't resist suffixing – that prohibitive. She was correct in her raillery – she's brainier than me anyway. Postcards, burps, to dip into others' letters, to slip into lungi and sandow vest the instant you return from office, to wear striped string drawers instead of elastic undies, and use homemade STs of discarded sari swatches and newspapers, and two languages for interlocution at home – your own lingo with your parents and their age, English with your own quartet – all, all that we were was so squalidly LMC: the castoff bedlinen for curtains, newspapers for tablemats – I've defined for Joyce what we were, how in Bhubaneshwar, repaying the housing society scrunched up Ma's salary, and month upon month she hocked, pawned, borrowed, to buy her provender. Joyce understood in a wink, she's really quick-witted' – asserts Burfi in the besottedness, the early lambency, of his marriage – 'how we, you and I, hauled ourselves – the family, I mean – out of the ooze, just by making good, so that Baba and Ma, correctly, can show us off, like the first colour TV in the locality.'

Jamun at that age thrills in the origination of discord; so he forthwith recites to Shyamanand that the new Burfi has just declared that his wife's graces have disclosed to him the shoddy, outrageous lower-middle-classness of his previous avatar. Afterwards, Shyamanand and Burfi squabble halfheartedly, and Shyamanand, for corrupting his firstborn so, notches up yet one more grouse against Joyce, of which there already exist a dozen; when he's downhearted, lonely, feels untended, overlooked, he reanimates any one grudge, and consequently declines a rare airing with his grandchildren in Burfi's Maruti because he senses that Joyce won't welcome his presence; or he's peeved that Burfi hasn't asked after a recent letter from Chhana, infers that even the shrivelling of his care for his kin is due to his wife's straddling of his wits, next acquaints Burfi with the arrival of the letter, but does *not* hand it over, maintaining that it's too lower-middle-class for his wife and him; which doesn't disquiet Burfi immoderately, for Time's sedate sledgehammer *does* lame the bonds between kith and kin, but as creatures of the beaten track, he and Shyamanand just can't permit a chance to bicker to glide by.

'Chhana's so thoughtless,' runs on Urmila, in a relaxed whine. 'At the end of the letter, simply because she must eke out at least one page – otherwise an eight-line note after weeks looks too ludicrous – she's scribbled: "Last week, I suffered a spurt of piles, but after a day or two the sonofabitch subsided, thank God. I'll write again soon. My love to all," etcetera. So goofy; she should know that piles is *not* like, well, electricity – it doesn't just come and go. And why must she use expletives in her letters to us? And which sane person'd chat about her *piles* in a letter? So much for your father's immaculate family – Chhana was fifteen when she first showed up to stay. She'd spent three years in the same class in school. Your Baba swaggered to his sister, "Send her to me. In six months, I'll reform her into a brilliant student." Huh. And to me, he shammed, "She can lend you a hand with Burfi." Huh! And he jeers at *my* family, exploiting Belu's freakishness as an instance! "If I hadn't been charitable enough to marry you," he blubbered at me once, "you'd've lurched into the sewer, where you and your kin rightfully belong" – but you were there when he – yes, you were, that frightening squall on that September evening, some weeks after his stroke, of course you were, because you half-heaved, half-hauled him out to the verandah for the sunset. I was hotly restless at the tension on your face, and he by then had a fertile stubble, silvery . . .' like a venerable Hollywood POW, recalls Jamun, masterminding an enthralling getaway from under the ice-blue Aryan eyes of a fiendish, Teutonic camp commandant.

He doesn't interrupt Urmila, even though he dislikes her indiscreet commentary in the presence of her grandchildren – perhaps because her tempered whine is almost lulling, at one with the warm wafts from the sea and the smirking sun. Her husband is her obsessive topic – his incivility, his nutrition, his gluttonous appetite, in that peculiar order. For thirty-seven years she's been harrowed by her catastrophic marriage. So has her husband. That he needs her company only as a butt for his derision, as an ear for his ridicule of the absent, gnaws her beyond repression. Her mien, the bleakness in her features, her being itself, envenoms him too. In turn they crab about each other to whichever of their sons is disposed to listen; Urmila crabs more than Shyamanand.

For days he won't speak to her or answer her, even when her questions concern his welfare, his nourishment, his existence. 'Since your tummy's upset, will you drink a glass of lassi at lunch? . . . That shirt that you've been rotting in for ages – why don't you send it to the dhobi?' In reply, he slouches even more implacably over the bank passbooks on his desk, or hoists the science periodical in his hand to wall off her lugubrious face, or, with irksome staginess, as a final expedient, hobbles out of the room. She weeps almost every time from impotence and rage; her pulped face is as much an image of home as their diminutive unkept garden, or the leavings of lunch on the dining table that Aya won't evacuate till dinner; Urmila's subdued lamentation is as household as the tearfulness of a widow being bullied by her petulant daughters-in-law in a Hindi weepie on Sunday TV.

Times out of number, in his featureless college years, Jamun has returned home at an unpredicted hour to stumble on his mother huddled in their house's most sombre room, blubbering, or quiescent after sobbing – a shadowy contour in the owl-light of the downstairs drawing room, with ashen strands all anyhow about her bloodless face, as though a giant fist has randomly lobbed her into a nook. 'What is it this time? Your favourite ogre? Or your BP? Piles? Corns? Arthritis? Aya? She isn't letting you clean up her droppings, or what? Or is it a letter from Burfi, trying to cadge the entire savings of the softest touch in the cosmos?'

When the pique spawned by the day has thus been voided on her, the family sink, Urmila's features disintegrate afresh; hearing her sobs, staring at her delicately shrivelled skin, Jamun inflames with the tenderness of contrition and, without warning, finds that the root of his throat has gorged. Then, hugging her, nestling against her neck, nosing the striae of Pond's Dreamflower talcum on her throat, kissing her tears, feels marvellous, like a virile, veined forearm bridling, cradling, hushing the thunder in his heart. 'What's it this time, Ma? Please tell me. I want to see you smile. Through your tears, I want to see your smile, like the sun.'

Seven times out of ten, Shyamanand's fathered her woe.

'Oof, you're such a goose, Ma, for allowing us to harrow you in a thousand ways.' He kisses her eyelids. 'We must've harangued you numberless times to retaliate, return like for like, but you're as mulish as an ass – oh, how idiotic that sounds. But if Baba's not speaking to you, then don't ask him a thing! He must learn through discomfort how vital you are for him. When I'm sullen, and heartless, and abusive with you, you only dribble tears and call me my father's son. Instead, you *must* draw blood in return, lash for lash. Though your tears' – he twinkles at her, hoping to rouse her to a smile – 'are a passable weapon. Yet you've never ever practised our advice on any matter – stop that daylong nibbling at that cheap clay, it'll enrich your mouth with cancer. Stop threshing about all the time over Baba's welfare – he isn't worth it. Did Baba sleep well last night? Is Baba constipated today? Phew, wouldn't you rather mull over some other subject? Perhaps you wouldn't. But isn't it enervating, killing, to be rebuffed time after time by every single creature around you? By Baba, your children, Aya, Aya's cronies, your relatives in Calcutta who write only when they've to grouse against you? Your one retort is that all mothers are decreed to be the family punching bag. Oof, Ma, you're an A-one bore.'

'You shouldn't say such things to your mother,' she murmurs

with pensive disapproval, between blowing her nose into the fringe of her sari.

Her inflexion surprises him. Her sons've belittled her as tremendously dreary a thousand times before. As she trudges to the door, she suffixes dispiritedly, 'And if your Baba hears that you called me a whore, he'll, instead of rebuking *you*, scoff at me even more for not having nurtured you rightly.'

'Ma! You're insane!' He is flabbergasted, as though, wholly without warning, invisible talons have clenched at his heart, tried to puncture it into repose. 'God. I didn't call you a whore, I said *Bore – B*.' He can't swallow the leadenness of her retort. Her deadness alarms him. 'But if your child calls you a whore, you should be livid, berserk with fury! How can you react so lumpishly!' He even starts to kindle. 'And you actually presume that *I* could use smut to describe you? My God, Ma, what sort of a ghoul of a son d'you imagine me to be?' He checks himself out of a kind of terror as his mother begins to blubber anew.

'Blame me! Taunt me! Day in day out, till the death of time, all of you jeering at me, thwacking me over the knuckles, licking your lips at each pinch, gunning for me as for balloons at a fair! D'you fancy I don't know? "Ma, you still haven't stitched that button on my shirt . . . Ma, you forgot to give Baba his after-lunch capsules . . ." Ma this, and Ma that! I can't – no, don't touch me!' She screeches weakly at him and, with untypical spiritedness, jounces off the hand that he, to hearten himself more than her, unconsciously extends forward. In the snarl of his wits careen the grisly thoughts that perhaps he doesn't know his mother *at all*, that, very likely, the ordeal of fostering a paralysed husband is stealthily deranging her. He at least enjoys the allures of college – Kasturi, Kuki and his other chums; he can steal away at six-thirty in the morning to jam himself into the university bus, can skip all his classes to trip for four hours on marijuana in an anonymous hostel room, can dishevelledly speculate whether and where he can that afternoon unclothe Kasturi, can, enervated and sullen, return home at any hour between seven p.m. and the next dawn, always to find his mother waiting – bloodless, careworn and waiting – sometimes to hear Shyamanand forebode, 'In your entire life, no one will wait for you as we've waited. To no one else will you matter even a fraction as much'; can extenuate his truancy with mumbled lies – the bus conked out, or he lost track of time amidst the leathered tomes in the library. He thus can slink away from his responsibilities; Urmila, however, has no byways of deliverance.

'I'm going to make myself some tea,' she announces, intentionally altering her tone and the subject. 'Would you like a cup? And have you nibbled at anything since the morning? Because you look ghastly as usual, peaked – as though you're tuberculous. You've totally lost the cherub of your adolescence . . . Ask your father whether he too wants tea. Now that you're back, you can bicker with him, and keep him off my back awhile.'

Yet Shyamanand is no rogue. He only hankers after the love of his children, and is befuddled and piqued that they plainly prefer their mother; of course, he can never grasp that she's simply a better human being, softer, more merciful. Instead, the years of fosterage creepingly persuade him that the fondness between mother and sons is potent only because it's genetic, is the primal sexual bond between father and daughter, and mother and son; this conviction itself pillories him because it is he who's always yearned to sire sons, and chortled in triumph even at the birth of his grandsons. 'How'll you escape,' he whoops to Burfi, 'the bliss of manliness? So what if your wife, that dear adorer of matriliny, pants for daughters?' He'd been apprehensive in Jamun's case, jittery that a second male child would be a godsend beyond his portion.

Hence he's exquisitely taunted to see his sons cleave unto their mother, and the eldest crawl from her to his wife.

'Please don't bother me, Jamun, with this drivel. All that I implore of your mother is that she not speak to me, on any matter. Is that too much to hope for? I want to sidestep all discord, friction. I'm sorry, but your mother frets me dreadfully. Her droopy, doleful face, her washed-out voice – a martyr hanging on despite indescribable torment – the monotony of her world, all tea, food and TV – her entire disposition, her stodgy questions that drag out the day – Should she cook curry or fry the fish? Would you like chillies in the dal? – fatuous questions because nothing in our house improves, ever – *everything* about your mother galls me. She conducts herself as though without her I'd croak, *instantly*, and at the same time, the tuckered out tedium on her features when she's helping me with anything – my bath or my clothes – far exceeds the irksomeness even on yours. You know full well that the most well-meaning exchange between your mother and me can detonate a squabble, so I wish to shun all dialogue with her.'

'Great, but your heroics won't work, not with your body in this state. With one operative arm and leg, you just have to depend on Ma and me. And we aren't really hellhounds, are we?'

When Pista and Doom start to fidget, Jamun proposes that they return home. 'We've been here for almost forty-five minutes. Not bad, considering the fuss you kicked up.'

But Urmila seems averse to struggling up from the bench, to losing three peaceful listeners. She's begun her analysis, voiced scores of times in the foregoing two months, of exactly how Shyamanand has expended some of his beloved money on resurrecting her, only because he yearns for someone to needle and goad, and because he realizes that he'll be gradually abandoned by his brood on Urmila's death, like an object no longer of value, a fusty dressing gown, or a gramophone when one has bought a CD, etcetera.

'That's *your* wishful thinking,' Jamun caustically interrupts her, half-nettled because he isn't certain that she isn't correct; he credits her with singular, impressionistic astuteness because she trusts the heart.

'In those horrible years when I didn't have the cash for soap and bread, when my salary was chewed up by the ridiculous claims of middleclassness – income tax, school fees, Provident Fund subscriptions, titanic deductions for loans for this house –

Aya'd ever so often sizzle at me, "Tell your damn husband not to squirrel away his small change for the future. There is no future. Assert yourself against this farcical arrangement, by which he stashes away his money while yours frisks out of your fist like a frog." But I could never carry weight with anybody – your father, Aya, you two, anybody. And dredging cash out of your Baba is as smooth as milking a bullock – or Burfi, I should add. Now – how derisive it is! – life will jeer at him again and again.

'I'll never forget one particular scene from his hospital spell a decade ago. His limbs were lumpish, stagnant. His left eye started out like a marble embedded in a jelly of blood – crimson and cream. His left cheek'd been yanked down, and reminded me somehow of linen being tugged off a clothesline by a grumpy servant. In his paralysis he didn't want to be gawped at by anyone, I guess, because he strained to curl himself up, away from me, when I neared the bed, but he couldn't – his entire left flank was frozen. He moaned with the struggle, a gentle, dull mewling. The notion then jolted me – that with minds, with souls, like ours, the real miracle was that our bodies didn't warp and buckle for decades! Within us all twitches and froths so much wrath and envy, malignity, churlishness, yearning – all weltering – that the body must, by and by, slump, moulder to express this enervation. At last, Baba's frozenness seemed to declare, this is the real me, undistorted; in this ice flesh is sheathed the real life.' Urmila, silent for a moment in remembrance, then tousles Pista's hair and murmurs bemusedly, 'You two need haircuts. Come, time to shuffle back, check what your grandfather's been up to.'

# 5

# THE COLD SWEAT YEARS

Jamun was then seventeen, or thereabouts, at the start of the cold sweat years. In fifteen months much befalls his family. Burfi marries Joyce – altogether confounding Shyamanand – and is yanked away from home by work. At fifty-eight, Shyamanand retires from government service. Urmila endures the ordeal of a perturbingly late menopause. They quit their government flatlet of a decade and occupy their very own shred of earth, of rock and desert sand, by the sea. A dying Aya is shunted to a charitable TB clinic. Jamun and Kasturi, for the first time in their lives, mount each other, love it, and reconnoitre thereafter, for ever and ever, for cloistered space. Urmila rebuffs Shyamanand's conditional offer to repay her debts. She surprises everyone by agreeing to spend a fortnight with Burfi two thousand kilometres away. In her absence, a blood clot gags an artery somewhere in Shyamanand's skull and benumbs his left arm and leg. The stroke also chokes his vocability, shrinks it to a sort of slurred moan.

July. Hot rain in the afternoon. Shyamanand presumes that he's alone at home. He feels intolerably listless, subsides into a basket chair in the downstairs verandah. Other houses, unsightly in their incompletion, have sprouted all about him. He likes the notion of frenzied brick-and-cement activity in the neighbourhood; it suggests that he's done well to raise a house when and where he did. Yet he's also peeved that in the last few months he's lost a prospect of the sea. The rain seems to immure him in its mugginess.

Jamun and Kasturi are upstairs. In the new house, Jamun can presume the entire first floor to be his own – a heady reverie – can daydream how, when, in what position, he'll have it off with whom, in which room. While Urmila's away, he can even effectuate a hunk of one fantasy, cajole Kasturi to undress upstairs, convince her that no one ever ascends the stairs, ever fetches up on the first floor save in the fake-winter weeks, when they come looking for the sun.

Both of them say 'bye to Shyamanand quite early in the morning. 'Just can't skip today's classes. Too crucial. Don't forget at lunch to finish off that leftover kheer, and if that bastard electrician shows up, please remember the bulb in the fridge.' Then they exit by the gate, but slink down the long flank of the house, scramble over the boundary wall, edge in by the side door and, snickering with the tension of proximal sexual fulfilment, tiptoe up the stairs.

After his retirement, Shyamanand has in fact become the watchdog of his newly-built house. On weekdays, after watching Jamun hare off to the university virtually at sunrise, he mooches about till Urmila scoots, at nine, all helter-skelter, for her office bus. Till six in the evening, when she returns, he's alone, friendless but for his anxieties and the instructions for the day that his wife and son assign to him. 'Don't pay the dhobi until he satisfactorily explains that violet blotch on my bedspread.' This injunction, for instance, will flounder in his mind alongside the concern: if I don't bribe the Corporation Surveyor when he drops in for the taxes, by how much will he jack up the dues for this year? 'When the electricity vanishes for three hours this afternoon, will you remember to boil the milk?' Burfi is now distant, unlikely to return to this nest other than evanescently; in due time Jamun'll also take wing: then what've I struggled to erect this house for? A home is for one's children. When Urmila and I die, who'll occupy and care for this house? For a dwelling needs to be fostered as much as a child or a parent. My sons, empty of sentiment, will lease the house out to some moneyed stranger, who'll be displeased with its tectonics, will propound hideous alterations, to which they'll readily assent; our edifice will be as effaced as our remembrance.

Watchdog. Day after day after day, for months, Shyamanand positions himself behind the curtains of the drawing room to spy on the gate, or the outmoded tallboy in the dining room to watch the boundary wall of the house, and five yards beyond it, the compound wall of the estate, behind which infringe the fishermen, the beach and the sea.

He rather enjoys the cameo of snooper, though his misgivings about vandals are not wholly groundless. The housing colony is new – even unexpected, since it's been erected on land that the Corporation never objectively believed could be reclaimed from the wastelands that sprawl, like layabouts, by the sea. Within months surge on that barrenness imitation chalets, villas, manors, lodges and, diffident among these vulgarities, the smaller, shyly imaginative bungalows of those who, like Shyam-anand, raise a home with some of a mother's passion. The stir of construction over a good many acres – precisely the steadfast bustle of ants about their business – allure to the colony the wastrels, scroungers, tramps, the irremediably down and out, all rooting about for the odd job, their daily bread, the fast buck; some of these become the inept nightguards of timber and expensive stone, and the observers of the unlatched backdoors on some yawning afternoon. The buzz of the neighbourhood – of an audacious midday housebreak in the outlaying quarter of the estate, or of gold earrings gashed off a screaming housewife on the colony's most teeming street by a deft pillionrider, or of the knifing at his doorstep, of the acquaintance of an acquaintance, by a rebuffed salesman – disconcerts the residents; at fifty-five plus, most of them only half-relish the notion of being pioneers, as it were, in the colonization of some acres of wasteland. Many of them, disinclined to view their prudence as panic, cordon their verandahs and pattern their windows with iron grilles of hideous design. 'These grille patterns of all these houses,' observes Burfi on his first sojourn, 'would *instantly* send any thief for a long shit. Quite brilliant.' A handful of families pick up enormous curs with tongues out of a cartoon strip; deplorably, the curs are scared shitless of the neighbourhood strays, are adroit only at furtively fucking the local bitches; other households economize and, though dogless, append dictums of warning on their nameplates:

'Chandrakant Mohanty. Joint Medical Superintendent (Retired). Former Additional Health Officer. 64 Sagar Estate. Beware of Dog.' For those who don't comprehend the caution, beside the bellpush, perhaps, will be a portrait, on a tin plate, of a cur, usually a hybrid of Mickey Mouse and the Phantom.

Possibly Shyamanand doesn't wish to squander any money on a pet, or on admonitions against it, electing rather to spy on his own house from within – to twitch at each jangle of the doorbell, every clang of the gate, to suspect, and wrangle with, and scoff at the assertions of identity of, unknowns through closed windows: of inspectors of the Corporation water supply meters, and footweary saleswomen (salespersons!) from the local bakeries vending cookies that stink of egg and vanilla, and fund collectors for vicinal welfare organizations – to garner for the evening, when Urmila and Jamun return, alarmist anecdotes of the day, of larcenies and thuggery snookered by his cleverness.

Now and then, Urmila and Jamun do return home together. If by four in the afternoon, Jamun is nauseated by the route of his day – by the company, the smut and hilarity, the stupefaction of pot – he buses the ten kilometres to his mother's office so that they can both take her department bus home.

He enjoys the long ride with her, snug, becalming; his guilt at shunning his parents for the whole day is dulled. Her usual moroseness is magically effaced whenever she sees him at the door of her room. However, when they plod the few steps from the bus stop to the house, they feel – at the image of Shyamanand immured in the house, rambling from room to room with his unsociability – shyly dejected, much as though they've been whooping it up at his expense, as though he's incarcerated himself only so that they can junket without a care.

Jamun presses the doorbell, but hears no responding tinny first notes of Jingle Bells. The bell is one of the million items of dissension between Shyamanand and his son. Jamun considers it vulgar, a bell befitting that sort of household in which the refrigerator, television, telephone and stereo system are all crammed into the drawing room, as luxuries to humble the visitor with. On this subject, as on practically all others, the sojourning Burfi sides with Jamun against Shyamanand, and Urmila is weakly neutral. 'Jeez,' Burfi remarks, 'Jeez. Thank God I don't stay in a house where the doorbell tinkles out fucking Jingle Bells. Why doesn't Baba prance around dressed up as Hanuman instead?'

No electricity. 'Revolting,' grumbles Urmila, subsiding into a verandah basketchair. 'No more voting for me. Our electric meter's probably ticking away, though – perhaps they're charging us for sweating it out.'

'We could complain, if you like, to the Department of Maya and Public Grievances, heh-heh.' Jamun continues to knock on the front door, louder each time. His knuckles start to hurt. 'What's the matter with Baba? Without the fan, he can't be snoozing that heavily.' He thumps the door a couple of times more, and bridles himself from glancing at Urmila. 'I'll check the back. Perhaps he's in the loo or something.'

On the wall alongside the lately transplanted cactus, with the juice of a few squeezed neem leaves, has been illegibly scrawled a couple of Hindi words that Jamun intuitively knows to be smut. Brow corrugated by anxiety, speculating confusedly over which visitor to the house could've scribbled the filth, he tests the side and rear doors. Bolted. He hears Urmila pummelling on the front door. He has to resolve the problem somehow, if only to stall her dreadful buffeting.

He ends by clambering up to the first-floor rear verandah by way of the grille and the overhang of the kitchen windows. It isn't easy. He's further enervated by his uneasiness and the lassitude of the ebbing elation of marijuana. The door to the verandah is luckily unlatched. He lurches down the steps three at a time. Shyamanand is in bed, unmoving, with eyes shut. Jamun halts only to check whether his chest is heaving, then darts to let Urmila in.

Shyamanand *is* asleep, a dead, macabre hibernation. They stare at him, both rattled and relieved, half-scared to wake him up. The febrile stillness of the room is disturbed by the stifled stridor of traffic and Shyamanand's sluggish, rasping inhalations. Urmila, never to remain quiet for long, begins, with a few clucking sounds, to murmur the expected anxieties. 'How can he doze like a corpse in this swelter? . . . Through all that thwacking on the door . . . Is it his medicines, should we call in that new quack that he's been . . .'

Jamun yanks back the dusty curtains. He suddenly notes that Shyamanand's face appears unusually dark. He isn't certain whether the light is beguiling him, or whether his father's skin has actually blackened – without warning, overnight – or again, whether the overshadowing has in fact been a stealthy process of weeks, and Jamun it is who is marking it even now. But the darkening is eerie, direful. The blood seems to've curdled just beneath the skin of the face and, in a manner, decided not to return to the heart. The jellying appears to've softened the skin too, like that of an overripe fruit.

About his hairline are huddled some grey, translucent slugs. In a second Jamun realizes that they are globes of cold, cold sweat, marshalled on Shyamanand's forehead like snails at a symposium. The largeness and viscosity of the pellets spellbind him. They seem exudations more from the brain than from the skin, like the oozing on the lid of a faulty, scalding pressure cooker, as though the tumult in the cauldron of his skull has concussed him into this comatoseness that surpasses heat and sound, has vaporized through the skin to cool and coagulate on his forehead, each cold slug a token for every thousand disappointed desires of a long, miserable life.

A faded T-shirt, Burfi's reject, now soaked in sweat; a chequered lungi so shabby that even Jamun would've dithered to wear it to drop a letter in the dark; but Shyamanand is a monumental hoarder of trifles, to each of which is affixed for him an evocation, a sentiment; he would've lived abundantly better had he learnt to transmit the feeling from the objects to the creatures connected with them, but he's always found it easier to cherish the inanimate rather than the vital.

'I'll just change my clothes and return,' whispers Urmila. 'Don't wake him.'

Jamun subsides into the chair behind his father's writing desk. He's been frightened by the entire episode. He reminds himself that it's not yet done with. He glances now and then at Shyamanand's profile, overshadowed, goodlooking, dormant. When his father dies, he broods entangledly, the circumstances'll be identical; Shyamanand will be alone, impounded by choice, in a prison house of his own making; the electricity will unofficially fail; to Shyamanand, the mugginess around him will, somehow, arbitrarily, image the vanity of living, he'll slouch about the house, sweating, opening cupboards and unlocking memories till, overmastered, he'll gulp down a handful of his Calmposes, and abate into this numbness; and, sluggishly, cold, opalescent, plump maggots of sweat will foregather on his forehead.

With his handkerchief he wipes Shyamanand's brow and neck. For the millionth time in his life, he suddenly, in a panic that time's running out, wants to expiate himself before his parents for the wrongs that he must've done them, yearns to convince them that he, despite his vulnerabilities, is truly grateful to them for the gift of life.

As a child, terrified of night, when he had to traverse the verandah in the gloom of midnight to reach the lavatory, he'd pluck at Shyamanand's vest or Urmila's petticoat, and clench an adult hand in his passage through the dark. When, in his pubescence, intimidated by the bicycle, reluctant to master it, he'd tried to evade his cycling lessons by a thousand idiotic stratagems, Shyamanand'd never derided him; instead, had hired a second bike, and, riding composedly alongside Jamun, his left hand steering the handlebars of his son's machine, evening after evening, for weeks, had bolstered him to glide like the wind. Shyamanand had looked bizarre on the hired, ramshackle cycles – stout, with a faultless nose and a head of silvered wool – much too stately to pedal. He hadn't much revelled in the rides either.

If my life itself, introspects Jamun convulsedly – within him the butterflies of contrition set aflutter by remembrance – isn't evidence enough for the debt that I owe my begetters, then nothing in this existence is meaningful. But we're all feeble, he assents to himself, and heedless, glutted with vanity, and languish only after trumpery; and in a flash there remains no time to articulate one's love to those to whom one owes love. He presses his forehead against the glass of the desk, but no comfort there.

Shyamanand awakes some two hours after, a little before dinner. Yes, he swallowed two Calmposes at four in the afternoon. Because Kishori, Aya's chum, and the libertine of the sewers, showed up, out of the blue, purposing to cadge a loan and a meal off her. That she'd been shunted to a hospice a few weeks before frustrated him acutely. He exposed his desperation by even trying to sponge some cash off Shyamanand; Shyamanand instead reviled him with terrific vigour, calling him, in passing, a rapist and a low-caste gigolo. Kishori, nettled, in turn snarled and threatened him. Kishori *was* a frightening figure, cadaverous, maroon-mouthed, in a buttonless shirt that flaunted the fuzz on his chest and forearms, yellow-eyed. Shyamanand bolted the door and spied from behind the window curtains.

'And how's that ratnagarbha? Is her womb still spawning pus and faeces?' Thus, Kishori also yawped his rage at the absent Urmila for a minute, narrates Shyamanand, and then scrawled his choler on the wall before shoving off.

'Ratnagarbha? Why should that fucker call Ma ratnagarbha? Doesn't it mean, one whose womb has – well – spawned jewels? Sounds far too elegant a word for that sonofabitch.'

An ineffable adjustment in the countenances of Shyamanand and Urmila, like the passage of a shadow; a shift of the eyes from one innocuous object to another, from the rice ladle to the bangles on Urmila's wrist. 'It's a name for me,' she divulges lukewarmly, 'that Belu coined in a letter, after you two'd been born. Aya must've told her Kishori about it.'

'Odd that I've never heard ratnagarbha before, of you, from anyone.'

'You shouldn't've gulped down two Calmposes.' Urmila swivels to Shyamanand to shift to what to her, presumably, is a graver subject. 'That Kishori can't be priced that high. Particularly since you've given up that bald quack's medicines. You shouldn't have, you know, not without consulting – or at least telling – him. While you were asleep, both Jamun and I noticed how sort of black you've become, as though your blood is clotting. Why don't you meet Haldia or someone else with these new symptoms?'

'Tchhah. Symptoms? Of what?' Even Shyamanand sounds glad to sidestep the discussion on Kishori. 'I'm perfectly fine. That pill that Haldia's prescribed – Pulsantin? Punsaltin? or whatever – costs two rupees per capsule. Six rupees a day! Just for a fortnight, he chirps at me at every visit, but I've been bolting three of those every day for months now. And to what end? As for my darkening, you two've never heard of a tan or what? I slog for two hours every morning in the garden, in the sun, not that you two'd've noticed. You want me to call in Haldia for an anti-suntan lotion or something? No, enough of his bloody cupidity. I can cure myself, thank you, when next my BP bounces up to the moon.'

After dinner, Shyamanand submits afresh to the effect of the Calmposes and returns to bed. Urmila and Jamun loll in the easychairs in the verandah. Jamun sips a post-dinner whisky. Not that he particularly wants a nightcap, but he's seventeen. On his sojourns, Burfi has initiated the custom, which Shyamanand and Urmila've been too elated with his presence to cavil against, of smoking and tippling under the eyes of his parents, a practice to which he's also invited his younger brother, for in numbers lies strength when a taboo is being circumvented – and on Burfi's departure, Jamun has continued the custom, the only way, really, of consolidating a concession.

He is still a little perplexed by the events of the day. The visit of a measly wraith of one's yesteryears does not warrant two Calmposes, certainly not with the obdurate, cold and sardonic Shyamanand. Very likely, muses Jamun, the actual significance of the day's happenings, of which Shyamanand and Urmila are more than aware, is snarled in that hunk of their past that he does not know. Just then, Urmila astounds him by asking him for a cigarette.

'Boy. Boy! Are you sure? . . .' He gawps at her hold and light the cigarette, and exhale smoke alternately through mouth and nostrils, most seasonedly. 'I'm stunned. Is this your method of getting even with me for boozing in your presence? I'm also hugely impressed, especially by the manner in which you crinkle up your eyes against the smoke . . . Exquisitely wrapt-in-far-off-philosophic-thought . . . You could revolutionize the Marlboro ad . . .' But beneath his chaff, he *is* startled. His mother puffing away is as jolting an image as that of his parents entwined in passion. Yet he can't accept that her smoking is the upshot of the anxiety of Kishori's visit.

'I'm worried,' begins Urmila all at once, 'about your Baba, about his health. Now that I'm padding off to spend two weeks with Burfi, I'm even more disturbed. Your Baba started consulting this Haldia just about three months ago, didn't he? You should remember, *you* brought the news that a posh clinic'd opened up overnight beside the flyover to Dost Garden. Kuki's mother recommended Haldia too. Well, in the last few weeks, that fat vet seems to've crammed your father with the *world's* medicines – three capsules in the morning, two at lunch, four tablets at bedtime. Haven't you marked a change in him, a strangeness more than a change? These marathon walks twice a day, that brutal digging and pruning in the lawn for hours in the sun, the gawkish efforts at housewifery, to clean up his cupboard, his room – just where's your Baba tapping his vigour from? He's never, in the twenty-five years that I've endured him, *never* revealed a chip of his present energy. His most characteristic, his *instinctive*, pose has been supine, browsing through junk in scant light, with his mind on other things. So whatever has Haldia been packing into him?

'Two or three days ago, your father suddenly left off gobbling these pills, stopped *all* of them, without even telling that crook!

He asserts that he's nauseated by this dependence on medication, and by Haldia's manner, that he wants to heal himself with self-reliance – the sort of trash that overfills the wits of those with time on their hands, like the retired. But the true reason, I think, is that he adores his petty cash too intensely to spend it even for his own wellbeing.'

'Has Baba changed after he stopped his pills? Become less energetic or something?' Questions just to keep Urmila going, to assure her of the attentiveness of her audience.

She doesn't respond for so long that Jamun peers at her in the dark, fancying that she hasn't heard. He begins to repeat the questions when she speaks, passionlessly. 'I must confide in someone, because I'm scared. Had Aya been here, I would've conferred with her. I wish she was with me now. I miss her – the woman's talk. Will you understand, or will you gibe me – in your smugness and your insobriety? In the last three weeks, your Baba, with his unprecedented pep, has tried to sleep with me five times.'

A sensation, like a groundswell, traverses Jamun's skin, seemingly from left wrist to the brink of the right shoulderblade. 'He hasn't touched me for eighteen years. We haven't gone to bed in the same room since you were conceived.' She exhales dejectedly. 'Had Burfi heard this, he'd've broken in with, "Quite naturally. The birth of a baby with Jamun's looks should daunt any couple from all further tupping."'

Quietness, for a time. The sounds of night, of restful laughter from behind a wall, the malcontent honking of thwarted traffic, the nasal hum of mosquitoes on the prowl. 'I was – I am – very frightened. When he sidled into my room at eleven at night, and I drowsy, yet fretful at the speed of the ceiling fan – minutes, whole *minutes* before I understood what he wanted. When he perched on the frame of the bed, and I finally realized, I felt as though I'd budged to the rockingchair by the window, and was rocking and gaping – from there – at Baba and me, bitter, incredulous.'

The most fanciful notions careen about in Jamun's skull,

ricocheting off one another with the delirium of a squash ball in play. For an instant he suspects that Urmila, pricked by her hatred and spite, has trumped up the tale; next, that her fantasy, spawned by her repression and her hankering, has scrambled with the real life till she's mistaken one for the other. But what she's recounted, to him it seems, just can't have occurred. His mind cannot conjoin Shyamanand's stately, silver-domed mien and the notion of a tense, stubborn penis; neither can he conceive his mother's nakedness. Other lumber, too, hustles his wits: what positions'd they copulate in? In her menopausal state, they wouldn't need condoms, or would they? However would his cheeks and chin nestle in the crook of her shoulder? Would the ruts of a lifetime on her face dissolve in the tenderness of coition? Jamun tries to make out his mother's expression in the gloom. But she's speaking again. 'The last time was three nights ago, the one you spent God knows where. So now what? I'm not even sure whether capsules *can* galvanize you like this. It's distasteful, somehow – this artificial boost. And it's possible that your Baba's done with those pills out of repugnance, because they roused him to touch me.'

Jamun discerns in her outpouring a kind of exhilaration at the idea that, despite his conduct for over two decades, Shyamanand actually needed her, even physically. A tincture of devilry as well, in her disclosure of such intimacies.

The verity of which, he knows, he can never confirm from Shyamanand, not because he'd be too embarrassed, or his questions singularly ludicrous ('Is it true that you sweated to get it up last night?'), but because when Shyamanand denies Urmila's assertion, and one parent is thereby shown to be a liar, Jamun's pity would seesaw between Urmila's crumpled face and Shyamanand's gagged silence till it brewed with the rage of impotence; and he'd once more be embroiled in the exhausting business of taking sides.

Even in his late teenage, he is, now and then, disconcerted that he feels for his parents a love that is only the tenderness of remorse, just a sorrow, a shame at their unhappiness. His affection for them is in fact pity, yet he also believes that it's truer than Burfi's thoughtless, fitful attachment. Concomitantly, Jamun presumes, unspokenly, that *he* is his parents' darling, their heart's-blood.

He's certainly awakened in them much less disquiet than Burfi, has demanded less of them. Just a few rupees a month from Shyamanand – for his train pass and his cigarettes. Urmila he hardly ever pesters for money – perhaps because the collegiate Burfi'd cadged off her nonstop – and in any case, her salary's gobbled up by the house – by the cook's wages and the gas cylinders. Whenever Jamun needs a little extra, he touches Shyamanand, who always coughs up – always lukewarmly – but always; in part because Jamun's requirements tend to be reasonable, in part because Shyamanand's post-retirement gratuity has been considerably more than anticipated. The windfall's even goaded Jamun to suggest that Shyamanand could fork out a chunk of it towards paying off Urmila's decades-long debts.

'Don't show off your birdbrain when you don't know the facts. Once this house was built and I had the cash, how many times've I probed your mother for the details of her indebtedness? "Just tell me how much you owe to whom." But she's wilfully refused, for years. If my money, ten thousand rupees of it, is to be used to settle your mother's borrowings, haven't I a right to know to whom she's hocked herself over the years, in front of whom she's derogated herself? But no! She resists infuriatedly! I must lavish on her the ten thousand with no questions tacked on. I didn't give her the cash, she screeches, when she needed it the most – for milk, Calmpose and the electricity bill! – so how dare I quiz her on her loan sharks? Idiotic, mulish woman. She doesn't want me to discover that she has, in her time, wheedled in front of Aya for pittances, and perhaps in front of Aya's lovebird Kishori too. The illiterate peons in her office have doled out to her, and some of her subordinates also – all at preposterous rates of interest. They snickered at her – nonstop – for being such a shoddy housewife, such a crummy manager of her money, and at me too they must've sniggered, for God knows how she vilified me to them.

'But your mother is masochistic. She craves to feel persecuted, harrowed – it's her way of tugging at attention – look, everybody! My husband's so unpleasant, so miserly, that I've to beg and borrow from the lumpen just to keep body and soul together. The one defence that I can pick out for your mother's conduct is that with so much heartache in this world, it *is* better to be masochistic.'

Jamun watches Shyamanand's features glow to enunciate the words of scorn. Disparagement is always much easier to voice. The pity that his father touches off in Jamun is rarer and stronger than that provoked by Urmila. Now and then, he's affected by it altogether independently of any utterance, demeanour, gesture or act of his father, when what moves him is a nebulous, ineffable sensation of the beggarliness of existence, the web of a shabby life – as when he drops in on Shyamanand at his office and sees him behind his desk, a silver-haired, distinguished head behind a tiny desk, unnoticed in the hall of ten inconsequential civil servants; at other times too, when Shyamanand disappoints him – when Jamun, for instance, pumps him for enlightenment on the most piffling matter, and Shyamanand concedes his inability to supply it – even on those occasions, Jamun's disappointment is more compunction, a hazy gentleness, than disenchantment.

As when, at the disgruntled age of twelve, he encounters Radhakrishnan in his textbook of English essays. 'Oof. Bastard. Why's he so bloody shitty? Baba, what does "putative" mean? And "pheno" . . . "phenomeno" . . . "phenomenal"?'

'I don't know, Jamun. Why don't you look up the dictionary?' In his own way, Shyamanand too has mapped out the fosterage of his children. They must, in due time, learn to be fittingly independent in all matters, even to stumbling on the delight of themselves unearthing the meaning of words.

'You sure you don't know? Would be much easier than opening a bloody dictionary.'

Shyamanand fibs only on exceedingly rare and what he considers crucial occasions. 'No, both the words seem new to me. What were they . . . puta – what ? . . . You'll've to rouse yourself to reach that Chambers. Always better to, you know, can be certain then.'

'Yeah, sure, but later. These two bloody words can't be that hot if bloody even you haven't heard of them.' After a few more lines of that killing essay, he eyes his father over the edge of his reader. He looks downcast, befuddled. 'You mean Radhakrishnan's English is better then yours?' His expression discloses to Shyamanand that, for Jamun, the question could be pivotal to his appraisal of his father; its reply might decide Shyamanand's worth as a wellspring of sagacity for this world.

'Well, yes, I think. He's a very learned man. A savant. A humanist. Look, for example, at the words he uses. Putative. Phenomenal. A genius.'

The disappointment in Jamun's features is more a commiseration at Shyamanand's having to concede his secondbestness. 'And Nehru?' shoving his chin out at his text. 'Nehru also knows more English than you?'

'Oh, no no. Nehru didn't know anything about anything – except to pluck roses for his jackets – however could he be a model for English?'

Now with his head on Kasturi's tummy, his fingers dilatorily guiding the gooseflesh on her thighs, his body disgorged and twingeing, his mind becalmed like the sea, Jamun gazes at the afternoon cloudburst sketching streamlets through the smudge that July has deposited on the windows. Kasturi and he've been in bed upstairs, muted and ravelled, since the early morning. Now that their rut has enervated itself, he wants her to leave so that he can return to his other lives. He tranquilly waits for her to suggest that she should be going. They'll slink out the way they sneaked in, through the side door and over the boundary wall, and feign that they've at that very instant returned, all fagged out, after eight hours in the university.

Shyamanand is not immediately visible. Jamun wonders

whether he's once more snapped up a handful of Calmposes to while the afternoon away. He *is* in his room, characteristically supine. 'Hi. Just got back. Phew, what a day –' A half-gasp as Shyamanand haltingly swivels towards him a haunted, stranger's face.

Shyamanand has sat in the varandah, blindly observing the rain, struggling to disregard the dreadful, ice-cold uneasiness that oozes all over him, as though a bulky stopper, somewhere in his belly, has been brutally unplugged. He's looked down at his body, at his hands, curled like foetuses, in his lap. His flesh and frame seem alien, an oppressive lumber that he has to tote as a duty, a final responsibility, to his room; if only he gains his bed, he feels, he can yield this frightful incubus, and at last be still.

He finds that he can't get up from his chair. The bidding to rise somehow never reaches his limbs, instead becomes clogged in the benumbing sludge that is now his blood. When sitting, insensate, grows more insupportable than the idea of standing up, he, with a prodigious effort, lunges upward, and instinctively, crabbedly, clutches at the wall to check himself from tumbling. His left leg does not take any weight, and feels like an outsize cricket bat trussed to his hip. He supports himself against the wall and on his right leg. In his bewilderment, he's bitterly scared.

Heaving himself along the wall, he reaches the door of his room, and drags himself past the cupboard. Its mirror stuns him. A frenzy of ivory hair above the features of a nightmare. The entire left half of the face has been zestfully yanked down, as by a malevolent child; the eye, crimson and terrified, balloons out like a caricature. He touches his cheek, and tries to prop up its skin. It feels glacial, as though wafer-thin frost has veneered his real skin.

He slumps on to his bed, on his dead hand. His nerves seem sound enough, he thinks confusedly, to transmit pain. He jerks up his left leg with his good hand, and topples on to his pillow. He is shuddering with dread and fatigue. The bounty of two prime sons, but where are they when they're needed the most.

Between his stroke and Jamun's appearance, time must've glided by, but Shyamanand doesn't sense much of it. At one point the Jaico wallclock that Chhana's gifted Urmila and him seems to say two-thirty; at another, seven-fifteen. He time and again shut his eyes, praying that when he opens them he'll again be back in his old world. He writhes and twitches about in a hundred different positions; each is intolerable after a breath or two. His throat is altogether dry, and he again and again swallows his spit, audibly, like the lapping of the sea on shingle. His mouth won't shut, his lips have withered.

He knows, but can't face, that something hideous has happened – is happening – to him. In the tumult in his skull also skirrs the notion that the crucial symptom of a heart attack is an insupportable pain in the chest – perhaps he hasn't suffered one.

A blood clot somewhere in the brain, proclaims Haldia. But getting Shyamanand to him isn't that easy. Jamun can't drive, he's never shown the least interest in learning how to , so their own car is of no use. He telephones two local taxi stands; at one, the cabs refuse to drive towards Dost Garden. They won't, grouses the lout on the phone, come across any return fare in that part of the city. At the other, no one disturbs his siesta to pick up the receiver. Jamun calls Haldia and ashamedly explains. Haldia surprises him by despatching his own car and chauffeur.

Who – podgy, safari-suited, smartassed – helps most unwillingly to shoulder and haul Shyamanand from his bed to the car. While Jamun and the driver struggle with his sandals, Shyamanand, clenching Jamun's shoulder for support, mumbles to him, 'I'll be too heavy for you. When we move, I'll rest my weight on this fat bugger, as much of it as I can.'

At Haldia's clinic, a swarthy, hirsute matron badgers Jamun with, 'Have you arranged for a night sister? Who's to tend to the patient at night? Give him his water and his bedpan? Isn't he your father? Maybe you yourself'd wish to stay. I could recommend a tip-top nurse though – my own daughter, terrifically seasoned, fifty rupees a night, most reasonable.'

Haldia and his perfume waft by. The redolence seems to exude from the doctor's downy skull. 'Nothing at all to fret about, dear . . . Your papa hasn't lost his consciousness – just a tiny cerebral thrombosis . . . His speech'll pick up not to worry . . . Only his left side's packed up, which is – I mean, had his right failed, would've been a deal more nasty, his memory and perception might've been damaged, he wouldn't've been able to do a good many routine things –' Haldia halts on his way out to think of a truly dire example. 'Couldn't've signed a cheque, for instance. Have you contacted your mamma, dear?'

Jamun telephones Kasturi and telegrams his mother and Burfi. Kasturi says that she'll come over right away. 'I've arranged for a night nurse for my father,' Jamun declares, grasping her by the shoulders in his ill-disciplined excitement, 'so we could spend the nights together, at least till Ma returns. She and Burfi'll receive the news only tomorrow – at the earliest. Posts and Telegraphs can also be banked on to fuck up the text of the telegram: "BABA STROKING NURSES AT HOME. COME SOON." And then there's Indian Airlines, the Ol' Faithless, a multicrore-rupee Russian Roulette Corporation. For your mother you could cook up –'

'But aren't you,' Kasturi looks truly, disagreeably perplexed, 'anxious firstly for your father? I already feel sinful that he was becoming paralysed downstairs at the very time that you and I – all but plumb above his head – were billing and cooing to each other. Like Mohandas mounting Kasturba in the adjacent room while his father snuffed it. I'd've presumed that, with your lofty driving forces of duty and compunction, you'd've darted to stay the night beside your father.'

But she moves in anyway, for two nights, carting her derision and her unease with her. In the mornings she sets out for the university and Jamun for Haldia's, to replace the night nurse, and to listen to Shyamanand's slurred bellyaching against her incompetence and his own condition. Then he feels guilty at having lain with Kasturi all night – but a guilt not insupportable, indeed a sinfulness unspokenly acknowledged as the spinoff of a greater pleasure. 'I could doss down here at night, Baba, in place of that cretin, but then who'd guard the house? Ma'll be in this evening, then we'll change things.'

Kasturi drives Shyamanand's Ambassador to the airport. Urmila looks dulled with uncertainty, but in her eyes seems to slink the tint of a sort of triumph. Burfi is markedly more reassuring. 'Terrific job, Jamun,' a thwack on the shoulder. 'If you hadn't returned in good time from college, God knows how much worse Baba would've been by now.' Jamun notes, as always, how Kasturi perks up whenever she meets Burfi.

'Now that Burfi's going to drive, we could maybe drop Kasturi home, Ma, on the way to Haldia's?'

'Uh . . . I want to reach there fast. Kasturi can easily grab a taxi or an auto from the nursing home.'

In the car, while Burfi belittles its state of disrepair, Urmila declares, in the voice of one who wishes her hearers to swallow that she's speaking only to herself, 'I should never, never've gone away. He needed me, though now he'll never concede it.' She reaches out to touch Jamun. 'Could Haldia get closer to the exact time of the stroke, to how many minutes or hours passed between the attack and your discovery of him? No? Because that's crucial, I was told, every second matters in the cure of thrombosis . . . Dreadful if he lay benumbed for hours and you were in the house somewhere and didn't know. Didn't your Baba beseech you at once to summon Chhana?'

She and Burfi are horrified when they see Shyamanand. Urmila begins to weep, chilled by the thump with which his paralysed face recalls that of Belu on the evening when, over forty years ago, he deadened his body with a glut of rat poison. Shyamanand's mien underneath the disfiguration, like Belu's, looks despairing and forlorn. He gawps at Urmila without blinking, but can't stare Burfi in the eye.

He stays in the nursing home for a fortnight. Despite Haldia's stratagems, he neither sleeps nor defecates for six days. 'Not to worry, my dear,' mews the doctor. 'I've known bowels which haven't moved for forty whole days.'

'At the butt end of which,' breathes Burfi into Shyamanand's ear, inciting his entire body to shudder with laughter, 'the bowels themselves began to resemble Haldia.'

Who calls in diverse electro- and physiotherapists, cardiologists, neurologists, to survey Shyamanand; each stays for seven minutes, asks the same questions and, while waddling out, sotto voce to Jamun, charges the earth. Shyamanand hates them all, and on the fourth day, after the quicksilver visit of a dietician with gulletgagging bad breath, begins to demur, with a singlemindedness and cogency that augurs well for his wits, that he's frittering away time and hard cash at Haldia's, and that he craves to return home. Each such clamour of his is parried by the vinegary curtness of the bewhiskered matron and the adamantine yellowness of the doctor's dentures.

Chhana telephones from Calcutta on the second day; Jamun says that he'll check with Shyamanand and let her know the following evening; Shyamanand pooh-poohs the notion, or rather, mumbles his pooh-pooh: 'Nonsense. She need not waste a good many hundreds just to come and goggle at me on this bed, struggling to defecate.' So Jamun tells Chhana, 'Rush. He declares that you needn't show up, but I presume that he's just acting gruff and cute; he's in fact dying to have all of us bob and bustle about him.'

The solicitous faces of his niece and his sons around his bed – a rare sight that swathes Shyamanand's soul in warmth. Chhana tries for a while to dredge some information out of the doctor on duty, but he – obese, leucodermic, stagnant – has no clue about anything. Burfi strokes and pinches Shyamanand's icy foreleg, and exhorts him to struggle to budge it. 'Can't you shift this bloody mace at all? Even a few inches?' Shyamanand can, and swerves his foot about on the crumpled hospital sheet like the death spasms of a plump reptile.

'I can't *raise* my leg though, not more than an inch or so, and not without bending my knee.' Shyamanand's new voice is screechy, more whingeing. He moistens – almost smacks – his lips for each syllable. His facial muscles – all blubber and skin – wobble alarmingly with the strain of enunciation. His buckled face maroons as he struggles again with his leg.

Burfi, ever on the lookout for novel, arduous callisthenics to test his body with, clasps the big toe of Shyamanand's left foot with his thumb and forefinger and, at arm's span, without crooking his elbow, tries to lift the benumbed limb to the height of his own shoulder. 'Boy. Oye, Jamun! This is a fantastic exercise!' Burfi cocks himself up on his toes and arches his back to yank Shyamanand's leg to a crest before restoring it to the mattress. 'Phew. Bugger, you should try this. Super for the forearm and tricep.' Chhana and Jamun cluster around the bed; to the snarl-like chortling of Shyamanand and the derisive encouragement of Burfi, Jamun begins chancing his arm with his father's leg.

Not since their puppyhood, it appears to Shyamanand, when they used to lark around together, indivisibly, before their irrevocable maturation tugged them adrift, have his sons sported with him in as joyous, as artless, a manner. He shuts his eyes and feels with delight Jamun snort and wheeze over his toe; he should die just then, he realizes with a sudden, extra squirt of rapture, in that very breath, for he'll never happen on a more opportune time. He blurredly recalls that a poem, or a line, that unerringly images his present sentiment, exists somewhere, that he can, perhaps, even recollect the phrases if he slugs his wits about a bit. 'Jamun, you boob. You're bending your bloody elbow.' Shyamanand's leg thuds down on the foam cushion. 'Oof – careful, you bugger! If you can't handle it, then lay off, but don't fuck up the leg.' 'Fuck you right back. You think I did that deliberately? Just fuck you.'

This kickoff of a squabble between his sons – once an everyday stridency, now rare, and dulcet, because it seems to recall a shard of their pasts – prods Shyamanand afresh to share with his children his gladness, and his fancy of death, but his tongue is too turgescent, lumpish, to be malleable.

He watches, with his grimace of a smile, Jamun riposte Burfi's vocal lunges. The brothers set themselves out in leisured positions about the room to keep up their slothful, trashy wrangle. 'Bloated namby-pamby fucker. If you didn't frig four times a day, you'd've been able to heave up Baba's leg.' 'Better than you, VD. At least, the entire world never shrieked with laughter whenever it saw the results of any exam that *I've* ever taken.' In their genial slanging match, they seem to've forgotten his affliction. Nothing had changed, it was good.

To the father, friction between his sons is a pointer to their affinity; that is, they are close enough to each other to, now and then, spit sparks. With the years, Shyamanand recalls sentimentally, Jamun's trained himself to more than hold his own against his elder brother, to match him jab for jab. 'Chuck me a cigarette, yaar, Walldrooler – shit, one can't even smoke in here – come, shall we step out for a drag? Will be back in a second, Baba.' Walldrooler. A happy coincidence, that Burfi's used the very nickname for Jamun that dredges up out of their pasts the scenes that Shyamanand himself has been, at that moment, daydreaming of, of the time before Jamun's articulation had ripened enough for him to parry with speech alone, when he'd banked instead, for expression, on clenched fists and the squeals of rage.

When he'd been four, and Burfi eight, and of an evening had played ice-pice together – or rather, Chhana and Jamun'd fruitfully wheedled his brother into joining them, because Burfi was eight, and far too weathered for silly ice-pice, and at least acquiesced only because his brother and cousin agreed to play the game in a novel way – wherein both Burfi and Chhana became dens, shut their eyes and, snickering, counted till hundred, while Jamun, atremble with excitation, waddled off to hide.

They nosed him out within seconds, every time, and hooted and cavorted about, while he, riddled, with tears tipping his eyes, goaded their guffaws to fuel him to detonate.

Months of this ice-pice before Burfi begins to feel really just too dreadfully adult, and once for all to wind up the witless sport, discloses to Jamun that as long as he keeps to his obnoxious, and comical, habit of licking the wall wherever he toddles, he'll never be able to camouflage himself from anybody, because the damp, rapidly evaporating smudges of his licks, like the trace of the moist heels of small shoes, will immutably guide his stalkers to him.

Good to hark back in this fashion to the years of their nurture, Shyamanand doughtily reminds himself, it'll keep his senses from his present frozenness. He observes Jamun push his spectacles up the bridge of his nose to read better the level of the glucose in the upside-down bottle above the bed. But nurture was frightfully labyrinthine, and one never knew what accrued from what. As a parent, for instance, one hadn't been opportunely aware that one's child savoured the lime on walls because he was probably deficient in calcium; when, less than a decade later, the boy needed glasses, one wasn't certain whether his vision'd been damaged by the negligence of a faulty upbringing, or whether it was true that, in any case, the children of thirty-five-plus mothers tended to physical weakliness.

So Shyamanand returns home in two weeks, uncontrollably happy. Joyce has attempted to transfigure his room – drape his bed in vivid linen, locate on his desk a few uncluttered inches for a carafe of gladioli. Burfi and Jamun half-buoy him from the car to his easychair by the window. They are startled to note that his rapture at returning home has edged Shyamanand to tears. 'When I suffer my next cerebral – no matter when, three months, or twenty years later – I'm not stirring from this room. All of you, please remember – next time, no Haldia, no hairy matrons, no enemas, no shock treatment. If I've crashed to the ground somewhere, just haul me to the bed, draw back all these curtains, play crescendo on your stereo that Gershwin that I like, and open, open wide these doors and windows, so that sparrows can streak in, with the moist wafts from the sea. That'd be enough for me. Then Heaven can wait.'

Shyamanand mends, but really stealthily, inch by inch, over years. That is, from being totally bedridden, he is able – with effort that is fitful, lengthened across a good many seasons, that is countered by prodigious bouts of morose, downhearted torpor – finally to hobble about aided by his thick bamboo walking stick, unescorted within the compound walls of his house. He improves because the hankering to live never actually abandons his limbs, despite his, from time to time, yawping and snarling out the opposite; furthermore, he recognizes, little by little, that with time the anxiety of his flesh and blood for his condition shrivels – through the routine stages, in waning order, of solicitude, inconstant care, weariness, irksomeness – to a variable blend of tedium, dutifulness and tempered vexation; the dwindling concern of Urmila and Jamun for his wellbeing disciplines Shyamanand to bank more and more on himself. But he recovers only up to a point: for the residue of his life, his left arm remains wholly, and his left leg in part, dead.

Urmila and Jamun privately dub them the cold sweat years – the sluggish, interminable, unremarked decade between Shyamanand's first cerebral stroke and Burfi's return on transfer to the city of his fosterage. Jamun conceives the phrase, and Urmila considers it so felicitous that all at once tears film her eyes when she first hears it; for her entire existence in those years has seemed to her to've been tyrannized by a medley of fear – terror that Shyamanand'll die on her hands, when she's alone in the house and floundering, in a cold sweat, with the telephone book for the right numbers; palpitation, like a clutch around her heart, that the others, the world, will squarely base the culpatibility of his death in her lubberliness; a disquietude with every breath that his strictures, as harrowing and as unexpected as arrows, incited by any subject under the sun, or even by the absence of subject, will maul her right now, this instant, or the next, or the next; an undercover trepidation that she herself will peg out most untowardly, with momentous chores undone, without having tasted the delight of a moment's repose.

Jamun is menaced too, in those years of cold sweat. The disconsolateness that exudes from Urmila's soul seems to've fattened like a contagion throughout the rooms, bedimmed and sullied them, so that the house itself demoralizes and appears to coldshoulder him. Her apprehensions, fuzzy enough in themselves, dribble into him too – after all, he *is* his mother's son, and has been engendered out of the marrow of his fosterers – but with even more fuzzy contours. Hence he also is secretly chilled, for instance, that both his parents, designedly, will die just when he alone is about, too sapped by panic to stall their deaths.

He is further unmanned by the responsibilities that his father's infirmity devolves on him. Minor, inescapable, enervating chores – learn the car; fret in the heat and welter of the workshop as the mechanics, sluggards all, open up the vehicle, listlessly run it down, and then forsake it to amble off to lay open some other car; fume punily in the electricity office against an outlandish bill; try halfheartedly to fathom the snarl of Municipal Tax laws; beat down prices at the fish bazaar.

Self-pity, their own disquietudes and Shyamanand's crusty demeanour, in the main, impede Urmila and Jamun from worrying inordinately about his affliction, about the paralysis itself, about how it must feel to have, without warning, one-half of one's body die, and yet not go the way of all flesh, to have to heave about leaden dumbbells in lieu of limbs. Most of the time, the stodgy businesses of living and nursing hinder them from any abiding sympathy for his trauma; and now and then, whenever Shyamanand is, or seems, outrageously peevish, they feel that his infirmity is a befitting visitation, even that the deities have let him off rather easily.

Once in a while, however, the derision of the deities for Shyamanand startles his wife and son out of their careworn apathy. Jamun, for instance, is stabbed, glancingly, by shame when he happens on his father struggling to grasp a bottle of hairoil in his left hand so that he can wrench open its seal with his right. 'Why didn't you call me?' he upbraids him as he takes the bottle away.

'Because I'm tired to death of having to wait and wait for someone else to tch with vexation before he plucks a few seconds off from mooching about to be kind to me.'

'Phew, that's a killer. Great, in some ways, you know, that the stroke whammed you and not Ma, for she's already pulped, and had she been benumbed like this, she wouldn't've endured, I think, her wits would've caved in within weeks –'

'– and she wouldn't have been able to bear the compassion – or compunction? – of her flesh and blood sour, with time, to exasperation and tedium, yes?'

'Vitriol. They should bottle your wit and peddle it as *the* wonderworker against the crud in a loo.'

But even as he kneads a palmful of hairoil into Shyamanand's scalp, with a vigour that is almost malevolent, he recalls and assents that time and time again, his father it is who's knuckled under the scourge of his affliction, and of the indifference of his family.

'I want to die!' He's pounded his impotent left arm and, with the snarling, warped features of a hysteric, screeched out his powerlessness. 'Please, please let me . . . die.' He's then blubbered something like that; very few would've understood him entirely, for his lips are still too buckled, and his steerage of his tongue too babyish, for him to enunciate lucidly; besides, the turmoil of the storm has smothered all other sound.

Late August. Sixish in the evening, the heavens grumbling, uneasy. Nevertheless, with considerable help from Jamun, Shyamanand, for the first time since his stroke, struggles up the stairs to survey the world from an easychair in the first-floor verandah. Urmila, certain that Shyamanand's abandonment of his bed denotes a complete recovery within weeks, and hence aquiver with excitation, leaves him to snuffle and wheeze and exclaim at the new world, and herself scurries down to make some tea. Jamun is on the phone with Kasturi when, from the sea, the high wind attacks.

In a wink, without warning, a hideous clatter as the lavatory window slams and splinters into a thousand slivers; the squall seems to thwack Shyamanand in the chest like a blow; he can't inhale. Dust, leaves, paper frenetically pirouetting in the air;

saplings and the boughs of bulkier trees curtsy distraughtly and, because the gale thrusts the sallower undersides of their leaves into view, look an anaemic green; large, hard splinters of rain, like warm glass on naked skin; and, suppressing all other sound, the boohoos and whoops of the wind. Gates clang and doors boom as adults scamper in and children dart out. By the time that Jamun reaches his father, Shyamanand, stunned by both the suddenness and the punch of the squall, is snivelling with fear. Jamun too is shaken by the storm, in particular by the smashing of the lavatory window – and by the expression beneath Shyamanand's lush stubble of a few weeks – a face like a chasm, like a child's at the instant of losing its balance. In that tumult, against the sting of the rain, he strives to heave him up, but his father has disintegrated too much even to stand, even with Jamun's support; they totter against the railing of the verandah. He then hustles and tugs Shyamanand in from the squall, clenching his jaws against the whimpering. 'Enough . . . I should die . . . This helpless . . .'

And Urmila? She careers helter-skelter up the stairs (seemingly having sloughed in the kitchen her piles and her arthritis), screeching out her anxiety: 'Jamun! Your Baba in the verandah! Oh God!' But upstairs, she sees her husband being aided on to Jamun's bed, and since she never wears her spectacles if she can survive without them, doesn't mark Shyamanand's shell-shocked face and, from relief, starts to gabble. 'Oh I'm so glad you're in, I feared that you'd still be outdoors, thrilling to the thunderstorm, not recognizing that this rain can be so perfidious, so I said to myself, this tea can wait, let me just first scuttle up and check whether they've shown the sense to creep in out of the –'

'God. God.' Shyamanand's moan halts her. 'Jamun, please ask her to go away.'

A slap wouldn't have stunned Urmila more. But then Shyamanand begins to snivel anew, as though his entreaty to his son had blitzed him all over again, to thresh about on the pillow as he was wont to under electrotherapy, ferally to wallop his dud arm with his sound one. His eyes bulge preposterously, as in a cartoon. Jamun is riveted by this transfigurement of his father into a hideous, bestubbled nursling. 'Please, God, I crave to die, please!'

In the seconds that Jamun, unmindful of the storm, from the foot of the bed, witnesses Shyamanand writhe, a something – a black curtain, a band of dark metal – is clawed off from just behind his forehead. So this was his father, his begetter, once beautiful and sapient, who'd shepherded him when he, a child, had been bullied by the dark, who'd piloted him through the middle of Calculus, had taught him how to cycle and swim – this accumulation of blubber shuddering on the bed, mentally annihilated by a storm, so this was his father, who'd begun, in his paralysis, to urinate in his jittery sleep – had once even defecated on the floor of his room because his sphincter hadn't held out till the lavatory, after which he'd slumped against the wall, half in his ordure, mumbling, 'Sorry. I'm sorry.' This was how we finished, reflects Jamun in a ferment, abandoned by our basest faculties, needing a son's arm to be guided to bed; this was the end of the wheel of life, its full circle, its fatuity before one's eyes when father became child in the years before dying.

The unexpectedness of her husband's incivility bruises Urmila the most. She does slew away, instinctively, to withstand Shyamanand's harshness; it registers with her that even in this, his extremity, his wits've found the time both to detest her and designedly to express his loathing. The ridiculous disparity between what she panted upstairs to expect and what she actually received pricks her to tears. She retorts almost ravingly, unwittingly, in a kind of self-defence. 'Then why *don't* you die, instead of just bleating about it! Your death'd at least release our lives –' She stops, appalled.

Shyamanand stops too – snivelling, that is. In that instant Jamun recognizes exhaustedly that he's, for the millionth time, going to witness a purposeless, enervating squabble between his parents, and that he'll be importuned by both of them to take sides.

'Yes, good. At last you reveal yourself. Good. Yes, of course I should die, what claim have I to want to – '

'I didn't say that! You know I didn't mean that – I – '

'Liar. You don't even have the spirit to own up to your real self.' Shyamanand turns to Jamun, gnarled features crimson with triumph and detestation. 'Now you bear her out, you mother's son. Assert to my face that she didn't screech just now that my death'd be welcome – come on, let me hear you fib.'

His mother's face decides him, as always. 'Well, Ma didn't *intend* to spout anything like that. Your asking her to buzz off was so heartless that she . . .' Jamun peters out when he discerns from his father's mien that he's been hurt enough. He has, with the curious acuity of late teenage, from time to time apprised Shyamanand that the tussle of fathers with mothers for the love of their sons is, for the fathers, hopeless from the start, because son is yoked to mother more sinewily than even daughter to father.

'Heartless! When compared to you cherubs, for sure I'm unmerciful, sadistic . . .' And so on, till the weeks accumulate into a decade. Shyamanand recuperates, by and by, sufficiently to be able to hobble about without help; walking sticks as an occasional gift for him become quite popular with Joyce, presents that he gratefully uses, but not without discomfort, since he likes to presume that he's too straightforward to relish giving to and receiving from those he abominates.

The years trudge by, Jamun plods through university. Fearful of the dispiritedness that his parents beget in him, he confusedly spends more and more time apart from them. When at home, he glides away upstairs and affects to study while listening to the stereo – for hours, or until Urmila's next spell of sobs tugs him down. In those years, he and Urmila continue secretly to chafe with guilt whenever they are lauded for their devotion to father and husband. With only one active hand, Shyamanand finds shaving irksome, hence he cultivates a lush beard that straggles down his chest and of which he becomes tolerably vain. The stroke alters his body in inconsequential ways too. The nails of his left foot and hand, for instance, begin to grow much more slowly than those of the right; they are pared half as often. In due time, the fact of the impairment does ooze through into his subconscious, for at ten one winter morning, he discloses that in his frightful dream of the previous night, in which he'd lain in the sludge at the bottom of a punt that was crewed by two noiseless, swarthy, wiry oarsmen – in that nightmare, he'd been transfixed even though he hadn't been bound, and within the dream itself he'd recognized, without surprise, that he could not stir because he was wholly paralysed.

# 6

# THE MOST FATEFUL EVENT

'Last evening, at his house, whatever' – asks Urmila, as she rearranges Joyce's roses in Doom's porridge mug – 'did Haldia keep you back for? Did he want more money? You know, I don't think he's understood my pacemaker one bit. I can make that out by the amount he smirks.'

But, 'Look! Look!' avidly yelps Pista just then from the door, thus delivering Jamun from a response. The kid can't even wait till his grandmother and uncle've swivelled, but immediately thrusts his right foot forward, sways insecurely before transferring his weight on to it, and seesaws yet again for balance before daring to shove his left foot ahead, and so on, crabbedly across the room, remembering to huff and snuffle before and after each tread. His right arm, braced, bent at the elbow, relies heavily on an invisible walking stick. His forehead puckers with befitting intentness and strain, though at each step the imp also titters in triumph, and looks askance at his grandmother to note how she's taking his parrotry of her manner of walking that morning. Doom stalks his brother, sniggering distraughtly, trying to ape the mimic, but failing because of the ferment of impatience. Shyamanand stands at the door, cackling his encouragement. Both Urmila and Jamun laugh, because Pista is imitating his grandmother so well as to be almost cruel, and simultaneously Jamun does wish, unwittingly, that the brat'd forthwith knock off the mimicry.

Pista fetches up at the bookcase, pirouettes, lurches and totters forward a few more paces, declares, 'Watching Thakuma struggling to walk this morning was so funny – like a kiddie trying his first steps – even Doom walks better! Thakuda says that when Thakuma moves, she's as steady as a drunken cripple! Like this!' He begins to parody his grandmother's walk again, pausing now and then to chortle teasingly at Urmila.

When his mimicry stops being droll and instead starts to drag a bit, Jamun and his mother, after commending the bugger's perception and flair for travesty, revert to the roses. The two monkeys mooch off to forage for an audience that'd be appreciative for longer.

Jamun next comes upon them about an hour later, when he descends for lunch. Urmila lies in her room. Pista ambles about her bed, repeatedly beseeching her to play chess with him, tch-ing with vexation whenever she responds that she wants to rest till lunch and then, out of boredom and balefulness, spoofing her steps again. 'See! See – this is how you plod – like a drunken cripple!'

'Oh, leave off, Pista. You're pushing up my BP like . . .' An adequate simile eludes Urmila, and she turns over, hoping perhaps that a view of her compressible, cushiony back will rebuff her grandchild. Plainly, she's been trying to deter him for quite a while, but he very likely has interpreted all her bids at dissuasion as stages in a game, for he prances up to the bed and starts to poke her in the back, as though inspecting its pliancy. 'Thakuma, d'you know how you looked when you went to the hospital? See – you looked like this,' and his eyes gyre up underneath their lids, his jaws unbrace, even his face seems to blench a bit in a first-rate imitation of an insentient countenance.

'That's enough, Pista. Stop riling Ma, and let's move for lunch.'

Perhaps Jamun's tone is too disdainful, withering, too abrupt, perhaps the boy is rankled by this dampening of his expectations, but Pista, before gliding away from the bed, without warning thwacks his grandmother in the spine.

'PISTA!' Shyamanand screeches from behind Jamun, from the door, so deafeningly, with such fury, that they all involuntarily twitch. He hobbles into the room, face lurid with rage. 'You beast. So this is what your damned parents knock into your head upstairs, is it – to wallop your grandmother – we don't matter at all, of course –' His arm jerks – the first motion of upraising his walking stick – but Jamun touches his father's shoulder long before his intent can be plain to Pista. Shyamanand's body shudders with passion. After a moment, poor Pista's legs fail him. Wholly stunned, he lurches forward two paces, slumps against the wall, slides to the floor, all elbows and knees, and begins to bawl soundlessly. 'You behave with us in this manner only because your parents treat us so dismissively, because you note every day that what we believe, speak and do doesn't penetrate them one inch. And you know that if I complain this evening to your father that you boxed your grandmother, the statement won't even enter his skull. And your mother'll probably gift you a chocolate for it . . .' Shyamanand peters out. For some seconds the room fills with his exhausted breathing. Jamun, who hasn't yet totally recuperated from his mother's straggling disclosures of the forenoon, glances at her, but she, seemingly insensible, gazes on them all without expression. Pista, still snivelling, revives enough to slink away and upstairs. Jamun clears his throat and suggests lunch. 'Later,' slurs Urmila drowsily, and labouredly curls up away from them.

Lunch, like every other activity in the house, is a delicate, fatiguing enterprise. For years, on weekdays, when Urmila's been in office and Jamun in the university, the menial of the month has, at one p.m. sharp, helped Shyamanand to stuff himself and, at two-thirty or so, has, amongst the flies in the kitchen, tucked into and pilfered prodigious quantities of leftovers. On the many days when the flunkey's played hookey, Shyamanand has had to look to himself with only his one good arm and leg (two and a half limbs actually, if one counts his left leg). Notwithstanding his tearjerking protestations, one *can* manage to care for oneself, tolerably well, with just one half of one's body alive. However, feeling tragic, he stands in front of the fridge and, with his right hand, gouges out and gulps down the gelid leavings of dinner – rice, dal, curd, fish (to the morsels of which are attached, like minuscule, tawny ice floes, frozen chunks of cooking oil), some vegetable mash, and whatever else the refrigerator might that afternoon contain – cheese, tomatoes, a sweet or two (more likely two). Later, ignoring the slight nausea of the hog, he telephones Urmila to inform her of the drudge's truancy, and then equably listens to her commiseration.

For years, on holidays, and when teenage despair prevents Jamun from attending at the university, lunch is a listless, potentially inflammable venture. He always tries to eat alone, but his parents, sick of each other, hoot and yell for him from the stairwell to come down and eat with them. He bellows back, 'I'm not hungry!'

'Well, come and sit with us while we eat.' And be the biased referee, is what they mean.

Then, after years, at their table for six, when the entire family is together, occasionally eat Shyamanand, Urmila, Burfi, Joyce, Pista, Doom and Jamun. From these meals, only the wiliest, the most vigilant, milk nutrition. They seemingly believe that the dining table is a sort of Hobbesian world in miniature, wherein only the fittest survive, and that, too, more on mutton and fish than rice and lowly spinach. The fittest are, in order, Burfi, Shyamanand and Jamun. Of these three, whoever first clutches the ladle masses up his own plate like an ideal growing boy in an advertisement for some wonderfood. Whoever grasps the ladle second, unspokenly detesting the first as the loser the champion, and fuzzily searching for revenge, while nattering with the less fortunate at the table, heaps up for himself an amount even more mountainous. Thus those who help themselves last usually feast on just rice and dal. Very swiftly, Joyce tires of the food habits of the house, and on her visits Chhana (sedate and dreadfully vain, who believes that to be slow is to detain the attention of others for longer) becomes more and more irregular at meals. Joyce sets up a separate kitchen upstairs, into which the ingress of those other than her brats and her aya is not encouraged, from which debouch, on holiday afternoons, the magical fumes of Occidental cooking, and from which goulashes and fondues gravitate to the dining table downstairs only when they've gone off a little.

On Urmila's thirty-seventh wedding anniversary, Shyamanand and Jamun are burping away their lunch and Jamun's puffing away at a cigarette when Doom, looking uncertain, sidles up to them, scratches his right knee out of a kind of misgiving, and quavers, 'Thakuma's on the floor, and is not getting up. I shouted in her ear, but she's not getting up.'

Breathless with the exertion, Jamun and Aya heave Urmila back on to the bed. She has urinated in her petticoat. 'You kids buzz off so that we can change Ma.' The kids don't budge. 'Pista, can you bring me Haldia's phone number? Thanks.' Shyamanand collapses on the bed and strokes Urmila's ashen strands back from a brow puckered with some gagged agony. 'Now what?' he falters to himself, twice. 'Now what?' Her mouth is open, like a cave on the face of a mountain. 'Maybe she's snoozing,' moots Pista unsurely. Her each inhalation seems the outcome of a slow and turbulent contest. Pista chats twice with Haldia's answering service. Burfi says that he's zipping home that very minute. After some fifteen minutes, just before the doctor calls back, Urmila starts to twitch and groan, gently. Her groans sound like shrieks from a remote dream.

Her sons stand about her bed. Jamun, worrying his lower lip, loosens the strings of her petticoat. 'What's she saying?' mutters Burfi, sallow with anxiety. 'She wants something, doesn't she? Something's pestering her.' Then, bending over her gunmetal face, long fingers rambling across her cheek, 'Ma, it's me, Burfi. Ma, what is it?' He straightens, grimaces at the wall, and shakes his head theatrically.

The moans swell in urgency, become quicker. The ruts in her temple deepen with the struggle, her eyes half-open, but sightlessly, her lips slip off her teeth, her skull starts to thresh about like a fish scooped out of a rivulet and tossed on to some shingle to die. Burfi clutches her shoulders, as much to bridle himself as her. 'Ma, what is it? What'd you like, tell me. Do you want water? Ma, are you thirsty?' A hint of a shift in pitch in her moaning, a sort of adjustment in its phasing, connotes that no is the answer. 'She understood me, God, what a relief . . . Ma, is the room too muggy? Shall I open another window? . . . What, d'you feel cold? Would you like me to switch off the fan? . . . I can't follow you, Ma, what're you trying to say . . . D'you want a third pillow? . . . Are you comfortable? Or shall we roll you over? . . . Is the light upsetting you? Shall I draw the curtains? . . . Maybe she'd enjoy a cold-water compress . . . Is some part of your body chafing you? . . . Oh shit, what an idiotic question . . .'

They continue to watch her purgatorical face – the skin the pallor of the sky at dawn, the dishevelled hair, the gullied forehead, the rictus of anguish on her lips, the string of gold about the neck – and the bloodless, forsaken hands, the cracked feet. Beside her, Shyamanand's spine has looped over in defeat. 'She won't return from Haldia's this time. I know it. In my bones, I know it.'

All at once, Aya squawks, rattling them all, 'Of course, I know what Ma wants!' She lunges forward, clacking distraughtly, 'She wants her hair combed! That's what she's missing! Don't you remember? After lunch she always sinks into that easy chair by the window and combs her hair for some fifteen minutes! Then in the evening, after her bath and before subsiding in front of the TV, she plaits and buns her hair – I know it! If you make her sit up, then I could brush down her hair.'

A flutter of Urmila's eyelids, like moths on the wing, and, amidst the twitchings of her head, a distinct affirmative nod. Burfi and Jamun tug her up from her shoulders, but Urmila can't sit straight in bed, and instead keeps listing over like a tipsy lush in some slapstick. Doom starts to titter. Finally, Jamun squats behind her and grasps her arms. Aya, murmuring in triumph at her own discernment, begins to unsnarl the luxuriant salt-and-pepper tresses. Urmila's moans mellow into weak purrs of cosiness. Her forehead eases, the jaws slacken, and over her features glides a sheen of light like a shadow across water.

Before they start out for the hospital, Burfi and Jamun climb up to the roof of the house to puff a hurried joint. Burfi's proposal – 'We'll need to be high, you realise, to grapple with those quacks and that carbolic acid. After all, it's Ma, and not just an aya or something' – readily assented to by his brother. Shyamanand quaveringly wails from the foot of the stairs, 'How much longer will you be? Every second is vital at this stage.' Jamun brays back, 'Coming, Baba! Burfi's pretending to rummage for some cash, hoping that we'll lose patience and beseech him to forget his contribution.'

The sons cart Urmila out to the rear seat of the car. She seems to be an abominably heavy, shoddily clothed, broken doll. Burfi sits in the back, her head in his lap.

At Haldia's, on the single visible stretcher at Reception, sprawls an orderly – uniformed, bestubbled, with feet as malodorous as his yawning mouth, into which Jamun rams a hundred-rupee note.

'Ten rupees'd've been enough for the fucker,' grouses Burfi as they trail the attendant, virtually waltzing behind the stretcher.

Doom'd been idling about when Jamun'd packed an essential bag for Urmila. To leaven the air, he'd bunged a foil of sedatives at the child. 'Here, have some of these, Doomdoomo, they'll develop you as an individual. Leonardo has four of them with every meal.' But Doom hadn't even picked up the strip from the floor. 'No, why should I? I'm not dying,' he'd retorted pipingly, and clumped out of the room.

At Intensive Care, Urmila and Malodorous are swished in. The bewhiskered matron shoves her knockers out at the brothers and orders them to wait beyond the glass doors. Burfi proposes that they find a spot where they can at least smoke a cigarette. 'Here we go-o-o again,' he warbles, and then appends, drily, 'being milked by Dr Rotunda for thousands and thousands and thousands of rupees. Shit. What a life.'

Jamun is chastened by his extreme exhaustion. Nothing else appears to wriggle into his skull. This is the real life, he ruminates messily, this fatigue, these aching calves, this bedpan world. We'll never know for certain whether Ma wished for anything other than the braiding of her hair. A primal remorse oozes through his veins. We can never express the true sentiments – love, devotion, kindness – we can never act humanely, while those whom we cherish are healthy and alive. At that moment, to Jamun, this thought seems as indubitable as the precept of Genesis that a man shall leave his father and his mother, and shall cleave unto his wife, and they shall be one flesh, and shall spawn a litter which in due time will leave its father and its mother to cleave to and be one flesh with a spouse. Thus existence has trundled along for thousands of years, and will chug on till Time itself peters out, and its hellish and dreadful designlessness is at last immaculately clear when one witnesses, at close quarters, the sickness of death.

The waiting room down the corridor is steel-blue and lugubrious. Jamun blows smoke rings at the nearest No Smoking plate, and watches Burfi whizz through a magazine. All at once, Burfi stops at a page, frowns at it and starts to read. Must be an article on kinky sex, muses Jamun.

'Listen to this, Chutiyam Sulphate . . . "Pierson is one of the three hundred or so children each year across the United States who murder one or both of their parents. Fathers are most often the victims . . . In court more and more children are arguing that they acted in self-defence, admitting readily to the crime but pointing to years of abuse that left them fearful for their lives . . . Sociz" – however that's pronounced – "Junatanov, who worked in his father's restaurant, hired a thug to kill his father. When the knife-wielding assailant failed, Junatanov's girlfriend crept into the hospital disguised as a nurse and injected the wounded victim with battery acid. That attempt also failed. Junatanov lined up another contract killer to finish the job – but this time the hired assassin was an undercover Los Angeles police officer . . . Last year a jury in LA acquitted him of all charges after hearing lurid testimony of years of physical, emotional and sexual abuse by his father. 'The jurors came up and hugged him,' said the Defence Attorney . . . In another case, Ludwig initially denied that he had been abused . . . 'Kids are so ashamed,' explains a psychiatrist, 'they even try to convince outsiders that they deserved the beatings. These kids are like prisoners of war. They can't think straight any more' . . . well over ninety per cent of children who commit parricide have suffered physical, sexual and mental abuse . . . Most such children are found to be suicidal . . . Pierson, a quiet and somewhat immature teenager, says that her 240-pound father began sexually abusing her when she was about eleven, progressing until he was having sexual intercourse with her as often as three times a day. She claimed that he even molested her in the car on the way to the hospital to visit her mother, who died some years ago . . ." Sombre stuff, isn't it? Baba should wade through this, and remember it whenever he bleats that in our time, the spaced-out Hindu tradition of undisputed reverence for one's elders has been degraded by the influence of the sordid West, where a child hasn't yet learnt to esteem its papa in between his four daily rapes of her. But then the West is youthful, and has much to imbibe on the subjects of tolerance and *maya*. Daddy's squat prick, looking much like the Police Commissioner in Mandrake, grinding into her mouth after every meal or something – that ingenuous, Polish, second-generation American must realize that Papa's phallus does not exist, that it's actually in her head, and not between her teeth.'

Jamun wishes to demur that he doesn't need to be diverted from their immediate extremity in this manner, but he isn't certain that Burfi's approach to the crisis isn't the correct one; if one conducted oneself as though one were only waiting in an anteroom for an inconsequential interview, or to endorse one's train tickets, then perhaps one could really push off after a while and not return morning, noon and night, day after day after day, just to stand about for a death.

They can see their mother only the following morning. 'She's better now, much better,' affirms a charlatan whom they haven't encountered before. He is colossal, in a turquoise safari suit and an Alfred E. Neuman face. He expresses himself in Hindi, Punjabi and English – by the sound of it – all at the same time. 'I declared her out of danger at'– for some reason, he peeps at his watch, which is about the size of a planet – 'four this morning. She's half-conscious, and her speech is somewhat intelligible. For sure, she'll tend to confuse time and space for a while – for instance, she fancies that she's at home now, and once or twice has asked after some Kishori and one Ratna Garbha – your maidservant or something, I presume. The instant that her system stabilizes, we'll ferry her off for a Cat-scan' – simpers – 'to worm out how her blood's been trifling with her brain.'

An interrogatory moan as they file into the cubicle; they can't discern much in the half-light that transudes through the black panes. Urmila's face is the ashen tint of the room.

'Ma, it's me, Burfi. Ma.' Her eyelids quiver, but she doesn't swivel her head towards the voice.

A twilight brain in a twilight room, a drugged sluggishness, a webbed silence. What rest, in an incorruptible, measureless freedom. In that pillowed owl-light, Urmila confounds her sons with her physicians, and twice demands of Neuman why Jamun doesn't come down for his tea. 'He fritters away all his time upstairs with Kasturi, shunning us,' she grumbles, or they presume she does. She wants to know whether twenty rupees has been deducted from the sweeper's pay and why Burfi has not remembered to turn off the pump after the cistern's topped up. So she unveils a subconscious that is almost wholly –.and embarrassingly – cramped and domesticated; yet these rodent-like scamperings within her skull seem unthinking, mechanical, and despite her slurred murmuring (what Alfred E. calls her 'strenuous cerebral activity'), in her insentience she is untrammelled and altogether free.

The Catscan den is elementary sci-fi – ochreous domes, winking computer screens, courteous bleeps, lubriciously gliding, rubber-swathed slabs, crystalline, schematic light, soundless footfalls, bespectacled moustached whitecoated whizzkids. Orderlies slide Urmila from her stretcher on to a ledge. Jamun marks that the left side of her face has buckled, much as Shyam-anand's had more than a decade earlier. Had it not been for her extinct, half-open eyes, the askew features would, for a moment, have looked pawky, sardonic, even attractive. She groans deeply, from her bowels, while Alfred E. struggles with and at last twists off her golden earrings. 'Can't have metal underneath the scanner,' he chortles. Jamun wants to stretch out and, like talons, clench Neuman's mammoth wrists, impede them from arousing an agony that skewers even Urmila's numbness and extorts such groans from her vitals. 'Old-fashioned earrings, these,' deplores Newman, pushing his upper lip all but into his nostrils, and spilling the rings into Jamun's palm. 'Like diffident virgins, they don't nestle in your paw without a little force.'

Elfin, golden marigolds. Jamun's eyes fringe with tears as he thumbs his mother's earrings. They are exceedingly dainty, patterned with mastery and restraint. As a thumbsucking toddler, he'd incessantly yawped and whinnied to be carried so that he could be within mauling reach of these rings and the flesh that had encased them. But that flesh had now departed, and in his hand the marigolds were heartrending, the terminal remains, like dice abandoned in the dupe's palm after a punishing and brutish game. He tries to hide his tears from Neuman's embarrassed glance.

In his initial days in the insurance office, Urmila'd telephone him now and then, chiefly to chuckle, and to 'see how it feels to hear you in a job, to conceive you actually jotting things down in a file, you, my own child. I should call your boss and disclose to him that you're horribly cantankerous and, not so long ago, regularly flew off the handle because I wouldn't permit you to tweak and grind my earlobes while you sucked away at your left thumb . . . Ah, but what's twenty years, Jamun . . .'

In the week that Urmila wastes away in hospital, his wits, in their disorder, ever so often conjoin the queerest, most disparate images. Her leaden countenance one forenoon, for example, with its unseeing eyes, which are flecked with the grey of a sort of bitter fear, suddenly, without reason, recalls for him the face of the lawn at home when it's not been hosed for days, when, beneath the chalklike topsoil, he's visualised the crust to be skeined by fissures, like an omnipotent's chastisement of their neglect. Other unrelated impressions also prod him to the brink of tears. When he stands futilely beside her bed, her exhalations waft to him the weakened fetor of carrion, as though her entrails are merrily rotting away. Throughout that day (and in his understanding, the two happenings – her breathing and the impression that his features have skewed – are cause-and-effect) he is overwhelmingly convinced that the left side of his own face has petrified and yet, somehow, at the same time, sagged dreadfully. Its skin feels glacial and inanimate. Time and time again, he buoys up his left cheek with his fingers, and (adopting the manner of a narcissist unthinkingly caressing his own face to encourage his dilatory introspection) unobtrusively massages it.

Hindi film ditties on television one evening. The sons, the daughter-in-law, the grandsons, easefully viewing and sneering at the beggary of the music. A weepy sixties idol cheeps and warbles to this screen goddess that she's far-out, a damn sight more gorgeous than the swollen moon, and much sexier than some Urdu word that Jamun surmises means a come-hither simper on the face of a sexbomb, and that Aya contends denotes simply the sun. Shyamanand wolfs down his dinner by himself in the dining room. After he's burped and wheezed the food down, he hobbles past the television on his way to Urmila's room. Perhaps the very sight of Joyce, her dome slanted in vacuous vanity, eyeing the screen with a daydreaming half-smirk, looking quite through her father-in-law, vexes him, because he abruptly draws up to ask the loungers, 'Shame on you all. Is this the hour that you consider suitable for Hindi movie muck? While your mother's dying in hospital?' He limps on across the room. He's begun to doss down in Urmila's bed from the evening of her departure for Haldia's, an act the irony of which bitterly entertains his children. 'What's he aiming to prove?' Burfi has scoffed. 'That he can glide into Ma's bed only when she's away in a nursing home? So he loves her only when she's absent and dying?'

'There's nothing unseemly or sinful,' counters Jamun, tense

with guiltiness at Shyamanand's comment, 'in lolling in front of a TV while Ma recuperates in Intensive Care. She isn't Indira Gandhi, you know, that we've to hurtle out into the streets and thwack our tits to voice our grief.'

'Grief! How can you even conceive,' sneers Shyamanand from the door, 'of sorrow in your bogus, looking-glass age? To you, a wimp in a Hindi movie, tweeting the tropes of intimacy, is more moving than your sinking mother.'

Was it that same evening, or the following, that Naidu and his hound look in to ask after Urmila? 'So? Is she on the mend?' bays Mr Naidu, wobbling on the balls of his feet in the centre of the drawing room, fuzzily hopeful that if he contracts his tummy and thrusts out his boobs, his five-foot-four'll somehow spiral to six feet, at which Joyce'd swoon with lust for him, instead of simpering witlessly at the television. 'Who's with her now?'

'God, I imagine,' murmurs Burfi, struggling to comb Doom's hair.

'No, I mean, who of the family's in the nursing home at this moment? Because I notice that all of you are here.'

'We assumed you knew. Ma's in Intensive Care and they head off relatives in there; we aren't needed in that situation either, just mooching about outside the glass doors, burning for a fag – '

'But someone should be there.' Surprise in Mr Naidu's inflection, and a gentle but distinct reproach. 'A blood relation should be with her all the time, a husband or a son. What are all of you slouching about here at home for? What if she – Heaven forbid – expires right now? A nurse'll telephone you to suggest that you zip across at once, because the case in Cubicle C has passed away. Would you like that? And if she regains lucidity and asks for one of you, she'll be told that her sons are at hand only at eleven in the morning and at sundown, so she'd better surface once more round about those times.'

For both Shyamanand and Mr Naidu, mourning has to be visible, for all to see; one simply can't laze about in front of a TV and tweet along with a Hindi hit parade if one is grieved; encumbered by despair, any devoted spouse or son should be shrivelled up in front of the glass of Intensive Care, night upon night, should start up only at each swoosh of the swing doors, and should disregard all the orderlies who sidle up to remind him that loitering in the corridors is prohibited.

At night, when he can't drop off, Jamun ruminates on these things. Intuitively, he disagrees with his father and Mr Naidu. But he doesn't hold, unlike them, that woe is no emotion for display, that passionlessly, in a Hindu way, one must learn that existence, which is immeasurably vaster than birth and mortality, paddles on independent of these events; and yet that, being itself, like Time and all other matters, must also fade out. No. Instead, over the years, while Jamun has grown up observing his parents squabble, while his gnarled emotional evolution has cramped him from voicing himself fully to Kasturi, while he's witnessed their marriage paralyse his father and slowly butcher his mother, he's begun to believe that living is elementally a petty, indecent, punishing business; its value lies in struggling against its meanness. In such a universe, remorse is weak selfishness, and mourning is remorse. When one grieves, one in fact only repines that one has not conducted oneself better. For Jamun, this sentiment is reinforced in the week that his mother takes to die. Regret is futile; there seems no point in behaving rightfully with Urmila in the terminal days of her life. Yet contrition is inexorable. He feels that he has to confront it face to face; through it he can learn to acknowledge his own shoddiness, his oafishness. Then, at other moments in that week, he's convinced that since they've all acquitted themselves abominably with Urmila, they fully deserve now to writhe with mortification.

Shyamanand disintegrates too, that week. One morning, he chokes on his tea and starts to wish that he himself were dead. 'No,' protests Burfi incisively, with Pista in his lap, and his hands on his child's shoulders, 'living is better than dying,' and suffixes, after a moment, 'Yes. We should pray for the best and brace ourselves for the worst.'

Jamun fondles Urmila's hair and watches an enormous vein in

her left temple throb fast and quick. Her fingers and arms are decoloured and chilled. To sob is greatly assuaging, and quite easy; whenever he snivels at his mother's bedside, he feels that he's fulfilling a duty, and redeeming himself a bit for his numberless churlishnesses.

Her entire corpse body judders with each inhalation. He wants to tell her that the inconceivable happened that afternoon, that while backing the car out of the house, he glanced at Shyamanand – whiling away his time in the vernadah, observing his family come and go – and spotted that his father's eyes were wet. I'm sorry, Shyamanand'd apologized, but I'd been brooding, and a moment ago I saw your mother's face vividly – how she'd fondle her earlobe while squinting at the TV – and I just couldn't restrain myself. Congratulations, Jamun yearns to purr to a sentient Urmila, your husband has at last sobbed for someone other than Chhana and himself.

A nurse's bloodless, beautiful hand, slim-fingered, finely veined, rests on Urmila's arm, a hideous contrast. Iced-water wads have been tucked into her armpits and patted down on her forehead. A silvery fluffiness of hair about the ears; above the left ear squats, like a frog, an oversize squashy bubo, which Neuman pronounces to be curdled blood. Yet some, muses Jamun muddledly, must've hankered for this body once, and, in a breath of enchantment, even decreed it more radiant than the swollen moon.

'If you overlook her sensations,' asserts Neuman, spanking his right flank with his stethoscope, 'she's really somewhat comfortable. If you set aside her emotions, that is.'

'I presume what the nerd means,' mutters Burfi, as Alfred E. lumbers off to confound some other careworn minds, 'is that Ma doesn't feel much pain. Her groans for sure don't support the bugger's idea. I guess quacks rake in even more cash when they're inarticulate.'

Like regret, guilt, grief and lamentation, death too is inexorable. One has to be all set to buzz off, okay, but after what age? Sixty-seven? Thirty-four? Thus, if one realizes at thirty-two, for instance, that one's number is up, one can justifiably feel defrauded of a few months of life? Rubbish, certainly. Perhaps one has to be ready to snuff it at *any* time – while polishing one's shoes, and tricycling about in the winter sun, on the shore, at the age of four. Doom should therefore be prepared to go the way of all flesh? Maybe the inevitability of mortality only connotes that death drops in at a particular age – and possibly that time of life for an individual is when his loved ones are tired of him or when he has mellowed into a vegetable.

Two mornings before Urmila cops it, Joyce and Doom emplane for Bombay. Joyce's soulmate Rani has lately shifted there, and Joyce pines to be with her; so the family discerns from Burfi's awkward, dishevelled explanations. In the five days that Urmila has till then spent at Haldia's, Joyce hasn't visited the nursing home even once. 'She doesn't like me, she won't miss me,' explains Joyce in the husky voice that she puts on when she's being sanctimonious, 'and I'm not a fraud. To bob about her bed looking pathetic, while speculating every second when it'd be okay to glide away – that's how you all behave there, anyway.' Joyce dilates her enormous eyes at Burfi.

'She's depressed,' Burfi struggles to extenuate his wife's conduct to Jamun, 'and maintains that there's an atmosphere of death in this house, and illness. She doesn't want this gloom permanently to dispirit her and the kids – particularly Doom. And none of us actually cares for Ma, she believes; if we cherished her, we'd've been, like Chachacha neighed the other evening, dossing down in the waiting rooms at Haldia's instead of looking in twice a day.'

'She's nuts.' Jamun can't curb himself. 'Worse than nuts. Not even a loon'd run out on the dying in this fashion – because the mood of the house isn't sunny and sparkling – like an ad for Kolynos.'

Burfi smirks without humour, trying to smother the turmoil within him. 'Maybe I should tag along with them – I could snuggle up too with Rani the butch, and pick up a few tricks.'

All at once his features crumple. 'Sometimes I wish she'd hurry up and croak.'

Neuman, in a tangerine safari suit, thrusts his John Lennon glasses up the bridge of his nose with a forefinger the girth of a dildo and announces a possible gangrene threat to Urmila's limbs. 'Do you mark these livid patches, soft and squelchy?'

Pista and Doom have visited the nursing home just once. Pista in particular has been averse to looking in on his grandmother. He secretly believes that she's fallen ill once again because he persisted in incensing her by parodying her walk. In her dim, chilled cubicle, Urmila frightens the children. All of a sudden, just when the brats are about to begin to explore the room, she starts to mewl loudly, like a derelict cat in a tree, in the garden, in the dark. Her skull too begins to thresh about, as though an invisible paw is repeatedly smacking her. The kids gawp, openmouthed. In that penumbral light, in alien surroundings, that bestial squealing from a swathed heap that a week before had been their homely, disregardable grandmother is truly fearsome.

Kasturi and Jamun drop Joyce and child off at the airport. Kasturi is a handful of days away from her lying-in. A long, snug quietness on the return drive into the city. 'We are all – at the middle point of the cycle, with allegiances and responsibilities before and after.' She sits in the car like an obese king with a breathing problem, for whom simply squatting is exertion enough. With eyes shut, she waffles away. 'We're now enduring the stress of grihasthi, when both our parents and our kids need fosterage. Isn't the classical codification of an individual life wise? Now and then I reflect on it – grihasthi is the eye of the storm, I suppose – though that isn't entirely correct, because the eye connotes stillness at the heart of tumult, doesn't it, and grihasthi is anything but. No, grihasthi is domesticity, the family, and a mortal life'd be fragmentary without it; for sure, the three other rungs are also significant to integrate a life, but the years before grihasthi seem to conduct you to it, and the age after grihasthi winds away from it – it's the hub, the umbilicus, the skein of birth and death, and one's so enmeshed in it, in the bonds and responsibilities of family, that one doesn't ruminate on the central questions, not much, anyway – but there isn't much spunk – oops, wrong word – left in the years after grihasthi, and vanaprastha and sannyas are euphemisms, aren't they, for rejection and dotage? Ergo, Jamun, grihasthi is all, that's why so many of us are sucked into it.'

Miss Hirsute starts to cluck as soon as they file into Intensive Care. 'Where've you been? The patient's been waiting since ten o'clock for her Trentol; last night, I told that other man who drops in here that we were running out of those injections, but he appears to've forgotten the second he breezed out of here. Now you've to trudge to Caulay Town for it, because the chemist downstairs exhausted his Trentol this morning. And hurry.' She then returns to her knitting; from its appearance, she seems to be ravelling a mammoth, grass-green, undie.

Hand in hand with Kasturi through the noisome alleyways of Caulay Town, while Shyamanand waits in the car. Jamun feels content to saunter with Kasturi again; the late afternoon recalls the similar hours of their university years, when, with scanty funds and a youthful itch for enlightenment, they'd foraged in the fusty cranny-shops of these bylanes for books. A pleasurable hubbub; rickshaws, backpackers, cattle, pedlars of philtres, Surds in Marutis, beggars with a gooey touch, neighing hawkers of export-reject clothes, cops fucking some citizen's happiness, junkies wasting away at the foot of lampposts, barrow boys clangingly delivering gas cylinders, the thundering din of disco-devotional chants from an askew shamiana. 'Kastu, a sale at Bharwaney's, look! Shall we pop in for a second?'

'God, you took ages!' whinges Shyamanand. 'What, did the druggist have to siphon the serum out of some shop assistant's veins? And some scruffy policeman started to pester me: "You can't park here, I'll tow you away," he kept smirking and hectoring me, thwacking his palm with his cane. "My son's just nipped down the lane for some crucial injections for his mother, who's in hospital," but that reptile wouldn't believe me. And if you were meaning to take so long, you could at least've left me in some shade.'

With Urmila's exhalations, Jamun finally knows what the phrase 'sickly sweet' truly conveys. Aya beneath the stairs had wheezed similarly, and tainted the air about her with this thick, candied unhealthiness, as though in her entrails, a rat'd been stifled in syrup. Throughout that week of his mother's hospitalization, he unthinkingly connects all fetid odours with her distended, insentient contour. When he drives by, the reek from the sea, or the zoo, or a refuse heap, or the abrupt waft of carrion, in recalling his mother's form, abides with him for minutes after he's crossed the actual source, and seems to effuse, instead, from her orifices. Each time that this occurs – and the instances are several – he admits to himself, yes, this is the knockout, and from Haldia's she's bequeathed me this fetor, which I shall ferry about with me as a legacy befitting the quality of her life.

Friday morning, six a.m. Tea in the verandah. No one else in the house is astir. An insinuation of a chill in the air, reminding Jamun that, with his mother absent, the household now contains nobody who can be pleasurably badgered for blankets. He muses on Kasturi's patter in the car on Wednesday, that they – he, Burfi, Kuki, Joyce, Kasturi herself and the like – have fetched up at a stage in their lives when they are twined with, and hence committed to, both the recently born and the dying, to both Shyamanand and Pista, Urmila and Doom. He assents to the idea, chiefly because Kasturi has voiced it; had it been articulated, for example, by Burfi, Jamun'd've construed that Burfi was using his children as a pretext to duck his turn to look in at the hospital.

Guilt continues to chafe him. He does, in jerks and snatches, believe in the creed: 'As far as possible without surrender, be on good terms with all persons.' But he further accepts that one has to be on even better terms – that is, one has to acquit oneself even more honourably – with one's kith and kin, and in particular with one's parents, because they've gifted one with life. Yet, in life, these precepts are forever being transgressed; indeed, their precise opposite always seems to occur, namely, that one is persistently more beastly, unfilial, baleful and heartless with those whom one most cherishes, is most restful with, like a mother; as though with them, one can be just oneself, naked and horrid; with them, one can't endure the strain of being considerate.

Shyamanand clumps out to the verandah, looking sloppy after a fretful night. Pista straggles down, hopeful of some sips of tea from his grandfather before Burfi wakes up and remonstrates. The telephone. Jamun answers. A voice from Haldia's declares that Mrs— in Cubicle C expired at zero four zero nine hours that morning. When he returns to the verandah, Pista is ducking rusks in Shyamanand's cup. 'My mother's promised me that if I finish up to Lesson Twelve of my bloody Hindi by the time she comes back from Bombay, she'll buy me the Rambo Special.'

Burfi and Jamun drive to the hospital at six-thirty. In Urmila's room, the divers machines are off and beneath her dead face is a body swaddled in white, a bit like a monstrous sanitary napkin. The sons sob, a warm and meagre dribble of tears. Hirsute click-clacks over to them to remark that the patient's pacemaker has been removed, and that since it's still in topnotch condition, they should remember to carry it with them before they leave because it could always be used once more.

'But we were told that its batteries were leaking. In fact, we'd presumed that had her pacemaker been working, she wouldn't've suffered her last attack.'

Hirsute gurgles with astonishment and jounces her football boobs about at the idea. Jamun doesn't possess the will to dispute.

Seven-thirty is dreadfully early for Haldia, but not so for Neuman, who clacks gossipily, as though death is hot news, like a burglary in the locality. 'In the last hours, the patient suffered a succession of explosions in her skull, a run of tiny strokes. Her body's altogether mouldered, you know. Are you meaning to park the body at home for long? Because her innards have putrefied, and relatives are likely to turn distraught over a corpse, and hug and clutch it, and hamper its being toted off to the crematorium; these hysterics crack up if, after a few hours, the cadaver they're half-worshipping exudes the wispiest pong – are any such inflammable near and dear ones waiting at home? . . . Good. I propose that you cart the body off to the ghat today itself, and not kowtow to any beseeching that the corpse be retained overnight in the house because some brother or cousin or nephew is whizzing in tomorrow from Buenos Aires or Lusaka, and he or she must, absolutely must, peep at least once at the dear, cold face of the patient – I should say, ex-patient – you mustn't knuckle under that kind of feverishness. Do light some incense around her bed, its smell always helps.'

Hirsute beckons to Jamun to assist her to fill in a couple of forms. 'Name . . . Age . . . Sex . . . Address . . . Your Name . . . Relationship with Deceased . . . Sons? You are her sons? Both of you? Really? I'd never've guessed by myself . . . Cause of Death . . . Place of Death . . .'

The stretcher. The van. Burfi and Jamun feel lightened when they step out of Intensive Care. For some idiotic reason Jamun is lulled that he is that morning wearing Joyce's latest present to him, a pair of cavernously roomy Levi's, into which he has with ease rammed prescriptions, the hospital receipts, residual medicines, his chequebook and ballpoint, a pouch that contains Urmila's necklace, earrings, bangles and pacemaker, her comb, a handful of notes, her face compact. As he plods alongside the stretcher, he irrationally believes that everything will be okay as long as he can continue to stuff things into his Levi's and thus keep his hands free to take on the world.

In the van Burfi possessively lodges Urmila's head in his own lap. 'However could anyone profess that in death one can look like sleep?' He is weeping soundlessly, with ease, as though his eyes are watering because of an irritant in them. 'When one is asleep, one's face is slack, even doughy, but this' – his fingers trip across Urmila's cheek – 'all the commonplaces that describe death are so befitting, aren't they? That a light, or a spark, or a glow within, that was most naked at the eyes, is now stubbed out. That what survives is a shell, an untenanted house, the desiccated flesh of the fruit from which the sap's been siphoned off – all the clichés about death wham you when you gaze at her lonely eyes and her mouth, when it doesn't fully hide the teeth.' With his fingers Burfi tries to clamp Urmila's lips together.

On the last sweep of the ocean road, Jamun asks his brother, 'Are bodies carted off to the crematorium always from houses? I mean, are the dead invariably brought home from the hospital before being ferried to the ghat or wherever? . . . We didn't do that with Aya. She slid, without any fuss, from that TB hospital to some van to the ghat . . . Burfi, is Ma to be burnt with wood or electricity or what? Where's the crematorium, anyway? Who'll instruct us on all this, Burfi, on what are hazily called "the last rites"? Baba is clueless, I'm certain. About what to wear and when to shave one's nut, even what to eat. I mean, we do intend to go through all that, don't we? What if we phone the crematorium, and some bugger yawps that they are overbooked, try next week?'

At home, they lay Urmila out on her bed and buffet open all the doors and windows. Solemn neighbours seem to emerge out of the walls. Pista dawdles from room to room, unenlightened. A lachrymose Aya lights a lamp between Urmila's head and the telephone. Jamun receives the wisdom of those who've borne with many deaths. Mr Naidu looks genuinely condolent and still manages to bore. 'Grief will overpower you later, without warning,' he assures, snuffling his moustaches into Jamun's face, 'in flashes, and it'll be elicited by the queerest, littlest things – a stranger in an adjacent room'll clear her throat exactly like her, and you will, all at once, be completely convinced, but only for an instant, that your mother will shuffle into the room in which you are, and ask you something totally mundane, whether you've had your second cup of tea, or whether you remembered to pay your college fees before the last date. And when the bus you're in drones to a halt at a red light, for a second, from somewhere, the lavender scent that she put on on certain days will flutter to you. Or when you're rooting about in the forgotten clutter of a drawer for, say, a ration card, and you happen on a twenty-year-old postcard from your mother, counselling you to spend your pocket money sensibly, and not to be impudent to your father – then, a yearning for her will crush you then.' An avuncular swat on Jamun's shoulder. 'But all that misery will bowl along, you know. Nothing is ageless except the bloody runs, ha-ha.' Mr Naidu pulls up when he realizes that he's chortling at an unfit place and moment; so he draws in his tummy and pokes Jamun's thorax with his cigarette packet. 'Look, I simply have to smoke my stamina stick – but perhaps I should sneak out. You don't want to plod about outside for a bit?'

Shyamanand subsides against the bedrest alongside Urmila's head and watches the hushed confusion of the room – much like a venerable, yet still Argus-eyed watchdog, of the species which fealty recalls from retirement for one last, dauntless vigil. On one of the times that Jamun passes the bed on some chore, Shyamanand hisses to him, 'Have you noticed that the Christian isn't present? It *is* significant, you realize, that at the instant of your mother's death, Joyce wasn't at home, or even in the city.' Pista slouches up to Burfi. 'Baba, can I go outside and play with Ramu? I've finished my homework.'

Jamun telephones and notes, with a kind of drab, distant surprise, that the voice from the crematorium is discerning and sympathetic, and that, seemingly, one *can* incinerate the dead without a bribe, without queueing up for days, without being badgered for one's School-Leaving Certificate and the corpse's Civil Supplies Card, and without filling in sixteen different forms in Hindi.

The van from the crematorium draws up at four in the afternoon. On the first-floor verandah, Aya, clutching an unenthusiastic Pista to her udders, starts to bawl most dreadfully as

Urmila is shouldered out. Pista's neighbourhood chums sidle up a couple of paces with fistfuls of petals for Urmila, chicken out and chuck them instead at her loadbearers. 'But where are the other women of the family?' demands Mr Naidu, fantasizing, perhaps, that Joyce, wildeyed and threnodic, should be sagging over the railing of the top verandah, with arms outstretched in doleful yearning to tug the cadaver of her darling mother-in-law out of the departing van.

A mammoth hall, black with burning. Pigeons fluttering and whirring away their lives near the ceiling; the several windows, expansive, munificent, are open to ensnare the dying light. Burfi haggles with six unclean adolescents and finally selects two. They are all priests attached to the crematorium, or so they gabble as they crowd one another, and for two thousand rupees will blether some decorous Sanskrit verses over Urmila before she is shoved in. Since he doesn't appear to be paying, Burfi at first is not disposed to bargain. Luckily, Jamun points out to him in time that Shyamanand and his sons are aiming to split the costs. Burfi whittles the two scummiest urchins down to a hundred rupees. They moult their Bruce Lee and Ninja Turtle T-shirts and anoint their foreheads with what looks like shit. The contused, purple lips and fleshless chest of the senior lout, by reminding him of Vaman, inflames Jamun with a spurt that makes him shudder at himself. He watches the sleazy stripling more than the dead face of his mother in the thirty minutes that the jokers waste over her remains.

'We should keep back the blood relations of the deceased,' commends to Shyamanand a podgy hireling of the crematorium, a sort of master of ceremonies. He hasn't pushed his belt through the loop above the seat of his biscuity trousers; the belt has capered up his dorsum, thus shaping a corniculate beige pouch over his arse. 'Where are they? Now and then we light on some near and dear ones whom the state of things whips up, and they lose their marbles, and at the very last moment, just before the body slides in, they do their damnedest to hitch a ride on it.'

Urmila is trundled into an outsize furnace at five forty-nine. The condolers shuffle up to Shyamanand, Burfi and Jamun, look manful and dribble away. The three of them drive home in a kind of sad, relaxed quietness, as though they are returning from a railway station, to which they've frenziedly careened to get a beloved friend to board on time, fearful throughout the rush that they won't pull it off, and after they've made it, have been thoroughly sucked out by the backwash of tension. Aya and Pista are perched on the culvert beside the gate, a bit timid of the darkened, empty house. Burfi and Jamun swathe themselves in their mourning dress, namely, yards and yards of unstitched cream cloth. Neither they nor Shyamanand quite know whether there exists a correct and tasteful way of enveloping oneself in a sort of bale of lining. They try out diverse styles; all look cute, Vivekanandavian. Burfi, vain even in sadness, starts to posture in front of the full-length mirror that's set in the cupboard in Shyamanand's room. 'Hey, this actually looks pretty neat . . . especially if you drape the stuff over one shoulder and under the other . . . Not bad, huh? . . . Are we to have these on for twelve days or thirteen? . . . You mean, continuously? . . . But how the fuck am I going to exercise with this outfit on? . . .'

Aya reminds them that for the days of mourning, they've to eat plain, vegetarian food, and, to stave off Urmila's spirit, wear iron next to the skin. 'An easy method'd be to slip a twine about your neck with an iron key or something on it.' She and Pista are sent off to forage in various shelves and canisters for iron objects; they can't ferret out any. Pista is fairly eager to see his father and uncle with some unwieldy thing about their collarbones, so he asks whether Shyamanand's ancient shaving mug'll serve. 'Couldn't you two put it on in turn? One in the day, the other at night? Shouldn't I also wear something? If I had my Rambo Special, I –'

'Shut up. Besides, it's enamel, not bloody iron . . . Let's just forget this entire iron business. Can't we, Baba? As it is, I could never be petrified of Ma's spirit – not *Ma's*, at any rate, if you know what I mean, and I don't mind if it hovers about my ears for the rest of my damned life.'

'And certainly, when Joyce returns from Bombay tonight, you'll be somewhat abashed to face her in this finery – and whatever will her exemplary Christian upbringing make of some obscurantist iron about your neck, bicep, or third finger?' Shyamanand pauses because Burfi doesn't seem to've heard a single word; with his back to the looking-glass, legs solidly apart, he's swivelled his nut around to a yogic degree to study what his bum looks like in mourning. 'The sonofabitch,' he is communing with himself, 'must *fall* well, like fucking water – God, this looks as though my sphincter's going nuts straining to hold back a whopping squirt . . . Sorry, Baba, were you saying something?'

'No, nothing important . . . The two of you'd better gulp down something before you zip off to the airport. It'd be unfair to expect of Indian Airlines that Joyce's airbus'll touch down on time – they haven't averaged a punctual plane a week since the moon landing. You might've to cool your heels there for hours. Did Aya remember to check when she bought this lining cloth how much was needed for each person? . . . Had Chhana been here, I'm positive that she'd've known what else one has to abide by during mourning. Did you read her last letter in which she's tried to explain why she can't come? Most dubious . . .'

At the airport car park, Burfi declines to debouch from the front seat. 'Not in this gear, please. We look like the fucking terrorist wing of some new, homosexual Buddhist sect. You watch. They won't even let you in.'

Jamun crosses the asphalt, feeling more selfconscious and awkward than melancholy. He is certain that in the saucers of amber light from the compound lamps, he must appear freakish, a tragedian out of a neighbourhood playlet. At every step he dreads to hear exclamations and derisive guffaws. 'To carry off togs like these,' Burfi has professed on the drive out of the city, 'you need the mug of a Chink.' Because he seems to have on his hands far too many yards, Jamun has wrapped the cloth about his legs so often that, he now discovers, he has virtually immured them; each tread of his carries him only a few inches forward. With these short, twinkling paces, like those of a very fat creature in a flurry, he fetches up at the foot-high rails of the enclosure and finds that his dress does not offer his legs enough leeway for him to step over them. A woman in a nearby car cackles, and he is sure that she's glimpsed him. Grinning to himself in embarrassment, he raises his robes to just below his crutch and hops over the spikes. But an idle cop, an undesirable, saunters up and wants to know what is what. By the time Jamun manages to persuade him that he isn't a Surd or Assamese or Mizo or Kashmiri or Pakistani or Tamilian or Sri Lankan terrorist, the board announces that Joyce's flight is forty minutes late.

In the car, Burfi unthinkingly gnaws his lower lip and starts to blether, 'Too late as usual, isn't she? She couldn't wait – "I'm entombed in your house," she spumed and bubbled, "by illness, death and the evocations of those who dislike me." She wasn't here, and Ma's gone, she'll never lay her eyes on her again, and now everything'll come apart –' He fidgets, tries to light a cigarette and, all of a sudden, gives way to tears. 'Every bloody second, I've been thanking my stars that I didn't chaperone them to Bombay. As long as you see her every day, she'll remain alive. I should've pushed that further. As long as you're at hand, watching her, she'll live. As long as you rivet your eyes on her, and *never* blink, she'll revive.' He scrabbles about for a rag to blow his nose into, once or twice fingers the fringes of his mourning outfit, and finally settles on the flannel in the glove compartment. After honking endlessly, he sighs and slews to an easier subject. 'One's diverse allegiances yank one – at the same time – in so many different directions. I mean, to whom is one *first* pledged? Is there any *one* to whom one is more beholden than to others? Parent? Or guardian? An aya? Spouse? Or one's favourite floosie? Or one's child? But which of them? One's first son or fourth daughter? Tchah.'

He potters about the house for half an hour the next morning, asking his brother whether he should exercise, suffixing that he'd *feel* better for it, and that life must go on. At eleven, in nipping, sunny weather, they all – Shyamanand, Burfi, Joyce, Jamun, Pista and Aya – drive to the crematorium to collect Urmila's ashes. Shyamanand and Aya remain in the car. The others are steered to a tiny, arid lawn. It is fringed by a slatternly hedge and two half-dead jacarandas. On a concrete bench, on its side, lies an open, blackened, queerly shaped container, much like the extracted glove compartment of a gigantic car. It contains some charred and ashen deposits, like the sooty flakes and chalk at the end of a long barbecue. Diffidently, Burfi stretches out towards the bench the bowl of burnt clay that Aya has picked up for them to be Urmila's last vessel.

Burfi has at first wished the receptacle to be in brass, 'or bronze, or some such metal, you know, class. This mud pot's damn lumpen, as though we didn't want to spend too much cash.' But Aya has illumined him, declaring that we should revert to the potter in a chastened shell, etcetera.

With a kind of spatula, an orderly spades a handful of ashes into the bowl. Burfi roofs it with an earthen saucer. They all stand about undecidedly. They'd blurredly supposed that they'd return home with every fleck of Urmila's remains, and not with a modest cupful. Or rather, in their befuddlement at an unprecedented experience, they'd supposed nothing, but when they actually face the singed chips of her bones, feel bizarre to be forsaking some ninety per cent of her to some hireling's whimsy.

'Any other service, saab?' asks the attendant, with the inflexions of one who covets a fat tip and your prompt, subsequent disappearance. His tone rouses them into simpering their thanks at him and sidling away. Burfi cradles the urn close to his chest, and snaps at Pista not to get under his feet.

Pista can't wholly believe that his grandmother is now an accumulation in a smudgy box, of cinders, scorched bones and ashes, and that his father is bearing away a slab of her, perhaps her foreleg or left shoulderblade. He begins to feel less awestruck as they shuffle further away from the orderly and his container, and to disgorge his inquisitiveness in an accelerating strafe of unanswered questions. 'That black box was really Thakuma? . . . but I thought once you burnt someone, he never came back . . . Can I take a bit of the ashes to school? . . . Can I travel to Haridwar with you, please? . . . Didn't you say that they burn many bodies a day? Then where're the others? . . . How d'you know this one was actually Thakuma? Could easily've been somebody else, couldn't it? . . . Couldn't some stranger have substituted his wife's, so that the cops never nose out her body? . . . What happens to the blood when it burns? It should become fat and thick, like kheer at Diwali . . . And the hair? . . . Was that white stuff bone? How do the bones shatter into such small snips? . . .'

No one hears the boy's questions. He registers with Jamun now and then, tottering as he tries to mince only on the limewashed stones that edge the footpath, tossing his interrogations into the air, ricocheting them off the sparrows and the gulmohars, with each tread the lank strands bobbing on his sizeable dome. Jamun realizes – but leadenly, dully – that Pista is in fact fairly pleased at his grandmother's death. Jamun isn't goaded enough to dissect why, but out of a kind of illwill, he slants towards Burfi and murmurs, 'Pista seems pretty thrilled, doesn't he, with this business. Gruesome little bugger.'

Burfi nods, without having seized a single word. At that selfsame instant, Jamun, all at once, is dreadfully ashamed at having divulged to Burfi his impression of Pista. It betokens to him both his balefulness and his lack of control. Malice, he jumbledly recalls, was the one sentiment that his mother'd never expressed, and certainly the only way to commemorate her was to emulate her, was to release oneself from the instincts in one that'd never been fostered by her. One had to atone for her passing by bettering oneself. Jamun reaches forward and tousles Pista's hair, but the dolt doesn't even wheel about.

On the drive back home, Shyamanand expressionlessly examines the earthen bowl and, gazing blindly out of the window, remarks that most of the ashes that Burfi has so reverentially carried to the car are actually bits of gutted coal.

Kuki shows up at eight the same evening, sleek, well brushed, in a shirt the shade and texture of his skin. 'I was away yesterday,' he stutters to Jamun, almost in self-defence. 'I didn't know till this afternoon, when Haldia phoned me. Sorry.'

'Can you curb yourself today from swigging your routine six pegs? We'll amble down to the beach instead, and I'll stick you to a daab or two.'

Casting about for a vacant bench, they saunter past the wastrels, the dope fiends, the turtledoves, the hawkers, the promenaders. 'Kuki, Haldia might not've told you, but at Ma's last checkup, which was the day before she was carted off to Intensive Care, he messed me up by declaring that her pacemaker was defunct because its batteries were oozing or were dud or something. But before I could figure out what I was to do with what he'd told me, she'd had her heart attack. I've been wondering this past week, you beefeater, whether you dumped on us a dildo for the price of a pacemaker.'

'Hey, don't fuck me up like this.' On the right fringe of Kuki's upper lip sprouts a rash like smeared lipstick. 'I'll definitely quiz Haldia on what he confided in you, but those pacemakers aren't toys, you know, cobbled together in Ulhasnagar or Kalyan by dropouts who chomp their fingernails and daydream of breakdancing in a Hindi movie. They're A-one stuff, and in my eight – no, nine – years in this racket, this is the first time that I hear of leaking cells in a pacemaker. Tell you what, give it to me, and I'll have Haldia test it; if it's sound, I could flog it again. Save you a cool fifteen thousand. But how're you all travelling to Haridwar? Have you worked that out?'

Changing the subject, Jamun senses, is Kuki's way of stating that to propose, after a death, to the supplier that his defective machine triggered off that death, is both futile and tasteless, because wholly speculative. Jamun can't decide how to react. 'We'll fly to Delhi, and rent a taxi or something there. A flunkey from Joyce's office is getting us the plane tickets. Us means

Burfi, Joyce and me. My father wants to accompany us, but we aren't so certain that he'll be able to endure the three hours with Indian Airlines and the five in a cab. Let's see.'

'Have you arranged for the drive from Delhi to Haridwar, or should I fix a car for you?'

'Could you?' A rotund girl hoots and points Jamun and his outfit out to a younger, even more rotund boy whose face, from cheeks to chin, is hidden behind rubescent candyfloss. 'Kasturi's husband is mooning about in Delhi nowadays. She's asked him to organize a taxi for us, but he seems a fairly hopeless guy.'

For the next two days, he and Burfi potter about the house in their pendulous and impure white, confronting the faces of commiseration. The rooms feel dreadfully silent. Jamun seems to hear only the drag of Shyamanand's left foot as he aimlessly shuffles about from room to hushed room. Father and sons sit for hours about Urmila's bed, and feel sad and companionable. In the sunlight that sidles in through the windows, swathed in the yards of homespun, Jamun begins to realize how befitting his clothing is. His dress, that he is to wear continuously for thirteen days, makes him feel penitent and unclean; only its wrinkles and limp crumpledness seem real, and in a manner venerable. After sundown, in the days of mourning, when he ambles down to the beach to take stock of what he knows of his mother's life, his vestments of sorrow make him stoop and cringe his shoulders. He feels that his feet, as they sieve through the sands, are particularly cracked and unclean; his robes appear to mantle him in a kind of sacredness, and he senses that in a way he'll miss them after he's peeled them off.

Shyamanand, Burfi, Joyce and Jamun fly to Delhi. Urmila is hand baggage, wrapped in a luridly-checkered kerchief, tied in jute string, eased into a dazzling, Perfection-Silk-And-Saree-House polythene bag. Burfi has demurred against the kerchief, preferring 'something less LMC, or we could leave the earthen bowl be – like, you know, ethnic,' till Aya's theatrically demanded of him whether he wishes to send his mother naked to her god. Burfi and Jamun are astonished to discover that Indian Airlines can provide Shyamanand a wheelchair after being supplicated just once. In the aircraft, a tubby woman with a mug like a fist all but dumps her dung-coloured attaché case on the ashes. 'Idiot,' Shyamanand snarls at her without explaining why. Inflight, transcending their sadness, they wolf down every fleck on their trays; Jamun angles for a second lemon tart, but is rebuffed so peevishly by the SC hostess that he demands of her a complaint slip, which she eventually fetches and flicks into his lap with a snicker of such insolence that he has balls left only to doodle freudianly on it.

A dove-grey Ambassador at Delhi airport, a ruffianly driver with tranquil eyes and a placard with Kuki's name on it. 'If you wish, we could first drive to Kasturi's husband's uncle's, waste some time there – you could shit, etcetera – and then shove off to Haridwar.' But Shyamanand maintains that his sphincter can see to its charge all day without help, thank you.

Four hours to Haridwar – dry, balmy, and frequently scary, for the tranquil one drives as though his pubis is being singed. One unsightly town after another amidst miles of nondescript fields. Sugarcane terrain. Wafts of new gur, and numberless Tikait types on charpais, farting the day away. Rural, and therefore unfamiliar, sights – of smoking brick kilns and bullocks hauling a pagoda of hay – and sounds – of the needlelike click-click of the motor of a distant rice mill, like Time running out. For lunch, and for a thirty-minute breather for Tranquil and his Ambassador, they pull in at a hoarding that shows the sniggering face of some peculiar creature, half-gazelle and half-Jerry Lewis, with a blurb alongside its antlers that splashes in outsize crimson letters: 'WELCOME ONE AND ALL TO DEER PARK!' The Park presents itself as one lime-green cafeteria and a succession of pissers against its north wall. Joyce asks Shyamanand whether cheese sandwiches can be eaten during mourning. 'I'm not sure, but we'd better not.'

Then once more the somnolence of the long drive. 'Perhaps

Pista should've come along,' suggests Jamun to the back of Shyamanand's cranium. 'He'd've loved this trip' – but Shyamanand has nodded off. Pista, indeed, has cajoled and beseeched that he be allowed to accompany them, and has been nonplussed, besides being miffed, at their refusal. In fact, the boy's been puzzled by much that has occurred after his grandmother's death. His parents, for instance, have become more attentive towards those they'd formerly overlooked. Every evening, well after dinner, Joyce has trickled downstairs with a mug of steaming cocoa for Shyamanand, and sat and made polite conversation while he's slurped it. Top quality pc – on the insinuation of a shiver in the night air, foretokening December, on Pista's dreadful performance in Mathematics and Hindi, of which the brat isn't even remorseful, on the recent lunatic increase in municipal taxes, on Aya's latest demand for a salary hike, and on yesterday's terrorist carnage in Punjab. An uncommon sight, Shyamanand and Joyce small talking – in ten years they couldn't have spoken to each other for more than three minutes at a go without one wilfully misunderstanding the other and freezing with outrage. Shyamanand too adjudges Joyce's conduct to be uncustomary, and comments to Jamun on the fourth evening, 'Her solicitude is a strain for her, and it discomforts me, for it seems to suggest that only the absence of one person was required to bring about care and consideration in this house, and that one person the most guiltless of us all, totally bare of malignity and deceit.' Two mornings later, on a Saturday, after Burfi's taken his father and his elder son out in his Maruti for a rare joyride, Shyamanand, with a kind of half-senescent fixity, repeats the idea. 'Couldn't Burfi have driven us about while his mother was alive?'

'You aren't being fair. Burfi's – and Joyce's – current considerateness is but natural after a death.' Unhappiness gushes up his gullet and muzzles Jamun. Grief spouts most easily, and it is welcome. The plainest discussion about Urmila, particularly with Shyamanand, suffices to ungag it. 'We should all try –' But he doesn't want to discourse, or prescribe. He truly and fervidly hopes that his mother's death will better their conduct with one another. Yet assertions such as Shyamanand's dispirit him, trouble him with the chasm between the perspectives of father and son. He then ponders whether, with Urmila's passing, Shyamanand is suffering at all – at least, in the way that he ought to suffer – and whether he's forgotten, or has ever recognized, the misery that he himself begot.

Not that Shyamanand exhibits no sign of sorrow. On the contrary. He irritates his sons a bit because they feel that he overdoes the desolation. For the first few evenings, he doesn't roost in front of the TV from six p.m. onwards, as had been his and Urmila's custom for years because, presumably, the thought of watching the crud recalls, with intolerable ache, how much they'd relished running it down together. Burfi and Jamun, however, on some evenings, do, in their creased, cream robes, park themselves before the box with its volume at zero; whenever Shyamanand spots them, he voices nothing, but seems to whisper – in the tap of his walking stick, the lumpishness of his dud arm, in the drag of his left foot – his heavyhearted, shocked rebuke of their conduct.

Yes, doubtless, Shyamanand misses his wife, but for sure not in the manner that his sons wish him to. Misery – a sort of rudderlessness – pricks him to try and situate the causes of Urmila's death in individuals other than himself. 'The churlishness with her – unvaried for years – of my daughter-in-law destroyed her. The feebleness too, of her son before his wife. Though with their own parents the sons are regular tigers.'

'Fuck,' hisses Burfi, seemingly to himself, 'what a mind,' gathers up his dress, and clumps off upstairs. Shyamanand peers at the doorway and introspects, after a while, 'Does he cry out for her at all? Do you?' He hesitates. 'The house feels altogether strange. Every object is familiar, commonplace and yet . . . peculiar, as though the rooms've been rearranged, the light fittings changed.'

'I feel differently.' Jamun speaks to deflect his father. 'I still sense Ma, everywhere, in a comfortable way. I imagine that at any moment I'll hear from an adjacent room the rustle of her sari, the clink of her bangles, or one of her wellworn questions: "Jamun, has Aya left for the bus stop to fetch Pista? It's almost one-thirty."'

He voices the truth but sketchily; for at those points of the day when he's very tired, or dispirited, or when – as in the small hours, at the instant of awakening – his guard is down, misery immures him like a prenatal fluid. He feels besmirched, as though something disgraceful has befallen him, a bane, a chastisement that now and for good has changed his placement in the world – and now and then as though an edge has sliced his bowels, and he's adrift, with the sea at his throat.

At such times, he pines to close his eyes in some pale room – the yawning windows of which are mountings for separate panel watercolours of the darkening sky – and have a large, warm palm batten down upon his eyelids and the ruts in his forehead, and remain there long after he's ebbed into a dreamless sleep.

Those moments of wretchedness do slip by, of course, sooner or later, for life is always there, isn't it, around the corner? The telephone will ring, or a Maruti, eructating some vulgar music, will almost run over his toes, yanking him out of his numbness, and compelling him to yawp some scurrility at its sunglasses-like windows. But he introspects – naturally – time and time again, on his sadness. All parents die, so every human being must experience the anguish, or the discomfiture, of their passing, of the snicking of a cord. No, obviously not every. Not those without memory. One's reaction to such a death was controlled by one's maturity and one's closeness to one's parents. Kuki's father, for instance – if that ugly family yarn of Kuki's was at all true – oughtn't to have felt a jot of sorrow at the exit of Kuki's grandfather. Perhaps one was ravaged, even if just for a time, only by the first death of a parent, and the second was like seeing your guest off at the end of the housewarming. Maybe one honestly lamented only a mother's passing, because one's body and soul never forgot that one was of her flesh. And certainly the sensation of having lost a part of oneself – as though the chunk beneath the left ribs had been gouged out, so to speak – was keener in his case because Urmila had hinged on him emotionally – as Shyamanand still did – like a kid to its mum. He'd now been grazed by death, and it would return, time after time after time, for Shyamanand, Aya, Burfi and Joyce, Kasturi and Kuki, even Pista and Doom. Surely each demise would muddle him less and less, toughen him till he could bestow neighbourly counsel on others at their bereavement. Surely.

With Urmila's death, they've grown, for the time being, gentle with one another. Jamun recognizes that this recent considerateness of theirs will not endure, and that its abatement will signal the close of their mourning for her. But in Shyamanand, alongside this caring, her departure appears to have planted a more persistent acrimony, so that when one death leads him to reminisce of others in his long, undistinguished life, of the deaths of his stepmother, his father, an older brother who yielded to diphtheria at the age of seven, he unwittingly dwells on – rather than what he might've reaped from each experience – more the comfortless, bitter sensations kindled by each event. 'When my father died of cholera, I was twenty-three,' he recounts to Jamun over their dinner of chapatis and hot milk, 'and two thousand kilometres away, in Simla, I received an unintelligible telegram, two days old, and fathomed that my father was sinking. Three more days for the journey by mail train and bus. Five whole days from the despatch of the telegram. In my suffocating third-class compartment, amidst the droppings of toddlers and the trunks of jawans, I prayed and craved that I'd see my father breathing. But he'd been cremated on the third day. Just his ashes and my brother's strained, unshaven face waited for me. I could've died with regret. I wasn't in any way certain what I was sorry for – all that I felt was that if I could've only met my father before he died, touched his feet, kissed his forehead, held water to his mouth, I'd've been reprieved for my transgressions against him. What transgressions? Simply our thousand trifling harshnesses against one another, daily, for a lifetime. That's why I feel that the two of you won't fret like I did, from guilt, because I wasn't at hand. What d'you think?'

Well, Jamun thinks a fair deal, in a scrambled, keyed-up manner, about his mother's passing, but exchanging his notions appears inconceivable. Would Baba or Burfi sympathize, for instance, with his sentiment that a mother's demise somehow behoved him to acquit himself better, more humanely, with all living beings, that he now felt, and keenly hoped that he'd continue to feel, towards all, a passionless and ascetic dutifulness? For passion was vexation and sorrow, and he'd now to set about to accomplish a stolidness even towards that sorrow. Truly, a death made one brood, didn't it. And if one scrutinized the matter, looked it in the eyes, and full in the face, then doubtless the value, the drift, the purport of existence was a burden likely to make one lose one's marbles. Of course, for that reason, if one were wise, one wouldn't reflect on the subject of the pith of death for more than a couple of seconds at a stretch. One could use Ma's case as an illustration. What had her life been for? Why had she come to life, and why had she survived for over sixty years? Surely, at bottom, for nothing? The aspiration of her existence had for sure not been happiness, which appears to him, uncertainly, to be one feasible vindication for living, the single glow amongst the anguish, malevolence, rancour and rage. But Ma'd never conceded to an instant of any species of delight in her drab childhood, her toilsome youth, or her catastrophic marriage. On this feature of hers, Baba'd once in a while observed, from his bed, from behind his journal, that individuals such as she wouldn't recognize joy even when it perched on their nose and nibbled at their cheeks. Yet whenever she'd been pumped, circuitously, on what she felt about these things, she'd steadily advanced that her life had been fruitful because after all, hadn't she fostered two good sons?

Haridwar. Bald recumbent hills, knolls. A scrubbed, piercing sky, and cloudlets like elfin white birds in a watercolour. Joyce's head pillowed on Burfi's shoulder. 'Where d'you wish to go?' demands the driver, swivelling his dome round at Jamun without decelerating an inch.

Jamun realizes with surprise that Tranquil hasn't been instructed on the object of the journey. 'We have to douse my mother's ashes in the Ganga.' The driver nods and the car careens away to the right at breathstopping speed.

Imperceptibly, the highway has whittled down to a lane. The bullying lorries and white Ambassadors have melted away. The town, however, is nowhere discernible. They scud past infirm saplings on what might be an embankment, and through buffalo, openmouthed children, oxcarts of gur, dungsmoke from invisible sources, dust. A bend or two, and they untidily pull up at what appears to be a fairsized canal. A handful of concrete steps between them and the avocado-green water. Hawkers, operating beneath awnings framed out of rent dhotis, spiritlessly bleat out the attractions of their wares – the commonplace pilgrimage stuff, rudraksha beads, shell pendants, statuettes, figurines, sandalwood sundries, vials and phials of the water of the Ganga. Burfi helps Shyamanand out of the car. Tranquil torpidly attempts to shoo away the fine-eyed urchins who foregather to gawp at the patriarch. The town – in the main on the opposite strand of the river, swarming up the hillocks like boyscouts on a crosscountry, predominantly in yellow and rosepinks blanched by the sun – looks pretty. They all feel tired and dull. 'Are we at the right place?' Shyamanand asks the world. 'The bustle seems to be all on the other bank. I don't even spot any touts here.'

'Maybe they're feeding somewhere. A two o-clock lunch of bananas and ganja at some temple.'

As though he's been tipped off, one does steal up to them just then – spindly, hairy, in a singlet and skull cap – and quizzingly shimmies his eyebrows at Jamun.

'No, we don't want a priest, no, for anybloodything . . . Is there any particular, sort of reserved, spot on the river for chucking ashes? . . . You sure? . . . But are you certain? . . . Baba, the bugger says that we can immerse this' – Jamun raises the earthen bowl in his hands an inch or two – 'anywhere. And should I ask him to find us a priest? But I've an inkling that he doubles up for one himself.'

This surmise is immediately ratified by the hairy man; to further validate which, his accessory, a skeletal adolescent, naked but for sodden carroty undies, with hydrocelic balls and elbows the girth of knees, hoarsely pronounces to Shyamanand, 'For the Ganga is the most sacred of mothers; for it, procreation and death are but one.'

Burfi doesn't like the situation. 'But we should line up a recitation or something, shouldn't we, an incantation, some Sanskrit verses?' But Shyamanand looks dreadfully old and uncertain, so they all shuffle again towards the steps. Joyce pulls out her camera, a gift from Philip Jonas, from her handbag, and begins clicking away. 'I guess we could dunk the remains even without the om mani padme hum or whatever,' suggests Jamun. He slips on his sunglasses in a sort of goofy protest against Joyce's and Burfi's ardour to freeze on snapshot even what he considers the most inappropriate events. The tout is deflected just then by the arrival, with a mewl from its brakes, of a crimson Contessa with black windows, the sort of car one'd reckon would be owned by somebody resembling any one of those four Hindujas.

Naked, pubescent urchins in the water, who leave off their romping for a time to watch Joyce, in her lilywhite sari, crouch and stretch for the dead-on angles. On their right, at the foot of the arch bridge, sits a compact, pinkwashed temple; its wall portrays a mammoth ad for hairoil – a visage that fuzzily recalls Shirdi's Sai Baba, and spurting away from his dome (and from his ears), like black, undisciplined waters, a squall of turbulent snakes of hair. Shyamanand is markedly indignant. 'How can they advertise hairoil here, of all places? Couldn't anyone deter them?'

'Jamun, can you duck back a step, please? I could then snap you and the ashes against that lunatic composition.'

When they'd brought Urmila back from Haldia's, and'd tugged and shoved to lay her down on her own bed, remembers Jamun, and he'd trailed off to rummage for the incense that Urmila always used to possess, he'd tousledly reflected that he appeared to command more selfrestraint than Burfi, didn't he, because on the drive from Haldia's, with Urmila's head in his lap, Burfi'd smoothed the strands about her ears and permitted himself to sob undismayed. Yet one could never, never be sure of people, for when he returned to his mother's room to declare that the incense didn't seem to be anywhere and that he, or someone else, or perhaps Burfi, would have to trudge down to that huckster on the beach for it, he was jolted to see Burfi behind his camera, focusing on Urmila's stonedead face, murmuring, 'Too still. We should've borrowed Kuki's Handycam.'

'But you don't shoot the dead!' Jamun had unguardedly exclaimed and, responding to Burfi's taken-aback, caught-in-the-act face, continued more measuredly, 'I mean, I don't think it's done – it looks pretty odd, as though we want to remember her most this way.' He'd stolen a glance at Urmila. Her complexion had blackened, and her lips seemed to have receded even more. 'I mean, I don't know, with a photograph of her like this in the family album, every time you stumble on it, you'd flip the page. You can't –'

But by then, Burfi had clicked. 'I don't see what's wrong.' With a sideglance at Shyamanand. 'After all, it's happened, hasn't it, the most fateful event of our lives.'

Entirely without warning, at that instant, Jamun had been reminded of a cartoon in some forgotten issue of *Mad* magazine, a takeoff of *Jaws*. One character lolling about on the deck of a yacht or pleasureboat, a second frisking around in the water, the simper on his mug elysian because he hadn't spotted the shark (with an extraordinary smirk on its face) zeroing on him. In the sequent panels of the cartoon, Jaws chomped away and the bather bleated at the yacht for deliverance. The pal on deck scooted in and, eyes alustrous, scooted out, not with a harpoon or carbine or something, but with a camera, to start clicking away. Of course, Jamun'd been in no humour to divulge to Burfi what his conduct had evoked for him.

Glacial, freezing, the Ganga is, avocado-green, and swiftly gliding. Wading a step or two in, with the residue of one's mother's body, is not easy. Shyamanand too wants to tread water with his sons, but its iciness and its rush stalls him on the last step. In the water, Burfi yammers theatrically and wonders just how those striplings can bob about in that cold. 'You and Jamun should hold the bowl together,' Shyamanand directs him, 'and slither in as far as you can. Pitch the ashes high and deep. Yes, now, throw.' They lob the clay pot. It sinks instantly, leaving behind in the world, but for the demented clicking of a camera, no whisper, no whiff, of evidence.

# 7

# SO

The unremarkable death of an old (no, middleaged) woman, sixty plus – a weepy wife, but a proud mother – but even that combination is not uncommon – indeed, the first all but always entails the second, doesn't it, in that when a husband and wife fall out, but don't separate, they are actuated, partly, by the itch to woo their brood away from each other while straining to demonstrate to it, in a thousand oblique ways, the general beastliness of the spouse. This tendency is indeed quite widespread, and is certainly conspicuous even in the subsequent relations between Burfi and Joyce, that is after their marriage really sours and Burfi begins his second extramarital affair, about which he breathes to Joyce not a syllable – but naturally! did you exclaim? No, in Burfi's case, not naturally, because, soon after his maiden adulterous fling had started to jade a bit, he *had* felt sheepish and had actually owned up to Joyce, and afterwards also unburdened himself, in turn, to Jamun, Urmila and Chhana, muttering, with sloshed, crimson-eyed gravity, 'My marriage's cracked up – and someone in the family must be told why.' Yet that too is widespread, isn't it, the affair, the fondling of the seven-year-itch – and one senses that one is growing up when the widespread, the commonplace, befalls oneself. One has ever so often heard and read, for instance, that for a marriage, the particularly dreadful, uphill years are one's late thirties and early forties, that one's most likely to be unfaithful, grumpy and disoriented then, and next, one observes and hears of somebody one knows – a neighbour, a brother-in-law – that even his marriage has cracked up; then one starts to believe that one's life will always startle one with those traits of the human temperament that've been disclosed a million times before, that the world is indeed composed of these cyclical, wellworn tracks that every generation shambles about on, age upon age, that nothing that falls to one's lot is new, that maturing and growing old really signifies encountering, in the particular, what has already occurred numberless times in the universal.

So. Neither Burfi's adultery nor the escalating wrangle with Joyce; instead, just a death in an ordinary family. This one too, like other families, has its skeletons that thrill rather than scandalize – illicit love, bisexuality, that sort of thing – but somehow, when one takes the family and not the individual, as the unit, nothing shocks anyway, as though the fellowship of one's blood itself is a kind of cushion, a buffer, or a diluting agent, for all singularities.

But a family, of course, has more than blood in common. Shyamanand, for instance, certainly bequeathed to Burfi both his yearning for money and his incapacity to hoard much of it; and Jamun did share with his mother an itch to snap his fingers at its frightful power. 'But to ignore the weight of cash,' he concedes, 'is damn hard, you know. We ourselves have suffered from not having enough of it. I mean, when we were young, weren't Ma and Baba hard up *because* they had to raise the two of us – and bloody Chhana? They became comfortably off only after we'd made it.'

'Yes,' comments Burfi, as though in concurrence, 'you and I'd be an asset to any parents.'

'True, even if only from the outside.'

'Don't be brainy, fucker. Gratitude between generations is a two-way thing. For not letting him down, for not slashing one's own wrists and for not ending up as a bus conductor or something, for not *embarrassing* him, any parent'd be proud of us.'

'True, even if only for our outsides.'

A sample of Jamun's salty wit – and of his spasmodic self-loathing for being absent for weeks on end from home and parent – and thus for acquitting himself shoddily with his blood.

'Where did I come across – but it's obvious, anyway – that only homo sapiens has this parental hangup? Meaning that in the other species, when the young are old enough, they're rebuffed and junked so that they can fend for themselves – tiger-cubs and stray puppies – but we clutch and claw the emotions of our spawn for ever.'

The family splinters with Urmila's passing. In the car, on the return drive from Haridwar, they – Shyamanand, Burfi, Joyce and Jamun – feel becalmed and restful, as after some convulsion. 'We've timed this business nicely so far. If the car doesn't conk out or go up in smoke, we should reach Delhi with an hour to spare for our airbus home. I hope, Baba, that you aren't too pooped?'

Shyamanand instead asks, without slewing his head around, 'Do any of you know where your mother kept her will?'

No's from Burfi and Jamun. From Joyce, an only-your-father-could've-raised-such-a-subject-at-this-moment glance. 'Perhaps,' suffixes Jamun, 'it's in her trunk. That's the only spot in the house that she could call her own. Everything that everyone else in the family didn't want to keep and couldn't toss away was dumped in her room, wasn't it. But her trunk was inviolate – maybe because she always kept it locked – like her desk in the office. Probably crammed with litter – our postcards to her when we were nine, Camays from Burfi's Europe jaunt, untouched.'

'I'd proposed to her that she change her will to include me as a beneficiary of the house – along with you two – but she couldn't, at that time, unearth the will, or so she said. We should find out from some legal type the correct position on this. If the will's never traced, then who gains the house?'

'Shouldn't all legal documents be registered with somebody to be valid? You know, a . . . well . . . registrar, or notary – someone who's halitotic and corrupt, and whose office is girdled by rolypoly touts in black jackets, also halitotic. In English whodunits, everyone seems to have a family solicitor.'

'Hindu law'll apply,' contributes Burfi, with a sideglance of censure at Jamun, 'in our case, I guess, so we'll all share equally. If we ever stumble on Ma's will, then of course we'll have to execute it. It's some kind of scandalous crime, isn't it, to be aware of a will and not to effect it?'

'But we could surely change the title deed to accommodate Baba. Neither you nor I'd protest.'

'Don't jump the gun, choot. We've first to take on the sharks at the Land Office. They'll compel us to kowtow in front of them a hundred times before they even fucking *begin* to skim through our application. Then they'll require from us the most incomprehensible documents, one by one, one every three months – depositions, affidavits, endorsements, attestations, warranties, testimonials – and expect with each visit a modest bribe. Don't you remember – or were you too young then – the trials of the Land Office that Ma and Baba endured while building the house? A good five years of struggle before its ownership's transferred to us.'

'Your mother,' interrupts Shyamanand, powerless, out of habit, to check himself, 'did very little – apart from signing the papers – to erect our house. I alone suffered those clerks and that Assistant Land Officer, the villainous contractors, the shifty suppliers of bricks, the dealers in cement, the carpenters and masons. Had even one of you backed me up that terrible year, I'd perhaps've eluded this.' With his right hand, he heaves up, by the wrist, his benumbed left arm.

The unlocking of Urmila's trunk is deferred for some days because all, quite naturally, wish to let the dead, and their possessions, be; furthermore, nobody knows where her keyring is. About a week after Haridwar, however, on the day that Doom returns from Bombay (conveyed by Rani, in tight jeans and dragonfly sunglasses), on the morning that Kasturi is confined, Jamun learns from their cook that Urmila had, six months ago, borrowed five hundred rupees from her, and (with a hideous, mincing pretence at embarrassment, playing with the end of her sari, simpering, dodging his eyes) could she be recouped please.

'Five hundred? I see,' reflecting all at once that the cook's indeed plumped for a realistic sum, that to confute her without losing either her or one's dignity'd be tough, that had she slithered up to Shyamanand instead with her claim, she'd presumably have changed his newborn, eggshell love for his dead wife to scorn (and not've reaped her notes either), that her first buttonholing Jamun clinches his position as his mother's successor, the steward of their household.

In all families, one member kicks off the day for the others, leaving his bed before the sun to unbolt some door, pick up the newspapers, put on the kettle. Urmila had been their starter for years, and had relished the quiet of the early morning. Even when ill, she'd tried to be up, to make and drink up her four cups of tea, before anyone else was about. After she was shifted to Haldia's, Pista's aya performed Urmila's early-morning chores for a couple of days before starting her bellyaching. Jamun took over from her quite agreeably, feeling, while fussing about in the kitchen or pouring Shyamanand a cup, the easeful right to claim a special relationship with she who was dead.

'Do you know what Ma wanted the money for? . . . I suppose she didn't give you a chit or something for it?'

'She'd've had to hand out chits, then, to one hell of a lot of us,' smirks the cook.

Warm blood seems to explode behind Jamun's temples. 'You should be ashamed of yourself for speaking of her this way.' He itches to claw the simper of timorousness off her face. 'No, I don't think we can pay you until you show me some proof – because she didn't need to borrow at all – you can quit if you please . . . How many of you are there, anyway?'

The cook isn't certain, but asserts that other than the dhobi and herself, there could be a dozen – fifty rupees here, two hundred there. 'She was fond of borrowing.'

'Let me see. I'll have to discuss this with Baba and Burfi . . . One of these days, we're going to open Ma's trunk – perhaps we'll dig up some proof in there – you're positive you don't know what she needed the cash for?'

'But how can I know?' Grimacing with defensiveness, pirouetting prettily, dwarfish, obese, wily; a rasping tongue that has never been schooled to speak gently. Jamun struggles with the fancy, spawned by his disquiet, to pink her against the kitchen sink with his six-foot prick, with which he'd next thwack the smirk off her mug. 'Obviously, she couldn't've taken the amount from her family, because you all would've probed. She did implore me and the dhobi not to leak to anybody.'

A mixup in Jamun's head. He wishes to focus on the cook's disclosure of Urmila's extraordinary conduct, but is muddled by the something in her that has, all on a sudden, evoked Kasibai – perhaps the sauciness with which her tight blouse squeezes out the flesh of her upper arms, or the sheen of avarice in her eyes at the idea of five hundred rupees – perhaps the stuff of her itself, the mosaic of vulgarity, unenlightenment, slumminess, tunnel vision, illbred voice, base material longings, that to bulge forth waits only for Jamun to cave in to her – which he doubtless would have, had they too tenanted a characterless flatlet in a disregarded town, cocooned by leaden rain for eight months of the year – he at the verandah door, lolling in a lounger, positioned so that he can eye both the drizzle and the mammoth haunches of Kasibai scouring the lavatory floor, speculating not, would he, but when.

The cook retires, jiggling her arse. He observes its jellylike jouncing and decides, for the time being, not to cough up even a rupee. The befuddlement over Urmila's possible indebtedness subsides when he, with a grimace, recognizes it as a detail of her quadruple life. The phrase is Burfi's, and denotes the notion, common enough, that each of us leads several existences of which one's near and dear ones are unaware, or only fuzzily aware.

The telephone. Kasturi's younger sister, garrulous and breathless (whom Kasturi's husband was to have married had he not been repulsed by her volubility), on the line. 'Hi, we haven't met for ages . . . How've you been? Very sorry to hear about your mother . . . Kastu left this minute for the hospital, looking like the Beyond – isn't this utterly too piquant? My sexbomb of a brother-in-law showed up just yesterday. "Hi, Cass," he cheeped to her. "Phew, if you don't mind my saying so, you seem to've swelled somewhat since your marriage.

Have you considered consulting a dietitican?" So cute, no? In the car, she reminded me to phone you – I'm terrifically relieved that she's hatching here and not in Calcutta, where she'd've littered, in an eighteen-hour traffic jam, into one of those craters – hell, chasms – on Central Avenue, and we'd've to name the bundle of joy Metrodeb, or Metrodebi, as the case may be – when do we see you?'

An eventful morning, for Rani and Doom return unannounced from Bombay some minutes after this phone call. Shyamanand, Burfi and Jamun are taken aback, in particular by Rani's jeans, T-shirt and sunglasses, not quite seemly wear for a visit to a house in which a mother has been dead for less than a fortnight. Rani is squat and swarthy, and doesn't take off her goggles while nattering to a cheerless, monosyllabic Shyamanand. But they are all distracted by Doom's phenomenal and wholly unexpected delight in getting back; he jettisons on the verandah his hand baggage, namely his toy recorder and his Hanuman mask, and, goaded by his ebullient joyfulness, starts to scamper in and out of the rooms, and up and down the stairs, chortling and cackling to himself and at every face that he passes, irregularly pulling up to twitch his nut up at the ceiling, squeeze his eyes shut and whoop. The walls themselves appear jolted by the child's hubbub, as though they too had taken to the hush of death. Shyamanand and his sons wish, involuntarily, that Doom be still, but reasonableness prevails and they say nothing to him, and half-shamefacedly enjoy the happy squeak of his sneakers on the steps, and his versions of the songs of *The Wizard of Oz* that flutter down to them, with uneven strengths, from different rooms.

Rani, however, has not showed up just as a chaperone for Doom. When Jamun goes up to remind Joyce, he finds her on the bed, Hamletically eyeing the dunes of clothes about her. The room looks stark and bright, for the curtains – picked by her, with her money – turquoise and orange on white – are drifts on the floor. He almost topples into an open suitcase at the threshold. It is glutted with more clothes, and looks like multicoloured dough rising. 'Oh. We imagined that Doom'd stay for a bit.'

She half-smiles. Very pretty. He can't muzzle himself. 'Are you hiving off with the curtains too?'

No, she proposes to stow them tidily in the cupboard by the door to the roof. She begins to regroup the clothes about her, clearly waiting to be quizzed why, then, the curtains had to be taken down. But Jamun doesn't speak, and seems to be going away, so she abruptly asks him whether she could have her silver rattle back, please.

What? He hasn't heard of this, ever.

'Some months ago – Doom's nursery school had just shut for the summer – your mother snatched away from him a beautiful silver rattle that'd orginally been my grandmother's. The racket, she squawked at Doom one afternoon, is pumping my blood pressure up and up and up. The brat called her a bloody thief and scurried, blubbering, to me. Neither of us has clapped eyes on that rattle since. I did sound your mother out more than once – do you brothers find it so hard to accept that a mother needn't be as angelic with the unchosen as she is with her sons? I did tell her of the sentimental importance of that rattle for me. The first time, she seemed not to follow – "Rattle? What rattle?" – that sort of thing. Later, her parrotcry became, "Now where did I put it?" Of course, I've groused to Burfi a hundred times, but I might as well try to prod a domesticated mongrel after it's gorged. I never could fathom what your mother really wanted with the rattle, beyond bullying Doom and spiting me.' Jamun quits the room here and to his back Joyce suffixes. 'Will you rake over her trunk for me, please?'

Urmila's trunk is underneath her bed, and is overlaid by dust. Jamun unlocks it, raises the lid and stops dead because, from beneath the redolence of naphthalene, the scents from the layers of saris resurrect his mother in a whiff. Warm, vivid saris, diaphanous like tracing paper, with the tones of ivory and biscuit, copper, lilac, tangerine, port; beneath the first few lodge a handful of Camay soaps, fusty because they've long since leaked their bouquet. Jamun feels will-less and cannot recall why he's opened the trunk. Each groove, each funnel amongst the clothes seems to exhale that singular perfume – somehow reddish and powdery, perhaps a brew of camphor and sandalwood – that Urmila had worn for decades. Abstractedly, aimlessly, he riffles through the strange and yet familiar stuff; a bulky polythene bag from Belu, crammed with the clay biscuits that she's covertly – and before her body'd conked out, openly – been addicted to; jars and bottles of unused, ritzy toiletries – in the main gifts from Burfi who, across the years, had also bought, as hasty afterthoughts, for his mother what he purported to gift his wife; dozens of old letters, all addressed to her office, a batch, in a muddled hand, from Belu, and even a couple of illegible, inconceivable inlands from Kishori; some bright, unused banknotes in the saris, of divers denominations, squirrelled away for years because too clean to be wasted, frequently resorted to in dire straits, but never without sighs; a canvas pouch of her discarded idols – a sindoor-smudged, framed picture postcard of Shiva, clay figurines of Kali and Ganapati – and of the outfit for domestic devotions, dinky, copper goblets and spoons, etcetera; as with everything else in that trunk, behind the pouch of idols too hangs a tale of a wrangle between Urmila and her husband.

For she'd been a fairly pious – though hardpressed – votary once, and had installed her josshouse in the middle shelf of her clothes cupboard. For years, in the mornings before she boarded her office bus, for a minute or two, she's mumbled some Sanskrit and fiddled about with the copper things before the gods and, at the same time, fulminated under her breath against the living – and Shyamanand in particular – for not conceding her more time for them. After her retirement and Shyamanand's stroke, her prayertime slides to the early afternoon, after her bath and before her spouse's lunch, which without warning has begun to start precisely, dead on, at one –

Tch, every piffling event and matter is knotted with every other bloody event and matter. You see, Urmila can't pray, obviously, before she bathes, and she can't, that is, doesn't wish to, bathe until Shyamanand has done with his morning crap – in case he tumbles in the bogs or can't rise from the loo seat or feels giddy or suffers his second attack or something and blubbers for help; entering the lavatory to assist him'd certainly make her feel dreadfully unclean, and insupportably so if she's already freshened and deodorized herself by then. But Shyamanand has from his cradle been frightfully constipated, and would've shat once a month and been content had he not been harangued from his puppyhood that all eupeptic mortals move banana-like turds just once diurnally, and that too in the morning. He is a lazy man, and his thrombosis has retarded him even further; thus his morning can tarry uptil twelve-thirty (*id est*, he is not a morning person!); after farting prodigiously till that hour (swilling tea, charmed by his bank passbooks) – most of his omissions are SBDs, altogether masterly, Silent But Deadly – he hobbles into the john, lugubriously (like a tailender inching out to grapple with a quartet of West Indian pacemen), grunts, sighs, groans, snorts and mutters for a time, and hobbles out and towards the dining room for lunch at one. I'm trying to systematize my life, reasons Shyamanand, but Urmila suspects (and Jamun seconds her against her father, as always) that he is systematizing simply to infuriate her, which is possible because for sixty years he's been markedly more – well, Hindu – about time and punctuality.

At one Shyamanand ferally pitches into – to belittle and wolf down – whatever is on the table. Urmila must be there, to help him to help himself and to accept the shit. In the cold sweat years, most of her mornings, therefore, are spent in waiting for him to move his bowels; she gains only a few minutes for a bath and a prayer. She doesn't pray the day she hears, from the bathroom, Shyamanand stagger against the refrigerator. She chugs out, half-scoured, gabbling, 'God! What happened! God!' In the minutes that she telephones Mr Naidu to send his servant to heave Shyamanand off the floor, her slapdash, routine devotions to her idols become trifling, almost ludicrous. She continues with them, however, till the Saturday that Jamun returns from the cornershop with a new brand of atta in a really cute canvas bag. Both its sides depict Krishna and his chicks stencilled in violet. To prevent herself from forsaking the bag to the creepy-crawlies in the kitchen cupboard, she introspects all afternoon on what to stow in it that will be valuable enough to match the cuteness of the bag, and decides finally on her gods.

At the bottom of the trunk, amongst old petticoats and what looks like a mosquito net, lie the silver rattle and Urmila's paperback of *The Good Earth*. On its flyleaf, Jamun reads his mother's maiden name and the year '1947', and beneath, in a more indigo ink and a faintly different script, her married name, '1950'. At the foot of the page, she'd once more, in her disciplined hand, inscribed her married name, but this time with Shyamanand's, '1950'. Jamun gazes at the page for a while and feels despondent. To him, the names, scrolled in two antipodal phases of Urmila's life, compress her wistfulness that perhaps her marriage'd turn out all right. All at once, his eyes brim over.

And in the book is stowed away the black-and-white snapshot that he hasn't seen for fifteen years, a frontal of Urmila at sixteen, in pigtails and an impossible oldworld dress that looks like a creamish bra over a coloured blouse. It is the solitary photograph that her children have viewed of her past, of her existence before Shyamanand, for the chronicle of the family photo albums begins with the birth of Burfi.

The picture of the maidenly Urmila the sons clapped eyes on fortuitously; it had been mailed by Belu and put by, decades ago, in the Pearl Buck as a bookmark, and stumbled on to by Jamun while he'd been foraging in his mother's handbag for change for cigarettes.

'Wow, she was quite a bomb,' Burfi, aged twenty-one, mews. Into his eyes slithers a kind of reverence at how much time can ravage. Jamun in a sentimental fit ousts, from the right side of the hinged photoframe above the fridge, of the two portraits of the youthful Shyamanand, the simpering profile, and eases into its place Urmila's snap. The effect of the switch is quite marvellous, for then from the photoframe two radiant and young faces gaze out at the world together, as though made for each other, deeply in love. Certainly, Shyamanand is peeved that one of his flattering closeups has been so dislodged behind his back; Urmila is thoroughly incensed when he appears to suggest that Jamun has swapped the photographs at her beseeching.

About the lips there slinks the breath of a smile. At sixteen, for the camera, for the second, the eyes speak a contentment that they've never expressed in life. A girlish fleeciness across the forehead. Jamun's brow corrugates as he tussles with the sudden, elemental idea that this virginal, innocent girl didn't deserve what the years apportioned to her. Doubtless, his reaction is merely emotional; yet, he is humbled. 'Ma,' he mutters to the photograph, smiling in an upsurge of affection for her, 'the dictums about death are bloody true.' I mean, where are you now, exactly? How far have you roved in this fortnight? A billion kilometres, beyond Carl Sagan? Or have you only shuttled off to Benares? Or are you right here, in the dust of this room, amongst your analgesics and antacids, as invisible as your memories, and do you perch like a sparrow on these pelmets to observe us? From wherever you are, Ma, you are going to teach me, aren't you, and knock into my head till it clamps there, that death too is vanity?

The family splinters with Urmila's passing, and Shyamanand is abandoned – no, rather, Shyamanand feels that he is abandoned – by his sons. In the car from Haridwar to Delhi, they start to conflict over the sharing of the costs of Urmila's treatment. Jamun begins it, perhaps guilelessly. 'I shall have to get down to all those receipts, who shelled out how much to whom for what. A killing business, but we'll need to set ourselves in order, sooner or later.'

'What's the hurry?' Burfi smirks at him. 'We should let these sensitive issues be.' His pinks Jamun's thigh with his forefinger and, pointing to Shyamanand in the front seat, frowns at his brother to shut up.

Shyamanand waits for a minute to allow Jamun to continue, then asserts, without swivelling his head, 'No, those receipts should be scanned pretty quickly, and the total divided by three. The longer we shelve it, the more gruelling it'll be for some of us to lever out our share from someone we all know.'

Joyce, Jamun and Shyamanand begin to snigger. Burfi remonstrates, unpremeditatedly. 'But Chhana isn't around. We shouldn't split the expenses in her absence.' The other three chortle even more, and Shyamanand snorts, 'Chhana! Touch her for a pie! She's been bountiful enough to all of us.'

'No, balls-balls, so what. She's been ungrudging because she has the cash. If we judge by our bank balances, she could probably bear all Ma's costs without blinking.' Burfi breaks off, manifestly gagged by the uncharitableness of his own remark.

Joyce pushes in to veil the gawkish moment. 'You should remember, though, that Burfi's bank balance is zero for all activity but the buying of outlandish clothes. Four thousand for a zoot suit is a bargain, while fifty rupees for a textbook for Pista is daylight robbery, a disgrace.'

'That's because schoolbooks and Pista square with each other like acid rock and Vinobha Bhave. I mean, I – we – must slop hundreds and hundreds of rupees every year on tomes for that bugger, but is our concern ever reflected in his bloody annual report card? He's like –'

'I've been calculating' – Shyamanand thus prevents Burfi from slewing the conversation away – 'my personal expenditure on your mother, and it's close to forty thousand – bucks, as Pista has now begun to say. Jamun has laid out another fifteen thousand, but you –'

'We can discuss this later, please. We'll have loads of time once we return to the rut.'

'No, no, we won't,' horns in Shyamanand, unexpectedly. 'I know, I know.' He sniggers in the attending silence. 'You're all taking wing, beetling off, I hear – and our house and I are the sinking ship! You fancy that I don't have ears on your floor! "Now that Ma's turned up her toes, sticking on in this house will be intolerable . . . At last we can quit this place . . . This epidemic greyness here is most unhealthy." So shouldn't we settle accounts before you march out? Perhaps you mean to hustle me out and lease the place to some Sindhi for a whopping sum. You shouldn't've any trouble with that after you fish up her will.'

'Did you glimpse, a moment ago, those eucalyptuses by the road, draggling, withering? That was the – well – vitriol of your sarcasm . . . Look, Baba, I've been away from work for nearly three months now, and I should get back, shouldn't I. I showed up opportunely, and what I came for has occurred, so now I should return. I don't know what Burfi's plans are, but you mustn't assert – or feel – that you're being discarded. You know that's nonsense, and that your jabbering in this way only stings us. We'll work something out – you can come and stay with either one of us, or if you don't wish to leave home, we could arrange for someone trustworthy to be with you – a twenty-four-hour sort who'll make you your tea and escort you on your walks, foster you. The future isn't a rally of insoluble problems, but let's face them one by one. Shouldn't we therefore look to the remaining rites – the sradh, the nutshaving – and ensure that they're correctly observed?'

A thread of assuaging half-lies – this speech. For the brothers've been talking their futures over for some evenings now, and Shyamanand has featured in the chats mainly as a peripheral impediment. Joyce has pronounced that she's sick of being sapped by the demands of Burfi's family, and that she wishes to quit, at once, the house and, in the near future, the city; she's already applied in the office for a transfer, thereby forcing Burfi to reflect on doing likewise. 'After your rituals are finished – and they themselves are preposterous, for your distance from them – I'm not hanging around in this stinking place for even a second, please understand that.'

Jamun dislikes her using the word 'stinking', and is dispirited that he cannot riposte forthwith. Cocktail time, and he and Burfi are swilling tea. 'We need a break from one another, I feel, and this seems an apt time for parting.' Burfi lights a cigarette and is in two minds about offering Jamun one, and finally does so only because his hesitation was fairly clear. 'Have you decided when you're returning?'

Jamun departs two forenoons after the sradh, his skull pallid and cool because of the shaving. Chhana has telephoned from Calcutta to confirm to Shyamanand that she isn't in the least certain of the ins and outs of the various rites, but trusts that they are all being abided by; in their next letter to her, they enclose a photograph of Jamun, with glabrous cranium, slanting selfconsciously against the wall beside the cactus. Burfi doesn't razor his head because Joyce has stated that she'll shudder at seeing him without his hair, because then his ears'll stick out even more, like bloody trainsignals; so Burfi tells Shyamanand that he truly believes that the woe of bereavement can never be even fragmentarily – and hence shouldn't be at all – articulated by any symbolic externals.

'It'll look odd that of two brothers, one doesn't perform a rite for his mother, and that too the elder. Chat to Jamun, check if he's earnest about calling the barber tomorrow morning. Either both should or neither.'

Burfi is surprised by Shyamanand's counsel, and even more by Jamun's reaction; he'd rather go through with the shaving, because to him it seems a befitting symbol for starting anew.

'But it's okay even with Baba if you don't – as long as we both do the same thing!'

But Jamun is steadfast and sits the next morning in the barber's chair at the back of the house, beneath the mushrooming mango tree. The razor scrapes against the virgin flesh of his scalp, and behind it sneak in wafts to titillate the newly exposed skin. The windows of Urmila's room are open. The sun is good. The sparrows in the mango tree carry on a bedevilled chirruping. A transistor in the neighbourhood yowls out the commentary on some cliffhanging moment in some one-day cricket match. A pliant and pleasing inertness under the barber's hands. He feels clean and holy. Pista all but starts to bawl with envy when, on his return from school, he sees the new Jamun.

He screeches at Aya when she proposes lunch.

For Jamun, some of the goodbyes are undemanding. Telephone calls in the morning to Kasturi and Kuki, kisses, hugs and waves to Doom and Pista as they (Pista with sandwich in one hand and left shoe in the other) scoot for their school bus, and to Joyce and Burfi some two hours later as they scamper through the gate to Burfi's office car, each livid with the other for having delayed him/her. Bidding adieu to Shyamanand, however, is somewhat messier.

For one, he looks pretty ghastly this morning – ashen and insecure, and his eyes continually dart away from Jamun's features like a tongue. 'Oh . . . So you're pushing off? . . . Of course you are . . . Have you called for a taxi?' Jamun touches his father's feet. Fumblingly, almost tottering on his stick, Shyamanand kisses him on the forehead and the cheeks. His munificent beard tickles his son's face. 'You turned up in time for your mother, will you do the same for me? Or will you instead despatch a condolent telegram? . . . You should've married while your mother was alive. She'd've been jubiliant . . . Don't forget your bottle of water for the journey.' He tails Jamun and his travelling bag out to the verandah. 'This is the first time that I see you off without your mother . . . She'd've softly nibbled your left pinkie and, while you cavilled against her mumbojumbo, mumbled a prayer for your passage . . . Can one use "passage" for a train journey? I think not . . . Yesterday, you remarked that I'm luckier than many because I still have my sons to care for me – and if I wish for a change of air, or when I squabble with Burfi, I'm to phone or wire you, and you'll hotfoot up to whisk me away – and in any case, if Burfi and Joyce are transferred, I've to wean myself from this house and shift to your muggy, forgettable town . . . Verily, verily, I say unto thee, When thou wast young, thou girdest thyself, and walkedst whither thou wouldest; but when thou shalt be old, thou shalt stretch forth thy hands, and another shalt gird thee, and carry thee whither thou wouldest not . . . Jamun, there truly does come a time to die. When the Brahmin sees the son of his son, he is to perceive that the day has arrived for him to withdraw from the household and recede into the forest. Eternity does not exist; rather, it too has its season, and immortality is only continued existence in one's issue, and in the seed of one's issue . . . Will you ever get hold of this house again if you lease it out to a Marwari? They'll battle you in court for fifteen years, bribe everyone in sight and romp home . . . You can't even bolt and lock up the place and push off, because Naidu related to me a horror story last Sunday when he dropped in to swill our tea and exhaust my evening. It happened in the block between ours and that mosque. One family's been away from their house for some months – a commonplace tale, one parent dead, the survivor packed off to where he won't be a pest, none of the children greatly concerned about the property, and in any case they're dispersed all over the globe like a fraternity out of the Pentateuch. When one son returned to the city last month and rolled up to check on their house, he found complete strangers inhabiting it. People he'd never laid eyes on before – can you imagine? I'd've croaked on the spot, at my own front door. They haven't settled matters yet, Naidu avers, because the bastards who broke in and didn't glide away – and they're a family! woman and children, a bloody sorority of thugs – have now produced signed and stamped rent receipts as proof that they've been legal tenants of the house for months! The owners apparently've had to trudge to court, and one of them's suffered a heart attack. While Naidu waffled away, I kept imagining that much the same'd befall us when we forsake this house – my sweat of four years slopped just to finally lodge some housebreakers.'

Jamun's missed a chunk of Shyamanand's diffuseness because he's been keeping an eye out for his taxi. When he concentrates on his father again, he all at once appears to see a cruelly older version of the person of five minutes ago. Shyamanand's eyes have filmed with the tiredness of distress, and the skin – on his cheeks, throat, collarbones, forearms – has shrivelled and slumped, as though the meat beneath it has ebbed. His voice is reedier and more fretful. Jamun is ashamed that his foremost response is a kind of triumph for his mother, who'd time and again distraughtly, screechingly augured to Shyamanand that she'd predecease him, that he'd recognize her worth, her virtue, only after her death, and that, Godwilling, she'd return from There to attend his tribulation.

'Your father needs a wretch,' she's times out of number asserted, while combing her hair or picking up the comics that Doom has sprayed all over the drawing room, 'whom he can pester and harass for twenty-four hours of the day – "Ah, wouldn't this be Paradise if I could drink a glass of icecold Rooh Afza now? But who's there to make me one?" – That's him being crafty. After I'm taken, he'll have nobody to badger, and the absence of a victim will finish him off. Unless you all can recruit a slave only to be a buffer for his nonsense – "Hey, you, put on my shoes for me . . . Hey, you, how dare you sit on a chair in my presence!" – but such a patsy'll be difficult to find, and'll demand a wage of a thousand – and deserve one of at least two thousand – rupees, which amount neither your father nor either of his prodigal sons will pay.'

Jamun tries to point out to Shyamanand the sunnier side of things. 'You've Pista here to divert you, and Doom too – whenever Joyce looks in. Your bank accounts are here, your Term Deposits, Postal Savings, and . . . everything. Your own house. You won't be happier elsewhere.'

Shyamanand is a bit startled and hurt at Jamun's synopsis of his, Shyamanand's, interests, and'd like to know whether he's being derisive, but the taxi draws up just then and begins honking at once, and he still has much to say, or so he'd fancied. 'But you're leaving me with Burfi. That bonehead's marriage appears to be on the rocks – so he'll have no time for me . . . Write as soon as you reach, or shall I telephone your neighbour tomorrow, the man with the queer name . . . '

Jamun's train is on time and Hegiste – dumpy, swarthy, a sweating Gioconda – and his child, cola in hand, are on the platform. Embraces, pats on the head, you-shouldn't've-bothereds, most-sorry-to-hears. A rickshaw through the dank, high-density streets. A livid sky, swollen with rain. Past the cooperative bank, the unfinished municipal auditorium, Reddy's Superstores, the hooch kiosk, dead at nine in the morning, the donkeygrey gynae hospital. From each spout on the roof of their block of flats, the rain for weeks has marked its course down the walls – cascades of moss and slime on a once-yellow backdrop. The lawn of the block is still a tract of mud and bleached crabs. Kasibai is hanging up washing in the verandah. From the rickshaw Jamun can see only her mammoth belly between white blouse and white sari. She sights him when they alight and hoots his arrival into the flat. Vaman debouches on to the balcony, waves fatuously and bobs indoors again. He capers up to the rickshaw to take Jamun's bag. He's wearing Jamun's shorts and T-shirt. The shirt is actually a seven-year-old discard of Burfi's. It was originally lime-green, and its thorax reads: 'Tough Guys Don't Dance. They Hustle.' Vaman is sniggering with foolish exhilaration. He now parts his frizzy hair, Jamun notices, on the left, and his upper lip – puffy, purplish – is bedecked by a tentative, ridiculous moustache.

In the verandah, Kasibai sets before Jamun a cup of her tea – thick, sweet, dark, like diluted molasses – and asks how his father is taking his mother's death. Her Hindi is adequate for just the most primary communication.

'Ah, you've raised an uppermost matter.' Jamun unfolds, in his ghastly Marathi, that Shyamanand might come to live with them. While explaining why, he suddenly breaks off because he just can't visualize Kasibai and his father together, in the same room – he sipping tea, she banking against the doorpost – or in the same world. Like matter and antimatter – he, without warning, confusedly, recalls his Higher Secondary Physics – the two simply cannot meet. Kasibai is gazing at him. A blunt nose, a virile, leathery face. 'So how was Yavatmal? Did you win your land back?'

When Jamun received the telegram about Urmila's heart failure, Kasibai and Vaman had been in their village hundreds of kilometres away in the district of Yavatmal. They'd had to scoot there because Kasibai had all at once learnt that squatters had begun to encroach on the pocketsize cultivable land that she possessed. Thus she informed Jamun on his return from office on the Monday before the telegram.

'Oh, that sounds dreadful. Did you get a letter or something, or did someone from the village show up?' Jamun suspects her of fibbing, and on their afterdinner amble, Hegiste confirms to him that Kasibai is skirring home for altogether another reason. Like Kasibai, the Hegistes are Maharashtrian, and Mrs Hegiste routinely ferrets out from Kasibai the more covert stuff. Kasibai's never been rightfully married, and the man she steadily refers to as her husband, i.e. Vaman's begetter, is only the village stud whom she's cohabited with, off and on, for several years. Every time, more or less, the he-goat's inveigled a second nanny to move in with him for some months, Kasibai and her dunderhead lovechild've been turfed out – to bum around the countryside, to go to glory, or to an aunt, to sign on in the Congress Party, or whatever. From wherever she is, Kasibai's kept tabs on the jock – who is giraffelike and marooneyed, with a dacoit's whiskers sprawling across his jowls like a verdant pubic thatch, and is immutably cantankerous because of acidosis; she's careened back to him at every vacancy. 'She learnt this afternoon, from a visiting fluff from her bit of the world, that the cock's last sexpot snuffed it some weeks ago – encephalitis, deduces my wife from Kasibai's reportage.'

'But surely she can tell me the truth, instead of this bull about poachers on her land – unless coyness pricked her into a euphemism there, even though she's usually as bashful as the slut in a herd of rhino. D'you suspect she fears that I'll be jealous or something? Priceless.'

Hegiste simpers, but voices nothing. The links are convoluted here. He knows full well that Jamun tumbles his elephantine domestic; indeed, he itches for her himself, and Jamun and he are fraternal enough to discuss her with comic bawdiness.

Within bounds, of course. Jamun, for example, will never

divulge to Hegiste what he actually feels about Kasibai, and how hard he was thwacked in his vitals when, the first time, she swallowed him, gulped him in like warm honey, grunting with relish. Never once in the hugger-mugger years has Kasturi not spat him out, demurring sheepishly that she dislikes the taste, or contending laughingly that the hormones in semen'll give her a beard. With Kasturi, he's pumped himself out, all along, on the coldness of his own belly or the hollow of her throat, forsaken after love. But Kasibai has unclenched him, made him feel opulent, as though his juices – his lymph, his spittle – were inestimably precious.

He can never disclose to Hegiste that sexually, in his mind, his maidservant has thrown open the doors to towering caverns. One dark Saturday afternoon, he is underneath her, tonguing her, feeling her beginning to undulate, her thighs snuggling his ears, when the doorbell jangles, twice. She, muttering, gets up off his face to answer. Continuing to grumble, she slips on her blouse and sari in seconds and lumbers out of the room. The front door opens and Jamun overhears her snap. 'No, isn't in.' She returns, peeling off her clothes, dreadfully irate, and, naked, surmounts his face once more, hissing in Marathi, 'Your bloody Hegiste. I told him you weren't at home. The next time he ogles me, I'll clamp my thighs around his loaf and suffocate him.' And then, leering at the face beneath her corralled by her thlobs of puckered blubber, a googlylike modulation to a frightful bashfulness, 'Now where were we, my Jamun saheb!'

For months, the memory of that afternoon – both droll and carnal – sends gooseflesh cavorting all over him. It is her conduct, her deportment, that is so piquant; cunnilingus for her seems a bit like watching on video a Hindi blockbuster weepie – a familiar and wholeheartedly delightsome amusement, from which one resents being distracted by irritants like the doorbell and the telephone, and to which one returns at the earliest, within seconds if practicable, matter-of-factly, to carry on exactly from where one's been interrupted.

But the convoluted links. Mrs Hegiste, for sure, knows that Jamun tups his washerup and housekeeper, but even after months, doesn't quite know how to react. She's always believed – or, rather, presumed – that only weirdos – widowers, lonely-hearts, dissipated and dispossessed feudal lordlings, misogynists with incurable afflictions, cranks traumatized in childhood, bachelors with insanity in the family, oddballs like that – actually sleep with the lower orders; in contrast, Jamun is young, healthy, middle-class and seemingly sensible. She dislikes Kasibai because of the expression on the faces of her husband and even her bloody grandfather whenever they sight her. Yet Kasibai is the only other female Maharashtrian in the vicinity, her sole interlocutrix for a chinwag in Marathi.

And Vaman. Hegiste is downright certain that Jamun, now and then, also has it off with his maidservant's son, that the urchin is inseparable from his mother and very likely lies with her and Jamun. Neither Vaman nor Kasibai is sure of his age, but he enjoys the wits of a twelve-year-old, and his physique seems an underripe seventeenish. He's presumably never known anything other than kink, for Kasibai has once or twice implied to Mrs Hegiste that to torment her, in front of her eyes, Vaman's father the stallion has, ever so often, mounted his own son. Hegiste never alludes directly to Vaman's ruttish links with Jamun, and Jamun customarily disregards all the innuendo – his winks, the asides and cautions.

Sometimes, however, he does respond, perhaps to a whisper during lunchhour gossip at the office, or a nudge during a saunter for cigarettes, when he's introspecting – on nothing specially, but in a vague manner, on diverse families – Kasibai's, his own, Burfi's, Kasturi's, – and the fearsome intricacies of fosterage. 'Well, in a family, the most hideous things can happen without the wider world knowing – without even other members of the family catching on, and if the incident – the misadventure – has been adequately distanced by Time – the real cock of the walk – then it doesn't even remain grisly; it becomes sort of spicy.

'Consider, for example, the yarn of Kuki's family. Kuki's a childhood friend. We went to the same school in the same bus, and we've kept in touch all these years. He's now engaging, sleek and unscrupulous. His parents are divorced, and they split up while Kuki's mother was carrying. Curious, isn't it. The marriage failed because of Kuki's grandfather, who sounds redoubtable by any standard – and certifiable too. Forthwith upon his son's marriage, he wished to enjoy his daughter-in-law – and presumably requested his son to direct her to his room after dinner or something. Kuki's father is a ninny, because he actually blabbed to his wife the old satyr's designs. When she declined, the maddened and horny – always a feral combination – father-in-law, for some days, importuned his son to woo her. When that too didn't come off, the venerable ogre buggered his own issue, Kuki's father, instead. The tale stupefied me for days. I was flabbergasted that I – ordinary, commonplace me! – actually knew someone whose family background was this fable of horrors. And knew damnably well! Kuki and I'd been neighbours, we'd flown kites together, and when we'd run out of milk or tea, our aya'd usually send one of her sidekicks to their kitchen for replenishments. Outwardly, they were like us – though richer, of course – they'd been to Singapore, and had a fridge and TV almost a decade before we did, or could – and I suspect that from then on, I accepted that rectitude and lucre were connected, that Kuki's grandfather couldn't've conducted himself so had he not been on the gravy train, had he not viewed everything – individuals, events, relationships – materially. Kuki'd tell me that his mother frequently stated that her father-in-law – the fiend! – used to declare that his son was, after all, his seed; what was the son's, ergo, was also his, the begetter's. Apparently, Kuki was pricked enough by these pronouncements to demand of his mother why, by their reasoning, his grandfather hadn't used his son's toothbrush and his undies.

'"But he did, and mine too," was, ostensibly, Kuki's mother's reply. "He'd glide into our bathroom when I wasn't in, and swipe my lingerie off the towel rack."'

Hegiste doesn't intend ever to snoop into his friend's precise relations with his domestics; besides, he's pretty certain that his most lascivious imaginings will more approximate the reality than anything that Jamun might confess to him. Thus, if he and Mrs Hegiste, for instance, are disturbed at three a.m. by the detonating of Jamun's front door, the noisy snivelling of Vaman as he rattles down the stairs, by the titter of Mrs Hegiste's insomniac grandfather as he watches, from the verandah, Vaman trudge through the gate, Hegiste, six hours later, when they amble off to office, won't tease Jamun with any questions about the night; instead, he'll only curl up against Mrs and drowsily murmur, 'Jamun's riding his hippo and the stripling hasn't been allowed to join them. If he chooses, he can kneel by the bed, with one paw on his tool and a pinkie up his arsehole, and pirouette. So he's spurted off in a tizzy to presumably jerk off into the well behind the hooch kiosk.'

But if Hegiste ever pumps, and Jamun is straightforward, he'll concede that the most exacting bit of his carnal life is the interlocution with his participators. Times out of number, he's craved for a likeminded soul to share this grisly comedy with, to marvel with him at the chasm between the mentalities of his playmates and his own. Vaman, in particular, continues to jolt Jamun with the unintelligence, the callow materiality of his concerns. He is passive and vain before, during and after coition – indeed, throughout the day. He is most often found on Jamun's bed, lolling, emptyheadedly simpering at the looking-glass, waiting to be inflamed, or to be biffed on his skull by Kasibai and walloped off to some overdue chore. From time to time, in his unmodulated, grating hoarseness, his barbaric Marathi-Hindi, he'll sniffle or sigh, 'If you give me the cash, I could scoot off to Bombay, tuck into some healthy food – chicken biryani, mutton chops – so that my chest broadens, then I'd proffer myself for a superfine role . . .' Or, 'Do I need a haircut? Off Rocket Maidan, a new hairdresser's opened up, with all the dandy styles. Twenty-five rupees per trim – that's how skilled he is. Why don't you . . .?' For sure, Jamun ignores this drivel as best he can (or shoos the sluggard out for biscuits or cigarettes), just as he is deaf to Kasibai's tireless demands for a few thousand rupees to redeem some ten godforsaken square inches of land in Yavatmal.

'But I'm flat broke, Kasibai. Why don't you deposit the whopping salary that you lever out of me every month in a bank and pick up some interest instead of stashing it away in your pussy or spilling it on that dildo of a son?'

It is enervating, though, to speak smut to your maidservant because you believe that she'd like to hear the lingo that you presume she's been reared on, and then to observe her blanch with hurt. Jamun feels droopy and immature, ashamed of his existence. When he isn't enkindled by them, he is frequently disgusted by their boorishness, by the smacking sounds that Vaman emits while he chomps, by Kasibai's thunderous hawking and expectorating first thing in the morning; for the months that he's known them, he's haphazardly striven to educate them for his own peace of mind ('Flush, you fucker, flush! Why don't you ever remember that this handle is not fucking decorative! . . . Kasibai! Whatever're you – but that black isn't grime or crud! – you can't scrape – it's the material – oh, fuck your mind –', derisorily caving in here at having to hatch Hindi-Marathi equivalents of 'non-stick', 'frying pan' and (phew) 'teflon'), but without conspicuous progress, principally because he isn't interested in them as fellow creatures. Which stricture Jamun himself will parry with, 'Balls, they aren't my family, or anything like that . . . I'm not yoked to them by blood, or nurture, or the years. In any case, all these shackles can splinter; what endures is only a blind and unreasoning notion of duty. If we acquitted ourselves with others as they merited, then we wouldn't've abandoned our aya in a charitable hospital with just her TB and her diabetes for company. She wasn't us, so we exonerated ourselves.'

With a second tea in his hand, Jamun dawdles about the flat, pointing out to Kasibai the evidences of her slackness in his absence – the grime on the curtains, the crud in the kitchen sink. The furnishings are minimal and comfortless. On a desk borrowed from the office squats his turntable that revolves at bloody 30 r.p.m. Underneath the window that looks on to the verandah lies the divan without a mattress on which he turns in when he's put off by K and V. Alongside the kitchen door dangles last year's calender of the National Gallery, London, displaying for June Degas's *Beach Scene*. Had Kasturi ever cohabited with him, the flat would've bloomed with tulips and gladioli, warm rugs, and bamboo curtains to lineate the light. Such had her own room seemed – cordial, vivid – when he looked in on her the evening after mourning.

To finally cast off the yards of cream linen feels momentous. 'For good,' Jamun declares to Burfi as he stows away the folded, wrinkled cloth in the chest in the drawing room on which roosts the TV. 'Oops, sorry, no, once more yet – one down, one to go. Though I gather from Chachacha that you can't wear these robes ever again. Doesn't peeling these off truly feel like moulting? With a new skin, through into another life?'

'I presume that these subtleties'll suggest themselves to you afresh when Baba passes over. Meanwhile, when're you going to begin swilling again? Chhana phoned this morning to check if we'd nosed out the will; I fenced with: "Is this evening okay to resume vices on? Thank God Ma and I didn't inhabit different time zones – figuring out when mourning finishes, in that jumble, would've been phew."'

The shirt and trousers feel peculiar too, as though he was decking up for an occasion – an interview, or a colleague's wedding reception. Kasturi's parturition has been right as rain – a couple of hours or so of labour – and she and her healthy baby have returned home on the fourth day. Jamun shows up there at eight to run into the entire family in the living room – her husband, her babbling sister, the parents, her cadaverous grandfather. He congratulates them and they condole with him. Kasturi's husband is still bearded, but appears to've fattened a bit since his marriage. 'Kasturi and the baby are resting now,' leers the grandfather; he's always loathed Jamun. 'No, she awoke some fifteen minutes ago,' confutes the husband, 'and is at the moment only gawping besottedly at her effort. Would you like to chat to her right away or d'you want to watch some minutes of the night cricket first?'

Kasturi's face is towards the window; her eyes are shut. The room is suffused with the bouquet of flowers; Jamun sees them everywhere – maroon roses in a carafe on her desk, white lilies in a brass dustbin at the door, a fan of gladioli above her head, a gush of jasmine in a plastic jug on a hifi speaker alongside the window. The curtains are new, a bright interlacing of tangerine, pea-green and violet. Highcoloured mats on the floor, and two glowing batiks mounted on opposite walls. Through the open windows, the gusts from the sea are mollifying. He is discomposed by a forceful aura in the room of plenitude, of contentment and smugness, as though he's edged into a warm, ripe fruit; all that is paramount now is to struggle to sustain through one's life this easeful consummation.

Within reach of Kasturi is the crib. Kasturi looks glossless. Jamun's entrails seems to shimmy inside him; all at once flashes across his mind, with spotless lucency, an image from an obscure September evening: he's on the roof of his apartment block, watching the river, orange and thick; in the same instant, a resplendent white bird floats past the trees and a youthful mother, who's very recently borne, gracelessly descends the incline of the gynae hospital. The swan and the mother together prod in him an overpowering desire to be fecund, to yield issue.

Half-smiling at the evocation, he raises the rose-pink netting of the cradle to peep, for the first time, at his daughter. She looks the usual – reddish, contorted, wrinkled, displeased, distressed, unenlightened. Unthinkingly, Jamun chuckles at her, and to himself. 'Hello, my petite sexbomb.' The infant twitches somewhat and curls a lip at him, which he accepts as a sign of recognition. He speculates whether he can gather the baby in his arms. 'Your shaven head looks fine,' voices Kasturi. She is smiling. He kisses her on the cheek. 'I'd've visited you in the nursing home, but my mourning outfit'd've attracted a good many loafers.'

'Ah, never mind. So how've you been?' They're happy to gaze at each other, even a bit pink with a sort of awkwardness. 'You look radiant, Kasturi, and she is entrancing. Here, I've brought her a little something. You could start her off on it straight away, to ensure that she takes after her mother.'

Kasturi tears open the wrapping to discover two Lakme face powder compacts. She slopes against her pillows and shuts her eyes, smirking. Jamun stretches out for her hand. Thus they sit for a time, more or less in stillness. From the living room sputter in the muted excitements of night cricket.

Impossible – of course – that Jamun hasn't mulled over the snarl that he and Kasturi've enmeshed themselves in. But being self-absorbed, he's viewed it just as an item in the larger shambles of his life – that is, as a detail that he can only observe, inertly, as on a screen. For flickers of a second at a time – like prizing open a gravestone just to breathe in the cadaver – he's wondered precisely what Kasturi's trumped up for her husband, how she's okayed it with him. Perhaps she's faked the periods she's missed, or with him craftily used some contraceptive. Then Jamun's willed the lid shut, resolving not to speculate on the future, but to confront each of its freaks – like Shyamanand's meeting Kasibai – only when it glides up to him, like headlights emerging out of black fog.

'Does it hurt very much – your mother's absence?'

He rubs his cranium selfconsciously. 'Not all the time.' He closes his eyes and with braced fingers massages his scalp. It feels like a sheath over a knob. 'My mother knew of this.' He indicates the crib with his chin. 'Don't ask me how. I've never whispered a word of this to anyone. But she guessed or something – she knew. On the day that she suffered her coronary, in the morning – it was her wedding anniversary, and we were arranging roses in Doom's porridge mug – she gabbled a bit – bizarre exposés about her past which I didn't wholly buy – she kind of sotto voced, all on a sudden, holding the last rose in her left hand, "You and Kasturi've to do right by your child" – something like that. My first, my every first, reaction was nothing – a blank. I didn't look at her and didn't respond. Just then, somebody breezed in, or the telephone rang.' He opens his eyes and smirks diffidently at Kasturi. 'Whatever is a godfather? Can't I be one? Or a fosterfather? She'll grow up with the lifestory of the tragedienne of a Hindi weepie, and consume the final six reels of her life in searching for her actual begetter.' A puff from the window tingles his crown. 'Do you accept that knotty questions resolve themselves without mortal help? Of course, they might not be disentangled the way we'd wish them to. That afternoon, several months ago, we were on the sands, in stinging rain, and you –'

Further speculations are curtailed by the entry at this point of Kasturi's sister the brook, who breaks in to check whether Jamun wants tea, and tarries to natter. How curious the world is, ruminates Jamun, observing the brook's eyecatching pantyline. Here we are, Kasturi and I, and our infant, with an altogether capricious future to confront, doubting of Time's munificence, uncertain when we will next meet, and unable even to discuss our hopes and misgivings, to voice our intuitions, simply because of this arsehole that won't shut up. However, it's arguable, he reminds himself with a soundless guffaw, that, as Aya'd've said, this arsehole has been sent by God; to wit, Kasturi and I, at this instant, can do fuckall – can't even *talk* – about our lives. Just furtively clasp hands beneath this bedspread, I guess.

Breakfast on the morning of Jamun's return is at Hegiste's. One end of Hegiste's dining table bears their TV. Jamun sits next to Mrs Hegiste's grandfather and gluts himself on some Maharashtrian stuff. The grandfather rests his hand on Jamun's shoulder and begins toothlessly and unintelligibly to blether in Marathi. Mrs Hegiste translates into dissonant Hindi. 'The grief induced by death is a queer thing. One comes of age not when one has – uh – uh –'

Hegiste simpers at his wife's awkwardness and zestfully takes over. 'One truly comes of age not when one's experienced sex or masturbated or had one's first period, but when one's flesh and blood dies. Then one fuzzily senses how mysterious and confusing living is, that it's most sensible not to introspect at all on its pith. Bizarre my own situation was some forty-five years ago, when, within six weeks, my father knuckled under to cholera, my mother to the venom of a scorpion that she nearly squashed in the latrine one night, my eldest sister, whom I doted on, to appendicitis – and one first cousin foundered to the bowels of the Ganga at Kashi. Four stubbed out in six weeks. I recollect that in a way I didn't altogether grasp whom to sorrow for first, as though that was the cardinal issue to be decided. I felt embalmed and unthreatened: I'll no longer have to wait for grief. Afterwards, when I'd revived enough for my memory of the dead to be ambushed, ever so often, by the unexpected sound or smell, I'd even feel contrite that my sadness was so much more for my sister and mother than my father. Lamenting for the dead is a peculiar business.'

Glasses of daab before Jamun and Hegiste set out for office. The grandfather, head bobbing, plods on. 'And your father'll come here to stay with you? Splendid, but will he adapt to the food and your Kasibai's cooking, and to this dankness twelve months of the year? He's about my age, and to be uprooted when one's rheumyeyed can be fiendish.'

Fuck the food, Jamun tells himself as they dawdle out to the gate, however will Shyamanand communicate here? His bloody Hindi isn't passable enough for him to follow Kasibai's. The instant I return from office, he'll beset me with his grouses against the day, the oafishness of Vaman and the slovenliness of his mother. As the minutes pass, the impossibility of Shyamanand's assimilation into his son's other life pounds Jamun with snowballing force. He'd have to beseech Burfi to cart Shyamanand with him when he's transferred. From Hegiste's or the office, he could phone home to say that he'd arrived safely, and somehow, though God knows how, skew the conversation so that he could, designlessly as it were, disclose to Shyamanand that his flat here had only one loo, which obviously the domestics also used. Nothing, he's aware, will head off Shyamanand as much as having to share his bog with the lumpen, or, for that matter, even his bowls and mugs. Vive la caste and la social inequality. And for sure, gravest of all, his father's presence will poleaxe his tumbling; one can't conceivably bid goodnight to one's father in one room and prance off to doss down with one's maidservant (and her asinine son!) in the next. Further, Vaman in particular can't be depended on to be circumspect. For Shyamanand's own dignity, Jamun doesn't want him ever to learn of his son's proclivities; he can suspect and arraign to his heart's content, but he must never incontrovertibly know.

'But what touched off her heart attack?' Hegiste, ceaselessly curious, unthinkingly aggregating thimblesful of fact. 'I've always supposed that with a pacemaker inside one, one's heart can't conk out.'

'We did her in together, I think. My sister-in-law gifted her some roses on her anniversary, the unexpectedness of which fairly flustered my mother. My father chortled and guffawed at the present, thus upsetting her even more; she in fact suffered a minor fit that morning. Nevertheless, I lugged her out for a walk to the beach – her first in years – God knows how that affected her.' When we returned from the beach, she blurted out to me some weird dope about her life – she must've been anyway rattled to divulge to me all that, and the revealing must've further discomposed her. 'My nephew, Pista, riled all of us by spoofing my mother's gait. Then the pacemaker itself. The quack superintending her had confided in me the evening before the attack that the damned pacemaker was faulty – its cells were leaking, like pus or something. Later, each and every motherfucker – the supplier and all the buggers at the clinic – poohpoohed the idea. By now, they must've taken the pacemaker away – why don't you donate it to the needy, they simpered, the anuses – and why don't we try and re-use it for you, could save you fifteen thousand? So now, I presume, we can't have it inspected. And the supplier – an old classmate of mine – provided us a free and comfortable ride from Delhi to Haridwar, for the ashes, a bit like a bribe, we all felt, because after the ease of the drive none of us had the heart to raise the matter with him – no, that isn't accurate – more that the tossing of the ashes into the Ganga was the end of it – the matter clocks out there, in the frigidity of the river.' And we all conduced to her winding up there. Even after her attack, when she was numb, we – her sons – delayed her because, fagged out and fearful, we craved a joint.

'Hello, Baba? Jamun here, from the office. How are you? . . . Yes, the journey was – no, actually, it wasn't fine in the least, the bloody AC was off for half the night, this mammoth Surd in the upper berth uncorked these viperous mooli farts every four minutes, and I had an eerie dream . . . Did you go for your walk yesterday? . . . No, but you mustn't give up the habit, Baba . . . Why, you could've asked Pista to accompany you . . . Oof, don't be silly, you don't beg for charity when you invite your grandson for a stroll . . . Did Aya or Joyce remember your afterdinner milk? . . .'

His last glimpse of Shyamanand has been through the scummy rear window of the taxi. Shyamanand is in the turquoise half-sweater that his wife knit two winters ago. He inclines against the thorax-high compound wall, has hooked his stick on the gate, and slowly waves his right hand in farewell. In the frame around him are the grey and white of his house, the arms of the giant cactus, a chunk of ashen sky, a shred of road, a snuffcoloured tempo, parked. The half-sweater and the cactus are conspicuously in focus, acute against the grey. He is condemned, isn't he, reflects Jamun, to the vexations of loneliness, to the recreations of hobbling about in the driveway on agreeable evenings, and of chinwagging across the boundary wall with any neighbour who pauses. Doesn't he feel dreadfully free, unbridled? With just walking stick and his benumbed limbs as his last liabilities?

In the dream that pesters Jamun in the train – a nightmare, save that everybody in it looks jaunty – Urmila stands in

Shyamanand's place alongside the compound wall, giggling and waving. Joyce is beside her, her hair tenderly disarranged across her features, tittering. Burfi and Jamun, on the roof of the house, wearing singlets and briefs, are cooking, sweating, stirring with long staffs a goulash in a huge cauldron. It isn't specified, but Shyamanand is dead. In the next frame, Urmila and her grandsons are on the seashore, facing the water, in blinding, metallic noonlight; they appear almost as three silhouettes against a screen of white heat. Hand in hand, they saunter into the sea, but it's no longer the sea; without warning, the three are instead on the broad steps at Haridwar, with the glacial water of the river deadening their shins. They are all beaming, and Doom starts to cackle, to oscillate in his delight, to turn his face up to the heavens and squeeze his eyes shut against the incandescence. His lips, at the edges, brown with the heat. Suddenly, with his free left hand, he thwacks his grandmother with frightful force in her underbelly. She totters, but Jamun never learns further, because the scene slides once more; a closeup of two huge, scarred, singed, exhausted feet, plodding with mesmeric regularity on scalding grey sand. They've been trudging for years, Jamun is aware, with an enormous burden; the shoulders of the pilgrim cushion a beam, at the ends of which sway two large, decrepit baskets; their shadows caper on the sand as the pilgrim clumps on.

Shyamanand arrives to stay with Jamun in the February of the succeeding year. A fortnight after his son's departure, he mails Jamun his first letter, a totally blank inland, clean but for the address on the outside. Jamun is unmanned by it, and telephones from office. 'What nonsense is this, why have you . . . ?'

Explaining to Shyamanand uses up some time; when he finally has it, he chortles and guffaws at his error. Jamun is further disquieted because his father's merriment sounds phoney, as though Shyamanand is persuading himself that the legpull was designed, and is successful. A second, three-page letter ten days after, to amend matters:

My darling Jamun,

Wasn't that incident with my inland droll! I related it to Burfi (in doublequick time, as he loped upstairs after office to shun me) and he retorted, from the head of the stairs, that if he ever received a letter with nothing in it from me, he'd fear that I was going off my rocker. 'Like son, like father,' I bayed up the stairwell.

Doom and Joyce dropped in yesterday. Heaven knows where they're nesting now, and with whom; why should I ask? The brat is bubblier at each meeting and disregards more and more whatever his mother voices. At lunch, he ignored his plate as much as he ignored her; she at last whinnied at him to get on with his food. Doom, agape, instinctively responded by parroting, as children will, the sounds, the pitch and cadence, the accents, of Joyce's speech – without actually articulating any intelligible word. Hearing him, I was abruptly reminded of your mother under stress; she too mimicked the tone and intonation of the other in an altercation – it was her first defence, for she was never a topnotch quarreller, she slanted much more to sentiment than to the cut and thrust of reason. Unexpected paltry events, like Doom parodying Joyce, evoke your mother dreadfully; and one relishes the acridness of remembrance, so one encourages oneself to remember.

On the second night after your departure, in the wee hours actually, I heard Urmila sneeze in her room. I swear. You wouldn't have forgotten her sneezing fits, those twenty-plus uninhibited thunderclaps in a chain, each of which alarmed Naidu's hound conspicuously; he'd tauten, cock up his ears and growl till socked on the skull by Naidu, to whom sometimes I itched to do the same. I heard only one sneeze though, that night, distinct and characteristic. Of course, you'll scoff that I imagined it.

Jamun tosses his head over this bit of the letter, sneering at humankind. Incredible that Shyamanand could've forgotten his conduct. Urmila's sneezing bouts had been truly marathon, and had occurred, for some reason, always in the late afternoon or early evening. Jamun and his nephews had treasured them ('Doom! Buck up, you bloody bloated snail, Thakuma's begun to sneeze!'), and ever so often swarmed about her to tot up the sneezes and to egg her on.

But Urmila's convulsions annoy Shyamanand, because he's resolved that every single item about her will rile him. He behaves despicably, twirling his head away – pronouncedly, exaggeratedly – with each sneeze, as though to dodge the germs, goggling at her balefully, theatrically leaving off whatever he's been saying, even limping out of the room – however can one be snubbed for sneezing?

The letter, continued.

I run into Burfi and his immediate family so seldom that I feel that I stay alone in this house. We've eaten together no more than four times since you pushed off. I suspect that Pista's been commanded to spend the minimum possible time with me. While your mother was alive, the monkey frequently sweated over his homework with us; now I can buttonhole him for just a couple of minutes before one of those women cheeps him away for something or the other. But even when I'm with Burfi or Pista or Doom, I feel utterly on my own, in a sense – a distressing sense – without bonds.

I continually see myself stumbling and sprawling while pottering about at home – in the dining room, for instance, while opening the fridge – injuring myself in the fall, and the cold floor against my cold cheek for an eternity; the cook does edge into the room at noon, and Aya at four, they gasp and charge out, but for some reason, help never steps in. With one frozen eye, I watch through the window the sky creep across its tints to black. Why do you leave me all alone? I quaver at Burfi when he drops in in the dead of night. He doesn't reply, but so stands in the doorway that I can make out only the left half of him; he is bisected lengthwise, and his right half, from hairline to floor, is entirely shadowed.

Such are my imaginings. But enough of them, and of my being alone. I've frittered away the past few days in struggling with the bank over your mother's pension. The extra money would be useful for such domestic trials as the cook's raise; she's uncivil and indelicate, but over the years I've inured myself to her cooking. Otherwise, as before, in the evenings I nest in front of the TV without registering anything. Though Sunday afternoon featured a first-rate BBC documentary on penguins in the Antarctic, and some of it set me off again, particularly how male emperor penguins foster their toddlers in exceedingly hostile weather, and how those funny birds enjoy just three months of quiet between two breeding cycles – the outworn, knackered question dispirited me all afternoon and evening, that wasn't there more to life than this, this dreadful procreation, this motiveless fecundity?

You never write first. Now that I've written (twice, if you count the inland!), will you at least reply soon?

With all my love,

Baba

Jamun is aware that Shyamanand's letter doesn't afford a complete picture of life at home. If he telephones Burfi in his office, for instance, he's likely to be fusilladed with just how fiendishly difficult their father has been. Jamun *is* unhappy that Shyamanand is unhappy, but he's also vexed by his own guilt, and by the selfish, emotional demands that his family members make on one another even in absence. He is sad, too, at the swiftness with which his mother's augury – about Shyamanand's misery after her passing – is being vindicated; at moments, he detests both his parents, one dead, one dying, for continually coercing him to choose between them; always, in their weaning of their sons away from each other, Shyamanand (as in the letter to Jamun) and Urmila have both, mindfully or semiconsciously, fibbed to them, or at least hidden from them bits of the truth.

Which neither Burfi nor Jamun've ever appealed to the other

parent to fill in; frankly, Jamun's been fearful of wounding one with the covert disclosures of the other. For instance, on the morning of Urmila's second heart attack, when she divulges to Jamun, while arranging roses, that she's aborted thrice in her life – and each time because of Shyamanand, twice because he wasn't ready to marry her, and once because he abhorred the idea of a second puling infant in the house – what *first* flashes into Jamun's mind is that he can never accost his father for corroboration; only secondarily, after a moment, does he reflect that Urmila might be lying without being wholly mindful of it, that she has for so long been musing on the wretchedness of her marriage that she's started to adulterate the actual with the imagined.

But that *was* a queer morning, wasn't it, in which Urmila dynamited an amicable silence with, 'You *should*'ve married Kasturi – since you can't curb yourselves even after she's become someone else's wife.' Her hands cradle Doom's porridge mug; her head and shoulders are black against the bright window. 'But I'm glad that you're keeping the baby. I myself've lost three.' Altogether unruffledly, as though she's chatting of buttons. 'Two before Burfi, and one between him and you. There could've been five of you. After the second abortion, Belu named me ratnagarbha. That hurt badly too. Years ago, when we used to stay in that government flatlet, your aya and I squabbled over something, and to spite me, she blurted out to Burfi my ratnagarbha life. I remember distinctly, we were on the roof, sevenish in the evening, Burfi was working out with his weights, and hating this wrangle distracting him from ten feet away. Perhaps he wished to squash my stunned embarrassment, or maybe he *really* detested the disturbance, or he presumed that Aya was lying, because he simply carried on with his puffing and grunting, and a moment after her outburst, wheezed, "Wise of you, Ma. With three extra arses in the house, the scrimmage for the loo every morning'd've been unendurable."'

Jamun is baffled and fuzzily wounded that he hasn't, and

Burfi has, known for years these snips of their mother's past; after her death, one evening, when he gets back from visiting Kasturi at home on her return from hospital, he's even more befuddled to hear from his brother, 'Big bloody deal. Joyce wanted to abort too, and we wouldn't've had Doom, so what. These aren't horror stories, they're just sad facts. I mean, most horror stories're just sad facts. And beneath the faces on the street and on television, in the shops and buses, within buildings and bungalows, underneath the hornrimmed spectacles, the lipstick, dentures, necklaces, earrings, cufflinks, watchstraps – inside everybody are scuttled these hundreds and thousands of trivial catastrophes. A woman gets knocked up – twice – before her marriage; she isn't growing any younger and when she does marry, her husband's not too crazy about her; he itches for his niece instead – his sister's daughter – and jockeys for her to lodge with them, on the pretext that he can help her with her studies while she lends a hand with the bundle of joy, i.e. yours truly; the brood of their mismarriage, of course, is not planned – accident upon bloody accident – and sex dries up after three abortions and two sons; the husband has a cockeyed go at a fling some years – Ma talked to you about that?'

'What's curious, Burfi, is that I probably sat beside her on the flight here – a Mrs Shireen Raizada, though now I can't recall her features – certainly sixty plus, and not Baba's type, whatever type that might be. She seemed as though she could've held her own against, say, the incivility of a Caucasian air hostess – it isn't a common name. What are Raizadas? Gujaratis? Would've been bizarre had I know then – I could've slewed round to her once in a while and simpered foxily.'

Jamun would've found precious little to say to Ms Raizada. Only that she, some thirty years ago, for a couple of months, had been three rungs above his father in the same office, that Shyamanand had taken to her, but that (Urmila was confident that) his lower-middle-class diffidence had bridled him from acting upon it (just as it had hobbled him from thrusting himself on to Chhana – beyond the persistent avuncular squeezing and tweaking during English lessons, beyond the graceless deflection of conversations to her infertility so that he could tingle in her awkwardness); that by that stage of their marriage, husband and wife had forgotten what coition was, and bedded down in separate rooms, but that on one feverish July night, Shyamanand, unrecognizably drunk, had tottered into Urmila's room and on to her bed, mumbling, spluttering, 'Shireen, you can't, you will, Shireen, like a calm mother you will, my Shireen,' had mounted Urmila, who'd struggled confusedly under him for the two minutes that he'd taken. Jamun was born exactly nine months later, exactly.

'Most of the time, Ma fretted more for you than for Baba – particularly after your flame Kasturi married that other guy. "Who'll take care of Jamun when he's old?" Not realizing that you need babysitting right through your life. Your acute pronouncements on how to live fucked her up a lot. "I'll marry only after the two of you cop it . . . What do I want with children? . . . Aren't you my children?" Well, now that just one of them remains, why don't you cart him off with you, hero?'

December. Shyamanand and Jamun correspond regularly. Shyamanand's letters are a detailed account of his leaden days. January. Kasturi's first letter, in her usual ghastly hand, that the baby is fine, and has he mulled over any names. On the first Sunday in February, Burfi phones Jamun at Hegiste's to declare that his and Joyce's transfers to Bombay have come through, and so what about Shyamanand? 'He's cracked up,' continues Burfi excitedly, 'shrivelled up too, lost weight, totally insomniac – he's fixed a buzzer next to his bed, which he presses a dozen times a night, and when one of us goes down he blubbers that he can't sleep, and begs that someone stay and chat to him. I'm being driven up the wall, man. Last Tuesday – some bloody school holiday – he asked Pista to help him bathe, and inside the bathroom to soap his balls for him. I mean, what the fuck. So Joyce's hit the ceiling and forbidden both kids from hanging about Baba. I don't see why you can't keep him for – '

'But his letters are okay – heavyhearted, that's all. He hasn't – '

'What's wrong with you? Ma suffered a heart attack and you took four days to show up! D'you like them only when they're well or what?'

Quiet for a moment or two. 'How'll you send him? His BP'll very likely prevent him from flying. A train?'

'Yes.' Burfi is of course calmer now. 'Your Kasturi's husband – an okay guy – is pushing off on the twenty-second for Madras. By the – I've forgotten which train, but it halts at your town. Kasturi'd phoned for your pincode or something, and we chatted of this and that. Her husband's agreed to escort Baba down. You'll no doubt be at the station –

'And the house?'

The house is to be locked up, because they all abhor the idea of somebody else occupying it. Both Burfi and Joyce are rooting about amongst the hirelings in their offices for a diffident bachelor with a housing problem who can be convinced that to become a caretaker-sentry for their house will actually be to his benefit. Two months later, Burfi will start to bellyache that by not renting it out, he and Jamun are forfeiting thousands of rupees per month, but that's two months later.

Jamun tells Kasibai of the date of Shyamanand's arrival. 'We'll give him my bedroom. Put the TV in there. Vaman might've to doss down on the floor in that room for some days. He'll have to help my father bathe and all that. We should all welcome him at the station. It'll please him.'

'Don't worry. The old are really fairly simple to manage. I wore out some months once, tending one great-grandmother. Their demands can be elementary. They begin to doze more and more every day, and to drink mugs of warm milk; when they turn seventy-two, they sigh and set their sights on seventy-three, I know them.'

On the twenty-third, Jamun tries to call the station from Hegiste's, but can't get through. 'Fucking telecom. Let's just presume that the train's on time.' Kasibai wears a biscuity sari that he hasn't noticed before; she of course puts it on the Maharashtrian way, with one pleated end that swoops down her fat crotch and up her rump to be fluffily tucked into her dorsum, therefore her bum looks like a Herbie-car. Her peerless scion is in one of Jamun's jeans, altered rather tastefully by Kasibai; he's pruned, oiled and brushed his hair, and appears ghoulish, but wellmeaning.

An amiable, almost horizontal drizzle while they wait on the platform. Hegiste shows up at eleven-thirty with a shaky wheelchair of the gynae hospital. The train is fifteen minutes late. Shyamanand is in his creamish kurta-pyjama, crumpled and all-anyhow after the journey. Jamun is stunned at how much his father's withered in three months; he is, or appears, a couple of inches shorter than he was. His once-silver hair is now acid-yellow, and he takes a second or two to recognize his son. The fancy flashes into Jamun's mind that his father has been supplanted by a scifi clone from another globe, the inhabitants of which are slightly smaller versions of ourselves. 'Hello, Baba, you look good.' He touches Shyamanand's feet and they enfold each other. 'Hi, Agastya. Many thanks. How was the journey?'

Shyamanand doesn't budge, but waits for the chair to be hauled and jolted into place under him; he feels so tuckered out that he can't even rely on his right leg any more, and he mustn't make an ass of himself in front of Jamun's friends. Amidst considerable confusion – hissed directives and yanking of paralysed limbs – Hegiste and Vaman help Shyamanand into his seat.

The hoot of the train. Jamun once more thanks and says goodbye to Agastya. He turns after the train starts to glide, and sees the last frame of one phase of his life – Kasibai stooped in front of Shyamanand's wheelchair, touching his sandals. Shyamanand's hand hovers over her head in uncertain blessing. Behind them is a gossamer rain. Well, not a bad beginning, reflects Jamun.